W9-BUT-677

BLEEDING HEARTS

SUSAN
WITTIG ALBERT

BLEEDING HEARTS

BERKLEY PRIME CRIME, NEW YORK

THE BERKLEY PUBLISHING GROUP
Published by the Penguin Group
Penguin Group (USA) Inc.
375 Hudson Street, New York, New York 10014, USA
Penguin Group (Canada), 90 Eglinton Avenue East, Suite 700, Toronto, Ontario M4P 2Y3, Canada
(a division of Pearson Penguin Canada Inc.)
Penguin Books Ltd., 80 Strand, London WC2R 0RL, England
Penguin Group Ireland, 25 St. Stephen's Green, Dublin 2, Ireland (a division of Penguin Books Ltd.)
Penguin Group (Australia), 250 Camberwell Road, Camberwell, Victoria 3124, Australia
(a division of Pearson Australia Group Pty. Ltd.)
Penguin Books India Pvt. Ltd., 11 Community Centre, Panchsheel Park, New Delhi—110 017, India
Penguin Group (NZ), Cnr. Airborne and Rosedale Roads, Albany, Auckland 1310, New Zealand
(a division of Pearson New Zealand Ltd.)
Penguin Books (South Africa) (Pty.) Ltd., 24 Sturdee Avenue, Rosebank, Johannesburg 2196,
South Africa

Penguin Books Ltd., Registered Offices: 80 Strand, London WC2R 0RL, England

This is an original publication of The Berkley Publishing Group.

This is a work of fiction. Names, characters, places, and incidents either are the product of the author's imagination or are used fictitiously, and any resemblance to actual persons, living or dead, business establishments, events, or locales is entirely coincidental. The publisher does not have any control over and does not assume any responsibility for author or third-party websites or their content.

PUBLISHER'S NOTE: The recipes contained in this book are to be followed exactly as written. The publisher is not responsible for your specific health or allergy needs that may require medical supervision. The publisher is not responsible for any adverse reactions to the recipes contained in this book.

First edition: April 2006 **MAY 1 0 2006**

Library of Congress Cataloging-in-Publication Data

Albert, Susan Wittig.
   Bleeding hearts / by Susan Wittig Albert.—1st ed.
    p. cm
   ISBN 0-425-20799-4
    1. Women merchants—Texas—Fiction.   2. Texas—Fiction.   I. Title.

   PS3551.L2637B57 2006
   813'.54—dc22

                                    2006040653

PRINTED IN THE UNITED STATES OF AMERICA

10 9 8 7 6 5 4 3 2

NOTE TO THE READER

Bleeding Hearts is a work of fiction, and all of the incidents, people, and places—yes, even Pecan Springs—are the product of my undisciplined imagination or are used in a fictitious way.

However, I am especially indebted to two nonfiction writers whose reporting on Texas high school football helped shape this story. Thanks go to H. G. Bissinger, author of *Friday Night Lights*, and journalist Danny Robbins, whose stories about coaches' sexual misconduct ran in the *Houston Chronicle* in 2001. Their work gave me the background details I needed to make *Bleeding Hearts* a more realistic book.

All of the herbs described in this book are real, and while all are "natural" and most (used in moderation) are nontoxic, their unwise use can have unfortunate consequences, especially when they are combined with prescription drugs. If you plan to use any medicinal plant, please do your homework, consult with the appropriate professionals, and use your common sense. You will be careful, won't you? China and I would be deeply distressed to learn that we had lost any of our readers because of their careless or uninformed use of these powerful plants.

—Susan Wittig Albert
Bertram, Texas

Chapter One

Bleeding heart (*Dicentra formosa*) is a shade-loving perennial herb, native to the Orient and happiest in cool, moist woodlands. The plant belongs to the *Papaveraceae* family (which also includes the opium poppy, from which morphine is derived), and is said to have cardiovascular effects: it lowers heart rate and blood pressure. Misused, it may be deadly.

Bleeding heart takes its name from its unique blossoms, which are shaped like delicate, dangling hearts in shades of red, pink, lavender, or white. In some forms, the red inner petals give the appearance of drops of blood. Several relatives have descriptive common names: Mary's heart, Golden eardrops, and Dutchman's breeches.

What's happened in Pecan Spring over the last few weeks has given us all a great deal to think about—especially me, since the tragedies struck so close to home. Death is always hard to understand and accept, but harder still when death is murder and when murder is done in the name of love. It's a tragedy, that's all you can say. The saddest and most incomprehensible of tragedies—the kind of thing you don't think will happen in a small town, a town of close neighbors and friends, where people go to the high school football game on Friday night and church on Sunday and where everyone talks about the importance of morality and family values. When something happens to call those values into question, we're buffaloed. "We don't understand how this could have happened in our town, in any town," Hark Hibler, the editor of the Pecan Springs *Enterprise*, wrote in a recent editorial. "Our hearts bleed for everyone involved."

Hark is right. Our hearts do bleed—and that's why I'm telling this story. Because what happened in the dark corners of Pecan Springs isn't something that happened only here and nowhere else. It happens to girls and boys all over the country, and it keeps on happening because the ugly, dirty truth is too often swept under the rug and right back into those dark and secret corners. If this story is told, maybe others will be willing to tell their stories, too.

And maybe, just maybe, there will be fewer tragedies, and fewer bleeding hearts.

BUT tragedies and bleeding hearts were not on our minds—Ruby Wilcox's and mine—that morning in early February. It was nine-ish (our shops open at ten) and we were sitting over cups of hot tea at a table in our tearoom, having our usual first-of-the-month conference. This month, we were talking about all the things we had to do before Valentine's Day, which was only two weeks away. Ruby, bless her, had made a list. Underneath that goofy ya-ya exterior, there lurks the soul of a ruthless businesswoman. Actually, I'm glad she is so focused. Traffic in the shops has been pretty slow for the past few months—fewer tourists, more competition from the big chains, and a general downturn in the local economy. We've had to make a special effort to attract customers and to build other income. Ruby takes this as both a personal and a professional challenge.

"There's all the usual stuff, of course," she said, chewing on her pencil eraser. "We need to finish putting up the Valentine's Day decorations and check to see that all the specialty items are on the shelves. Decorate the tearoom—I'll buy some more lace hearts and red paper doilies. And I'll bring my collection of antique valentines for the tables."

"That ought to brighten things up," I agreed. Last year, Ruby's antique valentines evoked a chorus of oohs and aahs. "But the tearoom looks pretty fine as it is," I added, glancing around. When we built Thyme for Tea, Ruby chose the décor: hunter green wainscoting halfway up the old stone walls, green-painted tables and chairs with floral chintz napkins, terra-cotta pots of herbs on the tables, large pots of cactus on the floor, and a longhorn cow's skull hanging over the door, its horns draped with ivy. A Texas-style tearoom.

"It'll look finer when it's decorated." Ruby went on with her list. "And Cass and Janet need to check the Valentine's menus from last year. There's no point in reinventing the wheel." Pencil raised like a twirler's baton, she cocked an eyebrow at me. "The gardens? Anything you need to do out there?"

When Ruby gets into this mood, there's nothing to do but fall into line and march along behind her. "Oh, you bet," I said. "The pansies have to be set out, I'm going to pot up about four dozen scented geraniums, and we're expecting a shipment of assorted two- and four-inch herbs. Some go into the garden, some go out on the display rack. Oh, and the roses have to be pruned."

Here in the Texas Hill Country, roses start putting out their new growth in March, so it's a good rule to have the pruning finished by Valentine's Day. Since there are dozens of antique rosebushes in the herb gardens around the shops, I do a lot of pruning. And since I hate to wear garden gloves, my February hands are a sight for sore eyes. Which is a problem, since my husband and I celebrate Valentine's Day in a big way, with presents and a romantic dinner out. I was giving him a pair of cowboy boots, with red stitching on the black leather tops. I wondered what he was giving me.

"If you're in the garden, will Laurel be in the shop?" Ruby asked.

I nodded. "Full time through Valentine's Day." Laurel Riley handles Thyme and Seasons when I have garden and landscaping work to do. A few months ago, she completed her certification as a Master Herbalist, so she is now an officially certified nutrition and health consultant. I encourage her to make contacts and hand out her cards to the customers, with the idea of building up her consulting practice. And of course, having a nutrition and medicinal herbs expert behind the counter is a very good thing. Between the two of us, we're able to answer any question we're likely to get.

"Laurel's great," Ruby said. She went back to her list. "Now, let's see. On the tearoom special events schedule, we have a tea for the executive board of the high school parent-teacher group, the Garden Guild luncheon, and the regular Valentine's Tea. And Party Thyme is due at the Martins on Friday night—" She stopped. "No, wait. Mrs. Martin cancelled that dinner—her mother has to have surgery—and I scheduled . . ." Frowning, she began shuffling through her notes. "Now, who did I put down for that date?"

While Ruby is trying to locate the name, let me take a minute to clue you in. Ruby Wilcox—a six-foot-something gal with a willowy figure, rowdy red curls, gingery freckles, and blue eyes (except when she's wearing her green or brown contacts)—is the proprietor of the Crystal Cave, a New Age shop where you can stock up on all the weird stuff you need for the serious exploration of inner and outer space: rune stones, astrological charts, crystal balls, magic wands, books about the healing journey, and so on. Ruby's personal style drives the Pecan Springs fashion police crazy. Today, she was wearing blue spandex pants and a dark blue turtleneck tunic spattered with silvery stars, suns, and galaxies, accessorized with a floating scarf in shades of blue, purple, and silver, saucer-sized silvery hoop earrings, a silver belt, silver slippers, and blue nails sprinkled with silver. She was a vision from the edge of the universe.

My name is China Bayles. I am short and stocky to Ruby's tall and willowy; I prefer jeans, tees, and anything wash-and-wear; and where Ruby has her head in the stars, I usually have both hands in the dirt. Eight or nine years ago, I left my practice as a criminal attorney in Houston and bought a century-old building on Crockett Street in the town of Pecan Springs, halfway between Austin and San Antonio, on the eastern edge of the Texas Hill Country. The ample yard is filled with gardens, which connect with the gardens around the Craft Emporium on one side and the children's bookstore, Hobbit House, on the other. At the back, on the alley, sits Thyme Cottage, a remodeled stone stable that I use for classes and workshops and rent occasionally as a bed-and-breakfast.

The two-story main building, built of locally quarried limestone, now houses Thyme and Seasons Herb Shop, Ruby's Crystal Cave, and our tearoom, Thyme for Tea. The tearoom is located in the space that used to be my apartment, until I married Mike McQuaid and moved with him and his son, Brian, into the old Victorian house on Limekiln Road. Because I'm a skeptical realist by nature and inclined to see the darker side of any situation, I figured that Ruby and I would be old and gray before Thyme for Tea turned a profit—if it ever did. Ruby, on the other hand, is a starry-eyed optimist. She looked into her crystal ball and predicted that our enterprise would be a profitable one. She was right. When she does the books at the end of the month, she points out the bottom line with a twinkle and an I-told-you-so grin. The tearoom has been up and down a few times, but the general trend is up, and even I have to agree that Thyme for Tea was one of Ruby's better ideas.

So I've learned to pay attention when Ruby dreams up something new. When she suggested expanding our business by adding a catering service called Party Thyme (which Ruby calls our "traveling circus"), who was I to rain on her parade? When we began this project, Party Thyme was just Ruby and I and Janet (our past-prime-time cook), with the help of several girls we borrowed from the Pecan Springs high school culinary arts classes. Unfortunately, just as business picked up, Janet's knees gave out, and Ruby and I were faced with the dismaying prospect of handling all the work ourselves. And then help arrived from an entirely unexpected quarter, in the person of—

The outside door burst open. A substantial form blocked the morning sunlight and a bright voice pealed, like a cheerful bell: "Hi, guys!"

It was the unexpected quarter herself. Cassandra Wilde. She was loaded with plastic grocery bags, and she wore a red chile ristra around her neck like an outsize boa.

"Hey, Cass," Ruby said, looking up from her notes. "Do you happen to remember who we put down for Friday night, after Mrs. Martin cancelled on us?"

"Sure," Cass said, over her shoulder. "The Duffys." She carried her bags into the kitchen and thumped them onto the counter. Hearing activity in the kitchen, Khat K'o Kung, the regal Siamese who lives at Thyme and Seasons, went to lend a helpful paw. Ruby, a wanna-be sleuth, named Khat in honor of Kao K'o Kung, Qwilleran's talented Siamese in the Cat Who mysteries. Khat insists that Ruby has it backward, and that Kao K'o Kung is named after *him*.

"Oh, right," Ruby said, and scribbled something on her calendar. "The Duffys."

"Yeah, and I'm looking forward to it," Cass said. "I'm a major fan of Coach Duffy's, you know. And what's more, he's a new Thymely Gourmet customer. I ran into him when I stopped at the Diner this morning. He asked me to make a month of dinners and put them in the freezer at his house—a surprise for Mrs. Duffy." She paused, looking down at her feet. "Hello, Khat. What's on your mind this morning?"

Khat remarked that he'd already eaten, but, a bit of something extra would not go amiss. He is a cat of action (his motto is "The early cat catches the early mouse"), but he is also a philosophical creature ("Every cat should rule his passions or his passions will overrule him"). So he assumed a meditative posture, curled his dark tail over his chocolate paws, and waited, the perfect picture of cat-in-the-present-moment.

"How about a bit of liver?" Cass opened the refrigerator, found a container of cooked liver, and zapped it briefly in the microwave before setting it down in front of Khat. He uncurled his tail, sniffed the liver twice, very delicately, and addressed it with the devout attention of a Buddhist monk at prayer. Cass poured herself a cup of tea from the pot on the counter and came to join us, carrying a paper bag. She grinned at me as she sat down.

"Jelly doughnuts, courtesy of Lila Jennings," she said, and I rolled my eyes. Of all the basic food groups—ice cream, chocolates, chicken fried steak, and artichoke hearts with hollandaise sauce—jelly doughnuts from Lila's Nueces Street Diner are my absolute favorite. Never mind that

I'd already had cereal and orange juice at home, or that I really do try to curb my consumption of fat and sugar. Show me a jelly doughnut and all my good intentions fly right out the window. "Save some for me," she added, as I snatched the bag. "And Ruby."

I took a raspberry doughnut and handed the bag back to her. Cass, our new partner, is a beautiful, bountiful blonde, light of spirit and much lighter on her feet than you might expect from someone her size—"my sweet, sassy, sexy size twenty-two," she says modestly. "All curves, and nothing to lose." Cass is not shy.

"Ruby is organizing our lives from now until Valentine's Day," I said, licking the sugar off my fingers. "She's making sure that every single one of our multiple enterprises turns a tidy profit. So we have to pay attention."

"I'm all ears," Cass said, taking a jelly doughnut and handing the bag to Ruby. "Where profit is concerned, I'm just as greedy as the next one. Remember, though, all work and no play makes us Party Thyme girls very grouchy. Be sure and schedule some R and R."

I have to admit that bringing Cassandra Wilde into our partnership has been a good thing, although I wasn't terribly crazy about the idea in the first place. Ruby and I have been together for nearly ten years. It's like being married: I know what she's thinking, she knows what I'm feeling, and we get along very well about ninety percent of the time. A third person, I feared, would inevitably change that balance. And it's easier to get a divorce than it is to dissolve a business partnership that's gone on the rocks. I worried that Ruby and I would find ourselves up to our eyebrows in a mess we couldn't get out of easily. The cautious side of my nature reminded me that two's company, while three almost always turns out to be a crowd.

But Cass had a smart idea and a great deal of persistence—"I'm your original pushy broad," she said with a grin—and it was hard to turn her

8

down. Her idea was another business enterprise: a personal chef service called The Thymely Gourmet, a spin-off of Party Thyme, which is of course a spin-off of Thyme for Tea and Thyme and Seasons, what's known in the business world as horizontal integration. Cass seemed to have the perfect background for it. She's been in the food industry for years and was recently certified as a personal chef by the American Culinary Foundation. What's more, she has enormous energy, a reservoir of cheerfulness that never seems to go dry, and the ability to see what needs to be done and do it without fuss. After three months of working with her on a trial basis, Ruby and I were ready to make it official. Our twosome became a threesome, and the Thymely Gourmet became an integral part of our expanding business. But don't think I accepted the idea without reservations. It was every bit as scary as getting married, with all the added complications of bigamy. Now there were three ways to go wrong, instead of just two.

"So Cass is doing Friday night at the Duffys," Ruby said, making a note on her list. "And Saturday evening, China and I have a hanging party at Carol Bruce's house, for the Scrappers." The Pecan Springs Scrappers is the name of our local quilting group, of which Ruby is a longtime member.

"A hanging party?" I widened my eyes. "As in old Westerns? Who's getting hung?"

Cass snickered. "Maybe it was a Scrapper who got caught stealing another Scrapper's quilt pieces. Or a Scrapper who can't sew a straight seam. Or a Scrapper who—"

"The hanging party," Ruby said, ignoring Cass, "will be held at Carol's house, after the hanging—that is, the installation of our first annual quilt show at The Springs Hotel."

"Oh, *that* kind of hanging." I sighed. "Rats. I was hoping for a little excitement. Things have been pretty tame around this place lately." It was true. There were some thrills and chills about the time Ruby starred in *A Man for All Reasons* the previous October, but the intervening months had been dark and a little dreary. Dullsville, as Cass had put it.

"The Duffy party is the last event on the Party Thyme calendar," Ruby said, studying her list. "We need to bring in some more business."

"The Thymely Gourmet has two new customers, actually," Cass put in. "So we're doing okay there."

"Two?" Ruby asked, impressed. "Wow. That makes—what? Twelve?" Of course, they aren't all regulars. Some people ask Cass to prepare a week's worth of meals every now and then, while others have her stock their freezers every month. And occasionally she'll get a wife who wants her to fix a husband's meals while she's out of town, or somebody who's trying a new diet, or—

"Fourteen," Cass replied. "Coach Duffy is Number Thirteen, and his neighbor, Chuck Manning, is Number Fourteen. He and the coach both want to surprise their wives. And Mr. Manning is the president of the Panthers Booster Club." She grinned. "If he likes us, maybe he'll spread the word to his Booster buddies."

"If you run out of Boosters, you can come to my house," I suggested helpfully. "I could sure use a couple of weeks of precooked gourmet meals."

"Of course she can," Ruby said, closing her calendar. She gave me a benevolent smile. "If you cross her palm with silver."

"Hey, come on," I grumbled. "The partners ought to get some perks."

Cass handed me the paper bag. "Have another doughnut."

Chapter Two

Women have no business whatsoever trying to cook chili. It's a man's dish.

Don Russell,
cofounder, San Marcos, Texas, Chilympiad

When McQuaid and I first decided to move in together, I was living behind the shop and McQuaid and Brian had a small house near the campus. Realizing that we needed a lot more space, we leased a ramshackle, white-painted Victorian on Limekiln Road, a few miles west of town, and the year after we got married, we bought it. The house, sheltered by huge pecan trees, sits at the end of a half-mile gravel lane. It has an L-shaped porch with a swing, a screened porch off the kitchen, five bedrooms, and three acres of land—room enough to ensure that we don't rub one another raw. I claimed the third-floor windowed turret for my herb library and the sunny area behind the house for a garden, while McQuaid immediately latched on to the garage workshop (with an adjacent locked room for his guns), and Brian took a second-floor bedroom overlooking the creek, with its mossy waterfall and maidenhair ferns and the wild Hill Country woodland that stretches for miles beyond. The place, which we call Meadow Brook, suits all three of us, even though the house is definitely a pain in the rear. The walls always need painting, the roof always needs shingling, the grass always needs mowing, and if we don't fix the termite damage under the kitchen pretty soon, the floor may fall in. Maintenance on this place is like paperwork at the shop. We could put every spare minute into it and never get caught up.

A pot of McQuaid's prize-winning chili was simmering on the kitchen stove when I came home after work that night. A bowl of coleslaw sat on the table, and I could smell the hot, rich fragrance of corn bread in the oven—jalapeño corn bread, baked in Mother McQuaid's old cast-iron skillet. Tonight was my husband's turn to cook, and he had obviously put his heart and soul into it. I was grateful. I'd been pruning roses all day. I was ready for some home cooking.

Howard Cosell, McQuaid's grumpy old basset hound, was ready, too. He strolled out of the pantry, where he had no doubt been on reconnaissance, scouting for chocolate cookies. Howard's favorite times of the day are breakfast, lunch, and dinner, separated by reasonably long naps in his Basset Basket beside my old Home Comfort gas range. Howard tolerates me (mostly because I'm in charge of groceries), he's affectionate toward Brian, but he thinks the sun rises and sets on McQuaid, the alpha male. He glanced around the kitchen, peered under the stove, and then up at me, with a mournful, where-have-you-put-him-now kind of look.

McQuaid wasn't in the kitchen. Howard and I located him in his office, his feet on his desk and the phone to his ear. Howard ambled over, sat on his haunches, and rested his chin on McQuaid's knee, gazing up at him with those adoring basset eyes that say, plainer than words, *Anything I can get for you, Pop? Pipe, slippers, a beer?* I wouldn't go so far as Howard, probably (I draw the line at putting my chin on McQuaid's knee). But if marriage has taken any of the shine off the romance, I haven't noticed it. McQuaid's features are too rugged to be called handsome, but he's tall, dark, and sexy. And while I don't have another husband to compare him to, I'm persuaded that he's the best. He's a patient man, even-tempered and fair, which is more than you can say for a lot of alpha males.

"Sure, I can handle that," McQuaid said into the telephone, fondling Howard's ears with his free hand. "Fly? Nah, I'll drive—that way, I won't have to rent a car. If I leave early in the morning, I can be there by dinnertime." Cradling the phone with his shoulder, he scribbled something down on a notepad. "Yeah, sure. Sounds right to me, Dell. Glad to do it."

"Do what?" I asked, as he put the phone down.

I met McQuaid when I was still practicing criminal law and he was still a cop—we were on opposite sides of the legal fence, so to speak. By the time we got married, both of us had left our careers. I owned the herb shop and he was teaching criminal justice courses at Central Texas State University. But while I've never once thought about going back to the law, McQuaid has always missed investigating—that's the part he liked best about being a cop—and he's occasionally flirted with the idea of going back to law enforcement. For a few months, he served as Pecan Springs' acting police chief, and on another occasion, he took an undercover assignment with the Texas Rangers. He got badly shot up on that case, though, and I hoped the misadventure would put an end to his yearning to return to police work.

And then, nine months or so ago, he surprised me with the announcement that he was hanging out his shingle as a private investigator. I wasn't thrilled. I've seen dozens of movies featuring PIs, and every one of them involves a couple of wild automobile chases and an obligatory shoot-'em-up scene—not to mention free-flowing booze and half-clad lassies. Real life ain't the movies, of course. I trust McQuaid to stay out of situations he can't handle, and being a private investigator is no doubt safer than being a law enforcement officer. But still . . .

13

"Nothing for you to worry about, China, my love." McQuaid gave me a boyish grin and bent over and rubbed Howard's nose. "You, either, Howard, old boy. A little white-collar crime, that's all. A guy in Albuquerque has asked me to investigate a theft of computer software."

Albuquerque. I'm sure it's just a coincidence, but McQuaid's dingbat ex-wife recently moved to Albuquerque. Mostly, McQuaid tries to stay out of her affairs, but when she gets herself in serious trouble—Sally plays the ingenue, the femme fatale, and the villain in her own long-running schizophrenic soap opera—he seems to feel an obligation to step in and bail her out. The last time, she fell in love with a high-flying stockbroker who not only broke her heart but also tried to break her bank account. When McQuaid took it upon himself to put an end to these transactions, Sally was not at all grateful for his interference. The one good thing she's done—the big gift she handed to McQuaid on her way out of their marriage—was to allow him to have uncontested custody of Brian. It's sad for the boy that his mother doesn't take much of an interest in his life, but when she does, it's likely to be disastrous, like the time she kidnapped Brian and then tried to commit suicide by jumping out a hotel window. So I'm just as glad she's in New Mexico. Except that now—

"Yeah." McQuaid went back to fiddling with the notes on his desk. "This one sounds like a quickie. I should be able to get the whole thing wrapped in . . . oh, two weeks or so."

"Two weeks!" I threw up my hands in dismay. "But that means you'll be gone over Valentine's Day! You'll miss our Valentine's dinner, and Brian's Science Fair, and Howard's appointment with the vet." Howard, for whom a trip to the vet is a definite bummer, gave me an apprehensive look and made for the door. "Not to mention the trip to the ranch," I added.

My mother, with whom I have been on somewhat better terms for the past few years, had called the day before with an invitation—a summons, actually, since she seemed rather urgent about it—to drive down to the ranch on Sunday. When I asked her why, she'd say only that it had something to do with my father, who died in an automobile accident when I was in my late twenties. Leatha remarried not long ago, and she and her husband, Sam, live on an exotic game ranch, the Tres Equis Ranch. Brian is crazy about Sam and the ranch, and since he had a school holiday on Monday and the shop is closed as well, the three of us had planned a relaxing two-day getaway.

"Aw, honey," McQuaid said, and put his arms around me. "I'm really sorry about missing our Valentine's dinner and dumping all that other stuff on you. But this investigation involves one of the biggest software developers in the Southwest. If I do a good job, it'll mean referrals, and you know how important that is, especially when you're just getting started."

He put his finger under my chin, lifted it gently, and gave me a sweet, husbandly kiss. "You'll forgive me, won't you?"

He kissed me again, not gently this time, and not very much like a husband, either. This kiss showed signs of continuing indefinitely, to the intense delight of both of us, but suddenly he pulled away, lifted his head, and sniffed.

"What's that I smell?" he demanded.

"I think it's your corn bread burning. Of course, I'm not the detective in this family, and I could be wrong, but—"

But I was talking to McQuaid's back. There's nothing he hates more than burned corn bread. Unless, of course, it's being thwarted when he has his heart set on conducting a criminal investigation. And I did promise him, when he started this new enterprise, that if he kept his nose out of trouble, I'd keep my nose out of his business.

So it looked as if my husband was headed for an exciting couple of weeks in Albuquerque, the same city where his flaky ex-wife lives, while Brian and I did the best we could by ourselves. Boring, big-time. Dullsville, as Cass would put it.

I couldn't have been more wrong.

I sometimes swear that Brian, now fifteen, is getting taller and more broad-shouldered by the minute—and more good-looking, too. He's inherited his father's dark hair and blue eyes, although he does not have his father's broken nose, which McQuaid earned when he was a college quarterback. For years, I have harbored the wistful hope that Brian might escape the thwacks and thumps and concussions and other hazards of high school football. McQuaid, who remembers his sports career with the fondness of an old soldier for the bloody battlegrounds of his youth, does not join me in this, and secretly hoped that Brian would try out for the freshman squad.

But I got my wish. While Brian likes pro football, he is a brainy kid who prefers crawling through caves on his knees and elbows to organized team sports, and lizards, frogs, spiders, and snakes to girls.

Except for Jake, that is. Jake is Jacqueline Keene, a cheerful, athletic girl, who is also cute, smart, and practical. Judging from the casual way they behave toward each other, I wouldn't go so far as to call her Brian's girlfriend. But what do moms know, especially a mom who hasn't been a teen for a couple of centuries and can't begin to describe the courting practices of today's young? Jake is definitely a girl and certainly a friend, so maybe she qualifies. Anyway, she was joining us for dinner tonight.

"Chili!" she said, taking a big sniff. "My favorite!"

"Smells like Dad burned the corn bread again," Brian observed critically.

"Don't make him feel bad," I said, opening a jar of applesauce. "Jake, if you want to help, you can dish out four servings of applesauce, and sprinkle some cinnamon, nutmeg, and cloves on top of each. When we're ready for dessert, we can put the dishes in the microwave and then top them with vanilla ice cream and chopped pecans. Brian, you can feed Howard."

"I need to check on my lizards first," Brian said.

"Dog before dinner, lizards after dessert," I said firmly. Mom-speak isn't something that comes naturally to me, you understand. While I've known Brian since he was a first-grader and have even subbed for the Tooth Fairy when his dad wasn't available, I've been an official mom for only a couple of years. But I've already learned the basic mom-vocabulary: *wash your hands, clean your room, stop teasing the dog, no burping at the table.* And more important: *good job, nice work, super kid,* and *I love you,* delivered with generous hugs.

Heaving a huge sigh of resignation, Brian went to feed Howard, who was already stationed at his dog-food bowl, thumping his tail encouragingly. I finished setting the table while Jake gave me the play-by-play of the latest girls' basketball game, which the Lady Panthers lost, 48–34.

Girls' basketball is definitely not a high-priority sport at Pecan Springs High, where almost every nickel of the athletic budget and about ninety-nine point nine percent of the effort goes to the football program. This is, after all, Texas, where football is king and the football coach is next to

God. Where the Pecan Springs Panthers have gone to State six times in the last fifteen years, and brought home the championship trophy four times. Panther magic, it's called. And where lots of men and quite a few women feel that life wouldn't be worth living if they couldn't look forward to those Friday night football games.

But football season is thankfully over, and it's the Lady Panthers' turn. Jake's mom, Annie, and I go to the basketball games and cheer. Annie and I are both proud of Jake's lithe, trim figure, her strength and endurance, and her bouncy good humor, even when the game doesn't go as planned. If you measure the season by the number of wins, it hasn't been the greatest, but losing doesn't seem to get the girls down, the way it does the boys. Jake says they play for the fun of it; watching them, I believe her. And of course, the girls' basketball squad has nothing to lose but the game, unlike the boys' football team, upon whose success is staked the school's reputation, its future, its past, its whole identity—and by extension, that of Pecan Springs.

Today, however, Jake did not seem as bright and bouncy as usual, and I wondered if something was bothering her. I wanted to ask, but there wasn't much time for girl talk. McQuaid came in, I ladled the chili into big blue bowls while he cut up the corn bread (rescued in the nick of time), and we sat down to good food and conversation and, well, family values. There's nothing like a hot meal for bringing families together.

Thirty minutes later, the chili and corn bread were only a pleasant memory. McQuaid went up to pack for his trip to New Mexico, and I left Brian and Jake to tackle the cleanup while I took a cup of coffee and went into the office to do some inventory work on the computer. It was some time after that when I went back to the kitchen for a coffee refill, pausing at the door when—to my surprise—I heard Jake crying.

"It's okay," Brian was saying, in an uncomfortable sort of way. "Just hang in there, Jake, and it'll work out. It's not that bad. Really."

Jake's voice was muffled. "That's all you know," she said, sniffling. "It's not okay. There's nothing I can do. Nothing."

"You could . . . well, I guess you could tell somebody." Brian sounded awkward and uncertain, as if he didn't really believe what he was saying.

"Tell who?" Jake demanded bitterly. "Not my mom, that's for sure. One of the teachers? Forget it. Anyway, what could they do? What can anybody do?" She blew her nose. "And don't you try to get involved, Brian McQuaid. It'll only make things worse. I have to handle this myself. I don't know how, but I'll think of something."

Poor Jake. Whatever dilemma she was confronting—friends doing drugs, somebody cheating on exams, somebody pregnant—she sounded utterly hopeless, and I found myself feeling her sadness and pain as sharply as if it were my own. My own high school days were pretty unspeakable, what I can remember of them. Between unhappiness at school and unhappiness at home—my mother was an alcoholic social butterfly whom I scorned, my dad a legal-eagle workaholic whom I adored but rarely saw—I was not a happy camper, and the days were a painful blur. My father brought home plenty of money, and we lived in an expensive house in Houston's upscale River Oaks. But our affluence only made my situation worse. I was a hippie, more or less, with an interest in social issues, which meant that I was completely out of step with my wealthy classmates, whose idea of an urgent social issue was getting invited to the Senior Prom. And I was a loner: I didn't play a band instrument, I wasn't interested in sports or dancing or clubs, and debating was my only passion. Identity crises? I suffered at least one a day, sometimes two.

I turned away from the door. My coffee refill could wait. I didn't want to embarrass the kids by walking in on them. Whatever was bothering Jake was something she meant to keep private, even from her mother, and respecting the personal privacy of others has always been a major issue for me. I know, of course, that there are times in your child's life when you have to step in, but I do it gingerly, and with trepidation. One of the toughest mom-lessons I've had to learn is when to interfere and when to stay the heck out.

But it's hard, oh, it's hard. And every time I have to make this choice, I have the awful feeling that I've made the wrong one.

I had that feeling now.

Chapter Three

Dicentra cucullaria, bleeding heart's white-flowering cousin, was used by Menominee Indians as a powerful love charm and aphrodisiac. The blossom was thrown by a young man at the girl he fancied; if it hit her, she was bound to fall in love with him. The young man chewed the plant's root and then breathed on the object of his affection. It was believed that the fragrance of his breath would charm her, even against her will.

Ah, the best-laid plans.

Party Thyme has taught us that things almost never go the way we think they're going to go—but that the event almost always turns out okay anyway. Because McQuaid had gone to Albuquerque, I was at loose ends on Friday night. Which meant that when one of the Bowers twins got the flu (Mandy and Missy are the current Party Thyme helpers, and very good ones, too), I was available to help Cass with the Duffy party.

And as it turned out, this was a very good thing, because at the last minute Ruby's current love interest, Colin Fowler, came up with a pair of tickets to a Jerry Jeff Walker concert in Austin, and Ruby wasn't going to miss it. She met Colin four or five months ago and has found him irresistible, her Prince Charming come at last.

Personally, I have to say that I am not smitten with Colin, for reasons I won't go into just at this moment. But my opinion on this subject doesn't count for much—for anything at all, when you get right down to it. When it comes to love, Ruby always follows her heart—which some-times sets her up for huge disappointments, in part because her romantic expectations are higher than any mortal man could possibly meet. For instance, she's never happy when Colin leaves on one of his business trips. And while he stays at her house most of the time, he's kept his own place, which she sees as a sign that he is something less than fully com-mitted. So when Colin suggests a night out together, Ruby moves heaven and earth to make it possible, and her gal-pals take up the slack.

So that's how I wound up in Glenda Duffy's elegant kitchen on Friday night, with an apron tied around my middle and Cass's party treats stacked up in tiers around Missy Bowers and me, with forty or fifty party-goers about to descend on the Duffy house.

Pecan Springs may like to think of itself as unique, but it has the same sort of social strata as many other small towns. In addition to two flavors of royalty (the old and the new), there are the bourgeoisie, the plebeians, and (we're a college town) the intelligentsia. The old royalty—the Sei-denstickers and Krauthammers, the Weisses and the Schwartzes—are the families whose ancestors came here from Germany in the 1850s, and a tough time they had of it, too, pouring sweat and tears and blood into the unforgiving Texas wilderness. The new royalty, on the other hand, came along before the Second World War, buying their way into the town's aristocracy with various combinations of cows, oil, railroads, and bank-ing. Once the aristocratic ranks were formed, they immediately closed. Now, the only way to be royal is to be born one or marry one—although most Pecan Springers wouldn't bother, since the Old Guard is history, and the town, as people like to say, is movin' on.

And then there are the bourgeoisie, Pecan Springs' movers and shak-ers. Doctors and lawyers and merchant chiefs—people who have made a name for themselves in the professions and commerce. People like Hark Hibler, editor of the *Enterprise*; Carol Bruce, who coordinates volunteers at the Adams County Hospital; and Chuck Manning, who owns Manning Real Estate and presides over the Panther Boosters. People like the local vet, and the principal of the high school, and the administrator at the nursing home. People like Ruby and me and our friends, who keep the shops and stores and belong to the Chamber of Commerce and speak up at the City Council meetings and help with the Pecan Festival every October and the Christmas Tree lighting on the square in December. Our advertising funds the local newspaper, our taxes pave the streets and pay the police, and our profits (when there are any) are spent locally, which is a lot more than you can say about Wal-Mart and Office Depot.

The intelligentsia? They keep to themselves, mostly. We have the usual town-gown split, and even though McQuaid is nominally a member of the CTSU faculty, we don't see much of the people on the Hill. And the plebeians—well, you know who they are and what they do to keep the rest of us clean, comfortable, cozy, and well-fed. They never, ever get enough credit. Most of the time, as the owner of a successful business and prominent member of the community, I am a bourgeois. That Friday night, standing in Glenda Duffy's kitchen, wearing an apron and unpacking boxes with our high-school helper Missy Bowers, I was a plebeian, and beneath notice.

Which is probably why Glenda Duffy scarcely noticed Missy and me when she came into the kitchen to make sure that everything was being set up properly. In terms of social status, the Duffys were a kind of anomaly, and their democratic guest list for the night included people from all strata of Pecan Springs society—except for plebeians, of course, although we would be there, too, doing our jobs in the kitchen.

23

Glenda herself is a second cousin to the Seidenstickers, one of the Pecan Springs royal families (the Seidenstickers founded the *Enterprise*), and she has a look somewhere between that of Princess Di and a Dallas Cowboy cheerleader. That night, she was wearing a slim white dress with a seriously décolleté neckline that showed off her sun-bronzed arms, lean, and strong from hours on the Country Club's tennis courts. Her golden hair was twirled and swirled, her nails and skin were flawless, and she wore pearls at her throat, a gold charm bracelet with dangling mini-footballs on one slim arm, and a to-die-for diamond ring on her left hand. I had the feeling that this was a woman who'd gotten everything she'd ever dreamed of, a woman who had never suffered an identity crisis in her life. She had absolutely no doubt about who she was: Glenda Seidensticker Duffy, royalty by birth and a different kind of royalty—football royalty—by marriage.

Of course, football coaches and their wives are exactly as human as the rest of us—but not in a football-crazy town. Hometown football is a matter of hometown pride, and the coach—especially a coach with a couple of winning seasons under his belt—has a special status. His salary is more than double that of the highest-paid teacher, and he teaches no classes. Perkins Ford dealership gives him the free use of a Ford pickup truck every year—this year, one of those nifty crew cab pickups that McQuaid has been coveting. And Manning Real Estate (that's Chuck Manning, the Booster Club president) arranged a very good deal on the house of the Duffys' choice, while the bank gave them a preferential interest rate.

And where Tim Duffy is concerned, everybody agrees that the perks are well-earned. When he moved to Pecan Springs from the head coaching job at little Friendship, Texas, the Panthers had just lost their previous coach to a massive coronary in the locker room. Coach Duffy charged the boys up, petted and prodded and propelled them into back-to-back trips to State, and brought home not one but two championship trophies. And next year, everybody says, considering the talent, considering the coaching, considering this, considering that, there's no reason in the world why the Panthers can't be Numero Uno yet again. In the eyes of the students, the alums, the Boosters, and anybody else infected by Friday Night Fever, Tim Duffy has hung the moon. And with his thick blond hair and meltdown smile, his linebacker's shoulders and his quarterback's lean hips and thighs, he is every inch a Greek god. So what the heck. Why not just declare him king and be done with it?

Queen Glenda was finishing her cursory inspection when her husband came into the kitchen. He put his arms around her from behind and squeezed. She squealed in protest and when he tried to kiss her, she made the usual playful female noises about smeared lipstick and mussed hair. But then she glanced up and noticed Missy watching them. Her eyes widened suddenly, and an expression of something like horrified surprise replaced the playfulness.

But then, in an instant, it was gone. Very deliberately, she turned to her husband and touched his mouth with proprietary fingers, giving him a long, slow glance that promised, plain as day, that he'd get what was coming to him when everyone had left and they were alone. It was a touch that staked her claim with a flat absoluteness—Tim Duffy belonged to her and nobody else—and a glance that . . . well, it smoldered, that's what it did. Glenda Duffy was sexually aroused by her husband, and by the fact that he was *hers* and nobody else's. And she didn't mind letting other people know about it.

Coach Duffy, however, was still feeling playful, for he chuckled as he let his wife go and swatted her shapely rear as she left the room, provoking another female squeal. Then he turned, and catching Missy's eye, gave her the kind of wink that guys sometimes give female plebeians when their wives aren't looking.

I didn't have time to mull things over just then, although I would give that little scene plenty of thought later. At that moment, Missy dropped a plate, and Coach Duffy offered to show her where the broom closet was. Then Cass bounced cheerfully into the room, and I was swept into the methodical madness of party catering: boxes and dishes and silver to be unpacked, already-prepared food to be arranged on trays and in dishes, liquor and wine bottles to be opened, ice buckets to be filled, coffee to be brewed, and trays and trays and more trays to be carried. And then, when the party was all over, the whole thing had to be done again, but in reverse, like playing a movie backward, where all the leaves get sucked back onto the trees or the presents get pulled back into their boxes and the boxes are magically rewrapped and the bows retied.

When it was all over, and Glenda Duffy's kitchen had been restored to its previous pristine condition, we three plebeians were glad to receive Glenda Duffy's pleased compliments. "Great job, ladies. Wonderful food, terrific service, and a super clean-up. Thank you!"

Cass handed her the invoice, the Queen wrote us a check (including a nice tip), and we said good night. Cass and I dropped Missy off at home, then drove Big Red Mama, our secondhand van, back to the shops and unloaded her, as we always do after a party, no matter how late it is. It had been a good job well done. Surely, the next time the King and Queen threw a party, we'd get the job.

Neither of us could know, of course, that the Duffys wouldn't be giving any more parties.

Chapter Four

CASS'S SPINACH-BASIL ROLL-UPS

1 10 ounce package chopped spinach, thawed, drained
1 cup fresh basil, finely chopped
2 tablespoons olive oil
½ cup onions, finely chopped
2 cloves garlic, very finely minced
1 cup mayonnaise (low-fat or fat-free is fine)
½ cup sour cream (low-fat or fat-free)
½ cup Parmesan cheese
9 burrito-size flour tortillas

Combine spinach and basil. Put into a sieve and gently press out the water. Sauté onions and garlic in olive oil (don't burn the garlic). Drain and combine with spinach and basil. Mix in mayonnaise, sour cream, and Parmesan. Spread over tortillas. Roll up tightly, jelly-roll fashion. Wrap in plastic wrap and chill 4 to 6 hours. Cut into ½-inch-thick slices. Makes about six dozen slices.

It was long after midnight when I finally got to bed, but I still had to get up early on Saturday morning and go to the shop. The flu bug that had been hopping around town had bitten Laurel, and she'd left an apologetic message on my answering machine, saying she'd be a little late and hoped I wouldn't mind opening up. So at quarter to ten on a cool, cloudy Saturday morning, I unlocked the front door of Thyme and Seasons, stepped inside, and took a long, deep, satisfying breath of the fragrant air, rich with roses and lavender and mint.

No matter how tired I am, my weariness always seems to evaporate when I walk into my herb shop. Year to year, nothing much changes at Thyme and Seasons, and yet it somehow always looks new and different to me. Just now, you'll see the Valentine's wreaths hanging on the wall—they were delivered last week by Donna Fletcher, who owns a flower farm not far from town and keeps me supplied with stunning dried-flower creations. I always display a shelf of herbal soaps, but those heart-shaped bars just arrived, the work of a friend who lives in New Braunfels and makes terrific bath products. Those are her herbal bubble baths and bath powders, too. The culinary and crafting herbs in the glass jars are freshly dried and the herbal tinctures in dark bottles—well, they keep practically forever, as do the pretty herbal vinegars on that shelf over there, all of them made by Verna Roberts, who got her start in a class I taught a few years ago and now markets her vinegars all over central Texas. The books on the bookshelves include old favorites (there's Marge Clark's *The Best of Thymes* and Susan Belsinger's *Flowers in the Kitchen*) and new releases (the Brooklyn Botanic Garden's *Designing an Herb Garden*), and the subjects range from cookbooks to gardening books, crafting books, books on herbal medicines and herbal lore.

And of course there are the dried plants waiting for you to craft them into wreaths and swags and bouquets: artemisia, goldenrod, baby's breath, purple statice, all grown in the gardens here at Thyme and Seasons. If you don't want to do the crafting yourself, buy one of the Flower Farm wreaths, or a chile ristra or a garlic braid made by the Sisters of the Holy Heart at St. Theresa's Monastery, west of Pecan Springs. Or maybe you'd prefer to knit a scarf from a skein of plant-dyed mohair yarn, spun from the fine fleece of the angora goats Allison Selby raises on her farm near Indigo, east of Pecan Springs. One of the things I love about Thyme and Seasons is being able to look around and name the person who has grown or harvested or crafted each individual item, and knowing exactly what it's made of, and where, and that it was treated with respect and affection. It's a feeling I treasure.

I came to herbs like most people, the long way around. My grandmother China—my father's mother, the woman I'm named for—always had herbs in her garden in New Orleans. When I was growing up, I loved green things but couldn't see how they could be part of my career, since I knew I had to be a lawyer, like my father, and his father, and *his* father. The law ran in the family, and that's all there was to it.

Of course, my father wanted me to be a boy, in which case I would have been Robert Edward Bayles, III. But boy or girl, I did my level best to carry on the family tradition. I wanted to be just like my father and grandfather and great-grandfather, to share in that mysterious power they wielded so easily, so casually, as men, as professionals, as respected citizens. So I went to law school, graduated near the top of my class, chose to go into criminal law, and joined a large Houston firm that specialized in justice for all, but particularly for bad guys with big bank accounts—all with the hope of pleasing my father, or at least getting him to notice me.

But it proved to be a silly, futile hope, for Dad didn't bother. Like a great many fathers, he was too busy pursuing his own important achievements— his law practice, his political connections, his highly placed friends—to pay any attention to mine. Looking back, the only father-daughter thing I can remember the two of us doing together seems like an anomaly, rather. When I was still in college, he took me to a firing range, taught me to shoot, and gave me a gun. But that was it. As far as my father was concerned, his final obligation to me ended when I graduated from law school. Anything I did after that, I did on my own.

And all the time, deep in my heart, I knew there was something I would rather be doing, and I did as much of it as I could in the few spare moments left over from my hectic life at the law firm. I grew plants in a greenhouse window, I read about herbs, I learned to cook and craft. Then my father drowned when his car went off a bridge and into a bayou outside of Houston, and I began to take stock of what I had done with my life, and why. Eventually I came to the decision that I was on the wrong road and it was time for a U-turn. I cashed in my retirement fund, left the firm, and . . . well, here I am, standing in the doorway of my herb shop, sniffing the roses.

I was roused from my reflections by the sound of footsteps crunching on the gravel path. I turned to see Lisa Simon, the principal at Pecan Springs High School, coming toward me.

"Hi, Lisa," I said. "Did you enjoy the party last night?" I had seen her name on the guest list, along with a great many other Pecan Springs notables. Obviously, the Duffys cut a wide social swath.

"It was very . . . nice," she replied, with an odd hesitation. "I didn't see you there, though—did I?" I get to wear jeans and a sweater to work, but even when Lisa isn't working—today was Saturday—she has to dress the part. She was wearing a dark skirt, a dark turtleneck, and a wool blazer.

"I was in the kitchen," I said with a grin, and flicked on the lights. "Party Thyme catered, which explains the great food and super service."

"Well, if you're angling for a compliment, you've got it," Lisa said with an answering smile. "Cass's spinach-basil roll-ups were terrific, and everybody raved about the meatballs. I don't know if I can afford you, but I'd love to have you handle my husband's birthday party next month."

"I'll ask Ruby to give you a call," I said, closing the door behind us and turning on the lights. "Sometimes we can reduce the cost—for instance, if we just do the food and you do the setup, the serving, and the cleanup." I refrained from asking why the high school principal couldn't afford a caterer when the football coach could, and went behind the counter. "Excuse me while I do a bit of early-morning housekeeping here," I said, getting out the cash register drawer, which is always cleverly hidden under the dust rags. "As you can see, you're the first customer."

Lisa glanced around, nervously, I thought. "Actually, I didn't come to shop. I was hoping you and I could have a private conversation."

"This is about as private as it's likely to be," I said, putting the drawer into the cash register. I've known Lisa ever since she came to Pecan Springs a couple of years ago, and I like her, although I wouldn't have her job for any amount of money. I know how difficult it's been for her to find her place among the galaxies of fixed stars (mostly male) on the school district's administrative roster.

"I hope this isn't about Brian," I added, turning to adjust the thermostat. "He's behaving himself, isn't he?"

"Of course he is," Lisa said warmly. "He's one of our best students— he has lots of academic promise and a good sense of who he is." I turned back and she met my curious glance. "Actually, this is about a bit of confidential investigating I'd like you to do. Now, don't say no before you hear what it is," she added hurriedly, raising a hand as if to forestall my refusal. "I'm here at Charlie Lipton's suggestion."

I cocked an eyebrow at her. Charlie isn't just a fine friend and the best lawyer in Pecan Springs, he's a good ol' boy who carries more guilty secrets than anybody else in town—the secrets of all his clients. He knows where the bodies are buried, where the dirty linen is stashed, and whose closets are full of skeletons. But what Charlie had to do with Lisa Simon, I couldn't fathom—until I remembered that he had been president of the school board the year Lisa was hired. She probably felt she could confide in him. Anyway, she had named the magic name. If Charlie Lipton had thought of me when she went to him with her problem, there must be a reason. A good reason.

"I'll help if I can," I said, going to the big rack of potted herbs. I keep it inside on cold nights, so the plants won't freeze if the temperature dips. "Would you mind holding the door?" I pushed the rack out to its usual spot beside the gravel path, made sure that the price signs were in place, and came back in. "So what's up?"

Lisa took a deep breath. "What's up is that I got an anonymous phone call last week, from a woman. A young woman, judging from her voice. She made a . . . well, a pretty serious charge against Coach Duffy."

"Duffy?" I blinked at her. "Did I hear that right?"

"I'm afraid you did." Lisa was somber. "I thought her charge was serious enough to warrant an investigation by the school district's legal office, but Claude Legler—he's the chief lawyer—doesn't agree. He says it's only an allegation, and anonymous. It might be a former student with a grudge, trying to stir up trouble. If we try to do anything about it, we risk litigation."

"Legler's right," I said. This is America after all, and people really *are* innocent until they are proven guilty. Or at least, that's how it's supposed to work. On the other hand—

I turned the sign on the door from CLOSED to OPEN. "Did the caller make any attempt to validate the charges? Provide any information you could follow up on? Informally, I mean."

"Not very much," Lisa replied. "That's the problem, China. All she had to offer were hints and insinuations. Deep Throat kind of stuff. Deep voice, too. She didn't offer anything concrete, except for one piece of information, which might or might not be accurate." She paused. "She did say she'd call later, with more. Something very important, she said."

I had heard that one before. It was the old informant-offers-information-a-piece-at-a-time trick. First the bait, then more and tastier bait, then the hook. "Has she? Called back, I mean."

"Not yet. This just happened, though." She was grim. "Of course, I went straight to Legler, and when he said there was nothing we could do unless we had some definite, verified facts to move on, I was really upset at him. But after I thought about it, I could see his point. Duffy's on a winning streak and popular with just about everybody in town—students, alums, Boosters, everybody. And Glenda . . . well, I don't know all the details, but I understand that she's related to the most influential family in Pecan Springs."

"You can say that again," I said. "The Seidenstickers don't control public opinion the way they did a decade or two ago, maybe, but they still swing a lot of weight."

"Right." Lisa took a deep breath. "Obviously, an official investigation isn't in the cards—not on what little we have. Still, I have a bad feeling. What happens if there's something to this? What if we do nothing and this person decides to go to one of the Austin or San Antonio TV stations? This whole thing could blow up in our faces."

I agreed. This was potential political dynamite, pure and simple, and Lisa was sitting on the keg with a match in her hand. Most coaches and teachers are basically good people, doing a job that the rest of us wouldn't touch with a ten-foot pole, and doing it very well. But every now and then, you'll pick up a newspaper and read that a coach is alleged to have accepted an illicit gift, or tampered with a star athlete's grades to keep him eligible, or misappropriated school property for personal use. If the coach has had a losing season or two, he'd better hire a good attorney, because the school board is going to throw the book at him. It's a big book, too. The board can press all appropriate criminal charges, as well as hauling the offender up before the State Board of Educator Certification, which can suspend his Texas teaching certificate for a certain period, or rescind it for eternity—and they do, too.

But when the coach is a winner, it's a very different situation. Then the board members have second thoughts. And third thoughts, and fourth thoughts. They might think for months without taking action. And with good reason. A winning coach usually has plenty of political strength and legal savvy on his bench, and is backed by vocal friends and fans who will cheer for their man 'til the cows come home. Here in Texas, where high school football is its own empire, coaches with clout have been known to bring down weak principals and hapless school boards even before the first whistle blows. I didn't blame Claude Legler for not wanting to suit up for this particular game. Make the wrong call, and you're out.

Which left Lisa in an extremely awkward position, knowing something that might or might not be true, and might or might not be potentially damaging to her school and her students, but lacking the muscle to tackle the situation. I sighed. I'm a sucker for the underdog.

"Okay," I said. "Where do I come in?"

She gave me a relieved smile. "Well, Legler says we need something more definite. Charlie Lipton and I are hoping you can dig it up."

"My husband's an investigator. You know that, don't you?" Charlie did, of course. McQuaid had already worked on a couple of his cases. "He's a lot better at digging stuff up than I am. If it's a matter of the fee, I'm sure he'd—"

"No." Lisa shook her head firmly. "This requires a woman's touch. And just as important, you're a former attorney. You know how to ask questions."

I frowned. "Well, I suppose I might—"

"Good," Lisa said. "The caller gave me the name of somebody who is supposed to have some information about a problem in Duffy's earlier school, down in Friendship. Charlie told me that your mother lives not far from there, and your husband mentioned to him that you were driving down to see her this weekend. If so, maybe you could go to this person's house and ask some questions. I have a special fund I can tap for your expenses."

I brushed aside the suggestion of payment. "Is that all you want me to do, Lisa? Just ask questions? What about talking to the school officials and looking at the school's records? If the problem was serious, it would be documented, wouldn't it?"

"No again," Lisa said. "Or at least, that's what the caller says. It was all hushed up. Covered over, for months and months, while the school administration 'looked into' the problem. And then Duffy was offered the coaching position here in Pecan Springs and turned in his resignation. The good ol' boys' network," she added grittily. "I'm sure you know how it works."

I did, although in this case, I suspected that the job offer might have as much to do with Glenda Duffy's Pecan Springs connections as with the old boys' coaching network. I regarded her curiously. "But the Duffys have been here for several years, so what you're telling me is practically ancient history. What are you planning to do with the information I dig up? Assuming there is any, of course. I might come up empty."

Lisa looked troubled. "It depends on what you find out." She glanced through the door window. A couple of women were standing outside, looking at the rack of potted herbs and discussing the merits of the scented geraniums they held in their hands. "Looks like we're about to be interrupted."

"Yes," I said. "Well, as it happens, Brian and I are going down to Kerrville on Sunday. The store is closed on Monday and it's a school holiday, so we're planning to drive back on Monday evening. Friendship isn't far from there. I suppose I could drive down on Monday and have a little chat with this person, whoever he is."

"She," Lisa said. "It's a woman." She smiled in relief. "Oh, China, I don't know how to thank you. I—"

There would have been more, but just at that moment, the phone rang. And when I put the receiver down, the two customers outside had made up their minds to buy the scented geraniums and were coming inside to pay for them.

"Looks like things are about to get busy," I said. "Could I call you later today and get the details? The name and address of the woman I need to talk to, and how she's involved."

"I wrote everything down on the back of my card, with the hope that you would agree," Lisa said, handing it to me. "And that's my office

36

number, and my cell. I'd appreciate it if you'd call me after you talk with her, so I'll know how to proceed."

"Sure. I can do that." The lawyer part of me added, "But I also need to know the nature of the allegation. What are we talking about? Misappropriation of school funds? Covering up for ineligible players?"

"I wish it were that simple," Lisa said. She leaned forward and whispered two words.

I winced. "As bad as that?"

"As bad as that," she said ruefully.

Chapter Five

Bleeding heart is the name given to several traditional quilt patterns that feature red heart-shaped motifs with a geometrical teardrop. One popular Victorian pattern featured an appliquéd basket filled with bleeding heart flowers in shades of pink and gold; another used embroidered sprays of bleeding hearts in an intricate interwoven design. The quilting was often done in various heart-shaped stitching patterns, with a continuous border of hearts.

Ruby Wilcox
Program Notes
Pecan Springs Scrappers Quilt Show

Saturdays are usually so busy that the hours have wings, and it's time to close before I barely get started. That Saturday was more hectic than usual, because the tearoom was full for lunch, and we had to get the food ready for the Scrappers' hanging party later that afternoon. But Janet's knee was better so she cooked, and lunch went without a hitch. Laurel came in for a couple of hours at the busiest time, and the two of us managed the customers in both shops while Ruby and Missy Bowers handled the tearoom. Meanwhile, Cass made up the party goodies and packed everything but the refrigerated items into Big Red Mama. It was chaos, of course, but the chaos was mostly organized.

In the middle of the afternoon, when things slowed down, Ruby dashed out with her quilt and digital camera to the Springs Hotel, to hang her entry and take photos. She had already shown the quilt to us: a beautiful wall quilt with overlapping appliquéd hearts arranged in a heart-shaped design. I was hoping to display it in the tearoom once the show was over, along with several of the other quilts from the competition. If you haven't seen Ruby's fiber art, drop over to her house some weekend, and she'll show you her quilts and woven shawls and the rug she's just finished hooking. Two years ago, she helped to get the Pecan Springs Scrappers underway, and this quilt show, the first one the guild has ever done, was her idea. The Scrappers had been working on it for months now. It was called "Parade of Hearts" (since the quilts were going to be on display all through February, the month of hearts) and all the entries were supposed to have a heart theme.

When Ruby got back from the hotel, she was bubbling over with enthusiasm. "We have thirty-two entries!" she crowed happily. "Can you believe it? For our first show? Come on, you guys, you have to see these pictures."

Obediently, Janet and Cass and I followed Ruby to her tiny office, where she took the disk out of her camera, slipped it into the computer, and brought up the pictures. She had taken quite a few.

"Wow," Cass said admiringly. "Rows and rows and rows of hearts. Every kind of heart imaginable." She looked at me. It was my turn.

"Overwhelming," I murmured. "Looks like thousands of hours of work." Of course, it was impressive, and I am the first one to admire a beautiful quilt. But what can you say about quilts en masse?

"Looks like a whole lotta beds gonna be gettin' new bedcovers," Janet said cryptically. Short and dumpling-shaped, with keen blue eyes, she has the habit of calling a spade a spade, and isn't one to pay compliments. She squinted at Ruby's photos. "To tell the good Lord's truth, I don't see a one that looks like the quilts my mama used to make."

"I don't think there were many traditional quilts entered, Janet," Ruby said. "Most of these are art quilts—you know, designed to show off the quilter's creativity."

"Art quilts, huh?" Janet said sourly. "Heck fire, some of 'em ain't big 'nough to cover my toesies, much less keep my butt warm at night." She planted her finger on the monitor screen. "These here itsy-bitsy ones, fer instance. What're they for?"

"Oh, those are doll quilts," Ruby said. "They're a special class. We've divided the entries into bed quilts, wall quilts, doll quilts, and wearables. We'll be giving awards in those categories, and special awards for creativity, use of color, innovative techniques, and so on." She flipped to another photo. "This one, for instance. Audrey Manning took pictures of each of her children and grandchildren, printed them on different fabrics, cut them out in the shape of hearts, stuffed and quilted them trapunto style, and then appliquéd them onto a family tree, with everybody's names on the branches." She regarded it admiringly. "Why, it's not only a work of art, it's a family treasure."

"Audrey Manning?" Cass said. "She's the one I'm cooking for next week. Her husband wants it to be a surprise. I'm to cook the meals here, then hide them in the Mannings' freezer, the day before her birthday."

Janet was still staring at the picture of Audrey Manning's quilt. "Hrrmph," she said. "When I was a girl growin' up on the ranch, a quilt was something your mama and your grandma and your aunts made outta flour sacks and old aprons and wore-out dresses that was too tired to hand me down. None of this artsy-fartsy show-off stuff for them, jes' common ol' Wedding Ring and Drunkard's Path, which ever'body knows how to do." She put her fists on her hips. "And how come somebody's gotta go and put their whole fam'ly tree on a quilt? Ain't the fam'ly Bible good 'nough?" She shook her head in disgust. "S'cuse me," she muttered. "I gotta finish cleanin' up the kitchen so's I can go home. My knees is killin' me."

"Dear old Janet," Cass chuckled, after she'd gone. "She keeps us honest, doesn't she?"

"Which of the quilts do you think is going to take Best of Show, Ruby?" I asked.

"If I were doing the judging, it would be Carol Bruce's quilt," Ruby said, "although people are saying that Audrey has a shot at it. That trapunto work is a nice touch." She brought up a photo of a quilt that featured a circle of interlocking hearts. "This is Carol's. It's an original design, a wonderful selection of colors and fabrics, and exquisite needlework. And there's a very moving story behind it. Carol designed and pieced the quilt when she was undergoing chemotherapy for breast cancer. She's in my support group, and every one of those hearts has the name on it of one of the women in our group, and some sort of symbol of the woman's experience."

"Which heart is yours?" I asked. Ruby lost a breast to cancer a couple of years ago. She chose not to have reconstructive surgery ("I don't want a foreign object in my body," she says, when anyone asks).

"This one," Ruby said, pointing. "Carol embroidered my flower on it. See? Very appropriate for the theme of the contest, wouldn't you say?"

"Yep, that's your tattoo, for sure," I said. When the scar healed, Ruby had a spray of bleeding heart blossoms tattooed over it. She'll show it to you, if you ask politely.

"Great quilt," Cass said. She straightened up. "Want me to help you guys with the party this evening? I'd love to meet these Scrappers."

"I thought you had a big date tonight," Ruby said.

"He canceled," Cass said.

"Too bad," I said sympathetically. Ruby told me that Cass had been married once, before she came to Pecan Springs, but her husband had died in an accident. In the time we've known her, she's almost never dated.

Cass's shrug was philosophical. "It happens. I'm not devastated. He was doing some false advertising, which I definitely do not need. I'm saving myself for a prince. Frogs need not apply." She eyed us. "Well, do you want me to help, or shall I climb back into my tower and wait for the next prince who happens along?"

"Oh, by all means, help," Ruby said. "Climbing towers is no way to spend a Saturday evening. Right, China?"

"Oh, right," I said. "Absolutely." I grinned at Cass. "Hang in there, babe. Your prince will come." Or maybe he already had. Maybe the prince was the guy who died.

"Really?" Cass said, giving me a half-skeptical, half-amused glance. "And just where is that written? Anyway, I'm getting used to playing the-cheese-stands-alone. The game ain't half bad, let me tell you, especially when you think of the jerks out there who want to play with you."

"Of course," Ruby said comfortingly. "And as everybody knows, cheese only gets stronger and better the longer it hangs around. I'd a whole lot rather be a moldy hunk of cheddar than a wimpy little jar of cheese spread. Wouldn't you?"

Since neither Cass nor I could think of a suitable answer, we left it alone.

* * *

THE Scrappers' party was much smaller and very different from the Duffys' party the night before, although some of the same women were there. Ruby, Cass, and I brought in the food and supplies and put them in the kitchen; Carol and the others carried it out to the table and everybody helped themselves. We were all in casual clothes, mostly jeans and slacks, and since there were no guys, minimal makeup. I didn't see a single game face. My kind of party.

The talk, naturally, was all about quilts, quilting, quilt shows, quilt fabrics, new ways to make a quilt, and the grand opening of Ruth Ann Gilman's new quilt shop, PatchWorks, which was scheduled for the following Thursday in the Emporium, the craft and boutique mall located in the two-story Victorian next door to Thyme and Seasons. Everybody was excited, partly because Ruth Ann is a longtime Scrapper and they love her, but also because they will no longer have to drive to Austin or San Antonio in search of their quilt fix. I'm glad, too. I'm not a quilter (although of course anything is possible), but I'm thinking that having a quilt shop right next door might mean more traffic for Thyme and Seasons. I haven't taken a scientific poll on the subject, but I'm willing to bet that women who like to quilt also enjoy herbs.

After about an hour, everybody agreed that the hanging had been a great success and the hanging party was just what was needed to wind it up, but it was time to head home and see what the Significant Others had been up to while the girls were enjoying themselves. Several people pitched in to load Big Red Mama, so called because she's big, red, and boxy, exactly the sort of vehicle we need to haul all our stuff around in. Many hands made quick work.

When Cass and I were aboard, Ruby said, "Would you mind if we took a swing past the hotel on our way back? Carol forgot to leave the guest book for viewers to sign, and she asked me to do it."

"Sure," Cass said. "All that talk about quilts whetted my appetite to see them, up close and personal."

"Even if some of them aren't big enough to cover your toesies?" I asked with a grin.

"Hey," Cass retorted blithely. "I have the tiniest toesies in the world. It's the rest of me that's big and gorgeous."

The show was hung just off the lobby of the Springs Hotel, the classiest hotel in town, where shows and exhibits are often held. When we went in, though, I looked around, frowning. "Where's the security guard?" I asked, seeing nothing but a stiff trio of potted palms and a pair of desk clerks who looked about two years younger than Brian.

"Who needs a security guard?" Ruby replied, with a toss of her head. "Heavens to Betsy, China—this is Pecan Springs."

"Yeah, right," I growled. "But everybody says those quilts are priceless. What happens if one of them disappears?" The lawyer part of me added, "Did you have the exhibitors sign a liability waiver, so the Scrappers aren't responsible in case of loss? I mean, what happens if there's a fire? Or a flood, or theft, or—"

"Oh, China," Ruby said lightly, "don't be such a worrywart. There's not going to be a fire. And nobody's going to steal a quilt, for heaven's sake. We talked about some sort of liability thing, and somebody—Audrey, I think—was supposed to write it up, but I bet she forgot. Anyway, it's not important. You can see for yourself that the only way to get into the hotel is to walk right in front of the registration desk in the lobby."

"Oh, come on," I hooted. "There are a dozen ways to get into and out of this hotel, and everybody knows exactly where they are."

It's true. Almost every organization in town has its annual banquet at The Springs, and when there's a big family reunion and Uncle Clyde and Aunt SueEllen don't want to share the sleeper sofa in the den with the resident dog and cats, they check in here.

"Not to worry," Ruby said soothingly. "The hotel management promised that the clerks would keep an eye on everything for us."

"I think China's right," Cass said. "There's a lot of valuable stuff here, in terms of the time people put into it. Maybe the Scrappers can take turns being on duty. You know, sign up for shifts."

"That's a good suggestion," Ruby said. "But everybody's pretty busy right now. I'll put it down on the list of things to think about next year."

So much for security. Cass and I exchanged glances and shrugs and watched as Ruby put the guest book on a small table beside the door. Then she motioned to us and we followed her into a wide, windowless hallway, where the quilts were hung on both sides, illuminated by lights on a ceiling track. A white card was fastened to the wall beside each quilt or quilted wearable, displaying the quilter's name, the name of the entry, and the class in which it was entered. As I walked along, I was amazed at the ingenuity and skill of the quilters—what patience it must take for those millions of tiny stitches!—and began to compile a mental list of the pieces I'd like to see on display in our tearoom (but with signed liability waivers from the artists, of course). We could organize an event around the exhibit, and advertise it in the newspaper, which might bring us a few new customers. We could have a Heart-to-Heart Tea, and a reading of poems about hearts. We could—

"Hey, Ruby," Cass said. She'd been strolling along ahead of us, taking it all in, but she stopped when she came to a big blank area on the wall.

She pointed to the hanging rod that lay on the carpet. "Looks like some-body took this one down."

"Took it down? But they're not supposed to, now that the show's started," Ruby said, sounding irritated. "Whose is it, Cass?"

Cass leaned forward and read from the card. "Carol Bruce, Circle of Hearts."

"Carol?" Ruby blinked, frowned, looked puzzled. "But why would Carol take her quilt down? I can't imagine— I mean, I talked to her at the party, and she didn't say anything about . . ." Her voice trailed away uneasily.

I didn't like the looks of this, but I didn't want to be an alarmist. "Do you have Carol's phone number? You could call her and clear up the mys-tery, and then we won't have to wonder."

"Well, I don't know," Ruby said uncertainly. "I hate to bother her. It's Saturday night, after all, and she and her husband were planning to go out. She's probably getting ready."

"Yeah, but still," Cass said. She glanced up at the blank area as if she were measuring the dimensions of the absent quilt. "Maybe she noticed a spot on it, or she had to fix some threads, or—"

Ruby shook her head. "Once a quilt's up, it has to stay up. That's spelled out in the rules. And you know Carol. She's fanatic about follow-ing the rules. Why, the other day, we were at the supermarket, and she—"

"For Pete's sake, Ruby," Cass said, "*call* her already. The suspense is driving me crazy."

Ruby reached into her purse, took out her cellular phone, and punched in some numbers. "Carol?" she said into the phone. She turned so she didn't have to look at Cass and me. "Listen, Carol, we brought the guest book, the way you wanted. And we're here at the hotel, where the quilts are hung, and— Yes, yes, it looks great, it looks wonderful, but that's not why I'm calling. Carol, do you have your quilt?"

There was a pause, then, "Because it's not here, that's why."

Another pause. "No, no, I'm not joking. You mean, you don't know anything about this?" Ruby scrunched up her face and held the phone out from her ear. Even standing a few paces away, Cass and I could hear Carol's shrieks. We didn't have to catch every word to know what she was saying. Her quilt, her beautiful quilt, the quilt that everybody agreed would probably win Best of Show, had been stolen.

"I just can't imagine who would have done such a thing," Ruby said at last, sounding flustered. "This is horrible, Carol. I'm really, really, *really* sorry." She said a subdued good-bye and clicked off her phone.

"Oy vey," Cass said in a low voice.

Ruby put her phone in her purse. Her face was pale, her mouth thin and pinched. "You were right, China. If you want to say *I told you so,* it's okay."

"And just how would that help?" I asked. "Come on, let's go talk to those two kids at the desk. Maybe they'll know something."

But questioning the desk clerks took us exactly nowhere. Neither of them had seen anything all afternoon, except for dozens of women racing in and out with boxes and bags and armfuls of stuff. I had the clerks write down their names and contact information and gave it to Ruby.

"What's this for?" she asked numbly.

"For the police report." I gave her a stern look. "The guild *is* going to file a missing-quilt report, isn't it?"

Ruby sighed. "You're right, of course. I'll do that this very evening." She paused, thought, brightened, and looked back down at the piece of paper. "But maybe I'll do some poking around on my own, too," she went on, in what I have come to recognize as her Nancy Drew voice. When Ruby was a girl, she adored Nancy, and now that she's a grownup, she likes nothing better than finding a mystery—the weirder the better—that needs a solution. "The police have too much on their plates to fool around with something like this. I mean, it's a big deal for the guild, but it's got to be petty potatoes to the cops."

Petty potatoes? I rolled my eyes.

Cass, however, was intrigued. "It certainly couldn't hurt for the Scrappers to have their own internal investigation." And then, with enthusiasm, she added, "I'll give you a hand, Ruby. Maybe we can start by talking to all the Scrappers who were here today. Somebody might have seen something suspicious."

Oh, great. Now we had Bess teamed up with Nancy. But I'd be darned if I was going to play George. I glanced at my watch.

"Sorry to break this up just as you two girl sleuths are laying your devious plans, but I have to get back to the shop and get my car, so I can pick up my kid." Brian was at Jake's this afternoon, doing whatever teens do when grownups aren't looking. "It's pizza-and-a-movie night. McQuaid may not be here, but the show must go on."

"Oh?" Cass asked. "Where's McQuaid?"

"He's in Albuquerque on a case," I said. "Software theft."

Ruby arched her eyebrows at me. "Isn't what's-her-name in Albuquerque?"

"Yeah," I said, in a sour, none-of-your-beeswax tone. I didn't need Ruby feeling sorry for me just because my husband, in an excess of helpfulness, was probably going to phone his flaky ex-wife to see how she was getting along, and the two of them would probably wind up having dinner at some nifty gourmet restaurant.

I sighed, a long, self-pitying sigh. "Come on, guys, let's go. It's getting late."

"Of course," Ruby said sympathetically. She knows how I feel about Dingbat. "Come on, Cass. I have to get home, too. Colin is expecting me."

I was about to make a snotty and entirely illogical remark about Ruby putting her current love interest ahead of her gal pals, but Cass—who was still thinking about the mystery—broke in with another idea.

"We could take written statements from everybody," she offered. "Then we could compare the differences and see if anybody's lying."

"Come *on*, Cass," I said testily.

Really. One Nancy Drew in my life is enough.

Chapter Six

You might not think of the prickly pear cactus (*Opuntia* spp.) in connection with Valentine's Day, but it certainly has a long-standing connection with the heart. The plant is a perennial succulent with flat, fleshy edible pads (*nopales*) covered with long, sharp spines. The pink buds bloom into flowers with nearly transparent, tissuelike petals, ranging in color from yellow to orange, pink, and magenta; the fruits (*tuna*) ripen in the early autumn to a lovely shade of purple and are used to make delicious juices and jellies. The Aztecs employed the plant to strengthen the heart and treat heart murmur and angina. This traditional use is partially supported by recent scientific studies showing that the fibrous pectin in the pulp protects the heart by lowering levels of "bad" cholesterol. It also stabilizes blood'sugar levels, making it effective against type II diabetes.

The drive from Pecan Springs to Kerrville is one of the prettiest in the entire state of Texas. Brian and I take the back way, across Devil's Backbone, the spine of the Edwards Plateau. To the east, the tide of civilization that surges along the I-35 corridor is like a tsunami spreading across the landscape, leaving a litter of houses, shopping malls, and acres of asphalt and concrete in its wake. But out here, the land is open and wild, much as it was when the nomadic Indians trekked through it. At US 281, we headed south to State Route 46, where we turned west again through Honey Creek (named for the nearby honeycomb limestone formations) and Bergheim and Boerne, settlements created by the same Germans who established Pecan Springs. We crossed Interstate 10 and headed for Bandera, once a staging area for cattle drives up the Western Trail, then made our way west on 470 to Utopia, where early Spanish explorers found silver and dug a mine shaft into nearby Sugarloaf Mountain. Tres Equis Ranch isn't far from there, on the Sabinal River.

I'm always struck by the varied topography and the changes in general climate as I take this two-hour drive south and west. The rocks throughout this part of Texas are primarily limestones and shales deposited in shallow Cretaceous seas, over 100 million years ago. Along Devil's Backbone and south on US 281, the layered rock is folded and tilted, so that every road cut holds a surprise. Farther south, there's less folding and tilting but more erosion, and there are dozens of shallow creeks filled with water so clear you can see every pebble and flashing fish. Around Pecan Springs and west across the Backbone, February was still too early for the most familiar wildflowers; the April bluebonnets and Indian paintbrush and white prickly poppies were only a pleasant dream. But the yaupon hollies were studded with scarlet fruit, and the dark green cedars—these low, shrubby trees, are actually Eastern red junipers—were heavy with blue berries. Both yaupon and juniper can get you high: juniper berries are an essential ingredient in gin, and yaupon berries were used by Native Americans to produce a medicinal and ceremonial intoxicant.

The cedars were hosting a convention of brown-and-buff cedar waxwings, dapper birds with neat black masks and tails that look as if they've been dipped in yellow paint, who surf south to Texas on the surging crest of the first blue norther. Waxwings are amiable, egalitarian birds with pleasant table manners, never bickering over dessert like aggressive jays and testy titmice. You'll sometimes see ten or fifteen of them sitting shoulder-to-shoulder on a branch, ceremoniously passing a berry from one polite beak to another until one of the birds decides it has his name on it. If the berry makes it to the last bird, back up the row it goes again. And when they gorge themselves on too many fermented berries, they get definitely drunk, although there's no information on whether or not they suffer hangovers.

In the February landscape, the dominant colors were green, brown, gray, and bronze. The naked mesquites and hackberrys stood out like trees sketched in charcoal. The open, rock-covered hillsides were strewn with patches of gray-green prickly pear, whose culinary and medicinal uses offset its reputation as an armed and dangerous nuisance. And deep in the ravines, I could see the bronzy flowers of an early-blooming huisache (once cultivated to provide oils for French perfumes) and the occasional flicker of rough-leafed dogwoods, glowing like candles among the darker, duller trees. In the Hill Country, wildflowers are a decorative accessory in a landscape that's already beautiful—and bountiful—without them.

Brian had been silent for most of the drive, listening to his Walkman and looking out the window. We'd nearly reached the ranch when he took off his headphones and gave me one of those grave, questioning glances that always remind me of his father.

"Is he going to see her when he's in Albuquerque?"

I didn't have to ask who "he" and "her" was. "I don't know," I replied honestly. "We didn't talk about it." I paused. "Do you want him to see her?" I operate on the principle that kids don't talk much to grownups— seriously talk, I mean—and when they do, it's best to keep the conversation going. Which means answering their questions, and then asking one of your own.

"I don't know either," Brian said, with patient resignation. He understands his mother. "She's pretty much messed up, but she doesn't like anybody to . . . well, interfere." His voice cracked, the way it often does these days. "The last time, she was sorta mad."

"Yes," I said. "Some people don't like it when you give them advice they haven't asked for." I paused, searching for the next question, but Brian beat me to it.

"That's what Jake says, too," he said glumly. He mimicked her. " 'It's none of your business. Stay out of it.' But what do you do when the other person is going through stuff they can't handle? Serious stuff, I mean. Do you just stand back and watch while they get hurt?"

Brian is too young to be impaled on the horns of such an unforgiving moral dilemma, but he's always seemed to be older than I was at his age, if that makes any sense. I remembered the scene in the kitchen Thursday night, and thought I knew what he was talking about. But what was the "serious stuff" that Brian was afraid Jake couldn't handle?

I couldn't ask that question, however, since I'd been eavesdropping. So I said, in a thoughtful mom-voice, "Well, I guess it depends on how bad the serious stuff is, and how bad the hurt is likely to be. For instance, I wouldn't keep my mouth shut if I thought you were doing drugs. Not that you would," I added hastily. "It's just an example." Not a very good one, either, because moms have more authority over kids than kids have over one another.

He saw the flaw, too. "Yeah, but parents are *supposed* to tell kids when they're doing bad stuff." He was morose. "But what if you're not the person's parent, and you don't know how bad it is? I mean, like maybe it's really bad, or maybe it's—" He shrugged. "Just sorta medium bad." He looked at me, his eyes intensely, deeply troubled. "Should you stick your nose in anyway?"

I sighed. How to tell him that dealing with this daunting moral dilemma is part of the dues we pay for being caring, responsible members of the human race? How to say that entire libraries of books have been written by theologians, psychologists, sociologists, and lawyers on the complex subject of personal privacy, the limits of responsibility, and noninterference in the lives of other people—and that this was a question he'd be asking, in various forms, for the rest of his life?

I settled for something less intimidating and more personally relevant. "Brian, dear heart, that's not a question anybody can answer for you. You just have to keep watching the situation, and asking yourself whether you can actually help the person by getting involved, or whether this is one of those lessons that she has to learn for herself. Or he," I amended hastily, since I wasn't supposed to know that he was talking about Jake. "For himself."

"Yeah, I guess." He was silent for a minute, and then said, "Like Spock and Dr. McCoy, huh?"

"Come again?" I asked, startled.

He gave me one of those how-can-such-a-smart-person-be-so-dumb looks that children seem to instinctively master the minute they turn thirteen. "You know. The Prime Directive. The *Enterprise* can boldly go where nobody else had ever gone, but the crew isn't supposed to intervene in the evolution of other cultures. They can't change something that's going to happen anyway, whether it's bad or not, because that's the way it's supposed to happen, and everything else in the universe will come unglued if it doesn't. Spock's the one who wants to stick by that rule, but Bones is always wanting to fix stuff."

Ah, yes. The philosophy of *Star Trek*. "Well, on the intergalactic level, that's probably a good approach," I said cautiously. "But when it comes to dealing with another person—"

"Don't worry, Mom," he said, patting my hand. "I've got it all figured out. I'll do a Spock until I can't, and a Bones when I have to, and it'll be okay." Satisfied with this cryptic analysis, he looked out the window and something caught his eye. "Hey!" he exclaimed excitedly. "That was a *buffalo*! We must be almost there. Do you think Sam still has the horses he had last time we were here? Am I gonna getta go riding?"

I relaxed. From moral philosopher to Trekkie ethicist to cowboy in the space of two minutes. I could stop worrying. This kid has flexibility. He's going to be just fine.

LEATHA and Sam were waiting for us when we arrived at Tres Equis, at the end of a long gravel road studded with cattle guards, along a wild stretch of Sabinal River. Sam, a tall, lean, laconic man with a rancher's faraway eyes and easy, ambling stride, took possession of Brian and led him, chattering excitedly, in the direction of the corral. I gathered that there was not a moment to lose. The horses were waiting and it was time to saddle up, mount up, and ride out, pardner. We watched them go, then Leatha gave me a distracted hug and led me in the direction of the ranch kitchen to have a cup of tea and a piece of coffeecake.

When I left Houston and moved to Pecan Springs, my mother was still a River Oaks society matron: Southern-belle born and Southern-belle bred, with too much money, an empty life, and the same alcohol problem that had made me so miserably unhappy when I was a kid. If you'd asked me to estimate Leatha's chances for changing her life, I would have said slim to none. As close to a sure thing as you can get.

But I was wrong. Acting entirely on her own, my mother joined Alcoholics Anonymous and managed, miracle of miracles, to stop drinking. She joined a women's encounter group and began to think that maybe there was more to life than decorating the Houston social scene. Then she met and married Sam Richards, a widower with a handful of grown children, and went to live at Tres Equis, a four-thousand-acre nature sanctuary where Sam raises buffalo, antelope, wild sheep, and javelinas. Recently, she told me that the two of them are considering starting a bed-and-breakfast for the ecotourists—birders, naturalists, photographers, and wildlife lovers—who flock to South Texas in the winter.

The moral of this story is that people really can change, and really do, even when you're one hundred percent positive they won't. Sam's rugged Hill Country ranch is about as far from the River Oaks Country Club as you can get, and it's hard for me to imagine Leatha trading in her servants, mansion, and masseuse for a home on the lonesome range. But the transaction, however improbable, seems to have worked out. If Leatha's not happy, she doesn't let on. And if she's drinking, Sam hasn't said anything to me about it—although he might think it's none of my business.

But I haven't noticed any of the telltale signs. Leatha looks younger now than she did when she was a trophy widow, even if the skin sags under her eyes, her ash-blond hair has gone silver, and she's put on some pounds. The two of us weathered a stormy time together a year or so ago, when we feared that we might have inherited Huntington's disease, the frightening genetic illness that afflicted Leatha's aunt Tullie Coldwell. It was an ordeal that took us back to Jordan's Crossing, the Mississippi plantation on the banks of the Bloodroot River, where Leatha was raised and where I had spent all the summers of my childhood. And where, in addition to Aunt Tullie's fatal illness and its disastrous implications for our own futures, we had to cope with buried skeletons, misogyny, and murder. But tough as that time was, it gave me a clearer understanding of the family legacy from which I had tried to disinherit myself, and of my mother, and who she was and why. I can't say I'm glad these things happened, but they changed our relationship for the better, which pleases both of us.

Leatha and Sam recently remodeled the ranch kitchen, in preparation, I guessed, for their bed-and-breakfast enterprise. It sports a veggie sink, an indoor grill, a refrigerator big enough to house a side of beef, and on the wall, a long shelf filled with cookbooks. My mother, who never so much as boiled an egg when I was growing up, has been getting into cooking in a big way.

"Iced tea, dahlin'?" Leatha asked, in that liquid Mississippi drawl she's never lost. "It's hibiscus. I read the other day that's it's good for your heart. Helps cut cholesteral."

"Please," I said. It might be February, but Texans drink iced tea all year round, and hibiscus is always a hit with me.

She put a glass under the spigot of an electric iced tea maker and pushed a button. Ah, culinary wizardry—no tea kettle, no teapot. She handed me the tea with a meaningful glance. "You're lookin' good, honey. A little on the thin side, though."

I sat down at the butcher-block island counter. We go through this every time we see each other. "No, I am not pregnant, Leatha, and I don't intend to get that way, so you can just stop hoping."

Leatha laughed, that up-and-down-the-scale tinkling laugh that always irritated my father. "Now, did I say that? I didn't say a word, China, not one single, solitary word. Of course, I'd love to have a grandbaby. And I'm sure you've heard about that fifty-six-year-old woman who had twins—"

"More power to her. But I've got enough on my hands without taking on a baby. Anyway, you have a grandson. And quicker than we'd like, Brian will make me a grandma and you a great-grandma. Just be patient." I stirred honey into my tea.

"Great-grandma," Leatha said with a sigh. "I'm not sure I like the sound of that." She cut coffeecake for both of us and sat down across from me at the counter.

"Yum-yum," I said, after the first bite. "What's this?"

"I'm calling it 'Lemon Lovers' Coffeecake.' It's one of the recipes I'm trying out for our new bed-and-breakfast. I added some of those lemon herbs you gave me."

"It's delicious," I said. "And pretty, too." We ate in silence for a moment. Then, remembering why she had invited me to come down, I asked, "What's this about Dad?"

Leatha frowned, looked away, looked back, and down at her coffeecake. And then, finally, she replied, "I got a letter."

I put down my fork. "Not from Dad, I hope. He's been dead for . . . what is it? Fourteen years? Fifteen?"

"Sixteen, come Valentine's Day. I still miss him."

Still miss him? That surprised me. Looking back at my childhood through the eyes of an adult, I wouldn't say that my father was much of a husband. Their wedding portrait told the whole story, I'd always thought. Dressed in her ivory-satin wedding gown, Leatha sat slightly in front of him, gazing over her shoulder at his face, while he stood looking into the camera, his hand fixed on her shoulder, as if to keep her in her place. It was a metaphor for their relationship: he had made a place for her, and she consented to occupy it; she looked up to him, while he looked outward, into the world. Not much of a life in that, at least for her. I had the feeling that the marriage she had made with Sam was much more satisfying and rewarding than the one she had made with Robert Bayles.

But there wasn't much point in going into all that ancient history. "Gosh," I said. "Sixteen years. I didn't think it was that long ago." The silence stretched out, then was broken by the eerie, childlike cry of a peacock, one of Sam's exotic birds. "So who sent the letter?"

"A lawyer in Austin. The son of your father's secretary." Leatha looked away again. "His mother died, and he was going through her papers. He found an envelope with some stuff in it that belonged to Dad."

I frowned, hesitated, then said. "Secretary. Let's see—that would be Laura Danforth, wouldn't it?"

With the name came the memory of her: not so much of her physical appearance—Mrs. Danforth was a plain woman with mouse-brown hair and mouse-bright eyes, the sort of woman people never notice—but of her quiet intellect and calm, disciplined poise. To me, she had seemed remarkably bright and able, all the more, I suppose, because I had not yet met another woman like her. My father's firm—Stone, Bayles, Peck, and Dixon—dealt with complex matters of tax law, and Mrs. Danforth only had a bachelor's degree in English. But she understood his cases and the issues and the people involved, and she knew what he wanted and needed and had it ready the minute he asked for it. She was one of those indispensable, invisible women who keep the ships of commerce and state afloat and moving forward, but are seldom seen above deck and are never once permitted to put their hands to the helm.

Leatha was staring at me. "My goodness sakes, China," she said. "I had no idea you'd remember Mrs. Danforth."

"Well, she was his secretary for a long time," I said evasively.

Laura Danforth was more than my father's secretary. She was also his mistress, but I didn't think my mother knew that. In those days, Leatha had been so overwhelmed by her own misery that she was oblivious to everything else (including me), and Dad had been so absorbed in his work that his wife and only child might as well have lived on the moon. I did my best to connect with him, for all the good it did. He scarcely noticed, but I hung around his office as much as I could during my teen years, running errands, making coffee, ferrying books and journals to and from the law library. I pretended that I was serving an apprenticeship in the secret guild of lawyers—getting an insider's view, so to speak, of the profession I intended to enter.

I got an inside view of something else, while I was at it. I saw enough of the relationship between my father and Laura Danforth to know, with a daughter's intuition, that they were lovers. I saw it in the attentive way she looked at him, the easy way he spoke to her, the glint in his eyes, the answering light in hers. At the time, I didn't judge him harshly for this. I don't know whether I was still infatuated with him myself and thought that whatever he did was de facto right, or whether I simply admired the poised, intelligent Laura Danforth and scorned my alcoholic mother. It was a complex emotional brew to be bubbling in a teen's tumultuous breast.

"Yes, Mrs. Danforth worked for him for a long time," Leatha said. "But she's dead now, and her son is cleaning things up, and he says there are these papers. He wants to know what should be done with them, and since you're a lawyer, I thought I should ask you." She met my eyes and looked away, and in that awkward, sliding glance I read the truth: my mother had known about Laura Danforth's relationship to my father, and she was afraid that something in those papers would document it.

"Well, sure," I said without expression. "Could I see the letter?"

She took it out of the drawer directly in front of her, where she had put it, knowing that I would be sitting here drinking tea, and that I would ask to see it. It was a perfectly ordinary letter, and obviously written by a lawyer. In the process of disposing of his mother's papers pursuant to her recent death, Miles Danforth had found a large envelope containing what appeared to be personal letters and notes written by a previous employer, Mr. Robert Bayles, whom Mr. Danforth understood to be deceased, as well. Would it be convenient for Mr. Bayles's daughter or his widow to accept the file, or would she prefer him to destroy it unread? The letter was typed on thick, expensive stationery, and embossed with the name of Zwinger, Brady, Brandon, and Danforth, Attorneys at Law, at an address on Lavaca Street, in downtown Austin.

"Well," I said, folding the letter. "What do you want to do?"

Instead of answering, she stood and went to the window. Past her, at the corral, I could see Sam helping Bryan up on a brown mare: Sam looking up with a grin, Brian looking down with something like hero worship on his face, the two of them laughing.

"Look at that," she said. "What a sight."

I got up and went to stand beside her. "I think," I said quietly, "that Sam is a much better grandfather to Brian than Dad could have been."

She sighed. "I think so, too. Your father wasn't very fond of children."

"Tell me about it," I replied, with an ironic laugh. He had missed both my graduations, high school and college. He did attend my graduation from law school, but he didn't offer me a place in his firm. *"Later,"* he'd said. *"After you've got your feet wet."*

Later never came, of course. What I did in my career, I did for myself, without his help—which turned out to be a good thing, although I didn't think so at the time. When somebody pulls strings for you, you run the risk of becoming a puppet, and you never have the satisfaction that comes when your success is your own. But there was still a deep hurt, which I added to the hurt he had caused me and my mother over the years. The whole amounted to a deep and enduring pain.

"I guess it was for the best." There was a sad resignation in Leatha's voice. "That I couldn't have any more children, I mean."

I stared at her in complete surprise. "You *couldn't?*"

She shook her head. "After you were born, I got some sort of infection. I had to have a hysterectomy. I was devastated, of course. And your father was terribly upset with me for having a girl, and not being able to try again. He wanted a boy—another Robert Bayles." She chuckled wryly. "But he got even. Since he couldn't name you after himself, he named you after his mother."

"Really?" Another surprise. "I thought that was *your* choice!"

China. Earlier in my life, I had resented my unusual name, because people were always asking where it came from. I'd tell them I was named for Gram Bayles, who was conceived in Shanghai during the Boxer Rebellion—a lie, because Gram's mother had never set foot outside New Orleans. In high school, I called myself CeeBee—my initials—and developed an elaborate signature script. When I was in practice, I signed myself simply *C. Bayles.* It's only been in the last ten years that I've made my peace with my name.

"My choice?" Leatha laughed that rippling Southern-belle laugh.

"How silly! I hated that nasty old lady. She was always meddling in our affairs. I would never have named you after her."

Well. This was something else I hadn't suspected. I knew that Gram Bayles could be trying, but I hadn't guessed that my mother hated her. Either Leatha had been completely successful in hiding her feelings, or I had been too self-absorbed to pay attention—or both. At another time, I'd have to ask her about it, and about not having children. But there was something else on our agenda.

"What do you want to do about these letters of Dad's?" I asked.

She turned. "I want you to look at them. If they're something I should know, or something important I have to deal with, tell me. If not—" She searched my face for what I might already know, then turned back to the window, pressing her forehead against the glass. Her voice was edged with resignation, sad but firm. "If not, burn them. The past is past. I don't want anything more to do with it."

"Okay," I said. It seemed to be a reasonable solution. Dad's personal letters and notes couldn't be left in the insecure custody of an Austin law firm. And I had to admit to a nagging curiosity about what was in that envelope. It seemed entirely likely that those "personal letters and notes" were love letters, and I suspected that Leatha thought so, too. What else would Laura Danforth have kept through the sixteen years since my father's death?

"Thank you," Leatha said simply. "I knew I could count on you, China." She brightened. "Now, let's talk about something else. How's Ruby? And how are things at the shop?"

And for the rest of that day, while Brian and Sam rode the range, Leatha and I lolled around and talked about everything else but those letters. When the guys got back, Brian informed me that Sam knew where there were some endangered Mexican burrowing toads, and that tomorrow, they were going to study them. "When a burrowing toad is frightened," he said excitedly, "he blows himself up like a balloon. He eats nothing but termites."

"How good of him," I remarked. "Maybe we could take him home and put him in the crawl space under the kitchen, along with a few of his buddies and their wives and children. I'm sure we can provide enough termites to keep them happy for years."

That night, several friends drove in from neighboring ranches. One of the women brought a barbecued brisket and others brought ranch beans and a tortilla casserole and potato salad. Leatha had made a chocolate cake. The men stood around with their drinks talking cows and horses and politics and high school football—the Kerrville Antlers had done well the season before. Brian stood with them, drinking up every word, just one of the guys.

McQuaid would have enjoyed the evening, too, I thought, and I was sorry he couldn't be with us. I had talked to him on the phone and learned that he'd been so busy with the software investigation that he hadn't even thought about calling Sally. But aside from missing him, it was an altogether enjoyable occasion. I almost forgot to wonder what was in those letters that Laura Danforth had kept for so long.

Chapter Seven

The blue agave (*Agave tequilana weber* var. *azul*) might look like a cactus, but the plant is related to the lily and amaryllis. A succulent, it shares a common habitat with many cacti—dry, well-drained soil and a warm climate. A mature agave has leaves five to eight feet tall, and may grow to twelve feet in diameter. It may have a life span of twelve or fifteen years, depending on the growing conditions and climate.

The agave has broad, spiny leaves called *pencas*. Early Indians used the spines as sewing needles, made twine and paper from the fibrous leaves and soap from the roots, and employed the agave's juices for both religious and medicinal purposes. Traditionally it has been an all-purpose healer, used to treat everything from fever to dysentery, liver ailments, indigestion, and congestive heart failure.

But the plant is probably best known for its use in the brewing of tequila, a fermented liquor made from the heart, or *pina*, of the mature blue agave.

I had more than one errand in this part of Texas. So while Brian and Sam went prospecting for Mexican burrowing toads, I got into the car and drove about fifty miles south, past Uvalde on US 83, into Zavala County, to the town of Friendship, once a major shipping point for winter vegetables, such as spinach, carrots, tomatoes, peppers, and onions, and still home to a large canning factory that employs half the people in town. Friendship is located on the flat, arid Rio Grande River plain, where the average February temperature is sixty-nine degrees—warm enough to make it a winter tourist haven. The Rio Grande, which marks the border between the US and Mexico, is only about thirty miles away, as the crow flies. In the distance, you can see the derricks of the oil fields to the east and west.

Friendship welcomed me with a large roadside billboard trumpeting the fact that the Friendship Coyotes—the high school football team—had won three Class 3-A championships in the last five years, one of them in Tim Duffy's final year as coach. From the size of the billboard, one might guess that the town was proud of its football team. The guess was confirmed when my route took me past the gleaming football stadium, with acres of impeccable green turf and enough seating to accommodate the population of the entire county. Here in Friendship, Friday night football was obviously a very big deal.

The billboard and the stadium were powerful reminders of my reason for coming: to find out what I could about the truth of the allegation that an anonymous caller had made against Coach Duffy. It was the ugliest of allegations, without a doubt. It's one thing for a coach to be accused of pocketing a few dollars from the school's athletic fund, or tampering with an athlete's grades. It's quite another to be accused of sexual misconduct with a high school student.

Sexual misconduct.

I winced at the words, as I had winced when Lisa Simon had whispered them to me. I could understand why the high school principal felt she had to find out the truth, just as I could see why the school district's legal eagle didn't want to have anything to do with the matter. Unfortunately, the caller hadn't offered any facts to support the charge and had given Lisa few details. Only the name and address of someone—Margarita

Lopez—who might or might not know what had happened while Tim Duffy was Friendship's football coach, and might—or might not—be willing to talk about it. I wondered who she was. A school employee, current or former? A former student? The student who had been involved in the misconduct?

After several stops at convenience stores to ask directions, I finally found the address I was looking for, a small gray house with a bare front yard, bisected by a concrete walk. A maroon Mercury Marquis from the mid-1980s was parked on the gravel drive, a large gray cat sitting on the top. In the yard, a white-painted truck tire held a bed of straggly yellow pansies; behind it grew a stately blue agave. The tip of a bloom stalk was beginning to poke up through the spiny leaf cluster, which meant that the plant wasn't long for this world. Agaves put their whole heart into producing their flowers and fruit, and wither and die when their reproductive work is done.

My knock at the door eventually brought a woman to open it. "Margarita Lopez?" I asked.

"That's me," she said, in a raspy voice. Forty or forty-five, she was obviously not the student who had been involved in the misconduct. She was slender and petite, and had once been pretty. Now, her olive complexion was sallow and her face lined, her hair was streaked with gray, and she wore a tattered green sweater over a plaid shirt and jeans. She regarded me with bright, suspicious eyes. "Who're you?"

"My name is China Bayles," I said. I hadn't decided until this minute how I was going to approach the conversation, but those eyes—sharper than I might have expected, judging from the rest of her—decided me on straight-up truth. "Lisa Simon, the principal of a high school north of San Antonio asked me to talk to you. She thinks you might be able to give us some background about a problem that's come up. It has to do with a man who used to coach football here in Friendship. Tim Duffy."

The woman's eyes widened. For a minute, she didn't speak. Then her mouth tightened and she pushed open the screen. "You better come on in," she said. "This might take a while."

Inside, the cigarette smoke settled on me like a heavy smog, and the small living room was so dark that it took my eyes a while to adjust. Brown draperies covered the two windows, and a wrinkled brown rug lay on the floor. A shabby corduroy-covered couch and chair filled one corner and a large television set the other. There was a low table beside the TV, and over it hung a gold-framed painting of Our Lady of Sorrows, the Virgin's bleeding heart pierced by seven swords, the bright red blood falling in seven large drops onto her blue mantle. The shelf was covered by a clean white scarf, on which stood a framed photo of an attractive, dark-haired girl with a pretty smile, clearly a senior portrait. A spray of plastic flowers lay in front of the photo, and beside it was a flickering votive candle, with a half dozen small Mexican dolls.

The woman dislodged an orange tabby cat from the chair and motioned me to it. I sat reluctantly, knowing that when I got up, my backside would be covered with orange fur. The cat twitched its tail twice and stalked out of the room. Lopez sat down on the sofa and took a cigarette out of a crumpled package. She offered the pack to me.

"I don't smoke," I said. "But thanks."

She flicked a lighter to the cigarette, crumpled the package, and tossed it into the trash basket beside the sofa. The basket was filled with empty beer cans. "So okay." Her smoky voice was rich with a Spanish accent. "Why are you here?"

"About Tim Duffy," I repeated. "Lisa Simon is the principal of—"

"Yeah, that's what you said," she broke in, shooting me a smoldering glance from those intense dark eyes. "A high school north of San Antonio. So what's the bastard done now?"

"Nothing, as far as I know." I leaned forward. "Look, Mrs. Lopez. This is hard, because I don't know what I'm asking. But I hope you can help. Ms. Simon was told that when Tim Duffy was coaching at Friendship High, he was involved in some sort of sexual misconduct with a student. She was told that you might know something about it."

She closed her eyes and leaned back, resting her head against the sofa cushion. "Sexual misconduct," she said. "Something about it. Yeah, I know something about it." There was a profound bitterness in her voice.

"Would you tell me?" I asked gently.

There was a silence. After a minute she opened her eyes. "Tell you? Why should I tell you? I told them at the school, and it didn't help. What'll you do if I tell you?" She laughed sarcastically. "You gonna pull some strings, maybe? Like how about a noose around his pretty neck?"

"I don't know what I can do," I said. "I won't know until you tell me. Maybe I can help. Maybe I can't." My eyes went to the framed senior photograph on the television set, and I spoke on a sudden hunch. "That girl in the photo. Was she . . . did it have anything to do with her?"

"How'd you guess?" Another bitter laugh, then a silence. When she spoke, her voice held a jagged edge. "That's Angela. My daughter. My only child." She stood up, looking down at me, her head tilted to one side as if she were considering whether I was trustworthy. Finally, she said, "I got some Coke in the fridge. Diet. Want one?"

"Sure," I said, glad that she was making an offer I could accept. "Thanks."

While she was gone, I got up, went to Angela's photo, and studied it.

Seventeen, eighteen, was she? Her smile, fragile, seemed almost to tremble. Her eyes were vulnerable. She was posed bare-shouldered, in a black velvet, scoop-necked studio drape. On another girl, the drape might have looked sexy, but it only emphasized Angela's youth and innocence and the pure, sweet line of her throat. She wore a gold cross on a thin chain around her neck.

"She was embarrassed, wearing that off-the-shoulder thing," Lopez said, behind me. "Angela was modest, the way girls should be. She never liked showing herself. She wanted to wear a white blouse with a lace collar." She handed me a can of Coke. "But the principal said if she was going to be in the yearbook, she had to wear that black thing, like everybody else." She gave an ironic chuckle. "Or she could get her picture taken in her white blouse and pay to have it put in the back of the yearbook, with the ads."

I thought a lawyer's dark thoughts about the violation of the girl's constitutional right to freedom of expression, but I doubted if Angela's mother wanted to hear my opinion. We sat down again and popped our cans. She had brought a fresh pack of cigarettes from the kitchen. She lit one and sat back.

The narrative of her story, which she told in a flat, hard voice, could be summed up in a few sentences. When Angela was a junior, Mrs. Lopez had begun to suspect that her daughter was having a sexual relationship with Coach Duffy, for whom she worked as a student assistant. It had been going on for some time when the mother learned about it, and she wasn't successful in putting a stop to it. That only happened when the coach got another job and moved away.

A sexual *relationship*? That might sound consensual, but as far as the law is concerned, there's no such thing as an adult male—or female, for that matter—having consensual sex with a minor. I glanced again at the photo. Still, there was a puzzling incongruity here: a modest girl who preferred a white blouse to a black drape, but who was also sleeping with the football coach.

"What made you think they were having a relationship?"

"Little things, at first. Stuff she wouldn't've bought for herself. Cheap jewelry, a diary, a teddy bear with a football." Her laugh was brittle. "A great big teddy bear with a black and orange football helmet on its head, carrying a football. Would you believe?" She tipped up the Coke and drained the can. "Then I found the key to her diary. I'm not ashamed to say I read it," she added defiantly. "A daughter shouldn't have any secrets from her mother. A mother always ought to know the truth about what's going on in her girl's life."

"I see," I said, understanding. But diarists don't always tell the truth— and teenaged girls have high-octane fantasy lives.

Lopez pulled on her cigarette, blew out smoke, and scowled. "I was mad, I can tell you. I mean, *really* mad. What kind of man would play around with a sixteen-year-old girl? And him married, too."

I nodded, although the fact of his marriage was hardly material. If the allegation was proven, Tim Duffy—married or single—would be found guilty of indecency with a child, a second-degree felony that carries a two- to twenty-year sentence and a fine of up to ten thousand dollars, as well as mandatory registration as a sex offender. And on top of that, he'd lose his teaching certificate. He'd have to say good-bye to the bright lights and green turf, to the roar of the crowd, and the sweet victory of the state championship. But Tim Duffy *was* married, and Glenda Duffy didn't strike me as the kind of woman who would stand for something like that. He'd probably have to say good-bye to his marriage and half of the community property.

"Did you talk to Angela?" I asked.

"Are you kidding? The minute I read that stuff, I was waving her diary under her nose and asking her what the devil was going on. But she said she'd made it up. She had a crush on him, but what she wrote was just a story. Like in a romance magazine. So what could I say? Anyway, she burned it. She said it was all lies, and she was ashamed of it."

So, whatever the evidentiary value of the diary might have been, it was gone. "But you didn't believe her? You thought the diary told the truth?"

"I know Angela. I *knew* it was the truth," Lopez said with emphasis. "And when I finally got proof, I didn't fool around asking her. I took it straight to the school principal."

Ah. Now we were getting somewhere. "What kind of proof?"

"I found an email he wrote, all printed out and everything. Must've come off the school computer. She hid it in her notebook, but I found it when she was taking a bath." Her dark eyes flashed scornful hatred. "Would you *believe*? The bastard is a teacher, a coach, he's almost twenty years older than her, and he's writing to her like a lovesick puppy."

Ah, evidence—although emails certainly aren't bulletproof. I sat back. "I'd like to see it."

"You can't." She picked a fleck of tobacco off her lip. "I gave it to the principal."

Well, that was easy. I'd get it from him. "What's the principal's name?"

"Mr. Barstow. Larry Barstow. I told him what was going on, and what Coach Duffy was doing to my Angela, and I gave him the email. He told me not to discuss it with anybody else. He said he'd talk to the coach."

"Did he?"

She gave me a dark look. "He told me he did."

"And Duffy said . . . what?" I prompted.

"That there was nothing between him and Angela. That somebody else had written the email, maybe Angela herself. Like maybe she was trying to get him in trouble. Blackmail him or something." Her dark eyes were fierce. "But it's not true. I know my daughter. Barstow just wanted to cover it up so Duffy's reputation wouldn't get hurt. He was a big shot, state champion and all. The best thing to happen in Friendship since the movie theater closed. Like he could do no wrong."

So. Still no proof of sexual misconduct, at least, not the kind Claude Legler wanted. And looking at this from a defense attorney's point of view, I could see how this whole case could be spun into a teenaged girl's romantic fantasy. In fact, I was beginning to wonder whether Angela herself might have made the phone call to Lisa Simon. Like it or not, it was a possibility that had to be considered.

"So what happened after that?" I asked. "After the principal talked to the coach."

"Nothing," Lopez said flatly. "Not a thing. Mr. Barstow said he was going to look into it some more, but that was all I ever heard from him. I called every couple of weeks, but he never called me back. He just swept it under the rug. I talked to the police chief, too, but he acted like I was crazy. Anyway, he said it was the school's business, and it was up to the principal to do what he thought was right."

I shook my head. It sounded like everyone Mrs. Lopez had turned to had stonewalled her, which probably wasn't unusual in a case of this sort. If her allegation was true, it was a giant embarrassment to the school and the town. Nobody wanted a piece of it.

"Then I found out that the coach got a job at another school," she went on. "That was at the beginning of Angela's senior year. So I didn't push it. I was just glad he was gone, and Angela was safe."

Well, sure. Her daughter might be safe, but what about the girls in the coach's new school? A man who gets away with sexual misconduct—if that's what it was—is likely to keep on trying.

"And Angela?" I glanced at the photo. If she had been a high school junior during Duffy's last year as the Friendship coach—"She must be in college by now," I said. "A sophomore?"

"Yeah." Mrs. Lopez looked at me, her eyes suddenly flat and empty. "A sophomore. At Central Texas State. She was majoring in psychology."

"In Pecan Springs?" I was surprised that the woman didn't seem to make the connection between Duffy's new job and her daughter's choice of a college. But then I remembered that she had interrupted me before I could mention Pecan Springs. Maybe she didn't know that Duffy and Angela were living in the same town.

"Pecan Springs. But she's not living there now." Mrs. Lopez pushed her cigarette into the empty Coke can and put it down. Her mouth twisted painfully. "Now she's dead."

I stared at her, uncomprehending. "Dead?"

"Killed herself is what the college counselor told me." Her voice was hollow. "She said it happens sometimes, when girls get depressed. That was the counselor's explanation, anyway. She said Angela was depressed." She shook her head, disbelieving. "I told her that was crazy. My daughter was a good Catholic girl. She'd never have done a thing like that to herself. It had to have been an accident."

There was a long silence. Finally, I managed to say, "How did she—"

"Drugs." She took out another cigarette, tapped it on the table. "Nembutal is what it said in the autopsy report. On her birthday. January third."

I tried to think of something to say and failed. What can you say to a mother who has lost her only child, just a little over a month ago? Words would only deepen the raw wound, widen the unhealed laceration. I bit my lip. Was there any connection between Angela's suicide and her relationship with Duffy? Had they renewed their . . . affair, or whatever it was? She was no longer a minor, but—

"I didn't want her to go up there to school," Mrs. Lopez said. She lit the cigarette, put her head back against the sofa, and closed her eyes again. After a minute, eyes still closed, she went on. "I told her that Central Texas State was too big for her. I told her she was a kid from a little high school, and she wouldn't know a soul. She'd just get lost in the crowd."

The words were coming fast and hard now, strung together with strangled sobs. "I wanted her to take some business courses at the junior college in Uvalde and come back here and work in the bank or something. Marry a nice boy, you know? Settle down and have babies. That's what I told her, but would she listen? She had good grades, so she got a tuition scholarship. Board and room, too. She begged and begged and finally I said yes, she could go."

The tears were coursing freely down her cheeks, and she scrubbed them away with the back of her hand. "And now she's dead, and all I've got of her is some pictures and a box of stuff I brought back from her dorm."

"I'm sorry," I said inadequately.

"You want to see where she's buried, you don't have far to go. The cemetery's just a couple of streets down. She's way back in the corner, under the cottonwood tree. That's the only place the priest would let me put her, but that's okay. There's room for me there, too. And I got her a good headstone. It's got an angel on it, and a Blessed Lady to watch over her. You should go see it."

"I will." I pulled in my breath. "I'm sorry, Mrs. Lopez. Really, I am."

"Sure," she said. She dragged hard on the cigarette. "I'm sorry, you're sorry, we're all sorry." She looked at the painting of Our Lady of Sorrows that hung over what I now realized was an altar to her dead daughter. "See those drops of blood? She lost her only, just like me. She's got knives in her heart, like I've got in mine." Her voice dropped to a mutter. "Knives in the heart. Never stops hurting."

I cleared my throat. "If you don't mind," I said, "there are a couple of other questions. In her letters, did Angela mention that she had seen Duffy?"

A pause, a contemptuous *hmmph*. "See that bastard? Why the hell should she? That was all over with. She was going on with her life."

I nodded. There was no point in my telling her that Duffy lived in the same town. It would just deepen the hurt. "In Pecan Springs, did she live in an off-campus apartment or a dorm?"

"The dorm. You ought to talk to her roommate. Christie's her name. She knew Angela real well. She'll tell you my baby didn't kill herself." Lopez glanced at the clock and brightened. "Hey, by golly," she said, getting to her feet. "It's lunchtime already. What would you say to a bloody Mary? I make it with tequila, you know? I noticed a couple of weenies and some cheese in the fridge, and there's some potato chips, too. The package has been open awhile, but they're prob'ly still okay."

"Thanks, but I think I'll pass." The thought of tequila turned my stomach, and weenies and stale potato chips didn't do anything for me, either. But if Mrs. Lopez found it comforting to get sloshed in the middle of the day, I wasn't going to try to stop her.

Tequilia is an age-old cure for a bleeding heart.

Chapter Eight

Auntie Hannah, who had got on to the parsnip wine, sang a song about Bleeding Hearts and Death, & then another in which she said her heart was like a Bird's Nest; & then everybody laughed again; & then I went to bed.

Dylan Thomas
A Child's Christmas in Wales

Cemeterio Guadalupe lay behind the church, guarded by a pair of tall date palms standing watchfully on either side of a wrought iron entrance gate. From its name and appearance, I concluded that this cemetery was mostly Hispanic. The plots were closer together and more brightly decorated than in Anglo cemeteries, with colorful plastic flowers, amulets, offerings of food and cigarettes, even the occasional bottle of beer or tequilla. (However thirsty you are, it's considered *mucho* bad luck to steal from a grave.) Many of the plots were surrounded by cement curbs enclosing a single grave or the final resting place of an entire family, while others were surrounded by simple fences made of wooden stakes or by elaborate wrought iron fences. Many of the enclosures were topped with gravel; some were bare earth, every blade of grass carefully removed. There were a great many crosses, plain or decorated with mosaic tiles or metal inlays or photographs of the deceased. Hispanics celebrate their dead throughout the year, but especially on La Día de los Muertos, the day when families hold reunions at the cemetery, where the spirits of the dead are invited to join the festivities and share in the holiday food, music, flowers, candles, and incense. It's a reflection of Hispanics' respect for death, their belief that death is only a part of life, in the natural progression from this world to the next.

I found Angela's grave in the farthest corner of the cemetery, under a huge cottonwood tree. The disturbed earth was still bare and raw, but a cement curb already surrounded the double plot where Mrs. Lopez had said that she, too, intended to be buried. Angela's grave was topped by a modest granite marker, obviously new, on top of which stood a carved marble angel, its white wings protectively spread. On the grave was a large red basket filled with red and white plastic carnations—red, the color of blood, white, the color of purity. Beside the vase stood a picture of Our Lady of Sorrows, her bleeding heart pierced with knives.

I stood there for a moment, thinking sadly of life's bitter lessons and wondering just who the hell was in charge of the curriculum. Whether the charge against Duffy was true or false, a young woman—a promising young woman with her whole life before her—was dead. It was a crying shame.

I learned one more thing before I left Friendship. I stopped at the high school and found out from the secretary in the main office—an older woman with a stern face and the look of the school's chief disciplinarian—that Larry Barstow was no longer the principal there, for one very simple reason.

The man was dead. He had died the day after Angela Lopez's death made the headlines in Friendship's weekly newspaper.

Well. This piece of information gave me something to chew on. If I had hoped to learn something from Barstow about his conversation with Duffy, I was deeply disappointed. And if I was tempted to consider the possibility of foul play (it wasn't hard to imagine a scenario in which Barstow's knowledge about the accusation against Duffy might prove deadly), I would have been dead wrong. Barstow had had the very bad luck to get slammed by a bolt of lightning while he was playing golf.

But maybe it wasn't just bad luck. If you believe in divine retribution, you might suspect that Larry Barstow got what was coming to him. Would Angela Lopez still be alive if he had made an adequate investigation into her mother's accusation? Maybe, or maybe not. But at least he would have done his job, and that has to count for something.

I considered stopping at the Friendship police station to talk to the chief, but I doubted that I'd learn anything. Even if he remembered that Mrs. Lopez had come to him with some sort of wild story about the football coach, he had probably discounted it. But I still had plenty to think about as I drove back to the ranch that Monday afternoon. The raw grave, a mother's raw pain, and an ugly allegation that was impossible to prove or disprove, but perhaps not so impossible to believe.

Brian and I had dinner with Leatha and Sam and then headed back to Pecan Springs. On the way home, full of his exciting desert expedition, Brian informed me that he was going to specialize in burrowing toads when he went to college.

That was perfectly okay with me. Anything is better than football. And if this particular toad really does like to munch on termites, I can envision a great future for Brian.

ON Tuesday morning, I called Lisa Simon at the high school and told her what I'd found out—which, when you boiled it all down, amounted to several serious claims but precious few facts. The accuser was a mother with a drinking problem. The victim had burned her diary, and now she was dead. Both the victim and the alleged perpetrator had denied that anything had gone on between them. And the chief investigator had died without leaving a paper trail.

At least that's what I had gathered from the expression on the school secretary's face when I asked her if she knew of any files or records that Larry Barstow might have kept regarding allegations of misconduct against Coach Duffy.

"Misconduct?" She gave me a distasteful look. "That's impossible. I saw every piece of paper in Mr. Barstow's files, and there was nothing like *that*. Why, he and the coach were best friends—and the coach was one of our most outstanding faculty members. We were terribly sorry to lose him."

Lisa Simon was horrified when I told her about Angela Lopez's death the preceding month. "Thank God she wasn't one of our students," she said, and then, realizing how that might sound, added, "I'm so sorry for her mother. She must be distraught."

"Devastated. And drinking," I added.

Lisa sighed heavily. "Well, if nobody at Friendship High has any information, I guess I'll have to confront Duffy."

"It probably won't do any good," I said. "He's already denied the allegation once, and there's no compelling reason for him to admit to it, especially now that Angela is dead." I paused. "Mrs. Lopez said that her daughter lived in an on-campus dorm with somebody named Christie. Girls share secrets, and know a lot about each other's lives. I wonder if—"

"Oh, *would* you?" Lisa broke in with eager relief. "China, it would be terrific if you could find Angela's roommate and talk to her."

I was planning to do more than that, actually. As it happens, the

Pecan Springs chief of police, Sheila Dawson, is a good friend—and she used to be chief of campus security. Sheila and I already had a date for lunch today and I had phoned to give her a heads-up on one of our topics of conversation: Angela Lopez's suicide. She had promised to dig up the file on the case and tell me what she could about the circumstances.

But lunch was still a couple of hours away. In the meantime, I had to finish arranging the Valentine's display in the middle of the store, check in and shelve a box of herbal incense, and listen to Ruby's angst-laden report of her latest frustrations with Colin.

"We had a great time at the country music concert," she lamented, "but when he came over for dinner on Saturday night, he seemed . . . well, withdrawn. And at about ten, he said that he was expecting somebody to call him at home—a business call." She made a sad face. "So he didn't stay."

"A business call at ten o'clock on Saturday night?" I asked, giving her a quizzical look. She was wearing black today, a long black silky tunic, black pants, a black scarf tied around her frizzy red hair. She looked as if she were auditioning for Queen of the Night. Or maybe she was in mourning.

"Yeah, that's what I thought, too," Ruby replied dejectedly. "Who gets business calls at that hour? I didn't hear from him all day Sunday, but he showed up with Chinese takeout last night, and everything between us was just as always—wonderful." She sighed heavily. "I wish I understood him, China. Sometimes I think we're soul mates. Other times, he's the lover from hell."

I held my tongue. Ruby has brains, personality-plus, motivation, and energy—the kind of woman who could fly solo and manage just fine. But since her husband, Wade, ran off with a younger woman seven or eight years ago, she has gone through one disastrous "soul mate" after another, none of whom have measured up to her great expectations.

Which is odd, when you stop to think about it. Ruby is an extraordinarily intuitive woman, especially where people are concerned. She can take one look at a stranger and give you an amazingly accurate estimate of his likes, his dislikes, his motivations. Most of the time, she can even tell you his astrological sign. Unfortunately, these intuitive powers seem to fail when it matters most: when it comes to a guy she finds physically attractive. She can't seem to get past a pair of sexy eyes, or a come-hither-babe voice, or a seductive smile. And before you know it, her heart has been broken once again.

When I first met Colin Fowler, I had to agree that he might be the exception. He's no standout in terms of powerful good looks or supreme sexiness, like some of Ruby's earlier soul mates. He's just your regular Mr. Nice Guy, with a lean, athletic build, an engaging boy-next-door friendliness, and reddish-brown hair, thinning on top—but hey, nobody's perfect. He moved to Pecan Springs about six months ago and opened a store on the square. Good Earth Goods, which sells environmentally friendly stuff: cleaners, pet shampoo, energy-efficient lighting, insect repellents, and hemp products.

Yes, hemp products. Pants, shirts, shorts, sandals, as well as fabric, paper, shampoo, soap, lotion—all made from hemp, a plant that is nearly a twin of marijuana, but is grown for its valuable fiber, rather than its psychoactive properties. (Smoking hemp won't do much for you except make you cough.) Hemp is an age-old agricultural staple that once provided the fiber for rope, the canvas for sailing ships and prairie schooners, and the oil for lamps and cooking. Although it's been illegal to grow hemp in this country since the late 1940s, this renewable resource is legally grown around the world, and is used to create many twenty-first-century products: remarkably strong and lightweight building materials, wear-proof carpeting, even circuit boards. Colin is an active, out-there member of the Hemp Industries Association, traveling around the country, trying to persuade people that growing hemp makes good commercial sense, as well as being good for the environment.

All this, of course, is a plus for Colin, in Ruby's book—and it would be in mine, too, if it weren't for all the mystery about him. He lived in New Orleans before he came here, he told Ruby, although he certainly doesn't talk like a Louisiana native. He was married once, and is now divorced, Ruby says, although he doesn't want to discuss it. "It's over," he says. "What's the point?" In fact, Colin won't speak at all about his life before his arrival in Pecan Springs. "I'm here now," he says. "I live in the present. The present is where I want to be"—a philosophy to which Ruby, who also lives very much in the present, can hardly object.

And even that might not be a problem—except for a couple of disturbing events. Around Halloween, at the cast party for the community theater's production of *A Man for All Reasons*, I witnessed an encounter between Sheila and Colin from which I concluded that the two of them knew each other, both personally and professionally. A few days later, Sheila admitted as much to me, but insisted that whatever relationship they'd had was ended. She wasn't at liberty to tell me anything else, she said. And from other bits of evidence (McQuaid, for instance, said that he felt he might have met Colin during his years in Houston Homicide), it seems pretty clear that, at some point in his life, Colin was in law enforcement.

I haven't mentioned any of this to Ruby, since Sheila won't reveal what she knows about Colin, and McQuaid can't seem to remember the circumstances of their meeting—if there was one. Whatever happened in the past is Colin's secret, and it looks like it's going to stay that way. It's really none of my business, except that Ruby has so many ups and downs. There have been good weeks—say, right around Christmas, when she and Colin spent several days in Cozumel together. But there have been bad weeks, too, when he went away on business and didn't call. I'm tired of seeing Ruby looking wretched and feeling unworthy, and I am almost out of Kleenex. Right now, the safest strategy was distraction.

"How's your investigation going? Into the theft of Carol's quilt, I mean."

"Oh, that." Ruby blew her nose. "Well, I guess we're making progress. Carol turned in the police report. And Cass and I talked to everybody who helped hang the quilts, looking for possible leads." She made a face. "Nobody saw much of anything, unfortunately. Except for Kathleen, Carol's cousin. Last night, she told me that she noticed some guy—one of the hotel employees—studying the quilt very closely. He seemed to be unusually interested in it. I thought I'd run over to the hotel after you get back from lunch, and see if I can find the guy. Kathleen said he only had one arm, so he shouldn't be hard to locate."

"A one-armed quilt bandit," I said, shaking my head. "I hope you nab him." I paused. "Is Carol getting along okay? She must be very upset."

"She's devastated," Ruby replied. "She says that making the quilt was like giving birth, and now she feels like her child has been kidnapped." She pulled her brows together and added, in her Nancy Drew voice, "I've been thinking about means and opportunity, China. I made a list of everybody who had the opportunity—more or less. As for means, all somebody would have to do is pull the quilt off the hanging rod." She paused, frowning. "But then there's motive. That's a lot more important, don't you think? If I could figure out *why* the quilt was taken, I'd probably know who took it."

"Sounds reasonable," I said.

She eyed me. "Do you have any ideas?"

I searched for something. "Motive. Well, let's see. Does Carol have any enemies? Anybody who'd like to see her hurt or embarrassed?"

Ruby looked dubious. "Carol is such a sweetie, it's hard to imagine anybody wanting to cause her trouble—especially after all she's been through the past year with her cancer. But I'll give her a call and see if she can come up with any names." She paused. "And I'll also talk to Arlene Cohen. She knows Carol's friends—and she's the suspicious type. She might have noticed someone who didn't even cross Carol's radar. Somebody with a grudge, I mean." She narrowed her eyes. "You're right, China. The thief has got to be somebody who hates Carol—although I still want to talk to that one-armed guy at the hotel. And while I'm there, I'll talk to the manager. After all, the hotel's got a stake in this. The theft occurred on their property, didn't it?"

I smiled. Love might send Ruby over the top and into a helpless, hurtling nosedive, but her investigating instincts are a hundred percent on target.

She turned to go back to her shop. "Oh, by the way," she said. "Missy Bowers called a little while ago. She wanted to talk to you."

Missy Bowers, our Party Thyme helper. "Why does she want to talk to me? You're the one who handles the party scheduling."

"It's not about Party Thyme. She said it's something personal. She'll call back."

I nodded. Missy, like her twin sister, Mandy, is a top-notch student. She'd mentioned an interest in a legal career. She probably wanted to talk about that.

"Good," I said. "If I'm not here when she calls, tell her I'll call back."

I'D like to be a fly on the wall when the Texas Police Chiefs Association assembles for one of its regular meetings. A lot of the guys look like Pecan Springs' retired chief, Bubba Harris, who is barrel-chested, beer-bellied, and balding, with a cigar in his mouth, a white straw Stetson on his head, and a belt buckle the size of a squad car's hubcap. And then there's Chief Sheila Dawson, who looks as if she just stepped out of a fashion ad in *Texas Monthly* magazine. She is slim, blond, and gorgeously chic, whether she's wearing a blue police uniform with a gun on her hip, or a stylish suit with a gun in her Gucci. It's hard to imagine what the good ol' boys of the Police Chiefs Association make of this woman. But they all know she's the Real Deal. Before the City Council named her as Pecan Springs' police chief, Sheila was chief of security at Central Texas State University— and before that, she was a beat cop on some of the meanest streets in Dallas. You don't want to mess with her. Whether she's wearing a pink suit or a blue uniform, Sheila is one tough babe. She is also one smart cookie, which is what her friends call her.

Today, Smart Cookie was wearing her uniform, which set her apart from the rest of the customers at Lila Jennings's Nueces Street Diner, most of whom were dressed for the February cold in jeans, flannel shirts, and fleece-lined jackets. It was Tuesday, which meant that Lila was dishing up chicken and dumplings—those big, fluffy dumplings like your grandmother used to make—with a side of green beans with bacon and apple pie, a meal that's guaranteed to warm your bones, no matter how low the temperature dips. The warm spell that had allowed me to get out into the garden to prune the roses had been abruptly curtailed by a sudden blast of Arctic air, and the weather guru was actually predicting snow in the next couple of days. In fact, it was already so cold that the windows of the diner—an old Missouri and Pacific dining car that Lila and her dear-departed Ralph redeemed from the scrap heap and brought back to life—were all steamed up.

The diner's décor is right out of the fifties, with chrome-and-red tables and chairs, an old Wurlitzer jukebox, and Texas memorabilia on the walls, like the picture of famous Texas cowgirl Connie Reeves, who uttered the memorable line, "Always saddle your own horse." One full wall was devoted to old Panther football programs, framed newspaper clippings, autographed jerseys, pennants, and team photos. Prominent among them was a large framed photo of a scowling Coach Duffy in an action crouch, a whistle between his teeth and a clipboard in his hand. It was captioned "Kick ass and take names."

Sheila had already claimed the booth at the end of the counter, where she was hunched over a bowl of chicken and dumplings. "Sorry for not waiting," she said, as I sat down. "I've got to get back to the office. An officer on his first patrol rammed his squad car into the rear end of a school bus this morning." She made a face. "Nobody hurt, thank God, but the fallout is heavy."

"I'm glad I don't have your job." I inhaled deeply. "Chicken and dumplings. Just what I need." Lila, who was serving a slice of lemon pie with a mile-high meringue, heard me and glanced in my direction.

"Big bowl or little bowl?" she asked. Lila fits right into the diner's fifties' mode, with her green puckered-nylon uniform, ruffled apron, and perky white hat perched on her Andrews-Sister hairdo. "Side of green beans?"

"Big bowl," I replied, shrugging out of my jacket. "Yes to the green beans, but no pie." I love Lila's pie, but there are enough carbs in her dumplings to keep me going for a week.

"So tell me why you're interested in the Lopez girl's suicide," Sheila said, wiping her mouth with a napkin.

"It's complicated." I hung up my jacket and sat down, rubbing my hands to warm them. "You go first. What's the story?"

"In early January, Angela Lopez rented a room at The Longhorn, put on a frilly nightie, and ate a handful of Nembutal in some butterscotch pudding."

I frowned. The Longhorn isn't a little fleabag mom-and-pop. It's an upscale two-story hotel-type motel, not far from the campus, that caters to visiting parents and alumni attending college events. "She was alone when she rented the room?"

"That's what the desk clerk told the investigating officer." Sheila regarded me narrowly. "What's your interest in this, China?"

Lila appeared with a bowl of chicken and dumplings and a side of green beans for me, and a piece of luscious-looking apple pie for Sheila.

Sheila rolled her eyes at the pie, which was topped by a scoop of melting vanilla ice cream. "Lila, will you marry me?"

"Can't," Lila said briefly. She has no sense of humor. "I got my hands full right here. Anyway, it's Docia's pie." Docia is Lila's thirty-five-year old daughter, who works in the kitchen. Right now, I could hear her banging the pots, which meant that she was in a bad mood. "Doubt you want to marry her. Coffee?"

"Please." Sheila picked up her fork. "Cream."

"How you get away with it, I don't know," I said, eyeing Sheila's plate. "If that pie went past my lips, there'd be three more pounds on my hips tomorrow morning."

"I worry it off," Sheila said. "You would, too, if your cops kept ramming their cars into school buses." She picked up her fork. "So tell me how come you're interested in Lopez."

"I'd rather not say just yet," I replied. "She was wearing a frilly nightie?"

Sheila nodded, her mouth full of pie.

"Well, what else? Did she leave a note? Any phone calls made from the room? How about visitors? Anybody ask at the desk for her room number? And what about the autopsy report? I need to see a copy."

Sheila put down her fork. "Yes, there was a note. It said. 'I'm really sorry. I didn't mean it to end like this.' It's signed, and the handwriting matches. It's got her fingerprints all over it. The investigating officer saw no signs of foul play. The autopsy surgeon—the body went down to Bexar County—ruled the death a self-inflicted drug overdose." Her voice went up a notch. "What's more, the girl was taking antidepression drugs, which raises the risk of suicide. If you've got any contradictory evidence, China, let's have it. Now." Hearing the sharp edge in her voice, she caught herself. "Sorry," she muttered. "It's been a rough day already."

"Sounds like it," I said sympathetically. "I understand that her roommate's name is Christie."

"Yeah. Christie Norris."

"What about phone calls from the motel room?"

Sheila gave an exasperated hiss. "None mentioned in the report."

"Which means that the investigating officer didn't bother to ask."

"Maybe not. Or maybe the phone is on a direct outside line." She eyed me. "Either way, so what? What's your interest in this, China?"

"When Angela Lopez was a junior in high school, she had an affair with a man who is now a prominent citizen of Pecan Springs." I paused and added, "At least that's what her mother claims."

"A *junior!*" Sheila looked disgusted.

"Yeah. Statutory rape. And when she died, Angela was . . . what? Nineteen?"

"Twenty," Sheila said grimly. "She died on her birthday. Who is this prominent citizen?"

"If she was twenty, the statute of limitations had eight more years to run," I said reflectively. In Texas, a felony indictment for child sexual abuse can be brought for up to ten years from the victim's eighteenth birthday. Angela had eight more years to blow the whistle.

"Yeah." Sheila spoke between her teeth, spacing out the words. "Who . . . is . . . the . . . prominent . . . citizen?"

"I can't say."

"Look, China." Sheila's face was dark. "I know how you lawyers feel about protecting the rights of the accused, but don't you think you could make an exception in this case? We're not talking shoplifting, for Pete's sake."

I sighed. I keep my bar membership current, so I'm still a lawyer. And for better or worse, I believe in protecting the rights of the accused, which usually means not handing out freebies to the cops. But Sheila was going to keep after me until I gave her something. And she was right. We weren't talking shoplifting here.

"Okay, here's as much of the story as I can tell you. Lisa Simon, at the high school, received an anonymous tip that one of her faculty members

90

had a sexual relationship with a student several years ago, when he was teaching in another town. The tipster gave Lisa the name of a woman who was supposed to know something about it. I was asked to talk to the woman, who turned out to be Mrs. Lopez. She told me it was her daughter who'd been involved, and that the girl was dead."

"Grrr," Sheila said fiercely. "What about the school administration in the other town? Was there any investigation into Angela's allegations?"

"Angela didn't allege anything. It was the mother who made the allegations. She talked to the school principal, and he talked to the faculty member, who denied it. Angela denied it, too."

"I assume you talked to the principal. What does he say?"

I grinned briefly. "He's not in a position to say anything. He's dead." When Sheila's eyebrows went up, I added, "He was struck by lightning, the day after Angela died. Of course, I'm not suggesting that there's any connection between that lightning bolt and his failure to do a better investigation."

"I didn't think you were," Sheila said, with an echoing smile. "It's an interesting coincidence, that's all."

"But I am suggesting that you take another look at Angela's suicide," I said. "The mother was positive that her daughter—who was a Catholic—didn't kill herself." I finished off the last dumpling with serious regret, carbs or no carbs. "It's the nightie that's bothering me. Why would she go to the trouble?"

"Because she wanted to look pretty when she was found," Sheila said promptly. "That's common, especially when the victim is a young woman." She paused, frowning, her fork halfway to her mouth. "You don't think somebody else might have—"

"I don't know what I think," I said. "If I change my mind, I'll let you know." I paused. "However, there is something you might do to help. You can tell me how I can get in touch with Christie Norris."

"I'll find out and give you a call. After you've talked to her, let's talk again." When I nodded, she relaxed a little. "So. What's new in your life, China? Other than Angela Lopez."

"Well, let's see." I pursed my lips. "Valentine's Day is coming up, so we're pretty busy at the shops. And McQuaid has gone to Albuquerque, so Brian and I are batching for a while."

Sheila gave me a look. "Albuquerque? Isn't that where Dingbat lives?"

"Yes, but this trip doesn't have anything to do with Sally. He's on a case—software theft. I don't think he's got time to get involved with—"

"I hope not," Sheila said, forking up the last bite of pie. "I sincerely hope not. That woman is such bad news." She sat back. "Ruby brought in a report on a stolen quilt. She said she's playing detective."

"Yeah. She's hot on the trail of a guy with one arm." I grinned wryly. "Maybe it'll keep her mind off Colin Fowler."

"I wish to hell she'd drop that jerk." With an irritated gesture, Sheila pushed her plate away. Her voice was angry, impatient. "He's only going to make her unhappy."

I thought of Ruby's fragile vulnerability, her wistful hopes, and frowned. "It might help if you'd come clean on him, you know. You might save Ruby some serious heartache."

At that, Sheila's impatience seemed to evaporate. She put both hands over mine, and her voice softened. "I'm sorry, China. I'd give anything to be able to help Ruby, but I *can't*. Honest to God, I can't. All I can say is, if you've got any influence over her, get her to drop this guy *now*—before it's too late." She was squeezing my hands very hard, and her eyes were dark and urgent.

"Too late for what?"

"Just . . . too late."

"Yeah." I glanced down at our hands. "Hey," I said. "That's some grip. You've been working out."

She pulled her hands back. "Sorry," she muttered. "Guess I got carried away."

"Yeah, well, I'm sorry, too." I pursed my lips speculatively. "Maybe I should do a little research into Colin's past. I wonder if he's using an alias. You wouldn't happen to know that, would you?"

Sheila picked up her cop cap and jammed it on her head. "It's a rotten world," she said tersely, pushing herself out of the booth.

I thought of Ruby, hoping to build a committed relationship with a guy with a past—a dangerous past, if Sheila's dark hints could be trusted. And I thought of a young girl lying in a grave in a far corner of the Cemeterio Guadalupe, under a cottonwood tree. A grave with an angel standing guard, and red and white carnations, and Mary's heart bleeding over all.

"Yes," I said softly. "An absolutely rotten world."

Chapter Nine

THE SYMBOLISM OF HERBS AND FLOWERS

Envy: *Bramble.* Tears and rends everything it can cling to . . . The Briar and Thorn are old emblems of Pain, Envy, and Suffering, and are frequently alluded to by our poets.

Falsehood: *Deadly nightshade.* The fruit of which produces poison and death, and cannot be pointed out too soon to the innocent and unwary, that they may be prevented from gathering it.

Cruelty: *Stinging nettle.* Wounds the hand that presses it.

Thomas Miller
The Poetical Language of Flowers, 1847

 Ruby wore a dispirited look. "It turned out to be nothing, after all," she said, coming into the shop. "Darn."

"What turned out to be nothing?" I asked distractedly.

Cass and I were leafing through Lucinda Hutson's latest cookbook, looking for possible additions to Cass's Thymely Gourmet menus. We were drooling over the recipe for chicken breasts stuffed with chives and fresh herbs, and Cass had just remarked that it looked as if it would be perfect for freezing.

"The one-armed bandit," Ruby replied.

Cass frowned. "Now, that's what I call an information-rich answer." She paused. "I didn't think slot machines were legal in Texas."

"Not that kind of one-armed bandit," I said. "This is a guy with one arm. Somebody spotted him casing the quilt show—specifically, the missing quilt."

"Turns out he wasn't thinking of taking the quilt," Ruby said. She sounded disgusted. "His wife is a quilter. He liked Carol's design and thought he'd get his wife to bring her camera and take a photo, so she could go home and copy it."

"Copy it!" Cass snorted disgustedly. "That's immoral!"

"Illegal, too," I said. "Did you tell him that stealing an original quilt design is the same as stealing the quilt itself?"

"I don't think it would have made an impression on him," Ruby said ironically. "I did call Arlene, though, and asked her to put up a sign that explains about copyright and tells people that they can't take photographs. And while I had Arlene on the phone, I asked her to make up an enemies list."

"An enemies list!" Cass exclaimed, her eyebrows going up. "You're planning a hit?"

Ruby gave Cass an impatient look. "It's a matter of motive. Carol is too nice to notice whether she has any enemies who might hate her enough to steal her quilt, but Arlene has a nose for stuff like that."

"Did you talk to the hotel manager?" I asked.

"Yes, but all she'd say was that we should have posted a guard—which Arlene is taking care of today. We can't afford to lose another quilt." Ruby glanced at the book that lay open in front of us. "Oh, is that Lucinda Hutson's new cookbook?"

Ruby and I got acquainted with Lucinda, who lives in Austin, when we went to visit her garden, which has been featured in magazines and on Tom Spencer's KLRU-TV show, *Central Texas Gardener*.

Cass nodded. "I'm looking for inspiration."

"Here's something to inspire you." I pointed to a photo of a hollowed-out red cabbage filled with dip and surrounded by fresh vegetables. "Gorgeous, huh?"

"Stunning," Ruby said. "Wow, Cass. Maybe we could use that idea for our party catering. It would be a great centerpiece. We can give Lucinda the credit, too." She hooked her fingers into quotation marks. "As featured in Lucinda Hutson's *Herb Garden Cookbook*."

"Suits me," Cass said.

ASIDE from the quiet few minutes that Cass and I spent drooling over the recipes in Lucinda's cookbook, the afternoon was hectic, with a constant stream of customers in both shops, the tearoom, and the gardens—the kind of busy a businesswoman likes to see. The scented geraniums were disappearing fast, and we were running low on some of the culinary herbs that Pecan Springers set out early, like parsley, sage, and garlic, so I spent some time on the phone, ordering more. Then one of the journalism interns from the Pecan Springs *Enterprise* came in to interview Ruby and me and take pictures for a story on our Valentine's tea. And when Cass closed the tearoom at four, we had served thirty-two people—not bad for a chilly February day with off-and-on drizzle.

At four thirty, I left Laurel to close the shop and headed out to my car. It was my night to cook dinner, but Brian was eating at Jake's house and McQuaid was out of town, so I was off the hook. This was a good thing, because I had something else to do.

Right after lunch, Sheila had phoned with the dorm address and telephone number for Christie Norris, Angela Lopez's college roommate.

Unfortunately, she'd moved out of the dorm, and when I finally tracked down her new number, the young woman who answered the phone told me that Christie had gone to Dallas for a couple of days. She wasn't sure when she'd be back—duh, maybe tomorrow, maybe later. It sounded as if she didn't care very much, either. I left my name and number and the message that I was calling about Angela. I doubted that Christie would get the message, and even if she did, there wasn't any guarantee that she'd call. But it was the best I could do.

Interviewing Angela's former roommate wasn't the only bit of business on my list. I dug out the letter my mother had given me, and telephoned Miles Danforth. It took a while to thread my way through the maze of receptionists and secretaries at Zwinger, Brady, Brandon, and Danforth, but finally, he was on the line, an odd mixture of caution and interest in his voice.

Yes, he had the envelope of documents pertaining to Robert Bayles in his personal possession.

No, he would prefer not to mail the envelope; it was his opinion that the contents warranted a personal discussion.

Yes, this evening would be suitable, if I could get there as soon after five as possible. Obligingly, he provided directions, told me how to negotiate the intricacies of the parking garage, gave me a secret password that would get me past the security guard and up to the twenty-second floor with the least amount of hassle, and instructed me on operating the coded panel that would unlock the office, since the receptionist would have left for the day. Obviously, Zwinger, Brady, Brandon, and Danforth did not chase ambulances for a living.

The drive from Pecan Springs to Austin used to be easy and sometimes even fun, and I can remember when it didn't take much more than thirty-five or forty minutes. These days, though, I-35 is not the place you want to be at quarter to five. It was bumper to bumper northbound and southbound, with SUVs and long-haul truckers doing their best to intimidate those lesser beings (like me) who drive smaller vehicles. To make matters worse, the cold gray sky had begun to weep a steady rain and the highway was treacherously slick. A serious fender-bender backed up traffic at I-35 and Ben Cannon and an injury accident clogged the Colorado River bridge, so it was pushing six by the time I took the off-ramp and swung down Eleventh Street to Lavaca. I maneuvered my car into the designated visitor's space on the third level of the parking garage, and remarked "How 'bout them Cowboys?" (somebody's cute idea of a password, I guess) to the security guard. I hit the elevator button to the twenty-second floor, glad that office hours were over and nobody was around to stare at my informal attire: the jeans, brown turtleneck sweater, fleece-lined boots, and denim jacket I'd worn to work that morning. But heck, this is Austin. Anything goes. I was sorry I hadn't worn my Go Panthers baseball cap.

The offices of Zwinger, Brady, Brandon, and Danforth lived up to expectations. The receptionist's desk was polished mahogany, the velvet sofas and chairs were arranged in intimate conversational groupings, potted plants decorated the corners and large paintings the walls, and the carpet was so thick it swallowed every sound. The place was elegant, imposing, and intimidating, exactly as the designer had planned. No lawyer wants a client who feels in control.

Miles Danforth had heard the discreet chime that announced my arrival and stepped out of his office to beckon to me. As I walked down the hallway toward him, I saw that he was a lean, fit-looking man about my age, with sharp blue eyes and a neatly clipped black beard. He was dressed in tailored dark gray slacks, white shirt with the collar open, tie loose, and—yes—cowboy boots. Alligator cowboy boots, dyed ebony. As I said, this is Austin.

"China Bayles." His deep voice was cordial, and his face crinkled into a wicked grin that had something oddly familiar about it. He pointed his finger at me, like a gun. "Hey, I remember you! You were that shrimpy little kid with skinny legs and big eyes who used to hang out in my mom's office, getting in her way." He gave me an appreciative look, up and down. His glance came back to my face and lingered there. "Not bad, I'd say. Not bad at all."

I shook my head in disbelief. "And you were the boy with buck teeth—Buddy, wasn't it?—who used to jimmy the Coke machines in the basement and steal cigarettes from the partners' desks."

I probably hadn't seen Mrs. Danforth's son more than a half dozen times, and I'd never heard him called Miles, but my teenaged self had been profoundly impressed by his tight jeans and his sleight-of-hand when it came to pilfering those cigarettes—not to mention the fact that he'd been generous enough to share them, one steamy afternoon in the basement. I gave him another look, searching for the boy hidden somewhere deep inside the man. No wonder that smile seemed familiar.

"Yeah, Buddy," he said reminiscently. "That was Mom's pet name for me. You may be the only other person in the world who remembers that bit of trivia."

We were in his office now, and I glanced around. On the credenza behind the desk was a collection of framed snapshots: Miles Danforth with a girl of about nine or ten, dark-haired, pixielike, pretty. One wall was covered with diplomas and board certifications testifying to various professional competencies; another was filled with photos testifying to various top-level connections in the world of government and commerce. There were several photographs of the governor, a father-son presidential pair, past and present U.S. senators, figures from the entertainment industry, and other eminently recognizable people—most of them on the conservative side of the political fence. I guessed that Miles Danforth, Attorney at Law, was very much persona grata in Texas political circles. The scene framed by the large window confirmed my hunch: it was an imposing view of the state capital building, its flood-lit dome gleaming against the deepening twilight.

"You must've stopped stealing cigarettes," I remarked dryly.

"You got it. Don't know how, but I finally managed to put all those youthful misdeeds behind me and make something of myself." He picked up a gold cigarette box with a Presidential seal on the cover. "Here. Have one. These are legit."

"I'll pass, thank you, Miles." I had to fight the urge to call him Buddy. "I gave up smoking when I left the firm."

"I should give it up too," he said. He took a cigarette out of the box, lit it, and turned to look out the window. "Mother told me you'd gone into criminal law," he added, over his shoulder. "She kept an eye on you, you know, from a distance, after she left the firm."

"Oh? She didn't stay at Stone and Bayles?"

He shook his head. "She left just after your father died. She was so pleased when she read about you in the newspaper." He half-turned, his quizzical glance not quite neutral. "And she was disappointed when you left the profession. She thought you had a promising future."

I heard the implicit criticism, raised my eyebrows, and shrugged without replying. Lots of people expressed their disappointment, both at the time I made the leap and over the years since. But their opinions made no difference to me then, and they make no difference to me now. I've never regretted giving up my career, but if other people think I should, that's okay by me. They can have their cheap thrill.

He got the message. "Yeah, well. The law is a rat race, that's for damn sure." A wry smile tugged at his mouth. "You'll probably live a hell of a lot longer than I will. Less stress, more fun, shorter hours."

More fun, yes—but less stress and shorter hours? He should hang around Thyme and Seasons for a week or so. But there was no point in arguing.

"It's right for me," I said, and changed the subject. "I was sorry to hear about your mother's death, Miles. I admired her. She could have appeared in court for any of the partners at any time, if she'd had the credentials. She certainly had the brains. She knew where all the bodies were buried, too." A secretary who knows all the company secrets—and keeps them—is worth her weight in rubies in any firm, but especially in a law firm, which always has a great many secrets.

"The bodies." His eyebrows came together and an odd note came into his voice. "Yes, I suppose she did."

"I'm sorry I didn't keep in touch with her," I said. "The last time I saw her was at my father's funeral." She had worn a black suit and a small black hat with a veil, and she carried herself like a grieving widow. Why hadn't I stopped in to see her after Dad was killed, or taken her out to lunch? Was I afraid that Leatha would be hurt if she found out?

More likely, I thought now, I had wanted to disconnect myself from my father and anyone who'd been involved with him. I had been angry in those days, angry that he had taken himself out of my life. I had done what I could to forget him. Why, I couldn't even remember what he looked like—couldn't, even if I tried, conjure up a recollection of his face.

Miles cleared his throat. "Mother was a wonderful woman," he said, bringing me back to the present. "It's been a loss. More than I might have guessed," he added, half to himself. He put out his cigarette in a crystal ashtray.

"I'm sure." I paused. It was time to get on with it. "You wrote to my mother about some papers that your mother had kept."

He nodded. "Yes. But perhaps we should decide about dinner first. What would you say to Scholz's Bier Garten—it's only a short walk. Or is there somewhere else you'd rather go?"

"Dinner?" I blinked, genuinely surprised. "But I didn't plan to—"

"I'm sorry." He smiled. "I should have mentioned it when you called, but I was in the middle of something, and I didn't think of it until we'd hung up. There are . . . well, there are one or two things that need to be discussed, and I—" He stopped, eyeing me. "You don't want to go to dinner."

"It's not that," I said, trying to sound regretful about turning him down. He was certainly good-looking, and a rather nice person, not the sort of man who would automatically assume that any red-blooded girl would be dying to spend the evening with him. And he was, after all, the grownup version of the kid who had introduced me to filter cigarettes, with a few fumbling kisses on the side. "Ordinarily, I'd be glad to," I added. "I haven't been to Scholz Garten for years. This evening, though, I need to get back to Pecan Springs. My son's having dinner with a friend, and I don't like him to come home to an empty house." That was true, although Brian is allowed to stay out until nine thirty on school nights.

"Oh," he said, and his dark eyebrows came together in a disconcertingly familiar way. "A son. That's . . . nice. But being a single parent isn't easy." His eyes went to the photos on his credenza, which I supposed were photos of his daughter.

"I'm not a single parent," I said, wondering how in the world I could remember eyebrows over a span of—what was it?—three decades? "Brian's father is away on business for a few days," I added helpfully. "He's an ex–homicide detective. A private investigator."

"Oh." He ducked his head, embarrassed. "I'm sorry. I thought, since you called yourself China Bayles—" He ducked his head, embarrassed.

"I should have mentioned it," I said, feeling guilty and maybe even a little sorry for him. But that was ridiculous. My wedding ring was on my finger, where it's supposed to be. He just hadn't looked. And why should I mention my marital status to a perfect stranger? Well, maybe not a stranger. I flushed, thinking of those kisses.

"Well, then." Miles became businesslike. "Let's get to it, shall we?" He went to his desk, opened a drawer, and took out a bulging manila envelope. He gestured to the conversation area arranged in one corner of the large office, the requisite leather couch and leather chair at right angles to each other, and a coffee table with a large designer arrangement of tasteful silk flowers, an engraved business card holder, and a heavy onyx ashtray. I sat down in the chair.

"You've read the letter I wrote to your mother?" He sat on the sofa and put the envelope on the coffee table.

"Yes. She asked me to contact you." I thought of Leatha, and the awkward, sliding look I had found so revealing, the look that told me that she knew about the affair. I wondered whether Leatha would remember Buddy, and what she would think of him now. But perhaps she had never met him. She hadn't visited the office very often. That was my father's territory—and Laura Danforth's.

"My mother died about a month ago," he said, somewhat stiffly. "She had been terminally ill for about six months—cancer—and she was preparing for the end. She disposed of the bulk of her personal papers and obviously intended to dispose of everything before her death. But she became unexpectedly incapacitated, and apparently wasn't able to finish the task. There was a box under her bed. In it, among other things, I found these letters from your father—two dozen or so of them—and a few photographs." He looked down. "I think she wanted to keep them with her as long as she could. She was . . . devoted to him."

I was somber, thinking of Laura Danforth dying. Even as she died, she had remembered my father with love and devotion. She was probably the only woman who had ever cared for him in that way, and I found the thought unexpectedly moving.

My feelings must have shown on my face, for Miles shifted uncomfortably. "Yes. Well, when I found the letters, I wasn't sure what to do. I read one or two, and looked at some of the photos. And then I . . . well, I read the rest."

"I see," I said, wondering if he expected me to object to what he had done. Was I supposed to think that he had committed some sort of personal trespass, a violation of privacy, my father's and his mother's? But their affair had been over for decades, and both of them were dead. At this point in time, my father's letters could only be of . . . well, academic interest. They might help me to understand a man I barely knew, but then again, they might not. And beyond that, what use could they possibly be? I had already made up my mind that I wasn't going to share them with my mother. They could only cause her pain. It would have been better if Miles had chucked them into the fire.

He reached for one of the cigarettes in a porcelain bowl on the table, took a gold lighter out of his pocket, lit it, and almost echoed my thought. "When I finished, I was tempted to destroy them. But there's something in the last few letters that . . . well, I wondered—"

He turned the lighter in his fingers, as if trying to decide what to say. Finally, he looked up. "It's delicate, isn't it? I mean, I have no idea what your understanding is. And I don't know whether your mother . . . that is, whether your father ever told her about . . ."

His face flushed and he looked away again, seeming to lose track of his thoughts, an altogether unusual thing in an attorney. I studied him. Whatever he was struggling with, I thought, it must be intensely personal. Maybe the affair was news to him, and he was having trouble coming to terms with it. Maybe he had loved his mother very much—he was an only son, wasn't he?—and was jealous of the way she'd felt about my father. Or maybe there had been a very strong relationship between him and his father, and he resented his mother's lover.

But we weren't going to get anywhere if he kept on like this, starting to say something, breaking off, starting over. We had to stop beating around the bush and *talk* about it.

I sat forward. "I'll be honest with you, Miles. These letters aren't much of a surprise. When I was a teenager, I had the idea that your mother and my father were lovers. I might have been wrong, of course—teenage girls are pretty imaginative when it comes to sex—but that was how I saw it at the time. I wasn't terribly traumatized by the idea then, and I don't feel any different about it now. So if your mother saved the love letters my father wrote to her, it's okay. Whatever is in that envelope . . . well, it's there. That's all."

"That simplifies the situation somewhat," he said, with evident relief. "What about your mother?"

"Does she know? At the time—back then, I mean—I didn't think so. But when she gave me your letter and asked me to find out what sort of papers you had, it seemed to me that she did know. I'm not sure it matters very much, though. My father has been dead for sixteen years, and she is happily remarried. She told me to take a look at what you had. If there is something she should know, or something that requires her attention, I'm to tell her. If not, I'm to dispose of the papers myself."

"I see," he said, and then surprised me by adding, in a half-apologetic tone, "I have an idea that you'll want to tell her. What's in the letters, I mean."

"Tell her! Why? What in the world could my father have written to your mother that is worth repeating to *my* mother, all these years later?"

He got up, walked around the coffee table, and began to pace. "I don't know," he said distractedly. "Maybe you won't want to tell her. Maybe we should keep this between the two of us. After all, I'm not . . . that is, she isn't really involved. But I suppose you're the best judge. You know her, and I don't."

I was staring at him. "Why are you making such a fuss about this, Buddy? Two people had a brief affair. It's been over for years, and both of them are dead. They—"

"But it wasn't a brief affair!" He stopped pacing and turned to face me. "It started when my mother went to work at your father's firm, the same year he went into practice. The same year he married your mother. It lasted until he died. And after that, until *she* died."

"Oh." My father had taken a mistress at the same time he had taken a wife? In a very real sense, then, he had been a bigamist, married to both of them. The social wife and the office wife.

"Yes," he said. "All told, my mother loved him for thirty years."

Thirty years. I'd thought I was shock-proof, but the longevity of the relationship rocked me.

He picked up the envelope, took out a photo, and put it on the coffee table in front of me. It was a photo of three people, with a tent, a lake, and trees in the background. My father with a rod and reel, standing in his familiar arrogant slouch, smiling his familiar arrogant smile. Beside him stood a teenaged Buddy, proudly displaying a string of fish. Beside Buddy stood a young and pretty Laura Danforth, in shorts and a halter top, squinting into the sun. Dad's arm lay casually across Buddy's shoulder. I stared at the photo. My father on a camping trip with Buddy and his mother. I had never gone on a camping trip with my father and mother. My father had never asked *me* to go fishing.

"Well?" Miles asked. "Do you get it?"

I looked up. He was watching me with an ironic smile. "Get what?" I swallowed, unnerved. "What are you talking about?"

He shook his head. "Good lord, China. Look at the photo. Look at me. Why are you so dense?"

But of course I saw it. Saw it in the quirk of the mouth, in the dark, inquisitive brows, in the determined set of the jaw. Saw it, and finally had to accept it.

Miles Danforth—Buddy—was my brother.

Chapter Ten

Monkshood (*Aconitum napellus*). The generic name of this poisonous plant is derived from Greek *akon*, dart. Among other uses the plant was employed as a deadly bait against wolves. The juice was widely used in ancient times for poisoning wells and springs, usually as a defensive action against invading armies. It signifies deadliness, illicit love, remorse, vendetta and misanthropy.

Josephine Addison
The Illustrated Plant Lore

It was as if an earthquake had rocked my world. Think about it. How would *you* feel if somebody you hadn't seen for fifteen or twenty years suddenly reappeared and introduced himself as your brother?

Well, half brother. But it's a distinction without a difference. I had gone all through my life thinking of myself as an only child, and all of a sudden, I wasn't. My father had *two* children—and of course, he had known it. He had to have known it.

"He knew you were his son?" I asked uncertainly.

If my voice sounded thin and scratchy, Miles didn't seem to notice. "Of course he knew. But I didn't." He shook his head. "Didn't even suspect, until I read those letters. Oh, I was aware of the affair, of course. He was around the house a lot when I was growing up, and we traveled together sometimes. I called him Uncle Bob. Mom told me that my father

108

had been killed before I was born. She showed me pictures of him. She said they'd only been married a short time, and that his parents were dead, too, so now there was just the two of us." His voice became bitter. "Just the two of us—and *him*."

"She never tried to . . . well, explain? Why he was around so much, I mean."

"No. It was just a given. The elephant in the living room. Something you don't talk about."

The elephant in the living room. Like my mother's alcoholism, my father's absences. Things we never talked about, things we just accepted.

He sat down again and ground out his cigarette. "Can you imagine how I feel, finding out that my mother lied to me about something as important as my *paternity*?" His lips twisted. "Can you imagine what it's like to know that your old man refused to acknowledge that he was your father, even though he was around all the time when you were growing up?"

I opened my mouth to speak, but the words wouldn't come, which was okay, because Miles wasn't finished talking. He propped a boot on the coffee table and leaned back against the sofa, clasping his hands behind his head, not looking at me.

"I guess I'm not supposed to complain, just feel grateful that he picked up the tab for college and law school, and gave me my first job in his firm. He was always there, supporting me, rooting for me. All the things a father is supposed to do. Everything except acknowledge—"

All the things a father is supposed to do? Except that he did them for his son, not his daughter. For Buddy, not for me.

"Excuse me," I said bleakly. "I have to get home." I picked up the envelope and stood. "Don't bother," I added, as he scrambled to his feet. "I can find my way out."

"I'm sorry, China." Distractedly, he ran his hand through his hair. "I should have done a better job of telling you. I'm not very good at personal stuff. In that way, I'm like him, I guess. I—"

"It's okay, Buddy. Really. Don't worry about it." I put out my hand, then drew it back. It didn't feel right, shaking hands with my brother. You're supposed to hug brothers, aren't you? But that didn't feel right, either. I busied myself putting the envelope into my purse. "It'll take some getting used to, that's all."

He gave me an imploring look. "Don't go, please. There are things we have to—I mean, you have to read those letters, China. There's a really serious issue we need to—"

"I'm sure there is," I said. "I'm sure there are a lot of really serious issues." Starting with what I was going to tell my mother. "But not tonight. Listen, I'll call you. Okay?"

He took a card out of the business card holder, scribbled something on it, and thrust it into my hand. "My home number, and my cell. Phone as soon as you've read those letters. We really have to—"

"Yeah," I said. "Yeah, I will. Good night, Buddy."

THE drive back home was a blur. I wasn't even aware that I had arrived until Brian tapped on the car window.

"You gonna sit out here all night, Mom?" He was shivering, both hands in his pockets. "I'm making hot cocoa."

"What? Oh." I glanced up, startled, and realized where I was. "Thanks. I'm coming in."

The familiar kitchen—the Home Comfort stove, the scarred pine table, the Seth Thomas clock, the rag rug on the floor—seemed to wrap itself around me in a warm and welcoming embrace. I sat down at the table while Brian poured two mugs of steaming cocoa, popped a marshmallow into each, and dug into the cookie jar for some of the chocolate cookies Leatha had sent home with us. Howard Cosell trotted purposefully into the room, summoned, no doubt, by the rattle of the cookie jar lid. Howard has sonar ears. He was already drooling.

I cupped my hands around the mug, warming them. "How was your evening at Jake's?" I asked, trying to sound normal.

"Not too cool." Brian broke his cookie in two and shared it with Howard, who gulped it down and attended to the crumbs that had fallen to the floor. "Jake's got a problem."

"What kind of a problem?" I spooned up the gooey marshmallow and savored it.

"A *big* problem." He used his hands to sketch out something bigger than a breadbox. "A personal problem. Looks like Bones is going to have to break the rules," he added, glum.

"Bones?" I asked blankly, and then remembered. "Oh, yes. The Prime Directive. Dr. Fix-it."

"Right." He shook his head, grave and grown-up. "I don't like to get involved, but I don't see any other way. And Jake agrees, so it's okay. I mean, it's not like going behind her back."

"When you say 'get involved,' what do you mean?"

"I don't know yet." He looked away. "There's a lot at stake. It's kind of scary."

"I'll bet," I said, wishing I knew what we were talking about.

"But you don't have to worry," he added reassuringly. "I'll think of something."

"I'm sure you will." My fingers were cold, and the hot cocoa wasn't doing much to warm them up.

He eyed me with concern. "Mom, are you okay?"

"Not exactly." I reached for another cookie. My family—Leatha and me, I mean—had just expanded by one. Now there was Leatha, and me, and my brother. I had to wade through that envelope full of letters, and read all about my father's thirty-year-long office marriage. About his secret life, which involved camping trips with his office family, and who knows what else. I was faced with the prospect of telling my mother that my father had had that son he always wanted, after all—and that the son had a daughter. Suddenly it all seemed very complicated. Too complicated.

"But I'll be okay after I eat this cookie," I added, not wanting to worry Brian. "Chocolate's good for what ails you. Your dad didn't call, did he?"

"Oh. Yeah, he did. He said to tell you he'd call you at the shop tomorrow." He pulled down his mouth. "He's taking *her* out to dinner tonight."

I sighed. I didn't have to ask who *her* was.

BUDDY might feel urgent about those letters, but I certainly didn't. I shoved them onto a closet shelf, behind a stack of sweatshirts. Then I took a long, lavender-scented bubble bath and settled down to lose myself in a book. I turned out the light at ten thirty and went to sleep, but not very soundly. I was plagued by dreams in which Buddy chased me with a horribly rotten fish through the basement of my father's old office building, my father dancing just ahead, always out of reach of my outstretched arms, while Laura Danforth lurked in the background, carrying a briefcase full of letters. I didn't have to be a shrink to understand the significance of that one.

When the alarm clock rang on Wednesday morning, I got up and went to work just as I always did, although I felt dull and disconnected, as if I were flying on autopilot. A sleety rain greeted me as I stepped out the door—nice news for the bluebonnets that would be coming along in another couple of months, but not so nice for people. I went back inside and got my umbrella and a pair of mittens.

The rain made for a slow morning in the shop, so I got out the feather duster and began dusting the shelves. For me, this job is the indoor equivalent of pulling weeds, almost as soothing to a troubled spirit—and my spirit certainly was troubled. Any day now—or any minute—Leatha would call and ask whether I'd had a chance to take a look at the papers Miles Danforth had found. What was I going to tell her? The whole dirty, sordid story? Or half the story, or less than that? Maybe I should just say that the papers turned out to be junk and I'd thrown them away. She didn't need to know that her husband had fathered a son, and that while we thought he was attending all those weekend conferences, he was camping with the Other Woman and fishing with the Other Woman's Son. *His* son.

Of course, the more I thought about this, the faster and harder I dusted. If I kept it up at this rate, I'd run out of dust before I ran out of troubles. I had worked my way halfway around the shop (but no closer to a solution to the problem) when the phone rang. I jumped, startled.

Leatha?

No, thank heaven. It was McQuaid, checking in.

But while I was glad to hear his voice, neither of us had much to say. His investigation was "progressing." He and Sally had had a "decent" dinner and a "friendly" talk, and she seemed no more flaky than usual. He thought he might be home in another week, but not in time for

Valentine's Day, and would I mind standing in for him at Brian's teacher conference next Wednesday, which he'd forgotten all about? I muttered "okay" to that, and "uh-huh" to everything else. I considered telling him that he had just acquired a brother-in-law, but I didn't feel like going into the detailed and painful explanation that would have to follow this bombshell. I refrained.

For the same reason, I didn't tell Ruby, even when she began to probe.

"I know there's something going on with you," she said insistently, eyeing the duster in my hand. She was wearing purple leggings and an oversize orange sweater, with an orange and purple scarf looped around her neck—a colorful sight on a dark and gloomy day. "You're really down in the dumps. Is it McQuaid?"

"Of course it's not McQuaid," I said, flicking my duster furiously. "McQuaid is just fine, thank you." And even if he wasn't, I wasn't in any mood to discuss it.

She regarded me, hands on her hips, head tilted to one side. "Well, if it's not McQuaid, what is it? Is Brian in trouble? Is your mom having a crisis? Come on, China. Tell me what's wrong."

"There is nothing wrong," I said between my teeth. Brian seemed perfectly capable of handling anything that came his way, and my mother wasn't having a crisis—yet. She would, though, when I told her. If I told her. I knocked a bar of soap off the shelf and bent to pick it up. "I just feel like dusting, that's all. Don't you ever dust your shelves?"

"Not the way you do."

I rolled my eyes. It was time for a change of subject—and there was one subject that I could count on to do the trick. "What's the status of your investigation into the Mystery of the Missing Quilt?"

"Investigation?" Ruby turned down her mouth. "What investigation?

I've totally run out of leads. When the one-armed-bandit theory bombed, there was nowhere else to go."

I dusted around the jars of bath salts. "What about Arlene? Did she give you an enemies list? Did you check it?"

"Yes to both, but there were only two names on it." Ruby sighed heavily. "One moved to Miami last month. The other one is on a cruise in the Caribbean."

So much for Carol's enemies. "We should all be so lucky," I said.

"Something else did occur to me," Ruby said. "I think it's time to Ouija, China. We've had good luck with that in the past, you know."

"Ouija?" I frowned. Ruby teaches a course on sharpening your intuition. Tuning In to Your Right Brain, she calls it, because (she says) the right half of the brain is like a receiver, capable of connecting with the universe and intercepting all the signals coming in from . . . well, just coming in. I'm never entirely comfortable with Ruby's forays into the psychic beyond, although I do have to admit that some of her flights of fantasy have been remarkably on target.

"Of course," she replied enthusiastically. "Remember when Brian disappeared? I brought my Ouija board over to your house, and you spelled out this crazy word *gurps*, which none of us could understand. And when you and Sheila finally found Brian, he was at the Star Trek convention playing some weird game called Gurps. Ouija knew exactly where he was—or where he would be when you found him," she amended, with a smug look.

I remembered. But I also remembered the time, in a little town called Indigo, when Ruby's intuition led us to discover a very dead body in the basement of an abandoned school. If I recalled correctly, after that eerie episode, Ruby had sworn off using her powers to try to solve mysteries. It seemed as if she had forgotten about that lamentable event—although if you looked at the situation from the cops' viewpoint, it was a lucky discovery. That body could've been there for a very long time before anybody found it.

"I guess it's worth a shot," I said slowly. I still don't believe that there's anything to the Ouija board, but even I had to admit that something very strange had gone on with that *gurps* business, and in Indigo, as well.

"Wonderful," she said in a decided tone. "I'll call Carol and see if she can come over tonight—it's her quilt and she wants to find it more than any of the rest of us. You have to come, too. And Cass. We need people with lots of positive psychic energy. Ouija feeds on energy, you know."

"Oh, but I don't have anything to do with Carol's missing quilt," I replied hastily. I didn't have much positive energy, either. Not after last night.

"But you're an experienced Ouija person," Ruby reminded me, in all seriousness. "You were the one who spelled *gurps*, remember? Anyway, you don't have anything else to do tonight, do you?"

Nothing else to do but read a bunch of stupid old love letters, I reminded myself. "I guess not," I said. Maybe Ouija could give me some tips on how to deal with my newly discovered brother, or what to tell my mother. "Okay, I'll do it. What can I bring?"

"I'll let you know after I talk to Carol," Ruby said, and bustled off to her shop to start setting up her Ouija party.

I was hanging up the duster a few minutes before twelve, when the phone rang. This time, I was sure it was Leatha, and took a deep breath. I had pretty much decided that I would tell her I'd looked at the papers and they weren't worth keeping. There's probably a special place in hell reserved for daughters who lie to their mothers, but I had a good reason, a *very* good reason, to lie. I was protecting her from knowing that the man she had loved had lied to her every single day of their married lives, and that he had left a walking, talking proof of his perfidy behind him. I had her best interests at heart. Didn't I?

But the voice on the phone wasn't Leatha's. It was a younger woman, who identified herself as Christie Norris, Angela Lopez's roommate. I was a little startled, because meeting Buddy and finding out who he was had driven everything else from my mind. I had nearly forgotten about my conversation with Mrs. Lopez and my talk with Sheila about the girl's suicide. But hearing Angela's name brought it all back, along with the urgency I had felt when I started to look for Christie.

"What's this about?" the girl asked, in an attractive alto voice.

"Angela Lopez's mother suggested I talk to you. She thought you might be able to help." This wasn't quite true, but close enough.

I heard the quick intake of breath. There was a silence, then: "Help with what?"

"How about meeting me somewhere for lunch? There's more to this than we can go into over the telephone."

Another silence, as Christie considered this. "Would you mind coming to my apartment? I'm studying for an exam. I don't want to waste a lot of time running around."

"Sure, I can do that." I jotted down the address she gave me and said good-bye. Laurel was there to take care of the counter, and there was nothing happening in the tearoom that Cass and Janet couldn't handle. "I'm going out," I told Laurel. "Back in about an hour or so."

"Better take your mittens," Laurel said. "It's cold out there." She glanced out the window. "Snow tonight, according to the forecast. Would you believe?"

Chapter Eleven

Your heart is bleeding because the one you love doesn't love you back? Herbs and flowers have been used in love potions for centuries, often administered secretly, so that the lover was lured into loving before he knew what hit him. The most potent of these herbs was the pansy, which Oberon tells Puck to find for him in Shakespeare's *A Midsummer Night's Dream:*

> *Fetch me that flower; the herb I showed thee once:*
> *The juice of it on sleeping eyelids laid*
> *Will make or man or woman madly dote*
> *Upon the next live creature that it sees.*

On my way out of the shop, I snatched a couple of sandwiches from a batch Cass was making and wolfed them down as I drove across town in my white two-door Toyota—a replacement for my beloved blue Datsun, which I'd driven until it gave out from sheer exhaustion. Christie Norris's place was on the second floor of a three-story apartment villa not far from the CTSU campus, with an outside balcony walkway crowded with winter-killed plants and overflowing trashcans and bicycles chained to the balustrade. The apartment door was decorated with a large heart-shaped wreath made of smaller red hearts, and corny valentines were taped to the front window. From somewhere inside came loud music, and from somewhere above and below, more loud music. It was the middle of the day. Weren't these kids supposed to be in class?

I knocked. After a few minutes, the door opened about two inches and I was rewarded by the sight of one large brown eye and half of a girl's face. She was as tall as Ruby, which meant that I had to look up to her.

"Christie Norris?" I said pleasantly. "I'm China Bayles. I called a little earlier."

"Who is it, Christie?" a girl called from inside.

"It's for me," the tall girl replied over her shoulder, in that intriguing trombone voice. Her words were almost drowned out by the sound of George Strait singing "I Cross My Heart," and a couple of girls, laughing. Then there was the sound of breaking glass, a shriek, and more laughter.

Christie unhooked the chain, opened the door, and stepped back. She was lean and lanky in a cropped tee and tight jeans that rode low enough to show her belly button, and her dark brown hair was cut very short, like a boy's. Her brown eyes were cautious, and there was a set to her jaw that suggested determination and a strong mind.

"Let's go to my room," she said, with an impatient gesture in the direction of the laughter. "Otherwise, we won't be able to hear ourselves think." She went over to the stereo and turned it down. "I'm moving out this weekend. I can't study in all this chaos. And I'm on a scholarship. I can't afford to blow it."

I could see what she meant, and it wasn't just the music. The living room was strewn with clothes and papers, and there were two or three half-empty take-out containers on the coffee table. The air was thick with the blended fragrance of cinnamon incense and cigarettes. They'd all be getting a good dose of secondhand smoke.

"Will you be sharing with somebody else?" I asked, as I followed her down the hall.

"Well, sort of." She gave me a shy glance. "My boyfriend, Jon, has a place. We're both pre-med, and we take a lot of the same classes, so it'll be good. We can study together."

Sure, I thought wryly. No doubt they'd get a lot of studying done.

Christie opened a door onto a room about the size of my bathroom. It was furnished in the usual college-dorm style, but was unusually neat and tidy. A desk along one wall held a stack of books, a computer, and a microscope, with a printer on an adjacent shelf. A brick-and-board bookcase held more books, serious stuff: biology, zoology, chemistry, physics. But a ribbon-draped bulletin board was studded with photos and the kind of mementos you'd see in any college girl's dorm room, and on the shelf above the bed was a row of stuffed animals, including a teddy bear about the size of a three-year-old, wearing a football helmet and cradling a rubber football in its extended paws. And there were more photos. One of them was a blow-up of Christie and a girl I recognized as Angela together at a table, eating ice cream. Another pictured Christie and a guy, tall and good-looking, his arm casually draped around her shoulders. The guy she was moving in with, I guessed.

Christie went to the bed, kicked off her moccasins and sat, tucking her bare feet under her, yoga-style. Gingerly, I lowered myself into a bright orange beanbag chair beside the bed, feeling the stuffing shift beneath me. The door was closed, but somebody had turned the music up. I could feel the thump of the bass reverberating in the floor. I took my coat and mittens off.

Christie regarded me steadily. "How's Mrs. Lopez?"

She's drinking too much, I wanted to say, but settled for something I knew to be equally true, and more to the point. "She misses Angela."

"I'm sure she does." Christie looked down and picked at the chenille puffs on the bedspread. "Did you ever meet her? Angie, I mean."

"No," I said. "I'm sorry. She sounds like a . . . a wonderful person." That sounded lame and stupid to me, but Christie nodded.

"She was very sweet." She looked back at me. Her eyes were dark, her mouth set against whatever pain rose inside. "So why did Mrs. Lopez think you should talk to me?"

"She told me you didn't believe that Angela killed herself."

"Yeah," Christie replied in a low voice. "I don't know how she died. An accident, maybe. But I don't think she killed herself." She gave me another sharp glance. "Why are you asking these questions? You never even met Angie."

I glanced up at the shelf over her head, at the photo of the girls together, and two and two suddenly added up to a round, irrefutable four. "It was you who called Ms. Simon, wasn't it?" Lisa had said that the caller had a deep voice. Christie sounded like Lauren Bacall.

Christie frowned and her glance slid away. "Simon? I don't know what you're—"

"The high school principal. That's why I'm asking these questions. You called and gave her Mrs. Lopez's name. After Ms. Simon talked to you, she asked me to go to Friendship and see what I could find out."

"Really, Ms. Bayles." Two round red spots appeared high on her cheeks. "I have no idea what you're—"

"Let's don't dance around the truth," I said. The beanbag chair might be cool for kids, but it was not designed for adult comfort. I hoisted myself out of it, went to the desk, and pulled out the straight chair. I turned it around so I could straddle it, sat down, and rested my arms on the back. "Look, Christie. I know you're the person who made the phone call about Coach Duffy. I want you to tell me what you know about him and Angela."

121

The name Duffy rattled her. She bit her lip and gave me an apprehensive look. "Are you . . . are you a cop?"

"No. I'm a lawyer, although I'm not in practice. Lisa Simon spoke to me because she thought I might be of some help—behind the scenes. She can't initiate a formal investigation into Duffy's misconduct without knowing more of the story."

She considered that. "Well, I . . . I guess I . . ." She swallowed. "There's a . . . a lot to tell. I'm not sure where to start."

"Maybe it would help if I asked a few questions. Just to fill in the background." Some witnesses find it easier to tell the story if they're encouraged to begin with something nonthreatening. Something they don't mind talking about.

"Maybe," she said, eyeing me.

"Mrs. Lopez said that you and Angela roomed together. That was in the dorm?"

"Yeah." She relaxed a little, knitting her fingers together. "Dorm life can be a drag, but it wasn't bad, actually. Angela made it . . . easier, somehow."

"What was she like? How did you two get along?"

She looked thoughtful. "It was kind of surprising, how we clicked. You couldn't find two more different people, really. Angie was sweet and nice, and I liked her, but when she first came to college, she was sort of . . . well, unfocussed. About what she wanted to do, I mean. And naive. You know, unsophisticated. I'm not bad-mouthing her," she added hastily. "She'd never been anywhere but that dinky little South Texas town. She didn't have any experience. It wasn't her fault she was that way."

"Of course not." I glanced at the desk, with its microscope and computer. "Looks like you're anything but unfocussed."

"Yeah." She smiled crookedly. "That was one of the ways we were different. Me, I've known since I was twelve that I was going to be a doctor. I went to a big high school, where we had a strong science program. I already knew how to deal with the system. Angie didn't have a clue."

"Did the two of you get along?"

She nodded. "Because we were so different, maybe. She was sweet. Sometimes she took it too far, but you always knew she really cared. But she was . . . well, timid, because of where she came from. I helped her sign up for classes and encouraged her to stand up for herself when people tried to push her around." Her eyes suddenly filled with tears, and she brushed them away. "Sorry," she muttered. "It sounds like I'm being critical, but I'm not. She was wonderful, really. I always wished I could be more like her. She knew when I was feeling down, even when I couldn't tell her. She'd do whatever she could to make me feel better."

"Empathetic," I suggested.

"Yeah, that's it. She was empathetic. Sensitive to people's feelings. Anyway, during the second semester, she decided to major in psychology, which I thought was a good choice. It made sense for her, given the way she cared about people. And then last fall, she started doing some volunteer work with children. She began to seem a whole lot better after that. More sure of herself, I mean. In charge."

I hesitated. It was time to take her into the painful stuff. "When did she first tell you what happened between her and Coach Duffy?"

She sighed. "Not until after midterms during the second semester. I guess it took a while before she began to trust me." She paused. "Sometimes Angie was like a scared little kid, you know? She was really scared about that. About what had happened."

"Scared?"

"Yeah. When we first started talking about it, she had the idea that the whole thing was her fault. She thought she'd led him on—without meaning to, of course." Christie looked at me and her voice hardened. "Can you believe? That jerk actually made her think that she was to blame for what happened! That he couldn't help himself! Like he'd drunk some stupid love potion, or was bewitched or something, against his will. Like it was all her fault."

I could believe it. I'd seen cases where the abuser has been able to convince his victim that *he* is helpless and bewitched, totally under the spell of her irresistible beauty, her sexuality, her power. It's a clever shift of responsibility and guilt from the seducer to the seduced. Clever and frightening.

"Did you two talk about it much?"

"It seems like it was the *only* thing we talked about," Christie said ruefully, "for weeks and weeks. I got sick of hearing the gory details, but of course I never let her know that. She kept on talking and I kept on listening. I think she still loved him, in a way, you know? Talking helped."

Still loved him? Yes, victims often love their abusers. "Her mother said Angela was seeing a counselor. Did she tell the counselor about Duffy?"

Christie shook her head. "Angie said the counselor was too judgmental. Anyway, all she wanted to do was hand out pills."

"Antidepressants?"

"Yeah. But Angie didn't need pills. Talking was what she needed, really. Getting her head straight. It took a while, but I think she finally began to get it. What happened wasn't her fault, no matter what that turkey—Duffy, I mean—tried to get her to think." She clenched her hands. "Damn it, Angie was only sixteen! He was twice her age. No *way* was she responsible."

"I see," I said, watching her. "So she got it, finally. So then what?" I paused. "Did she just leave it there?"

"Not exactly." Christie began picking at the chenille again. "She . . . well, she started to think that maybe she ought to do something."

"Like what?" I said dryly. "Kill herself to call attention to what he had done?" If that's what it was, her desperate act had not achieved its purpose.

"No, no, *no!*" Christie shook her head violently. "She never once mentioned suicide. We talked about how men like Duffy don't do that kind of thing just once. It gets to be a habit. Since he got away with it with her, he was probably still doing it with some other young girl. And he'd keep doing it, until somebody stopped him."

I pictured the two girls talking together, thinking out loud about what could be done. I had a sudden sense of awful things set in motion, of an inevitable, irrevocable tragedy. "So Angela decided it was up to her to stop him?"

Christie nodded wordlessly.

I sucked in my breath. "How did she plan to do that? Was she going to press charges against him? Did she know that there was still plenty of time for that?"

Another nod. "She found out that the statute of limitations had a while to run. I don't remember how long, but it was, like, years. The problem was that she didn't want to have to testify in court. She figured it would get into the newspapers, and she didn't think it was fair to her mother to put her through all that stuff. Not to mention Duffy's family," she added. "She felt sorry for his wife. She said that Duffy was really nice."

"How did she know Mrs. Duffy?"

"Through her volunteer work. And while she would never come right out and say so, I think she still cared for Duffy, somewhere down deep.

So she had good reasons for not wanting to take him to court. She just wanted him to stop."

"But criminal court wasn't her only option," I said. "She could have filed a complaint with the school district and the state agency that issues teaching certificates. They would have conducted a formal investigation, but kept it out of the papers. It could have ended with a reprimand and the suspension of his teaching certificate." I knew of a case like this, where the teacher agreed to surrender his teaching certificate in lieu of revocation proceedings. Of course, suspension or revocation might have been almost as devastating to Duffy—and his wife—as a criminal trial. Both of them seemed to be heavily invested in his coaching career.

"I guess maybe we . . . she should have talked to a lawyer," Christie said, in a low voice. "But as it was . . ." Her words trailed off.

"So, as it was, you decided to do something else. What was it?"

She gave me a quick, defensive glance. "*I* didn't decide anything. It was Angie. I tried to tell her it wasn't a good idea to—" She flushed and bit her lip.

"A good idea to what?" I prompted.

"Well, she had this idea that she ought to get in touch with him. Let him know that she knew it wasn't right, what they had done. Put him on notice that he couldn't keep on doing stuff like that, or—"

"Or what?"

"Or she would accuse him. She'd drag it all out in the open, in court. She'd *make* him stop. She didn't intend to do it, she said. She was hoping that the threat would make him stop."

I let my breath out, exasperated and angry at the naïvete of this amateur blackmail. "Didn't she have any idea how dangerous that might be?"

Christie looked away. "I asked Angie if she worried that he might . . .

well, might try to stop her. But she said she knew him. He was basically a very sweet guy, and he'd never do anything to hurt her."

"Oh, right," I muttered, under my breath. And now Angela was dead—and Christie didn't seem to make the connection. Or maybe she made it, but wasn't ready to acknowledge it. Aloud, I said, "Did she know whether he was involved with another student, or was she just guessing?"

"She . . . she knew."

"How did she know? Was she spying on him? Was she stalking him?" Now, *that* would have been foolish. But maybe Angela had another motivation, something that Christie didn't know about, or didn't want to tell me. Maybe Angela regretted that the affair was over, and hated the idea of him with somebody else. Maybe she was jealous.

Christie looked at me, hesitating, was trying to decide how much she wanted to tell me. "How did she know? Well, she met a girl at the place where she was volunteering. A student at Pecan Springs High, who was working in the same program."

I felt my eyes widen. "So the girl told her?"

"Right. I don't know how it first came up, but the two of them started talking. Angie liked her—she said the girl was pretty mature for a high school kid—and they got to be friends. Like I said, Angie was really . . . well, sensitive. Like, she always had her antennae up. She would have been good in psychology."

"The high school student actually named Duffy?"

Christie nodded. "That was what finally made Angie decide. If he wasn't stopped, he'd just go on, one girl after another. He could ruin a lot of lives that way."

It didn't sound like a case of jealousy, but . . . "She couldn't persuade the girl to make a complaint?"

"I'm not sure she even tried." Reluctantly, she added, "Like I said, it was complicated. I know it sounds crazy, after what he did to her. She didn't like to admit it, but she felt like she should protect him. She didn't want him to get into trouble."

I'd seen that before, too, in cases of domestic violence. The victim is in love with the person who victimizes her—and sometimes, at some even deeper and more secret level, in love with the victimization itself. I pushed that thought away. "The high school student Angela met in the volunteer program—any idea of her name?"

Christie frowned. "If she mentioned it, I don't remember. Why? Is it important?"

Is it *important*? I kept my voice even. "It might be. So then what happened? This girl told Angie about Duffy. Then what?"

She gave me a guilty look. "Well, we were both pretty busy. It was the beginning of sophomore year, and the way our schedules worked out, we had a lot less time to talk. I don't exactly know what—"

I leaned forward over the back of the chair, impatient. "Did Angela see Duffy? Did she confront him with what she knew?"

"I . . . It's possible, but I'm not sure." Christie glanced away, then back. "Look, Ms. Bayles. All this was happening about the time I got involved with Jon. When he came into the picture, I wasn't around very much. I wasn't keeping track of what was going on with Angie." Her eyes suddenly filled with tears. "To tell the truth, I feel really awful about it. If I'd been there for her, if I'd been paying attention to what she was doing and thinking, I might have kept her from . . ." She swallowed audibly. "If she could've talked to me, she might not have done . . . whatever she did. I don't know what that was, but I can't get away from the idea that it's my fault."

There was enough guilt here to go around the world and back again. I returned to my question. "So you don't know whether or not Angie got in touch with Duffy? Whether or not she confronted him?"

Christie wiped her eyes with the back of her hand. "She talked about doing it, but I'm not sure if she actually did." She reached for a tissue on the bedside table and blew her nose. "Tyler might know. She sometimes talked stuff over with him."

"Tyler?"

"Tyler Cole. Angie went out with him sometimes, but I don't think there was anything romantic going on. No sex, I mean. They were just friends."

Another complication, but a possible lead. "How do I get in touch with Tyler?"

"Angie wrote down his cell number. It's still in my book. I'll give it to you."

"Did the police talk to him? After Angie died, I mean."

"I don't think so. I don't remember mentioning him. There wasn't any reason."

"And you didn't mention Duffy, either? To the police, I mean."

She shook her head. "I guess I should have," she said uneasily. "But I . . . well, there wasn't anything to tell, really. I didn't know whether she'd seen him."

I stared at her, words rising in my throat. *You didn't wonder whether she had confronted Duffy, or threatened him? You didn't wonder what he might have done to keep her quiet?*

But if Christie had wondered, she hadn't acted on it. She hadn't been curious enough, or concerned enough, or guilty enough, before Angela's death and after. I thought suddenly of Brian, reluctantly drawn into

Jake's problem, whatever it was. I shouldn't be so hard on Christie. This was a difficult issue, and one I had struggled with myself.

"Actually, I did do something." Christie blew her nose again. "After the funeral, I kept thinking about him—about Duffy, I mean. Then I called the high school principal. It wouldn't bring Angie back, but it might take that jerk out of commission, if anybody cared enough to investigate and find out what was going on. And in a couple more days, I intended to call her back and tell her Angie was dead. I figured that might shake her up a little." She looked at me defensively. "Maybe it wasn't much, what I did. But it was something."

Yes. Christie got credit for intervening after the fact. And it was her intervention that had prompted Lisa Simon to ask me to investigate. She was right—it was something.

I stood up and pushed the chair back under the desk. "A couple more things. You mentioned antidepressants. Was Angela taking them at the time she died?"

"The policeman asked about that. I told him she had some left over from the prescription the counselor gave her, but I don't think she was taking them. She seemed to be better. Not happy, exactly, but more sure of herself."

More like a girl with a mission, I thought bleakly. *A girl who had decided to take matters into her own hands.* "Did she tell you she was going to the Longhorn Motel? Had she ever stayed there before?"

"She didn't mention it—but I was with Jon all that weekend. I wondered about that motel, too, when the police officer told me where they'd found her. I'm sure she had never been there before. She was on a pretty tight budget. It wasn't the sort of place she could afford."

Unless, of course, somebody else gave her some money to pay the tab. Somebody like Coach Duffy.

Christie gave me an oblique look. "Are . . . are you going to investigate this?"

"I promised to let Ms. Simon know what I've found out," I said. "She'll have to decide where to go with it." I also intended to talk to the Pecan Springs chief of police, but Christie didn't need to know that.

Christie unfolded herself, got down off the bed, and went to the desk. She took out a little book, looked up a number, and wrote it, and another number, on a piece of paper. "This is the number Angie gave me for Tyler."

I fished in my purse and found a card. "And here's my number," I said. "If you think of anything else that might help, please give me a call."

"Yeah," she said. She gave me a hard look. "I hope somebody gets the bastard," she muttered darkly. "If it hadn't been for what he did to her back in high school, Angie would still be alive today."

I nodded, agreeing. That much, at least, was the truth. I glanced up at the shelf. "Is that Angela's teddy bear?" It had to be. Most bears don't wear a football helmet and carry a football.

"Yes. Her mother took the rest of her stuff, but that got left behind. I meant to send it, but I couldn't find a box big enough."

"I'll be going down to South Texas in a few weeks. Want me to take it to Mrs. Lopez?"

"I'd be glad if you would," Christie said. "I certainly don't want it." She climbed up on the bed, took it down, and handed it to me. "I never understood why Angie kept it."

I looked at the bear. It was holding a junior-size toy football. On it was written, in a loose, sloping script, *To Angie with love always, from Tim.* A heart was substituted for the *o* in "love."

"There are some things that are hard to understand," I said. Like men who prey on innocent young girls. I tucked the bear under my arm and picked up my jacket. "Good luck, Christie."

"Same to you," she said. "Don't forget your mittens."

Chapter Twelve

A few well-known herbs traditionally thought to have aphrodisiac qualities include basil, parsley root, anise, rosemary, passion-flower, celery, and garlic. A favorite aphrodisiac tea from India contained cinnamon, cardamom, ginger, peppercorns, cloves, nutmeg, saffron, honey, and black tea—all reputed to increase sexual attractiveness and prowess.

And then there were the antiaphrodisiacs, herbs that were thought to reduce sexual desire. These included winter savory, hops, rue, and vitex (also known as chaste tree). Of these, rue is perhaps the most famous. A Scottish saying suggests that a little rue goes a long way to ensure a young woman's virginity: *Rue in time is a maiden's posy.*

On the way back to the shop, I stopped at the *Enterprise* office to leave my Valentine's Day newspaper article—ahead of the deadline, for a change—then detoured past the police station, to see if I could catch Sheila in her office. Late last fall, the Police Department moved into a new building on the southeast corner of the square, diagonally across from the courthouse. Progress, of course, is usually a good thing—although many people complain that they miss the character of the attractive old building where the department used to work. In addition to the police department in the basement, it also housed the Tourist and Information Center on the main floor, the Parks and Utilities Department on the second, and a colony of Mexican free-tailed bats in the attic. But Parks and Utilities and Tourist and Information were embroiled in a nasty, long-running feud over parking spaces, and the bats smelled—not to mention that the basement was dark and crowded. There were just too many uniformed bodies per square foot, and the Police Department was glad to relocate.

But while the walls of the new cop shop may be freshly painted, the offices newly furnished, and the air noticeably free of the penetrating fragrance of bat guano, some things haven't changed. Dorrie Hull, for instance, the daytime dispatcher and receptionist. Dorrie's platinum Dolly-Parton big hair is an interesting contrast to her official uniform, her ten red-painted scimitar nails could be declared weapons of mass destruction, and the cloud of exotic perfume that wafts around her is every bit as potent as bat doo-doo. But Dorrie is plenty experienced, and don't let anybody tell you otherwise. Sheila wouldn't keep her around if she didn't do her job.

She looked up from her paperwork and smiled brightly. "Say hey, Miz Bayles. How ya doin' today, huh?"

"I'm doin' good," I said. If you tell Dorrie you're not doin' good, she wants to know all the whys and wherefores, and she won't quit until she's dug out every last one. "The boss around?"

"Yeah." Dorrie frowned darkly. "You c'n go in, but watch yerself. Mr. Graves just left. He was here about that school-bus accident yestiddy mornin'. The chief is prob'ly spittin' nails."

I registered the warning. Ben Graves is a member of the city council—a retro personality, politically ultraconservative, and a believer in strong-arm tactics. He is Sheila's most potent foe. Give him half a chance, and he'll have her scalp hanging from his belt. Sheila is always in a foul mood after he drops in.

I opened the door and peered cautiously around it. Sheila was standing at the window, hands clasped behind her back. There wasn't much of a view—just the parking lot, filled with pickup trucks and SUVs—but I doubted that she was interested in it, anyway.

"What is it now, Dorrie?" she growled, not looking around.

"It's me, Smart Cookie," I said, opening the door a little wider. "Is he gone? Is it safe?"

She turned. "Oh. Yeah, he's gone. Sorry, China. That jerk gets to me every time. Now he's after me about this school-bus incident. Wants the cop fired." She sighed. "What's up with you?"

I came in and sat down in the chair in front of her desk, which was neat and orderly, as usual. The photo of her and Blackie Blackwell—the Adams County sheriff to whom she was engaged for a couple of years—has been replaced with a plastic philodendron. The two of them broke up earlier in the year. It was the right decision for Sheila, but Blackie is taking it hard. McQuaid (a longtime friend of Blackie's) says that Sheila broke his heart. I don't doubt it, but what's done is done, and there's no going back. Blackie will get over it eventually.

"I've been talking to Christie Norris," I said.

"Norris?" Sheila sat down behind the desk, scrawled something on a piece of paper, and tossed it into her in-box. She was obviously still processing her conversation with Ben Graves. She stuck the pencil behind her ear. "Oh, right. The Lopez girl's roommate."

"Yeah. She also turns out to be the anonymous informant who tipped Lisa Simon that one of her faculty members had a prior sexual relationship with a high school student—Angela Lopez."

Sheila's glance strayed to the in-box. "Yeah?" Her tone was distracted.

"There's more. According to Christie, when Angela was working as a volunteer, she met a high-school student, a girl. The two got acquainted. I don't know how the subject came up, but the girl eventually told her that she was involved in a similar relationship—with the same man."

Sheila's glance, startled now, came back to me. "The prominent citizen you wouldn't identify yesterday?"

I nodded. "When Angela discovered that he was still up to his old tricks, she told Christie she intended to do something about it."

"Like what?" she asked wryly. "Kill herself to make him sorry for what he'd done?"

I shook my head. "I don't think so. It was more like put him on notice. Force him to stop fooling around with young girls. Cool it, chill out, or whatever the kids say these days."

I had Sheila's full attention now. She sat up straighter and her tone hardened. "Did she? Put him on notice, that is."

"Christie says she doesn't know. She got busy with a new boyfriend and Angela was left on her own. But she gave me the name of somebody else—another friend of Angela's. I'm going to see him, but I'd like to read the Lopez file first. Do you have any objection to that?"

Sheila gave me a thoughtful look. "I don't see a problem. On one condition."

"What's that?"

"You tell me this man's name. The man Lopez was involved with."

"I don't see a problem," I countered, "*if* I can also have access to the investigating officer." Back in my lawyering days, I learned that there are things—little things, some of them significant—that don't get into the police report, often because the officer is operating on a theory. Details that don't fit the theory get left out. Questioning the officer sometimes turns them up.

"Sounds okay to me." Sheila folded her arms. "So who is this pervert?"

"Alleged pervert," I corrected her.

She sighed impatiently. "Okay, okay. Alleged pervert. Who is he?"

"You're not going to like this," I said. "He's Tim Duffy."

She stared at me, aghast and incredulous. "You're kidding. Tim-the-Golden-Boy Duffy? The pride of the Panthers?"

"Yep." I folded my arms. "The Duffy who's married to the Seiden-sticker princess."

"Oh, *hell.*" Sheila breathed. "Tim Duffy is Ben Graves's best friend. Graves is always bragging about going places with him."

"He's everybody's best friend," I said evenly. "He's the coach that took them to the top. King of Friday night football."

Sheila gave me a grim look. "You've got proof of this alleged relationship between Duffy and Lopez? And I don't mean accusations, China. I mean *proof.*"

I had left the teddy bear sitting in the front seat of my car, cradling the football. *To Angie with love always, from Tim.* Proof of the relationship, yes, but I needed more. More proof, and a clearer understanding of why Angela Lopez had ended up dead.

"I'm working on it," I said. I unfolded my arms and leaned forward, elbows on my knees. "I don't need to spell this out, Sheila. You know as well as I do that a young girl who decides to blow the sexual misconduct whistle on a man like Duffy is taking an enormous risk. But Angela was too naïve and trusting to understand the danger. She told Christie that Duffy would never hurt her—he was too 'sweet.'" I shook my head. "He seems to have convinced her that she was the one who made him lose his head. So she probably didn't think of him as a threat."

Sheila narrowed her eyes. "And now she's dead."

"She's dead. But there's a lot we don't know," I added cautiously. "Maybe this is just a matter of sexual misconduct—in which case, the ball is in the school board's court. Or maybe it's a hell of a lot worse."

Sheila's mouth tightened. "What's your guess?"

"I don't know enough to have one. I don't know whether Angela was taking antidepressants, for instance, and whether that might have prompted her to suicide. I don't know if she actually confronted Duffy. If she did, I don't know whether he gave her a hard time, or threatened her, or sweet-talked her—played on her feelings for him, maybe. If that's what happened, I don't know how she would have taken that. Maybe she became so confused and despondent that she killed herself." I gave Sheila a straight, hard, meaningful look. "What's more, I don't know whether Duffy has an alibi for the time of her death. I don't know—"

"We can find out about that alibi pretty damn quick," Sheila gritted, reaching for the phone. "We can get him in here and—"

"No." I stood up and put my hand on hers. "Let's hold off, Sheila. Before we make any moves, I need to talk to this other friend of Angela's, a guy named Tyler Cole. I also want to read the file and talk to the investigating officer. We have to bring Lisa Simon into the loop. And she'll no doubt want to inform the school board's legal eagle." I smiled tightly. "Anyway, I doubt that our pal Duffy is going anywhere. He's got too much invested in Pecan Springs. His life is here. His wife's life is here." Queen Glenda. She would be absolutely devastated if she knew what Duffy was up to.

The muscle in Sheila's jaw was working. She shook her head. "I just can't believe it, China. The town worships that guy. Why, the Boosters are planning a Tim Duffy Appreciation Day the first weekend in March. They're giving him and Glenda an all-expense-paid trip to Hawaii for a second honeymoon. They—"

"Don't believe it," I put in. "Keep an open mind. It's too soon to be sure about anything yet, one way or another. There are too many unanswered questions."

Sheila pushed back her chair and stood up. "Innocent until proven guilty, right? I'll get that file. You've got time to read it now?"

"Yeah. Thanks, Smart Cookie."

"Any time," she said with dark sarcasm, going to the door. "Your friendly neighborhood police department, at your service." She shook her head. "Ben Graves is going to shit a brick," she muttered, and left the room.

While I was waiting for Sheila to come back with the file, I used my cell phone to call the shop to let Laurel know I'd been detained.

"Take your time," she said cheerfully. "It's getting colder and there's not much going on here. It's slow in the tearoom, too. Ruby said to tell you that the Ouija party is on for tonight, about seven thirty. There'll be food, so don't eat ahead of time. You don't have to bring anything, either." She paused. "Ruby invited me, but I can't come. I'm sorry. Sounds like fun."

"Oh, yeah," I said, without enthusiasm. "I'm just dying to know what Ouija has to say about that missing quilt."

Laurel chuckled. "And you got a couple of personal calls," she went on. "One was from your mom, wanting to know if you'd taken care of that business she asked you to look into."

I sighed. "And the other one?"

"A man named Buddy, who said he was an old friend of yours. He wanted to know if you'd read the letters he gave you." There was a note of barely disguised curiosity in her voice, and I wondered what she would say if I told her that the "old friend" was my half brother, and that the love letters had been written by our father to a woman who wasn't his wife. "He wants you to call him back. As soon as possible."

139

Oh, sure. Next week, maybe. Or next month. "If he phones again, tell him I'll get to the letters when I can. If Leatha calls back, tell her there's nothing to worry about—I'm taking care of everything."

And that's exactly what I was going to do. I was going to resolve that sordid business by chucking the entire envelope of love letters—unread—straight into the fireplace. I would do it tonight, right after Ruby's party. Leatha wouldn't ever know about Buddy, and Buddy and I were definitely *not* destined to be pals. We hadn't been in touch since those furtive teenage encounters in the basement of my father's office building, and I intended to leave it that way.

I had another call to make. I took out the cell phone number Christie had given me, and dialed again.

"Yo," a boy's voice said. "Tyler here." In the background, I heard the buzz of voices and the strident ringing of a cash register.

I explained who I was and what I wanted. There was an extended silence on the other end of the line, interrupted by a couple of dings and "Pizza's up! Super spicy Cajun chicken, double anchovies."

"Well, I don't know," the boy said, obviously reluctant. "There's not much I can tell you about her."

I turned on the charm, and after a few moments, he sighed and gave in. "I'm over here at Gino's Italian Pizza Kitchen, on Nueces. My shift is up in half an hour. Doubt if I can help you, but if you want to waste your time, that's up to you."

Pecan Springs is a small town, and nothing is very far away from anywhere else. Gino's is about five minutes from the police station, up the hill in the direction of the campus. "I'll be there in thirty," I said, as Sheila came through the door with a file folder under her arm. "Thanks, Tyler."

I spent the next twenty minutes hunched over a desk in an empty office, going methodically through the file, making notes. There weren't any major surprises, as far as I could tell. Angela had checked into The Longhorn about six o'clock in the evening of January third, a Saturday. She'd had a reservation for one person, one night, nonsmoking queen. She paid cash. The desk clerk hadn't noticed whether she'd had any luggage—people often took their bags straight from their car to their rooms—and didn't notice anything out of the ordinary about Angela or about the registration. Business as usual, and business had been brisk, with a CTSU basketball game on tap for that weekend.

The body was discovered at ten thirty the next morning by the maid who came to clean the room. Angela was lying on her left side in the bed, wearing a brief yellow nightie, which appeared to be new. Her jeans, shirt, underwear, and shoes were folded on a chair in the corner, with her purse. The purse contained the usual: wallet, keys, coins, lipstick, comb, a phone card, a five and three ones, a couple of mechanical pencils. On the bedside table, there was an empty plastic pudding cup (butterscotch) and a plastic spoon, beside a disposable plastic cup from the bathroom. The bathroom cup and spoon bore her fingerprints. Her prints were also found on the door, the TV remote control, the faucets in the bathroom sink, and the phone.

The phone. I looked again. The report didn't mention any phone calls, so why were Angela's prints on the phone? There were no other fresh prints except for an unidentified thumbprint on the bottom of the pudding cup—perhaps that of a grocery clerk.

And, of course, there was the note Sheila had already told me about, handwritten in purple ink on a torn piece of lined pink paper and propped against the lamp on the bedside table: "I'm really sorry. I didn't mean it to end like this." It was signed "Angie." The handwriting had checked out; the paper bore the print of the girl's right index finger. As a suicide note, it obviously left something to the imagination. But it seemed to clearly indicate that Angela had meant to take her life.

The report also included a brief summary of the questions that had been put to Christie Norris and to the college counselor, a woman named Jean Snyder, and their answers. As I already knew, Christie had insisted that her roommate wouldn't kill herself; her insistence was duly noted, but without explanation or elaboration. The counselor's answers were heavily qualified, but tended to reinforce the investigating officer's suicide theory.

"Let's put it this way," Snyder had told the investigator, in what must be a triumph of understatement. "I'm not surprised. Angela had a lot of unresolved issues around sex. Girls like that tend to fantasize about suicide. It's an effort to get the attention they crave." Left unexplored, however, was any role that the antidepressants Synder had prescribed might have played in Angela's death—or any other possible explanation for the way she had died.

I made a note of the counselor's name and contact information, then flipped the pages to the autopsy report. There was no indication that the deceased had had any recent sexual encounters, and she had never been pregnant. No signs of a struggle: no bruises or scratches, no broken nails. She had died of an overdose—about three grams—of Nembutal, the same drug that had killed Marilyn Monroe all those years ago. The theory was, apparently, that she had put the ground-up Nembutal into the pudding, and gotten it down that way. The toxicologist had also found traces of *flunitrazepam*—Rohypnol, or roofie, the date-rape drug—in her system.

I frowned. Why roofie? And three grams of Nembutal? That would be thirty 100-milligram tablets, available only by prescription. Where had she gotten it? Who had prescribed it? I leafed through the rest of the report, but there were no answers to these questions, and nothing to suggest that they had been asked. I scowled. One dead girl with access to antidepressants plus three grams of Nembutal add up to suicide—an easy equation. But what if it wasn't as simple as that?

I stared at the pages for a few moments, trying to focus, trying to center myself, as Ruby likes to say. The report was cool, objective, impersonal, a series of factual statements; you would never know the storms of chaotic emotions that swirled through the events behind it. Angela's passionate conviction that she had to "do something," whatever that was. Christie's guilt at turning away from her friend when she was most needed. Angela's mother's anguished grief. And Tim Duffy—how had he felt?

The photographs were objective and impersonal, as well. A shot of a pretty girl in a brief nightie lying on her side on a neatly made bed, legs curled up, one arm flung out, hair spread out over the pillow. A shot of the bedside table, another of the bathroom, another of the clothing folded on the chair. Everything neat and tidy. An orderly death.

I checked the last page of the report. The investigating officer had been Sophie Murdock. The attending justice of the peace was Maude Porterfield, who is probably the best JP (and certainly one of the oldest) in the entire state of Texas. I was pleased. I've known Maude Porterfield for several years. She has a sharp eye to go with her sharp tongue, and an opinion about everything—a woman to be admired. I'd like to hear her thoughts about Angela's death. I made a mental note to call her first chance I got.

Sophie was on four-to-midnight today Dorrie said, when I asked. She'd be available tomorrow, though. I could check with her then.

143

Chapter Thirteen

GINO'S SPECIAL ITALIAN PIZZA SAUSAGE

1½ pounds lean ground pork
1 teaspoon salt
1 teaspoon freshly ground black pepper
3½ teaspoon paprika
1 teaspoon fennel seed
¼ teaspoon red pepper, crushed
1 tablespoon chopped fresh parsley
1 teaspoon dried basil
1 teaspoon dried oregano
2 large cloves garlic, minced

Mix salt, pepper, spices, and herbs. Distribute evenly over pork and mix well. This sausage is best if made 12–24 hours before using. To prepare, crumble sausage in a medium-hot skillet. Cook until brown, stirring occasionally. Drain well. Sprinkle generously over the top of the pizza before baking.

Gino's Genuine Italian Pizza Kitchen served up Pecan Springs' very first pizza sometime back in the 1950s, and in spite of the franchised pizza joints that have sprung up since, it still does a brisk business. Gino is long gone—he was killed in a car wreck on I-35 about ten years ago—but the Kitchen still makes the best pizza in town, with the same thick crust, so much cheese that it strings when you pick up a slice, and mushrooms and sliced pepperoni and Gino's special Italian pizza sausage heaped generously over the top.

That special sausage is probably the reason customers are willing to put up with the gloomy interior—brown-painted wainscoting and fake beams across the fly-specked ceiling—and the racket that penetrates the plywood partition from the saloon and pool hall next door. Anyway, a lot of the customers are college kids who are at home with the flashing neon signs on the wall and the crack of billiard balls and the loud music that blares from the sound system. Grown-ups like me usually go through the drive-through, to avoid the wear and tear on our nerves.

The lunch crowd was gone and the place was mostly empty, except for a quartet of big-shouldered rowdies in a front booth. College football players, they looked like. I paid for a medium drink, filled the cup with ice and diet soda from the machine against the wall, and went to join the skinny kid who was sitting at a table in the back corner, wolfing down what was left of a medium pizza. Tyler Cole was no older than twenty or twenty-one I thought, just five or six years older than Brian. He had a spotty face, an incomplete moustache on his upper lip, and a sheaf of dirty-blond hair that kept falling into his eyes. I sat down and introduced myself.

He eyed me cautiously. "Not a cop, are you?"

I shook my head, moving my elbow to avoid the sticky spot—pizza sauce?—on the brown-painted table. "I'm a friend of Mrs. Lopez, Angela's mother. She asked me to talk to some of the people who knew Angela. She'd like to learn more than she was able to find out from the police report." It wasn't strictly true, but it seemed to satisfy him.

"So," he said, pushing a hunk of pizza into his mouth and talking around it. "What do you want to know?"

145

"I was wondering how you found out about Angela's death," I said conversationally, easing us into it. "Did the police tell you?"

"Nope. Christie Norris called me." His glance was pained. "Blew me away, I'll tell you. Totally wiped me out. I just couldn't believe it. Still can't. That Angie killed herself, I mean. She wasn't the type."

"So what did you think might have happened to her?"

He picked up his mug of root beer and took a swallow. "An accidental overdose, maybe. She was on antidepressants. She could've lost track of what she was taking. It happens, you know. Or—" He put down the mug.

"Or what?" I prompted.

There was a shout of rough laughter from the rowdies in the front booth.

"I dunno," he said with a shrug. "Anyway, I figured the cops would come around to ask me questions, but they didn't show. And then I heard that her death had been officially ruled a suicide, so I thought . . ." He raised his blond eyebrows. "Well, I figured there must be something going on with her that I didn't know. I mean, we were pretty good friends. We knew one another back in high school. But even good friends don't tell you everything. You know?"

"You're from Friendship?"

"Yeah. We were in the same class." He picked up the last slice of pizza. "We graduated together. But that's ancient history. And we were just friends, in case you're wondering." He looked at me, setting the record straight. "We weren't sleeping together or anything like that."

Just friends. Well, you don't have to be sleeping with a guy to talk to him about what's bothering you. I leaned forward. "Christie Norris said she thought Angela might have talked to you about something that happened to her when she was in high school—a relationship she'd had."

146

More shouts from up front, a bray of laughter, and the sound of something—a metal pizza tray, maybe—hitting the floor. Someone behind the counter—the manager, maybe, called out, "Hey, you guys, cool it. You want rough stuff, take it outdoors. We don't need that action here."

"Maybe she did." Tyler's mouth twisted. "Why do you want to know?"

"Because it might help me to understand how she died, and why. Did she tell you who he was?"

He looked at me, then away. "It was a secret. I don't think she would want me to—"

"Tyler," I said urgently. "Angela's *dead*. You said yourself that she wasn't the suicide type, so there must be something else behind it. I need to know what she told you. It's important."

"Oh, hell." He sucked in his breath, let it out with a whoosh. "All right, then. The guy who hit on her was Coach Duffy. She told me it went on for most of her junior year." He pulled his mouth down. "Hard to believe, I know. You wouldn't think a guy like that would want to screw around with a teenaged girl, even one as pretty as Angie. But she would never make something like that up. She was as straight as they come. Too straight for her own good, maybe."

"Too straight?"

"Yeah. She believed what people told her, even when they were lying. Like him." He cleared his throat. "Anyway, she said she had proof. In writing."

I was startled. "Proof? Letters, you mean?"

"Yeah. Stuff he wrote, back when he was banging her. She burned some, when her mother found them. But she hid the rest. At least, that's what she told me, and I believed her."

147

"Did you ever get a look at them?" I spoke low, under the loud voices coming from the front booth.

He shifted on the hard bench, his head down, not letting me see his face. "Hell, no. If she'd offered to let me read them, I would've said no." He was trying to be cool, but his voice had thinned and there was something in it he probably didn't intend me to hear. Anger. Bitter contempt. Personal injury. "Who'd want to read lovesick puke like that? From a guy like him, who everybody looked up to? Shit, I looked up to him, too. I thought Coach was the best there was, ever—then come to find out he'd been screwing this teenaged chick in the locker room. Destroys your faith in humankind, hearing something like that. Blows up all your illusions." He aimed a finger at me, as if it were a gun and I were an illusion, and said, "Ka-bam!"

"Yeah," I said sympathetically. "I can imagine."

I could, too. I knew exactly how Tyler Cole felt about reading those letters. I felt very much the same way about the file Buddy had given me—letters my father had written in the heat of an illicit affair. I didn't intend to read them, either.

The voices of the quartet up front had turned angry. There was the sound of a scuffle, the sharp bang of a chair going over, and the manager's startled "Hey, you guys! Can it, or I'm calling the cops!"

"Keep your shirt on," a rough male voice growled. "We're outta here." A door slammed. Out in the parking lot, a truck engine revved into life.

"Football players," the manager said disgustedly. "Think they own the world." Another slam, the oven door, this time.

"You wouldn't happen to know where she kept those letters," I remarked into the sudden quiet. Christie had said that her mother had taken all of Angie's stuff—and Mrs. Lopez hadn't mentioned any additional letters. So where were they? If I were a young woman with a stash of incriminating love letters, where would I hide them?

"I have no idea," Tyler said sourly. Losing illusions is a hard business, especially for the very young. "I never asked. She never said."

Nothing more to be gained there. I took a different tack. "I wonder— did Angie happen to mention a girl she met while she was doing volunteer work?"

"Yeah. Some kid who claimed she was involved with Duffy." He paused. "Well, I don't know that *involved* is the right word. I mean, I don't know how far it had gone. All I know is that Angie was upset when she heard the kid's story. Said he was hitting on her. The kid, I mean."

"Did she tell you the girl's name?"

"She might've." He pulled his brows together, thinking. "Yeah, I think she mentioned it once or twice. Jackie, maybe. Something like that."

Jackie. Well, that was a help. There couldn't be that many volunteer programs in Pecan Springs, and Angela must have worked in only one of them. I might actually have a prayer of finding this girl.

"You say that Angela was upset when she heard Jackie's story. Why?"

He gave me a crooked smile. "Well, why do you think? It hit her pretty hard, finding out that Coach was coming on to somebody else. To another underage kid."

"Because the girl was underage? Or—"

He shrugged. "Angie didn't exactly say. But I got the feeling she maybe had the idea that it had been just *her*, back when she was in high school. You know, like she was special. Like he'd been crazy just for her and nobody else." He chuckled ruefully. "So, yeah. She was upset. Guess you can understand that."

"Yes," I said, "I can."

"Anyway, when she found out that Coach had the hots for this girl, she wanted her to rat him out. But the girl said she'd handle it her own way. Said she was going to tell the jerk to buzz off and leave her alone." Tyler finished off his pizza and licked at a string of cheese that was decorating his moustache.

"Did she? Tell him to buzz off, I mean."

"I don't know. I never even saw the kid." He gave a bleak chuckle. "But that was the part that really rocked Angie. You know? Like, *she* could never have told him off like that, and here was this girl, who was ready to spit in his face." He shook his head. "And finding out that he was still coming on to young girls—well, that really bothered her. She said she wanted to try to do something about it. Like, maybe she thought it was her responsibility or something. Maybe because she didn't do it before."

I leaned forward. Christie had said almost the same thing. But Christie hadn't known what Angie planned to do. Maybe this boy did. "So what was she thinking of doing, Tyler? What was her plan?"

"Plan?" He shrugged. "You got me. She was pretty mysterious about it. She said she'd tell me—if it worked out."

I sat back, disappointed. "Well, what did you *think* she was going to do?"

"I dunno." He frowned. "Confront the dude, maybe. Tell him she was going to spill the beans if he didn't quit. Or she might've been thinking of talking to the cops. She did some research and found out that she could press charges against him if she wanted to, for a few more years, at any rate. Something about the statue of limitations." He stopped. "Statute, maybe. Yeah, statute."

"And what did you think of that?" I asked, to keep him talking. "About pressing charges, I mean."

"Me?" He gave me a raised-eyebrow look. "Well, I guess if I'd thought about it, I would've said she'd be taking a risk. Coach had a hell of a lot of clout back in Friendship, and he's got even more here. Like, if she went public, the shit would hit the fan, big-time. But she didn't ask my advice, and I didn't offer. It was her business. Not mine."

"Yeah," I muttered. Does everybody think alike on this? "The Prime Directive."

He gave me a look of pleased surprise. "Hey, yeah. That's it. Don't screw with other people's stuff. Things are going to happen the way they're going to happen."

"But the Prime Directive applies only to galactic societies," I objected, "not to individuals. And anyway, it's just fiction. Some screenwriter thought it up."

"It applies wherever it applies," Tyler said knowingly. A metallic musical chirp sounded. "Hang on," he said to me, and took his cell phone out of his pocket. "Yeah? Uh-huh. Right. Any minute now. Bye." He pocketed his phone and said, "Listen, I gotta go. I'm supposed to pick somebody up, and I'm late. Is there anything else you want to know?"

"Not at the moment," I said. "If I think of something, can I call you?"

"Sure. You got my number." He stood and gathered up his plate and utensils. "Like I said, I'm glad to help out. Angie was a friend."

I sat there for a few minutes after Tyler had gone, pondering the ironies of this statement. Angie had been his friend, yes. He was glad to help, yes. But only up to a point—the point where he took cover behind the Prime Directive. Beyond that, noninterference was the rule. Hands off. Nobody's business.

But where did that leave somebody like Angie, who might still be alive if one of her friends had intervened? Where, for that matter, did it leave the rest of us? Adrift, on our own, supposed to be capable of managing our own affairs? What happened when we weren't? What happened when we needed help and couldn't ask for it? These questions weren't comfortable for me—I had always insisted on my own independence, to the point of not wanting to get intimately involved with anyone who might seem inclined to take care of me. And maybe they had no answers. Maybe—

I stood up. It was time to get back to the shop. I had gotten more out of the exchange with Tyler than I had expected. Somewhere, there was a stash of Duffy's letters. And not long before she died, Angela had met somebody named Jackie while she was volunteering. Jackie had some sort of involvement with Duffy, and what's more, had told him off, or planned to. I knew more than I'd known when I came in, and I had Tyler to thank.

I suddenly remembered that all I'd had for lunch was the sandwiches I'd snagged on my way to see Christie, a couple of hours ago now. I sniffed.

Wasn't that Gino's special Italian sausage I could smell? A couple of slices of pizza was exactly what I needed, along about now.

Chapter Fourteen

RUBY'S FAVORITE DIVINATION INCENSE

2 parts sandalwood
1 part clove
1 part mace
1 part cinnamon
charcoal incense disks (can be purchased where incense supplies
  are sold)

Powder the first four ingredients in a mortar and pestle. Light a
charcoal disk and sprinkle a pinch of incense on it.

A few snow flurries were sifting through the air when I finished my pizza and headed back to the shop. Anxious to
share my discoveries, I immediately put in a call to Lisa Simon. Her secretary said she had gone to a meeting in Austin, however, and wouldn't
be back until later that evening. I left my home telephone number and
asked her to call me after ten. I tried Judge Porterfield, but got her secretary; I left a message saying I'd like to talk to her about Angela Lopez's
death. Then I phoned Christie, thinking that she might be able to suggest
where Angela might have stashed the letters that Tyler had told me about.
I got an answering machine there, too, so I left a number and a request
for a call-back, without much expectation of success. Christie's room-
mates seemed like the type to forget about taking messages.

My mind still on Angela, I paged through the phone book, looking for volunteer programs. What was it Christie had said? It was a program that involved children, wasn't it? I wished I'd been more specific in my questioning, and made a note to ask Christie when I talked to her again. And then it occurred to me that Angela might have told her mother about her work as a volunteer, and might even have mentioned Jackie's last name. I got Mrs. Lopez's number from Directory Service and phoned her. No answer—and no answering machine. As far as the telephone went, I was batting oh-for-five. Not exactly a standout record.

The rest of the afternoon wasn't much to write home about, either. When I closed the shop and cleared out the cash register at five, the totals were not inspiring, about what you'd expect for a chilly, drizzly Wednesday with snow in the air. But Ruby, always the optimist, reminded me that the Garden Guild was booked for a Valentine lunch in the tearoom tomorrow, so there'd be a gaggle of customers in the store. Tomorrow was also the grand opening of Ruth Ann Gilman's new quilt shop, Patch-Works, next door in the Craft Emporium, and some of her traffic was bound to detour in our direction. Today was slow, but we'd probably do okay for the week.

At the beginning of the school year, McQuaid and I gave Brian a cell phone—a cheap one that doesn't shoot video, play music, or wash windows. Of course, Brian thinks we got the phone for him, so he can keep in touch with his friends. Nope. We did it for us. The phone allows us to keep tabs on his comings and goings, schedule pickups and deliveries, and relay various instructions—as well as reassuring us that he's okay. While I was closing out the register, I called Brian (he was in the middle of a Science Club meeting) to see what he had on tap for the evening, and was reminded that he and his friend Barry were going to Austin for the monthly meeting of the U.S.S. Rhyanna, the local chapter of the Star Trek fan club, where Brian (a longtime Trekkie) is a cadet lieutenant. Barry's father, Joe, was picking them up. He'd be home around ten fifteen. I glanced out the window, wondering if maybe the weather was bad enough to tell Brian to stay home. Deciding it wasn't, I told him to call me when they left Austin, and hung up.

If I'd been looking for an excuse to get out of going to Ruby's Ouija party, Brian wasn't it, so I resigned myself to an evening of consulting the spooks, which (if it did nothing else) would take my mind off Angela. But since I didn't intend to go home and change—Ruby's get-togethers are always come-as-you-are and my jeans and green shirt-and-sweater combo were perfectly acceptable—I needed to find something to fill up the intervening couple of hours.

I didn't have to look very far. Having your own business may seem like an attractive idea, and most of the time it is. But if you're thinking of starting a shop of your own, just remember that you'll be shuffling about three tons of paper a week. Well, that may be an exaggeration, but not by much. My business is relatively small, but I still have to deal with stock orders, invoices, sales receipts, deposit tickets, bank statements, daily and weekly and monthly accounts, time sheets, state and federal tax reports, and so forth and so on, stretching out in the general direction of infinity. If record-keeping doesn't fire you with enthusiasm, you might want to become a park ranger or an Arctic explorer instead of opening a shop.

Khat showed up while I was stashing the cash register drawer under the counter. He wound himself around my ankles, purring purposefully. It's not too difficult to read Khat's mind at this hour of the evening, so I went to the tearoom kitchen, opened a can of cat food, and put some into his bowl. He stared down at it for a moment, the tip of his tail twitching.

Then he looked up, plaintively. But this was canned cat food! Where was his liver? Ruby and Cass *always* gave him liver for supper.

"Ruby and Cass aren't here, old buddy," I said. "I'm in charge of rations tonight. It's cat food or starve." I paused meaningfully. "Or you can always catch a mouse. Cats have been known to do that from time to time, you know."

Faced with this distasteful menu of choices, Khat shot me a dark look, lowered his head, and ate. I checked out the refrigerator, thinking that I might find a bite of something—maybe a sandwich—to tide me over until the party, where there was bound to be plenty of food. However, I struck out here, too. No sandwiches, no sandwich fixings, and we seemed to be out of bread. There was, instead, a note from Ruby lying on an empty plate on the top shelf of the fridge: *Cass, I. O. U. one dozen chicken salad sandwiches (for the Ouija party).*

With a sigh, I settled for a handful of Ritz crackers and a bowl of warmed-up tomato bisque, which I carried into my cubbyhole office, where I spent an hour and a half adding up numbers and writing checks, in a distracted sort of way. Somehow, I couldn't seem to get Angela Lopez out of my thoughts.

RUBY lives in a turn-of-the-century two-story Victorian, on a block with a dozen other Victorians: dignified dowager houses in decorous shades of grays and browns and ivories, sitting with their hands sedately folded and their ankles primly crossed behind their boxy front shrubberies, wearing their "Historic House" badges with a justifiable pride.

Ruby's house, however, is a horse of a different color: apple, fuschia, periwinkle, plum, and pumpkin, with apple-green wicker furniture on the front porch. If you happen to pass by when nobody's looking, you might see this Painted Lady dancing the Texas two-step across its wraparound yard. For several years, the neighbors tried without success to persuade Ruby to tone things down—which happened, after a fashion, as the paint began to naturally fade. Now, I notice, the Plain-Janes on either side are sporting touches of red and mauve and persimmon. Color is catching.

There were already a couple of cars in front of Ruby's house. I parked my Toyota in front of Cass's antique Saab, and got out, leaving Angela's teddy bear still sitting in the front seat, a forlorn passenger. I filled my lungs with the cold, crisp air. The temperature was dropping and the flurries had turned into gusty snow showers. Even if we got only an inch or two, we would all be as excited as kids with a new sled, since snow is an infrequent visitor to the Hill Country. We might be snowbound, too. Most of us haven't a clue about how to drive on icy, snowy roads, and Pecan Springs doesn't own any snow removal equipment.

Ruby's front door was slightly ajar, dropping a slant of golden light onto the porch. I pushed it open, went inside, and hung my coat on the pegs that line one wall, between an elegant faux-fur, a sleek suede coat, and a man's denim jacket with mud on the sleeve. Colin's, no doubt. There were other evidences of his occupation: a pair of men's boots in the corner, a cowboy hat on another peg. I wondered whether he would be joining us for the Ouija party, but doubted it. Ruby had hinted that he wasn't entirely in tune with her mystical efforts—another reason for me to wonder whether there was any future in the relationship. Ruby's mystical side is an integral, vital part of her personality. Colin would ignore it at his peril.

The interior of Ruby's house, which she bought from the estate of our friend Jo Gilbert, is even more colorful than the public exterior. Jo, who died a few years ago, had let the old place run down, and when Ruby moved in, she rolled up her sleeves and got busy. Throughout the downstairs, she restored the golden oak woodwork and floors and papered the walls in bright orange, yellow, even red, electrified with black-and-white stripes and checks and zigzags, like a Mary Englebreit painting. But for all this vibrant color, it's a comfortable house, filled with Ruby's favorite things: her own quilts and woven pieces on the walls, baskets and sculpture and bowls and artwork and books on the shelves, a large loom in one corner, and a star map painted on the dark blue living room ceiling. Also on display, on various tables and shelves, Ruby's magical tools: her crystals and Tarot cards, her rune stones and I Ching coins and incense burners.

Incense. I sniffed. Tonight, she was burning something woodsy and fresh. Ruby makes her own incense, which she packages and sells in the Crystal Cave and burns at home. Her house, like her shop, is always full of wonderful scents, subtle and evocative. This one reminded me of the East Texas piney woods after a rain.

I heard voices and laughter from the kitchen at the end of the hall, and headed in that direction. Last year, Ruby began to glimpse the decorative potential in watermelons. She added a watermelon border to her red-and-white striped kitchen wallpaper, painted the table red and the four chairs green and red, and put a watermelon rug under the table. It's colorful and cheerful, just like Ruby herself.

Carol Bruce and Cass were in the kitchen with Ruby, and they all greeted me. Carol is a square, sturdy woman with an intelligent expression and capable hands who looks exactly like what she is: a nurse. She lost her hair during chemo and it's just beginning to grow back, a shapeless brown mop, soft and fine, like babies' hair and very attractive. Seeing her reminded me that there was a serious reason behind tonight's frivolity. Somebody had stolen the quilt she had made to celebrate the women in her cancer support group, and we were there to uncover a clue to its whereabouts.

Well, maybe that was putting it too confidently. In my opinion, we were there to play with a toy that was supposed to point to letters or numbers printed across a board. Ruby was the one who insisted that the Ouija board might help us find the quilt, and she was dressed to fit the part of a psychic. She was wearing a silky, dark blue medieval-looking garment with silver and gold stars all over it, belted just under her breasts with a wide golden belt. Her red hair was combed out in frizzy halo. She looked like an Elfin queen.

Carol was holding up a quilt block for Ruby's inspection. "I made this for my quilt but didn't use it," she said. "I thought I'd bring it. I don't know if there's anything to this Ouija board business, but maybe it'll . . ." She grinned ruefully. "Oh, I don't know. Encourage the spirits or what-ever. Give them something to focus on."

"Wonderful!" Ruby enthused, taking it between her fingers. "It's a beautiful quilt block, Carol. I love that appliquéd heart—and your stitch-ing is so perfect."

"For me, stitching is like saying a mantra," Carol said. "It settles me down when everything is up in the air."

"Me, too," Ruby said. "It's as good as meditation." She put the block aside. "This will help, I'm sure. It'll give us something to focus on. Ouija works better when everyone is focused."

Cass put four glasses on the table. "You really believe there's some-thing to this Ouija business, do you, Ruby?"

Cass, who has a sharp sense of style, says she doesn't believe in dressing to camouflage her beautiful bulk. "Life is not about big boobs and thunder thighs," she is fond of saying. "Just because I'm shaped like Roseanne doesn't mean I can't dress like Cher." To prove it, she was wearing a pair of purple palazzo pants with a hip-length woolen vest vertically striped in shades of orange, red, and purple. Between her and Ruby, my jeans, and green shirt made me feel perfectly dowdy.

"Of course I believe there's something to the Ouija," Ruby said indignantly. "I can't guarantee that we'll be successful tonight, but it's certainly worth the effort." She turned to me. "Don't you agree, China?"

"Oh, absolutely," I said, in a hearty tone, noticing the tray of sandwiches on the table—the dozen chicken salad sandwiches Ruby had borrowed from the tearoom refrigerator, no doubt. They reminded me that all I'd had to eat today was a couple of slices of Gino's pizza, a bowl of soup, and a few measly crackers. I was hungry.

"Audrey's coming," Carol put in. She gave Ruby a questioning glance. "I hope you don't mind my inviting her. I ran into her today when she was visiting a friend at the hospital."

"Audrey?" Cass grinned. "Her husband has asked me to make two weeks' worth of dinners for them. A Valentine's surprise. You're not supposed to mention it, though."

Carol nodded. "When I told her that Ruby was going to use her Ouija board to find out who took the quilt, she said she thought it was a wonderful idea. She wanted to come."

"Not a problem," Ruby said. "After all, she helped with the enemies list. Not that you have any," she added cheerfully. "Everybody likes you, Carol." She sobered. "Which makes this theft so hard to understand."

It's true. Carol, who has a warm, motherly way about her, is the kind of person who becomes an instant friend. I think that's why she's so successful as a coordinator of the Hospital Auxiliary programs. She makes everybody want to pitch in and help.

Cass put another glass on the tray for Audrey, and got a pitcher of sparkling red punch out of the refrigerator. "I can't believe it has anything to do with you personally, Carol. Somebody probably just fell in love with that quilt and had to have it for their own. They didn't have the money to buy it, or they didn't think you'd sell it, or—"

"But *who?*" Carol asked, with a perplexed shake of her head. "None of the Scrappers would think of doing such a horrible thing. And there wasn't anybody in the hotel who might have taken it. When I think of all the love and work that went into it, I just feel sick. I—"

"Hello, all!" The back door swung open and Audrey Manning burst in. Audrey is a short, plump little woman with a full moon of a face and soft flesh that hangs from her upper arms. Emotional and impulsive, she always seems to burst into every room she enters. "Oh, Carol, I'm so glad you invited me!" she cried, in an excited, high-pitched voice. "I've never been to a Ouija party before. This is going to be such wonderful fun!"

Ruby put Carol's quilt block into the pocket of her caftan. "We shouldn't think of Ouija as 'fun,' " she began, in a serious tone, but Audrey wasn't listening.

"Leave it to you, Ruby, to think of asking your Ouija board about Carol's quilt. Honestly, you have the *brightest* ideas!" She set a covered dish on the table and said, in her usual bustling way, "I've brought salad. Are we almost ready to eat?" Audrey likes things organized, and if nobody else is organizing, she steps right in.

I didn't know about the others, but I was ready. I looked around. "What can I do to help?"

161

"You can put the shortcake hearts onto a plate," Carol suggested, "while I get out the cookies."

Audrey shrugged out of her coat and carried her salad out to the dining room table. Carol and I arranged the shortcakes and cookies. Ruby took the sandwiches and a stack of plates. Cass finished pouring the punch, then took the tray and followed Ruby. I brought the pitcher of punch and the silverware and napkins, Carol brought the dessert, and we were all set.

The next half hour was filled with the usual party-time business of fixing our plates, settling down in front of the living room fireplace, and eating, all the while exchanging the usual party chitchat. Audrey has a reputation as a gossip and she didn't disappoint, but the conversation was mostly about the Scrappers, the Scrappers' friends and neighbors, the opening of Ruth Ann's quilt shop, and so on. We carefully avoided the subject of the quilt show, from which Carol's quilt had been so unceremoniously and mysteriously removed, leaving Audrey's quilt the chief contender for Best-in-Show. It was a potentially awkward situation, and we stayed away from it. I'm neither a Scrapper nor a quilter, so I didn't have much to contribute to the conversation. To tell the truth, I wasn't even listening—until, that is, Audrey happened to mention the Duffys. It seems that they were Audrey and Chuck's neighbors on Bronwyn Avenue, and the two couples were on rather close terms.

"It's a terrible pity, and no one is sadder than I am about it," she said, finishing off her sandwich. "It looks like the Duffys are having their problems." She looked around the group. "I'm sure you won't let this get any further than the walls of this room."

I was about to say something when Cass spoke up.

"Oh, dear," she exclaimed. "I'm so sorry to hear that! They're such a handsome couple, both of them. I was noticing them at their party the other night—how stunning they look together. They seemed very much in love."

"Looks can be deceiving," Audrey said, with the air of someone who knows more than she's telling.

"This must be something new," I said, remembering what Sheila had told me. "Just today, I heard that the Boosters were planning to give the Duffys a second honeymoon in Hawaii."

"That's what makes this so terribly difficult," Audrey said, lowering her voice and leaning forward, as if she were afraid that somebody might be lurking just outside the window, listening in. "My husband is president of the Boosters, you know. The club was all set to give Tim and Glenda this incredible expense-paid trip to Hawaii over spring break. It was a donation from Burnham's Travel Agency, and quite a surprise, actually. You know how cheap old Mr. Burnham is—he counts every penny twice. But we were even more surprised when Tim asked Chuck to hold off. He said that he and Glenda were . . . well, going through a rocky time. Nothing they couldn't fix, but they'd rather wait and take the trip later, when things got straightened out."

A few problems, huh? Was it possible that Glenda Duffy had gotten wind of her husband's involvement with high school girls and had put the jerk on notice?

In a comforting tone, Cass said, "It sounds like they're working on it, which is good. It's always worse when there's a problem but neither one will admit it."

Audrey nodded in a solicitous way. "Chuck said he really felt sorry for Tim. He was apologetic and sort of hangdog and terribly embarrassed about turning down the trip. Of course, Chuck agreed without any argument. He didn't want to make things difficult for them." Her smile was smug. "So instead he talked to Jerry Weaver, at Weavers Electronics, and got Jerry to donate one of those big-screen TVs for the Duffys' recreation room. And old Mr. Burnham says he'll offer them the Hawaii trip next year—which would be even better, since it will be Tim and Glenda's tenth wedding anniversary. If they make it that far, cross your fingers." She held up both hands to show that her fingers were crossed. "Just before I left, Chuck called Tim and asked him to come over. He was going to give him the good news about the TV."

Ruby frowned slightly. "Maybe I shouldn't say this, but I've always had a weird feeling about Glenda Duffy. All the Seidenstickers are ambitious, but she's got more ambition than most."

Carol came to Glenda's defense, in that sweet, thoughtful way she has. "I'm not sure it's ambition, though, at least, not for herself. I think she just wants to see her husband live up to his potential. She's in charge of our Candy Stripers program, you know. The other morning, we had coffee together. She told me she thought Tim was wasting his talent coaching high school football. She's talked to one of her cousins about helping him get a college coaching position."

"A college position!" Audrey said, recoiling in wide-eyed alarm. "Oh, gosh, don't let the Boosters hear that! They love having a winning coach. Why, they're even talking about raising the money to build a bigger field house and expand the stadium."

"Expand the stadium!" I exclaimed. "But it's only a few years old." And twice as big as the stadium it replaced, with a field of grass so perfectly green, so perfectly mowed that most people think it's artificial.

"It's seven years old," Audrey corrected me knowledgeably. "And the locker room isn't nearly big enough for the new weight training equipment Tim wants to get." She bit her lip. "Oh, dear. Chuck will be absolutely brokenhearted when he hears that Glenda wants him to get a college coaching job."

"Don't tell him, then," Ruby said. She laughed a little. "Or maybe Glenda would *like* you to tell him. Maybe she's trying to up the ante." At Carol's questioning look, she added, "It might be easier for Tim to get a raise if the school board heard that his wife is encouraging him to move up to college coaching."

"Oh, don't be silly, Ruby," Audrey scoffed. "Glenda doesn't have a manipulative bone in her body. She's a very sweet person, and terribly insecure."

"Insecure!" Ruby hooted. "Not on your life, Audrey. That woman is more sure of herself than anybody I ever saw. After all, she's a Seiden-sticker."

"That's true, Ruby," Carol said hesitantly. "But I always have the feeling that, somewhere deep inside herself, Glenda is worried that somebody is going to come along and snatch everything away from her." She frowned, as if she had said more than she meant to say. "But really, I'm being too critical. Glenda is a very valuable member of our Hospital Auxiliary. She's always bringing in new Candy Stripers and helping with their training. She makes a special effort to get to know each one of them."

"Well, I for one hope Coach Duffy stays," Cass said, with emphasis. "He's such a neat guy. Everybody says he's so good with the kids. And every school feels good when its football team is winning."

Oh, sure, I thought with sad irony. *So good with the kids—especially the girls.* I wasn't especially fond of Glenda, but I had to feel sorry for her. Having a husband you couldn't trust was bad enough. Having a husband with a hankering for underage girls was a heck of a lot worse. I thought of Angela Lopez, dead in a motel room, and shivered. Having a husband like Tim Duffy would be a disaster, even if you were a Seidensticker. But of course I couldn't say that out loud. None of the others—not even Ruby—knew what I knew, and I hoped to keep it that way.

"If we're through eating," Ruby said, bringing us back to the task at hand, "it's time we got started with Ouija." She stood up and began to clear away the food.

"You'll have to tell me how this works, Ruby," Carol said, after we'd taken the dishes back to the kitchen and returned to the living room. Ruby put another log on the fire, the flames casting a flickering glow across the ceiling. "I'm a real dummy when it comes to all this psychic stuff. And to tell the truth, I'm a little afraid of it."

"So am I," Audrey confessed nervously, as Ruby went around the room, turning off the lamps and lighting candles here and there. "*The Sixth Sense* was a really spooky movie. It scared me. And *The Exorcist* gave me the willies for weeks." She bit her lip. "You don't suppose we'll actually find out what happened to the quilt, do you?"

"I don't know what we'll find out," Ruby replied honestly, "but I do know there's nothing to be afraid of. The Ouija board is nothing like what went on in those movies, Audrey. People have been using it for over a century. And they've been consulting oracles for a heck of a lot longer than that. Since the beginning of human history, actually. Any time the Greeks couldn't figure something out, they went to Delphi and asked the oracle." She bent over the cassette player and pushed a button. "Maybe a little music will help you relax." The soft, ethereal sound of a harp floated through the room.

"My cousin got a Ouija board for Christmas," Cass remarked. "She said it didn't do a thing for her, but maybe that's because it's just cardboard. Where did you get yours, Ruby?"

"I made it," Ruby replied, putting a wooden board on the coffee table. It was a wooden board, highly polished, with an attractive grain. She had painted the letters of the alphabet on it, and numbers from one to nine, all in gold. In one top corner was the word *yes*, in the other, *no*. In one bottom corner were the words, *It's not for you to know*, and in the other corner, *Ask later*. The moon and the sun were painted in the center, and around the edges, she had painted the twelve astrological signs, in a kind of swirling cosmic border.

"Ruby," I said admiringly, "it's a masterpiece."

Ruby smiled modestly. "I dreamed it."

Cass stared at her. "Honestly?"

"Cross my heart and hope to die," Ruby said, putting a votive candle on the coffee table and lighting it. "I got up out of bed and went to the garage. I'd seen an old cutting board out there, and I thought it would work. Colin sanded it smooth and I painted it." She smiled down at it. "It's exactly the way I dreamed it." She glanced at Cass. "It doesn't matter what the board is made of, though. It has more to do with your attitude, and your belief."

Carol leaned over it, regarding it doubtfully. "How does it talk?"

"It *talks*?" Audrey squeaked, her eyes wide. "What does it say?"

"It doesn't really talk," Ruby said soothingly. She opened a black velvet amulet pouch and took out a slender quartz crystal, several inches long. "We'll use this quartz as a pointer—a 'planchette,' it's called. As the questions are asked, the crystal glides across the board and points to symbols or letters or numbers. Somebody—Cass, maybe you can do this—will write them down. We have to remember, though, that Ouija doesn't always give us the letters in the right order. Sometimes we have to reassemble them in a way that makes sense, like Scrabble. And sometimes the words seem to have more than one meaning. It's up to us to figure out which is the right one."

As Cass went to the desk for some paper and a pen, Ruby took down a small pottery bowl, put a charcoal disk in it, and lit it with a match.

"What's that?" Audrey asked, frowning. For all Ruby's pep talk, she didn't seem any less apprehensive.

"Divination incense," Ruby said, uncorking a small glass bottle and sprinkling a powder over the charcoal. "Sometimes it helps to invoke an answer." She smiled briefly. "The spirits like sweet-smelling smoke."

"What questions do you think we should ask?" Carol said, as the incense wafted into the air. It smelled of cloves and cinnamon, two spices that have an eons-old reputation for enhancing clairvoyance. There's a long list of herbs that are said to have this effect, although I can't speak from personal experience. I'm too "left-brained," as right-brained Ruby puts it, to be readily susceptible to this sort of thing. Too logical, too pragmatic, and probably too skeptical. I tend to agree with McQuaid, who describes Ruby's Tarot and astrology and rune stones as "mystical claptrap"—although I am more willing than he is to stipulate that there are some things in this world that are not susceptible of quantitative analysis. Some of Ruby's weird stuff is make-believe. But some of it isn't, and I've learned that you have to *be* there to understand the difference.

"We could start with 'who took Carol's quilt?'" Cass offered helpfully. A flute had joined the harp in a kind of magical harmony.

"And why," I suggested, as Ruby passed the crystal through the curling smoke, whispering something under her breath.

"What are you doing?" Audrey asked suspiciously.

"Cleansing the crystal of negative influences," Ruby said quietly. "And blessing it, so that it does no harm."

At this, Audrey made a sharp noise under her breath, and I began to wonder why she had bothered to come.

"I only want to know where my quilt is," Carol said, coming back to the subject. "I don't really care who took it, or why. I just want to get it back, that's all." The candle flickered.

"Then we'll begin with that question," Ruby said, kneeling on the floor beside the coffee table. She took the quilt block out of her pocket and put it on the table. "Carol, you sit on the sofa, so we have the board between us. Everybody else gather around."

Audrey sat on the sofa next to Carol, and Cass and I sat on opposite sides of the coffee table, on the floor. Cass looked interested, Carol seemed uncertain, and Audrey's round face wore an apprehensive look. We all glanced expectantly at Ruby, whose fingers rested lightly on the crystal.

"Carol," she said, "will ask her question. As she asks it, the rest of us will focus on the question, and repeat it. The trick is for all of us to concentrate as hard as we can. We all have to think the same thought."

"What happens if we don't?" Cass wanted to know.

"Sometimes Ouija picks up other energies," Ruby explained. "If one person is thinking hard about something else, and the spirits tune in to that concern, Ouija's answer would relate to that issue, rather than the question we're all concerned with. If we're going to get any information, it's because we're all concentrating on the same thing. So focus just as hard as you can, and try to keep other thoughts out of your mind." She swept the crystal across the board several times, then across the quilt block lying on the table. "It might help for Carol to hold the quilt block," she added.

169

Carol picked up the quilt block and held it out, rather self-consciously, as if she thought this might be silly, but she wasn't sure. "The most important question for me is—" She paused. Her words were spaced and emphatic and her face was puckered with the effort to concentrate. "Where is it? Where is my quilt?"

"Where is it?" Cass murmured, staring intently at the quilt block.

"Wh . . . where is it?" Audrey stammered.

The smoke from the incense curled upward in a fragrant, spiraling twist, as if it were drawn by the music. Carol's quilt, I thought, looking at the block, a red heart appliquéd on white. Where is the quilt? Where can it be? All those beautiful hearts. Hearts, hearts. Red hearts, embroidered hearts, bleeding hearts. The fragrant smoke from the incense wafted in my direction. My eyes blurred, and I blinked to clear them. Bleeding hearts.

"Where?" I whispered. "*Where?*"

The crystal moved under Ruby's hand. "*B,*" Carol said, in a whisper.

Cass picked up the paper and pencil and wrote down a *b.*

Audrey shivered. "You're sure you didn't do that yourself, Ruby? Point to that letter, I mean."

"No, she didn't," Cass said, patting Audrey's arm reassuringly. "I was watching. Her eyes were shut. She couldn't see where the crystal was pointing."

Ruby didn't seem to hear us. Her eyes were still closed and she was swaying slightly, in rhythm with the music. The crystal began to move again.

"*R,*" Carol said, and Cass wrote it down.

There was a longish pause. "*O,*" Carol said, and almost immediately afterward, "*n.*"

"*Bron,*" Cass said. She glanced at Audrey. "Don't you live on Bronwyn?"

Audrey looked pale. "Yes, but you can't possibly think that—" She swallowed. "That's ridiculous!"

"Of course," Cass soothed. "I didn't mean to suggest—"

"Remember what Ruby told us," Carol cautioned in a low voice. "Sometimes it doesn't spell out the letters in the right order."

Ruby opened her eyes. "Focus, please," she pleaded. "I'm losing it."

We focussed obediently, and over the next few minutes, Ruby's crystal gave us three more letters: a *c*, an *o*, and an *s*. And then it stopped.

Audrey had wrapped her arms around herself. "Can we turn up the heat?" Her teeth rattled. "I'm . . . I'm freezing."

Ruby opened her eyes. "It feels like the session is over, at least for the moment. What do we have written down, Cass?"

Cass frowned down at the paper and spelled out the word. "B-R-O-N-C-O-S." She looked up. "Looks like *broncos* to me. Anybody think of any other word it might be?"

"Do we have to use all the letters?" Carol asked. "If we left out a *b* and an *o*, it might be *scorn.*"

"Or *croons,*" I ventured. Brian and I play Scrabble at least once a week. "Without the *b*, that is."

"We should use all of the letters Ouija gave us," Ruby said.

"Well, then," Cass said, "looks like we're stuck with *broncos.*"

Carol frowned, puzzled. "Broncos? As in horses?"

"As in a horse stable," Audrey suggested, brightening. "Maybe somebody hid the quilt in a stable."

"Or in Denver," Cass said. "Broncos is the name of the Denver football team."

Carol gave a skeptical chuckle. "You're not saying that somebody stole my quilt in Pecan Springs and took it all the way to *Denver*? Come on, Cass. Get real."

"Maybe we just have to think," Ruby said. "Sometimes Ouija doesn't say things clearly or straightforwardly."

"Well, I can't think of anything except being *cold*," Audrey said, clambering awkwardly to her feet. She looked at us, shivering. "Nobody else is cold?"

We all shook our heads. The temperature felt just right.

"I must be taking a chill or something," Audrey muttered. "I'm going home. Thanks for the evening, Ruby. It's been fun." She headed for the kitchen to get her coat, and a moment later, we heard the door shut behind her.

We traded uncomfortable glances. "Maybe it wasn't a good idea to invite her," Carol said regretfully. "I'm sorry."

"No problem," Ruby replied. "I could feel lots of energy coming through the crystal, and it felt so *right*. We still have a couple of questions, don't we?"

Cass nodded. "Who took the quilt. And why."

"I don't think we're getting anywhere," Carol said with a dispirited shrug. "But I don't suppose it will hurt to try again, if you really want to."

We didn't get very far. When we asked "who?" the crystal skittered around the board and finally pointed to the astrological sign of Scorpio. None of us was a Scorpio, and we couldn't think of anybody who was. Ruby muttered something about checking the signs of all the Scrappers, and we went on to the question "why?" But the crystal pointed to "Ask later," so we gave it up.

"You're really *not* moving that crystal?" Carol asked, frowning at the board.

"Not in the way you mean," Ruby said. "There's a kind of . . . well, a tingle. Like a low-level electrical current. It seems to be stronger in some directions than in others."

"Ah," Cass said, hoisting her bulk up from the floor. "Like an energy field or something."

Ruby nodded. "I move the crystal around, trying to feel where the tingle is strongest." She sighed. "I'm sorry we didn't get a better response. 'Ask later' isn't very helpful, and 'Scorpio' doesn't tell us much. But I can keep trying."

"We did get *broncos*," Cass said. "We can keep thinking about what it means. And I learned a lot." She grinned. "I can't wait to tell my cousin how this Ouija thing is supposed to work. Maybe she'll give it another chance."

"I learned a lot, too, Ruby," Carol said, getting up and giving her a hug. "Thanks for trying. It was a good idea, even if it didn't work out."

"Yeah, Ruby, it was really interesting," I said, stretching. "Gosh, it's been a long day. I'm ready to head for home."

"Not before I make us some hot chocolate," Ruby said. "We need to unwind."

Carol said she had to get home, so we said good night to her. Ruby, Cass, and I went to the kitchen, where Ruby made hot chocolate while Cass and I popped a batch of popcorn. We were unwinding nicely—sharing some serious stuff, some gossip, and some giggly girl-talk—when the kitchen door opened and Colin Fowler blew in, carrying a burst of cold air with him.

"Whew!" He shrugged out of the fleece-collared suede jacket that made him look like the Marlborough Man, only thinner and younger. "It's a real snowstorm out there."

Smiling and happy, Ruby got up to give him a quick kiss and get him some hot chocolate and popcorn, while we went around the table with introductions and pleasantries. Colin and I had met, of course, but Cass knew him only from Ruby's somewhat incoherent descriptions.

"Is that honest-to-goodness *snow* on your coat?" she wanted to know. She got up and went to the door, opened it, and another sweep of cold air came in. She returned to the table, wide-eyed. "Somebody on the radio said it was going to snow, but I didn't believe it." Cass is from the Northwest and even spent some time in Wyoming, so she's no doubt accustomed to snow. But she hasn't been in Texas long enough to witness one of our rare snowfalls.

"I was surprised, too," Colin said, sitting down and stretching out long, jean-clad legs. "But what do I know? I'm from southern Louisiana. Never snows there."

I studied him. His reddish-brown beard was graying here and there, his expression easygoing and cheerful, and his eyes were a warm, friendly brown. But if you looked closer, you might see something else behind those eyes—a tense, distrustful wariness, a kind of hyperalertness. The look of a man who has gotten into the habit of watching his back.

At the moment, though, he seemed relaxed and comfortable, and there was nothing at all unsettling in his eyes. He glanced around the table. "So how did the evening go? Did Ruby's spooks show up? Did they name the thief? Give you directions to the quilt?"

Ruby pouted. "It's not nice to make fun of Ouija."

He rolled his eyes at me, sharing his amusement, acknowledging me as a fellow skeptic. It was meant to be a compliment. "Well, did they?"

"It depends," I said. "What does the word *broncos* mean to you?"

"Denver," he said promptly. "Football."

"See?" Cass clapped her hands. "Told you. Carol's quilt has gone to Denver."

I leaned forward, eyeing him. "You're not a Scorpio, are you, Colin?"

"Oh, heavens, no," Ruby said. "He's a Libra, which is very different." She patted the back of his hand. "Scorpio is manipulative, secretive, and into power trips. Libra is balanced, fair, positive, enjoys intellectual activities and—"

"Admires beautiful women," Colin put in, with a teasing grin at Ruby. "Plays well with scissors and doesn't eat paste." He winked at me and added, "See? She's got me trained. I know just how Libras are supposed to behave." He turned to Cass with what seemed like genuine interest. "Where are you from, Cass? How long have you been in Texas?"

That's another thing about Colin. He always seems deeply interested in the person he's talking to, totally focussed, no wandering attention, no shifting gaze. He asks questions that—if they were asked by anybody else—might seem probing and personal, but the other person, charmed (or perhaps hypnotized) by his close attention, his apparently genuine interest, answers without hesitation. There's nothing flirtatious about him, or at least I don't see it that way. He simply seems to be fascinated with you and wants to know more. It's a technique that works on guys, too, not just women.

"I'm originally from Oregon." Cass replied. "I came here two years ago for a job with the CTSU Food Service. I met Ruby when I took one of her astrology classes. And then we worked together on a community theater production—the one that opened the Obermann Theater. About the same time, I started helping out with Party Thyme." She ran out of breath and took another. "And I had this bright idea for a personal chef business called The Thymely Gourmet, which seems to fit pretty well with all the other stuff that Ruby and China are doing."

"Doesn't just 'seem to fit,'" Ruby amended emphatically. "It fits perfectly. The three of us make a great team. Lots of good ideas and the energy to carry them out."

"I'll bet." Colin was looking at Cass's ring finger. "Not currently married, I take it. Kids?"

You see? If some other man had asked that question, you'd have thought he was prying into your personal life. But Cass hesitated only briefly.

"I was married, yes. Alan was killed in a climbing accident in Yosemite. Something happened to his rope, and he fell. We didn't have any kids." Alan. That was the first time Cass had mentioned her husband's name, or said where and when and how he died.

"I'm sorry," Colin said sympathetically. "A climbing accident. That's hard."

She nodded pragmatically. "But that's life. You move on." She tilted her head. "You? Married before? Children?"

He shook his head. "Yes and no. One wife, now ex, no kids. No family to speak of, actually."

"Where in southern Louisiana?" I asked, seeing an opening. "My father was from New Orleans, but I have to say that you don't sound like a native."

"I'm not a native," he said. "That was only my last port of call." And then, so quickly that it was hard to notice that he had evaded the question, added, "To tell the truth, I've been pretty footloose most of my life. Wandered around quite a lot until I got to Pecan Springs. Until I found

Ruby." He stood up, picked up his popcorn, and poured another cup of chocolate. "Glad to meet you, Cass. China, nice to see you again." He dropped a kiss on Ruby's hair and added, "Now, if you girls will excuse me, I have some reading to do upstairs." I didn't need a crystal ball to tell me that he intended to stay all night. It was an open declaration, and I wondered if it was meant for Ruby's consumption, or ours.

Whichever, Ruby certainly got the message. Her face was glowing, lit from the inside by her happiness. "I'll see you in a little bit," she said softly.

Watching Colin leave, Cass rolled her eyes and let out her breath in a long, admiring whuff. When he was safely out of the room, she said, "What a cute butt, Ruby. He's a real charmer, too—so sensitive and empathetic."

Yeah, right. I supposed he did the laundry. And windows, too. "Girls?" I asked dryly, raising one eyebrow.

"Oh, come on, China," Ruby said, frowning. "What do you want him to call us? Ladies? I know you don't like him, but you don't need to pick him apart." She looked at Cass. "More hot chocolate, Cass?"

Cass gave me a questioning look, and I knew she had picked up on Ruby's "You don't like him." But all she said was, "Thanks, but tomorrow's going to be a long one. I need to get home." She hoisted herself to her feet. "It was fun, Ruby, even if we didn't find out where the quilt is. Maybe we can try again sometime soon."

I stood. "I need to leave, too," I said. "Brian will be getting back from his Trekkie meeting."

Ruby didn't protest. Now that Colin was home, I suspected she would be happy if we left. And now that I thought about it, I was tired and ready for bed—even though sleeping alone when McQuaid is out of town doesn't actually mean sleeping alone. Howard Cosell always jumps into bed to take his place. Dollars to doughnuts, that's where Howard was at this very moment: flat on his back with all four huge paws in the air, snoring. I couldn't wait to join him.

But as things turned out, that wasn't going to happen for quite a while. It would another four or five hours before I joined Howard Cosell in bed—and even longer before I finally managed to get to sleep.

Chapter Fifteen

Children were often considered to need special protection against evil. They might be given a cross made of lavender, or an amulet filled with rosemary, dill, and lavender. Peony root was carved into beads and hung around the neck to protect against evil, or a child might wear a bracelet of cloves strung on red thread to repulse the devil.

China Bayles
"Herbs for Protection"
Pecan Springs *Enterprise*

Cass and I said good night and headed for our cars. The temperature had fallen several more degrees, and snowflakes spun through the iridescent halo that surrounded the streetlight. The flake-filled night was still and magical. The street was already covered with snow, and a light dusting frosted the windshield of my Toyota. I brushed it off with my sleeve, slid behind the wheel, and started the car. Turning on the defroster, I noticed that the dash clock read nine fifteen.

I frowned. Brian was supposed to call me when he and Barry started home, but I hadn't heard from him yet. I took out my cell phone. I wanted to make sure that Barry's father had picked the boys up at their Trekkie meeting in Austin. It looked like the streets were beginning to glaze, and I-35 might be worse. If they were stranded, I might have to go fetch.

It was a thoughtful, motherly plan, but it didn't work. Instead of Brian, I got a snippy metallic female robot who informed me: "The person you have called is unavailable. Try again later." Brian must have turned his phone off during the meeting and forgotten to turn it back on—although he's under orders to leave it on when he's out and about, so we can find him if we need him. Feeling irritated, I put my cell phone on the passenger seat. I'd call him back in a few minutes.

As I put down the phone, I noticed Angela Lopez's teddy bear, sitting in the passenger seat like a patient child, waiting for Mommy to return. The bear was wearing an orange-and-black helmet and cradling a football in its arms. On one side, Tim had signed the football. And on the other, in bold orange and black letters, was painted one word. *Broncos.* The hair prickled on the back of my neck, and gooseflesh rose on my arms.

Broncos. Denver *Broncos.*

I picked up the football—junior size, nine or ten inches long, brown rubber—and held it in my hands. Down its center length was a series of white hatch marks, meant to look like plastic lacing over a seam. But when I looked at it closely, I saw that the ball had been neatly slit along the seam, making it a perfect place for—

I turned on the dome light and fished around under the seat, pulling out the flat-bladed screwdriver I use to disengage the latch lock on the hood, which is slightly bent and doesn't always open as easily as it should. I inserted the blade into the slit, prying the stiff rubber edges apart so I could peer into the ball. Using the screwdriver to wedge open the slit, I turned the ball upside down and shook it. A folded piece of paper fell out into my lap. I wasn't surprised to see that it was a letter, handwritten. It began "My Angel," and ended, "Yours forever, Tim." I took another look. The football was stuffed with paper. I had found Angela's stash.

I sat back in the seat, feeling shaken and more than a little frightened. I couldn't even pretend to know what had been going on as we sat around the Ouija board and watched Ruby probe with her crystal, feeling for the strongest "tingle." When I'd tell her about the Broncos football and ask her what she thought had happened, she'd probably tell me that my question—*Where did Angela Lopez stash Tim Duffy's letters?*—had been much more urgent than the one we had come to ask. After all, it had been nagging at me for hours, ever since Tyler Cole had told me that Angela had kept at least some of Duffy's letters. So her supernatural spirits had responded to *my* question, instead of Carol's. No mystery there—at least for Ruby. She'd be delighted to learn that Ouija had plugged into the right channel after all.

But maybe there was another explanation, one that didn't involve Ruby's spooks. Maybe this was a simple case of mental telepathy, the kind of subliminal communication that sometimes happens between intimate friends. Maybe I had unconsciously guessed that Angela had hidden the letters in the football, and—again, without being aware of it—noticed the word *Broncos* on the ball. Maybe this idea had been brewing in some remote corner of my brain while Ruby was doing her trick with the quartz crystal, and I had communicated it to her. Possible, yes. Probable? I wasn't sure.

The windshield was steaming up, and I turned on the defroster full blast. Both explanations were equally squirrelly, of course. There wasn't much to choose between Ruby's supernatural spooks and a spooky case of Vulcan mind meld. But however the information had come to me, one simple, concrete, indisputable fact remained: Angela Lopez had stashed Tim Duffy's letters in her teddy bear's football. And now that I had possession of the evidence of Duffy's crime, I had no choice. I had to do something about it.

I turned on the wipers to clear the windshield of the melting flakes. I would read enough of the letters to be sure of what I had, and then turn the whole batch over to Lisa Simon, along with a written report summarizing my conversations with Mrs. Lopez, Christie Norris, and Tyler Cole. That would satisfy my obligations, moral and otherwise, and then I was out of it. Whatever happened after that would be up to Lisa, the legal eagle of the Pecan Springs ISD, and the State Board for Educator Certification. I was finished with this awful, sordid mess.

I put the car into gear. Unfortunately, that wasn't quite accurate. I wasn't finished. One thing still bothered me—and bothered me even more, now that I saw just how much evidence Angela had in her possession, and understood just how powerful a threat she must have seemed. Under these circumstances, I was not entirely sure that the medical examiner had gotten it right when he ruled that Angela Lopez had killed herself.

But if her death wasn't a suicide, that left only two possibilities. Either it was an accident—a theory that didn't fit the facts—or it was murder. And if it was murder, all the evidence pointed to Tim Duffy. I had to talk to Sheila. But not tonight. Brian would be home soon, and I needed to be there. Tomorrow morning was soon enough.

I pulled out of the parking space, made a couple of right turns, and headed south on Brazos Street. By the time I got to our turnoff, the snow was beginning to drift across the road. If it kept coming all night, which was beginning to look entirely possible, getting back to the main road in the morning might be an iffy proposition.

Before I went in the house, I punched in Brian's cell phone number again, thinking that it might be a good idea if he stayed all night at Barry's house in Pecan Springs. That way, if the school bus ran late in the morning—as it very likely would—he wouldn't have to miss his first class. He still didn't answer his phone, though, and now I was beginning to worry.

Howard Cosell was waiting for me at the kitchen door, smiling his gloomy basset smile, thumping his basset tail ecstatically. I didn't have to be psychic to read the thought zipping through his basset brain: *Yay! Mom's home, just in time to rustle up a bedtime snack for her favorite doggie.*

I fondled his ears, pulled off my jacket and snowy boots, and put down a spoonful of dog food—just a tad, because Howard's supposed to be on a diet. Howard gave me a reproachful look, and I shook my head. "That's it, pal," I said. "We promised the vet you'd lose that spare tire around your middle. After that, we can discuss an increase in your rations."

The blinking light on the answering machine caught my eye and I reached for it. Well, good. Brian had left a message. Maybe there was something wrong with his cell phone. Maybe—

I had two messages, the machine advised me briskly. The first one wasn't Brian; it was Buddy. "Hey, China," he said, in a spirited voice, obviously forced. "Just thought I'd check to see if you had a chance to look over those letters this evening. If not, soon, I hope. I'm anxious to hear what you make of them, particularly the last two. There's something there we need to look into. When you've read them, I'm sure you'll want to talk."

He was sure, was he? Well, he was wrong, dead wrong. I wasn't anxious to talk to him. In fact, I would be extremely happy if I never saw or heard from the man again. As soon as I had the time, I intended to toss those letters into the fireplace, one at a time, and gleefully watch the flames turn them into ashes. And then I planned to forget all about them. Remorselessly, I punched the Erase button. Go to hell, Buddy Danforth.

The second message was from McQuaid. He was well, he was busy, he was getting to the bottom of it, he hoped to tie up all the loose ends and be home before long, and he loved us. And oh, by the way, he'd just re-membered that he had an appointment with the dentist, and would I mind rescheduling it for him. I played it again, for the pleasure of hear-ing my husband's voice, and then erased that message, too.

But nothing from Brian. Still wearing my jacket, I checked the phone book for the number at Barry's house. Barry's mother, Janet, comes into the shop frequently, and while we're not bosom buddies, we're at least on hello-how-are-you terms.

"Hey, Janet," I said cheerily, when she came on the line. "I was won-dering if you had heard from our intergalactic travelers."

"Excuse me?" Janet sounded perplexed.

"Brian and Barry. Have they checked in with you? I asked Brian to phone me when Joe picked them up at the Trekkie meeting, but I guess he forgot. I tried calling, but he seems to have turned off his cell phone." I put a smarmy smile into my voice, since I was about to ask a favor. "I was thinking that maybe Brian could stay at your house tonight. It's snowing up a storm, and the school bus will probably be late in the morning."

"I'm sorry, China," Janet said, in a tone that just missed being prissy, "but I have no idea what you're talking about. Barry has had a nasty cold for several days, so I told him he couldn't go to the meeting. And Joe is in Houston this week, so he couldn't have picked the boys up even if they *had* gone, which they didn't." And then, in that virtuous and sweetly superior tone one mother uses when speaking to another mother whose child has been publicly naughty, she added, "Of course, if Brian would like to stay tonight, he's more than—"

"Oh, gosh, thanks a bunch," I broke in quickly, covering my confusion with more smarm. "You're really sweet to offer. But we won't bother you. I must have misunderstood what Brian told me. Good night, Janet."

I hung up the phone. Something wasn't right here. Brian isn't a perfect kid, by any stretch of the imagination, but he's never given us any major trouble. Still, there was a first time for everything, and it looked like tonight was the night. I began mentally toting up his offenses. He hadn't gone where he said he was going. He wasn't with the friend he told me he'd be with, and the adult who was supposed to be giving him a ride was in Houston, for Pete's sake. Plus he had turned off his phone to keep me from reaching him—and on the worst night of the winter, too. Where the dickens *was* the little twerp? I punched in his cell number, angrily now. Still no answer.

Well, there was nothing I could do, at least at the moment. But I would be waiting when that boy got home, by golly. In fact, when he walked in that door, I would be sitting right here in my kitchen rocking chair with a comfy shawl around my shoulders, sipping a cozy cup of hot tea and reading a book. And when he did—

I gritted my teeth. When he did, young Mr. Brian was going to get exactly what was coming to him. No privileges for two weeks, and that included television, computer, and nights out. No, make that three weeks. It was time he learned a lesson.

I took off my jacket, hung it up on the peg by the door, and was putting on the kettle to brew that hot cup of tea when the phone rang. Ah, *there* he is, I thought fiercely, reaching for the receiver. Boy, was that kid ever going to get it. And if he gave me any smart mouth, he'd forfeit his privileges for a month. Detention, that's what it would be. School, home, and nothing else.

It wasn't Brian. It was Sheila. Her voice was brusque and businesslike, her cop's voice—but there was a different urgency in it, something I couldn't identify.

"China, we've got a serious problem."

My heart began to pound, and I forgot all about detention. Sheila wouldn't be phoning at this hour of the night and in that tone of voice unless the problem was *seriously* serious. My mind went first to McQuaid. But he was out of town, and—

"Who?" I managed. "What problem?"

"It's Brian."

I made some sort of inarticulate noise. Brian? Oh, god, not Brian! An accident. Brian had been in an accident! Lord, make him be all right, I prayed fervently, my anger completely extinguished by a wave of chilling fear.

"Where?" I asked. "Is he all okay?"

"Hang on, China," Sheila said. "There's something I gotta do."

Voices in the background, and then the wail of a siren, soft at first, then louder and louder. An emergency vehicle arriving—arriving where? At the scene of an accident? The sound of car doors slamming, an engine starting, the crackling of a police radio. Another siren. More voices. Somebody sobbing. A girl?

It was an accident. A car crash. Brian had been hurt. Brian was—

My fingers were clutching the receiver so hard that my knuckles were white. My heart was racing. My mouth was cotton-ball dry and I seemed to have stopped breathing. I sucked in a lungful of air, then another. Suppose he was . . . What would I tell McQuaid? There's a magnetic board on the wall next to the phone, where people are supposed to (but never do) leave phone messages. Stuck to the board was a heart-shaped magnet, with I LOVE YOU written on it. I focused my eyes on it. *I love you Brian love you love*

"Sorry, China." Sheila was back on the line. "It's kind of crazy here."

"Where is here?" I demanded through clenched teeth, steeling myself for the worst. *love you Brian love.* "What's happened?"

"Here is behind the high school football stadium, in the parking lot." Sheila paused for the space of two breaths. "What's happened is that somebody's been shot."

Shot? Behind the football stadium? I felt limp with relief. Well, that settled that. It wasn't an auto accident, thank you, God. And Brian never has anything to do with guns or drugs or any kind of criminal stuff. I frowned. But Sheila had said that this involved Brian, and—

I clutched the receiver, my eyes fixed on the red heart magnet. "Who got shot?"

"Coach Duffy. He's dead."

The heart blurred. I blinked, incredulous. "Duffy? Tim Duffy?"

"Yeah. The guy we were talking about this very afternoon. Golden Boy Duffy. Pride of the Panthers." Sheila's voice changed. "Abuser of young women."

I made a low sound in my throat. And then, breathless, blurted: "Who? Who shot him?"

"That's not entirely clear—yet. I haven't talked to the witnesses. But I thought you ought to be with Brian when we start questioning him. Unless you want to bring in another lawyer."

"Questioning Brian?" What did Brian have to do with Tim Duffy being shot? Unless—

I sucked in my breath, feeling as if I'd just been socked in the solar plexus. McQuaid collected guns. He had lots of them, too many of them, enough to start a war. But he always kept them locked up. And anyway, Brian couldn't. He *wouldn't*. He had absolutely no reason. He didn't know about Duffy's history. There must be some mistake. Some other Brian.

"You're not . . . you're not talking about *my* Brian, are you?"

"Yeah. Your Brian." Sheila paused, and her voice softened. "Listen, China. We've got a helluva mess here, and it's not going to get any better—especially after the press gets wind of it. The boy needs you. Get over here as quick as you can."

"Tell him I'm on my way," I said, and slammed down the receiver. I was back into my boots and jacket and halfway out to the car before I remembered my handbag and keys. I raced back to get them. I was out the door and down the steps when I remembered that the burner was still on under the kettle.

Howard Cosell sat in the middle of the floor, perplexed at this flurry of disorganized activity. As I flew out the door for the last time, he watched me go, his ears drooping apprehensively.

THE high school is on the south side of town, a twenty-minute drive from our house, more or less, depending on the traffic. East on Lime Kiln Road to the supermarket where we shop for groceries. Right at the light on Pedernales, left where it dead-ends into Jefferson at the sewage treatment plant. Then right again at the bridge over the Pecan River, where you can almost always catch a catfish or two on the wooded, sloping bank. No catfish tonight, and no catfish fishers, with the snow still coming down and the pavement glazing over. Colin was right—the snow would be gone by noon tomorrow. But tonight, my Toyota felt skittish, as if it were wearing ice skates instead of tires, especially on the bridge, where it went into a skid and barely saved itself from kissing the concrete railing.

I didn't let myself think while I was driving. I consciously switched off the thoughts, the stream of words that go through your head all the time, even when you're not listening to them. I turned off the feelings, too. The disbelief that comes when you hear that somebody you know is unexpectedly dead. The cold fear that comes when you're told that somebody you love is somehow involved in the death. Instead of thinking or feeling, I hunched over the steering wheel and gripped it as if it were a life preserver, as if it were the only thing saving me from being pulled into the swirling whirlpool of snowflakes I could see in my headlights. By the time I passed the big brick sign announcing PECAN SPRINGS HIGH SCHOOL, THE HEART OF OUR COMMUNITY, my fingers were permanently frozen on the wheel and I was shaking, inside and out.

There's a big circle drive in front of the school, where the buses park while they're loading and unloading kids. Vehicles had driven around the circle in the last few minutes, leaving dark tire tracks in the fresh white snow. I followed them blindly, past the main building, dark inside, brightly lit outside by security lights, and took the cut-off that goes around the back of the school, to the football field. Still following the tire tracks, still not thinking or feeling, I drove through an open gate in a chain link fence.

The parking lot was ahead. The near-side stadium lights were on, illuminating the untracked blanket of sparkling snow that covered the field from sideline to sideline and end zone to end zone. The goal posts and bleachers and light standards all wore snowy caps, and the blowing snow created rainbow halos around the lights. I saw a huddle of vehicles and uniformed officers at the far edge of the parking lot, where it butts up against the cinder track that circles the field. Everything was in black and white, except for where red emergency flashers turned the snow red, like puddles of blood. It looked like the set of one of those reality cop TV shows.

I followed the tire marks across the lot and slid to a stop behind a Pecan Springs police unit, barely missing its rear bumper. I got out. A silver pickup—a Ford crew cab truck—sat off to one side, both front doors ajar, the dome light on. Several police units were pulled up around the pickup, their emergency jack lights focused on it like beacons, their radios spilling cop chatter. A couple of uniforms were stringing yellow crime-scene tape in a large loop around the truck. An EMS unit was there, too, the back doors open, an empty gurney waiting for a body. Waiting for Tim Duffy's body.

I looked back at the pickup. That must be Duffy, that black shadow slumped over the steering wheel. I swallowed my disbelief. This wasn't something I was watching on a cop show. This was real. This man was *dead*, and somebody had shot him. Somebody. But not Brian. No, not Brian.

I caught a glimpse of a uniform I know, Odell Marshall, and hurried toward him, my boots crunching on the glittering snow. I raised my voice. "Where's the chief, Odell?"

He turned, saw me, and frowned. "Hey, China Bayles. What're you doin' out on a night like this?"

"Chief called me, asked me to come." Not knowing how much Odell knew about what had happened, I didn't mention Brian. "Where is she?"

"Coach's office." Odell nodded toward the field house, a square, squat concrete block building that stands between the field and the school. He rubbed one leather-gloved hand roughly across his face. A big black man, six-four, with a linebacker's shoulders, Odell isn't somebody you'd want to meet in a dark alley. But his eyes had teared up.

"Can you believe it?" he choked. "Somebody offed the coach. Shot him right through the heart. Don't make no sense. No sense a-tall."

Through the heart. My lips were so stiff I could barely frame the words. "Who? Who shot him?" Not Brian. No, not—

"Dunno. Just got here m'self. All I know is he's dead." Odell jerked his head in the direction of the field house. "The chief's got a coupla kids in custody. S'pose it was them." He snuffled and wiped his nose on the back of his glove. "Best friggin' coach in the whole friggin' state," he muttered, "and somebody friggin' blew him away. Makes you wonder what kids these days is comin' to, don't it? I mean, drugs and drive-bys is one thing, but killin' the coach is another."

My blood had chilled to slush. I opened my mouth to speak but fear had frozen my throat and nothing came out. I raised a hand, turned, and leaving Odell to his head-shaking grief, stumbled for the field house.

As I crossed the parking lot, a white van with a satellite dish on top barrelled through the gate, hot-rodded across the snowy lot, and skidded to a stop in front of me. I looked up. Hell, I thought disgustedly. That's all we need: a TV crew. Lights. Camera. Action.

A perky young woman in a faux-fur jacket and cap jumped out, confronting me. "We're from KVUE-TV in Austin," she announced in a chirpy tone, flashing a press badge in my face. "We were out on the Inter-state, covering a wreck, when we got a tip that a couple of kids'd shot the high school coach." She glanced toward the cluster of cop cars around the pickup. "Is it true?"

I swallowed and tried to speak, but my throat was still frozen.

She turned back to me. "Is it true? Is he dead?"

I found my voice. "I have no idea," I growled. "But you'd better clear it with Chief Dawson before you put anything on the air." Sheila would want to keep a lid on things as long as possible—although it didn't look like that was going to be very long, now that the media was here. But I might as well not have bothered to open my mouth.

The reporter had dashed back to the truck. "Hey, Dick," she said to the driver. "Call the station and tell them we've got breaking news." Her voice was brimming with excitement. "Looks like some kids killed the coach. Nothing official yet, but get us an up-link and air time. Pronto."

"Hey!" Odell yelled, striding toward the van, one arm upraised. "What d'ya think you're doin'? Y'all shut them doors and keep them cameras in that truck. No pichurs 'less the chief says so."

Leaving the reporter and her camera man to argue it out with Odell—an argument with a foregone conclusion—I broke into a run. Reaching the field house, I ducked through the door, only to be strong-armed by a female cop.

"Nobody comes in here," she said, one hand firmly on my sleeve, her square body blocking my forward progress. She felt as big as a house, and just as sturdy. "Order of the chief of police."

I thrust out my jaw. "Back off," I said, in a low, tough voice. "You are holding my minor child. I am an attorney. You don't let me through, you've got trouble, big-time."

I don't know whether the officer was merely surprised or actually bullied, but she stepped back. I strode purposefully down the brightly lit hall, past the Pecan Springs Football Wall of Fame, hung with photos of handsome boys with slim hips and shoulders grotesquely exaggerated by outsize pads, decorated with red crepe-paper streamers and construction-paper hearts. Across the hall was strung a banner that read ♥VALENTINE'S DANCE FRIDAY NIGHT♥. And beyond that, on the right, stood a soldierly row of glass-topped pedestals displaying game balls, over which hung coaches' photos, larger than the boys'. Tim Duffy's was the largest of all, framed with red crepe-paper ruffles and topped with a huge heart struck through with a silver arrow shot by a coy cardboard cupid with a bow.

I didn't have far to go. Just past Duffy's photo, on my right, a soft drink machine stood at attention, humming efficiently. Past that, an open door. The Athletic Department office. Inside, I saw Sheila, dressed in a beige wool suit and matching cashmere turtleneck, her ash-blond hair caught up on one side with a tortoiseshell comb. She might have been a Houston deb out for a night on the town, or a young society matron headed for a charity do in Dallas. She was perched on the corner of a desk, kicking one high-heeled foot and talking on her cell phone—Coach Duffy's desk, I guessed, from the glamour photo of Glenda Duffy on the credenza. Sheila looked up and saw me as I came through the door, clicked off the phone, and dropped it into the Gucci bag on the desk beside her.

"Glad you're here," she said, getting off the desk and coming toward me. "I need to talk to Brian as soon as possible."

"Where is he?" I demanded roughly. "Is he okay?"

Sheila nodded to a smaller windowed office, off to the side. An assistant coach's cubby, probably. "He's in there, with Officer Murdock."

Murdock. Murdock. "Sophie Murdock?" The officer who had investigated Angela Lopez's death.

"Right. He's fine. Just a little upset. I'm hoping he'll calm down when he sees you, and we can get him to answer a few questions."

A *little* upset? Through the window, I could see that Brian's face was streaked with tears, his expression anguished. Physically, at least, he looked unharmed. Questioning, however, was another matter entirely. Nobody, not even my friend Smart Cookie, was going to question my son about a shooting death until I was certain that I knew exactly what the situation was. And maybe not even then.

I narrowed my eyes. "I saw Odell outside. He said Duffy was shot through the heart. Who was the shooter? Have you got the gun?"

"We don't know who the shooter was. And no, we haven't got the gun." Sheila crossed her arms and put her head on one side, regarding me. "We haven't even got the full story. We won't, until I can talk to Brian and hear what—"

"I want to know what happened, as far as you know it. Right now."

Sheila frowned. "Look, China, I really can't—"

"Look, Chief Dawson," I snapped. "I understand that you want to question my minor son. I can assure you that he will cooperate fully with your investigation, when the time comes. But you are not asking question one until I know exactly as much as you do about what went on out there in that parking lot tonight. Brian and I are not walking into this blind." I pointed my finger at her. "You got that?"

She sighed. "Yeah. I got it, Counselor." She leaned her fanny against the desk. "Okay, you want it, here it is. From what we can tell—from something we heard them say—it looks like the kids set Duffy up."

I clenched my jaw against a rising incredulity. Set Duffy up? Set him up to *shoot* him? Nonsense. No way. Whatever Brian had been up to, that was not it. He had more sense than that. I pulled in my breath. But maybe the kid he was with—

"Who's the other boy?"

Sheila shook her head. "Not a boy, China. A girl. Jacquelyn Keene." She nodded toward another windowed office, where I saw a uniformed policewoman seated at a table with her arm around a pretty blond girl, who was sobbing against her shoulder. "Her parents went to the Spurs game in San Antonio tonight. No cell phone, so they can't be reached for permission. There's not a chance in hell that I can talk to her in the next couple of hours. So that leaves Brian."

Jacquelyn? Startled, I looked again.

And then, suddenly, out of the chaotic whirlwind of the entire day's events, the pieces fell into place. Jacquelyn was Jackie, the high school student Angela Lopez had met in the volunteer program. The girl, according to Christie and Tyler, who was Tim Duffy's next target.

And Jackie was Brian's girlfriend. Jake, who had wept in my kitchen, who had told Brian that there was nothing he could do to help, that he mustn't get involved, that she would have to handle it alone.

But in the end, Brian hadn't let Jake handle it alone. He had persuaded her to let him help, and the two of them had come up with some sort of cockeyed scheme to trap the coach—at least that's what I was guessing. Maybe Jake had agreed to meet Duffy in the parking lot, and Brian was there to witness the encounter. Maybe Jake had somehow gotten hold of a gun and planned to use it to scare him. Maybe she didn't know it was loaded. Maybe—

I shivered, feeling very cold. No. Not a gun. Brian and Jake weren't stupid, individually or collectively. Whatever else they planned to do tonight—trap Duffy, scare him, make him leave her alone—neither Brian nor Jake would have, *could* have intended to threaten him with a gun, much less shoot him. It wasn't possible. I knew these kids. I'd stake my life on their innocence, if not their common sense.

Sheila was studying me. She turned to look at Jake, then back at me. "So. You know that girl, do you, China? And you know what she and Brian were up to?"

"She's Brian's girlfriend." I tightened my jaw, narrowed my eyes. "Whatever they were up to, she didn't shoot Duffy. And neither did Brian. Period. Paragraph. End of story."

"Oh, hey, we *know* that!" Sheila said quickly. She put out her hand, her eyes wide. "You didn't think . . . you couldn't—"

"Of course not." I straightened my shoulders, took two deep breaths, tried to appear nonchalant. "I know those kids better than that. But I had no idea what *you* thought. Not a clue, Chief."

"I am so sorry," Sheila said, shaking her head. "I should have finished the story. Look. Here's what we think we know. The girl—Jacquelyn—was in the pickup with the coach. Brian was behind the corner of the field house, with a digital camera."

Photos. A camera! The relief was making me giddy, and I almost laughed. So Brian *was* aiming to shoot the coach. To shoot his picture. A compromising picture. A picture that Jake could use as evidence, or maybe threaten to use as evidence. Sheila had been right. It had been a setup.

"Things were going pretty much according to plan," Sheila went on. "Brian came up behind the pickup while Duffy was putting a serious make on the girl. Brian was set to take a picture, when somebody walked up to the driver's side window and tapped on it. Duffy turned around and she shot him twice, in the heart."

"*She?*"

"Yeah. Brian had his cell phone in his pocket. He called nine-one-one. He and the girl were waiting when the first unit arrived. There. You know as much as I do." She tilted her head to one side, regarding me ironically. "*Now* are you ready for me to question Brian?"

It looked like I didn't have any choice.

Chapter Sixteen

According to Daniel E. Moerman, in *Native American Ethnobotany*, the Ponca Indians of South Dakota and Nebraska used the herb bloodroot (*Sanguinaria canadensis*) as a love charm. The Micmac Indians (Nova Scotia, Prince Edward Island, and New Brunswick) used this plant both as an aphrodisiac and (if it worked a little too well) an abortifacient.

"Mom!" Brian cried. He jumped out of his chair and flung himself into my arms, sobbing wildly. "Oh, Mom, I'm so sorry! I didn't mean to—"

It wasn't necessary for the police to hear what he hadn't meant to do. I put my hand over his mouth, gathering him tight against me, his grief tumultuous, his tears burning hot on my neck. I had to remind myself that he was fifteen.

"It's okay, Brian," I said, holding him. "It's going to be all right. I'm here now, and we'll get this all straightened out."

Officer Murdock, a handsome black woman with remarkable dimples and short-clipped, wiry gray hair, handed me a box of tissues. I took a handful and began to dab at Brian's face. "Maybe something cold and wet?" I suggested to her. In the background, I was aware that Sheila was talking on her phone, speaking in a low voice. "And a soft drink?"

The officer nodded and disappeared, coming back a moment later with a terry hand towel, wrung out, and a cold can of Coke. Brian mopped his face and head with the towel, making spikes of his dark hair. I popped the top of the can and handed it to him, noticing that his digital camera—the one Leatha and Sam had given him for Christmas—was on the desk.

"Better?" I asked.

He swigged the Coke. "Yeah." His shoulders weren't heaving, although his face was still mottled, his eyes puffy from crying. "Have you talked to Dad?"

"Not yet. I thought we'd clear up as much of this as we could before we bring him into it—especially since he can't get here right away."

"Yeah. I just thought that since he used to be a cop, he'd know . . ." He lifted his gaze, dark with concern. "Have you seen Jake? How's she holding up?"

"I saw her at a distance. She's upset, of course, but otherwise she looks okay. The chief doesn't want to talk to her until her parents get here." Sheila had finished her call and put her phone back in her bag.

"Yeah. They're at the Spurs game. They won't be home for a couple of hours." Brian finished the soda and set it down, looking from me to Sheila, whom he has met as an occasional guest at our house. He was standing a little taller. "I guess you want me to tell you about it."

"Yes," Sheila said. "This needs to be official. That's why your mom is here."

Brian grinned wryly. "I thought she was my lawyer. Are you going to read me my rights?"

"She is not going to read anything," I said firmly. "You're not under arrest, and you're going to cooperate."

"Okay," Brian said. "I was just making a joke, sort of." He sighed. "I guess this isn't a good time for jokes, huh?"

Sheila gestured at one of the chairs. "Why don't you sit there, Brian?" She sat on the edge of the desk. Officer Murdock went to the corner of the room, where Brian couldn't see her, and took out a notebook.

I took the chair beside Brian. "Chief Dawson is going to ask you some questions. If I think a question is inappropriate or if for any reason— any reason at all—I don't want you to answer it, I'll say so. Otherwise, I expect you to answer truthfully. I may have a few questions of my own, as well. And Officer Murdock is making a record of the conversation. Okay?"

He turned to look at Murdock. She gave him a thumbs-up and a flash of a dimpled grin. He turned back. "Yeah. Sure." He licked his lips apprehensively. My gut clenched. I was as nervous as he was, except that I was experienced enough not to show it.

Sheila leaned forward. "Okay. Let's start with the plan."

"The plan?" he asked uneasily.

"Yes. What did you and Jacquelyn—Jake—expect to happen tonight?"

Brian hesitated, choosing his words carefully. "We weren't exactly sure, I guess. The coach had been after Jake to . . . get together with him, outside of school. Finally she said yes, and told him tonight would be good. She was supposed to be waiting for him. They were . . . he said they were just going to sit in his truck and talk."

"Talk about what?" Sheila asked.

He shifted uncomfortably. "About what was going on. About how the coach . . . how he felt about her."

"Which was?"

He bit his lip and shot a glance at me. "Am I supposed to say? I mean, all I know is what Jake told me."

"Chief Dawson will ask her what she thought," I said. "Right now, we'd like to hear what *you* understood was going on. Your impressions of the situation." I managed a smile. "It's okay, Brian," I said quietly. "We have to know."

Brian thought about that for a moment. Then he sighed, took a deep breath, and it all came out in a rush. Sometime around Christmas, Jake had told him that the coach was after her—"hitting on her," as Brian put it, and that this had been going on for a couple of months. When it first began, she was flattered. ("Who wouldn't be?" Brian said. "After all, he's the coach.") She had flirted back, which was sort of fun. It made her feel special, and different, and older. Anyway, there was no harm in flirting.

But after a while, it stopped feeling like fun, Brian said, and Jake began going out of her way to avoid Duffy—which wasn't easy, since she was on the girls soccer and volleyball teams, and he hung around practice a lot, watching. And then she got involved with a volunteer program at the Adams County Hospital—Candy Canes, or something like that—working with sick kids. She became friends with one of the older volunteers, a college student. Her name was Angie.

So *that* was it! Angie must have been working in the program Carol Bruce had mentioned earlier that evening. The Candy Stripers program. Although now, of course, that information wasn't necessary, since we knew that Jake was the girl Angie had called Jackie.

"Angie." Sheila glanced at me, and I knew she was remembering our conversation that afternoon. She looked back at Brian. "You're talking about Angela Lopez, I assume."

Brian frowned. "You'll have to ask Jake. The only name I ever heard was Angie."

"It was Angela Lopez, all right," I said to Sheila. "I got a few more of the details when I talked to Tyler Cole this afternoon."

Brian swiveled to stare at me, surprised. "You *know* about this?"

"I know about part of it," I said. "Go on, son. You're doing a good job."

Brian nodded and complied. Angie told Jake that she had known the coach when she was in high school, not in Pecan Springs, but in the school where Duffy had coached before. She told Jake that Duffy had maneuvered her into the same situation, first with little flatteries, then with larger ones, finally telling her that he was crazy about her. She kept trying to say no, but he wouldn't leave her alone, and after a while she gave in and let him do whatever he wanted. Now, she wished she hadn't done it. She felt cheap, she said. Like a prostitute. She had tried to talk to a couple of friends, but they thought she was making it up just to seem important. She attempted to confess to her priest, but he wouldn't listen. He told her that the story was a product of her own sinful imagination and lectured her on the dangers of spreading sick rumors about such an outstanding man.

Officer Murdock cleared her throat. Sheila gave a despairing shake of the head, and I felt sick. Everyone had let Angela down—her friends, her school, her church. The only person who had stood up for her was her mother, but in the end, Mrs. Lopez had been as powerless as her daughter. In the end, Angela had had no defenders.

Brian made an effort to look confident. "I felt really sad when I heard about this girl," he said. "Angie, I mean. But I wasn't worried about Jake. I knew she'd never let this jerk treat her like that. When she got tired of putting up with his bullshit, she'd figure out a way to make him stop. Then she came up with this plan." He paused, and slid me a glance. "We did, I mean. I helped."

"But if Jake wanted it to stop," I put in reasonably, "why didn't she just blow the whistle? Why did she have to resort to pickup-truck dates and cameras?"

"Well, be*cause,*" Brian said. His look told me that this had been a very dumb question.

"Because why, specifically?" Sheila asked.

Brian refrained from rolling his eyes. "Because she knew nobody would believe her, any more than people believed that other girl. They'd accuse her of making it up." He appealed earnestly to me. "I mean, *look,* Mom. The coach is the most popular guy in this whole town. Haven't you been to any of the pep rallies or Booster Club meetings?"

I acknowledged that I had not had that opportunity.

"Well, he is," Brian said, then corrected himself, with a hangdog look. "*Was,* I mean. Everybody loved him. Nobody would ever believe he was hitting on Jake. It would be her word against his, and she's just a kid."

The sad voice of practical wisdom. "So what happened to make her decide that she had to do something?" I asked.

Brian laced his fingers together. "She read in the paper that the other girl killed herself—Angie, I mean. That . . . well, it scared her, I think."

"It scared her?" Sheila asked. She raised both eyebrows. "Why?"

"Because after that happened, there wasn't anything flattering or funny about it anymore. It was really serious, a matter of life and death. Jake knew she wouldn't end up killing herself, but what would happen if the coach started hitting on some other girl? She might not be strong like Jake. She might end up like Angie. Jake wanted to talk to somebody— Ms. Simon or one of the counselors—but it was just her word. She didn't have any evidence."

"The coach didn't write to her, or send her any email?" Sheila asked.

Brian shook his head. "He told her it was too dangerous."

"Angela had quite a few letters," I said wryly. "I think he must have learned not to leave the evidence lying around."

"So," Sheila said. She folded her arms. "Having no evidence, you and Jacquelyn decided to obtain some. Is that it?"

"Yeah." Brian ducked his head. "Maybe it sounds dumb now, but that was our plan. Jake would agree to get together with him, in his truck, behind the school, and I would take their pictures. We figured that tonight would be the best night to do it. Jake's folks were going to the Spurs game, and I—" He gave me a shamefaced look. "I could say I was at the Trekkie meeting in Austin. That way, I could stay out until ten o'clock."

"Why the truck?" Sheila asked. "And why behind the school?"

"Because we figured I could sneak up on the truck easier. And here—" He shrugged. "It's closer to Jake's house, for one thing. We could stash our bikes close by and run for them after we got the photos. And I guess it seemed safer, sort of. You don't think anything's going to happen at school." He shivered. "Especially somebody getting shot."

Sheila frowned. "Who else knew about your plan?"

Brian looked up at her. "Nobody," he said earnestly. "I swear it. We didn't dare tell a soul—we were too scared of a foul-up. It might look like we were . . . like Jake was trying to . . ." He bit his lip. "Well, you know. Like she was coming on to him, to cause trouble."

I understood. But I also understood what was behind Sheila's question. Somebody had shot Duffy. Was it just coincidence that it had happened at that moment, or did his killer know where Duffy was going to be?

"You waited for him, then?" Sheila asked.

"Yeah. We hid out in the library after everybody left school. It's not hard to do when you know your way around this place. When we got hungry, we bought some chips and candy and stuff out of the vending machines, and hung out inside the field house door until we saw him drive up. He was supposed to be here at eight. But he was late, and we had to wait longer than we thought."

"What time did he finally get here?" Sheila asked.

"About nine. We saw his truck, and Jake went out. I went out by the side door and around the building, with my camera. It was snowing pretty hard. He'd turned off his lights, and the stadium lights were out. The only light was the security light by the back door. By the time I got out there, Jake was in the truck."

Sheila leaned forward, her eyes intent. "Did you see anybody else?"

"Not really." He frowned. "Well, maybe. Sort of. As I was going out the side door, I saw some car lights, out by the gate. But it looked like the car was only turning around, so I didn't think any more about it. I was pretty worried about what was going on in the truck. I didn't want anything to happen to Jake—he's a big guy, and strong. But we wanted to get some good evidence, so she was going to have to let him do . . . something."

I regarded him with respect. It was a large dilemma for a pair of young kids. But even in a town the size of Pecan Springs, young people are presented with some pretty formidable decisions: whether to have sex, for instance, or do drugs, or smoke, or cheat on their homework. Whatever they do or don't do is risky, it seems. Youngsters these days become adults, and confront adult choices, far too fast. Brian and Jake had taken a very large risk, and had gotten into something that was much more frightening than they could imagine.

"So Jake was in the truck," Sheila said matter-of-factly, "and you were waiting to get a photo. Then what happened?"

"Well, I was supposed to go outside and wait until I heard Jake yell something like 'No, I don't want to.' And then I was going to run up to the truck and take a picture through the windshield. I set the focus at four feet, so the flash wouldn't screw it up. I figured I'd maybe get two or three shots of her fighting him off before he could jump out of the truck and chase me." He grinned ruefully. "It might take him longer if he had to zip up first."

I shuddered at the phrase, delivered with such an adult sangfroid. Brian was just fifteen, for Pete's sake! He was still a child. But child or no, he was embroiled in a very adult situation. "What were you going to do then?" I asked.

He picked up the empty soda can and turned it between his fingers. "Like I say, we figured he'd chase me, so I propped the side door open. I was supposed to run into the field house, duck through the school, and out the main door. I'd get my bike and ride down the jogging trail to Jake's house, which is only a couple of blocks if you go that way. When Duffy jumped out to chase me, Jake was supposed to jump out of the truck, too—only she'd stashed her bike beside the music room door. We figured the jogging trail would be good, because if we rode down the street, he'd catch up to us." He put the can back on the table. "Of course, we didn't know it was going to snow, which changed everything. I'm not sure we could have ridden the bikes in the snow, but we didn't get a chance to find out." He sighed. "Coach never got out of the truck."

Sheila cleared her throat. "What happened next?"

"I heard Jake hollering, and I figured it was time. So I ran around the pickup to get a picture."

"Which side of the truck were you on?" I asked.

"The passenger side. But you know what? I couldn't get a picture! I could sorta see Jake in the truck, pushing him away, but the windows were already steamed up, and there was no way I could do what I was supposed to do. I was trying to decide whether to jerk the door open and get Jake out of there, when I saw somebody on the other side of the truck. A shadow, really. It sort of raised up, like it'd been crouching down, and tapped on the driver's side window."

"This was the first time you knew the other person was there?" Sheila asked.

"Yeah. I thought maybe it was the cops, and Jake and I would be in some serious trouble."

"How did Duffy react?" I asked.

"It scared him. He jerked around to see who it was. And then there was this really loud bang and—" He covered his ears with his hands, as if he could still hear it. "Then there was another bang. Jake was screaming and trying to get out of the truck. I just sort of aimed the camera and shot. When the flash went off, I got a glimpse of her."

Sheila's expression became intense. "*Her?* A girl? Another student?"

That made sense. No telling how many girls Duffy had been fooling around with while he was waiting for Jake to fall into line. Perhaps one of them had discovered that he was meeting Jake and was jealous enough— and crazy enough—to come after him with a gun. An icy horror shivered up my spine. And she might not have stopped with Duffy. She might have shot Jake and Brian, too, and maybe even turned the gun on herself. We could have had four dead bodies out there in the snow.

"A girl?" Brian shook his head, frowning. "I don't think so. She had a hood or something over her head. The hood of a coat, I mean. It was pulled forward, like she meant to hide her face. But I thought it was a woman. An older woman."

An older woman? Of course, anybody over eighteen was an "older woman" to Brian, but another possibility had popped into my mind. Maybe Glenda Duffy had discovered that her husband was fooling around, and decided to take matters into her own hands. She would certainly have a motive, and she might have followed him, or known where he was going to be.

But that was silly, I scoffed. I couldn't believe that cool, composed Glenda Duffy would have summoned enough jealousy and anger to commit a crime of passion, especially in front of Duffy's companion. She might not have been caught, but her dead husband would have been found by the police, if not in flagrante delicto, then certainly in a compromising situation, and with a teenager, to boot. His sexual transgressions would be all over town in a couple of nanoseconds, for while the Seidenstickers might control the headlines in the *Enterprise*, the family-owned newspaper, they couldn't control Pecan Springs' other means of mass communication, the grapevine. No. However angry Glenda Duffy might be at her husband, she would not put the Seidensticker name in jeopardy by shooting him.

Sheila was reaching for Brian's digital camera, which sat on the desk. "You say you saw her when the flash went off. Did you check to see whether you were able to get a recognizable image?"

Brian shook his head. "I was too busy. The shooter ran off as soon as I took the picture. Jake was screaming about blood, and I was trying to call nine-one-one and—" He gave me a helpless look, and his voice squeaked. "Jake and me, we didn't have any idea that there was going to be a shooting. You've got to believe me, Mom. We would never have done anything like—"

"Of course I believe you," I said. I turned to see Sheila monkeying with the camera, trying to turn it on. "That's the power switch," I told her, pointing. "And then you click that little button to Play. And then you hit the Menu button, to make it go back to the last picture. You'll see it in the view screen."

Sheila made a face and handed me the camera. "All these cameras are different. You do it."

I turned on the camera, clicked the buttons, and brought up a picture on the view screen. It was the blurry image of a woman, half of her face hidden by the hood of her coat. But there was no mistaking who it was. I knew who had shot Tim Duffy—and in a way, I couldn't blame her.

"Take a look," I said grimly, handing the camera to Sheila.

Sheila studied the view screen. "Anybody you know?" she asked.

I sucked in my breath. "Yes, I'm afraid I do. I—"

"What's going on here?" a woman demanded. I turned to see Lisa Simon, framed in the doorway, clutching her coat tight around her. She was trying to maintain control, but I could hear the tremor in her voice. "Somebody phoned and said there'd been a shooting. I got here as soon as I could. What're all those vehicles out in the parking lot? What's happened?"

"I was the one who phoned," Sheila said, stepping forward. "I'm Chief Dawson. I'm sorry to tell you that Coach Duffy was shot. He's dead."

"Dead!" Lisa exclaimed in horror. "Oh, no!" Her hand went to her mouth.

Sheila nodded. "You might want to notify the appropriate school district officials as soon as possible. There's a TV crew outside right now, and we can't stop them from broadcasting, although they're not supposed to reveal any of the details. I've sent one of our officers to tell Mrs. Duffy. It's going to be a shock to everyone, and the sooner we get on with the notifications, the better."

Lisa looked at Brian, her eyes widening. "Oh, my God," she whispered.

"Brian, you didn't . . . you couldn't—" She swallowed. "And I saw Jacquelyn Keene out there, in the other office. She wasn't involved, was she?" She cast a pleading look at Sheila. "It was an accident, wasn't it?" And then, without stopping to hear the answer, said, "An accident. Yes. It had to be an accident."

I put my arm across Brian's shoulders. "Brian and Jacquelyn witnessed the shooting," I said, "but they had nothing to do with it. And no, it wasn't an accident. I'm afraid this is going to be very messy, Lisa. It's—"

"Not an accident?" Lisa cried frantically. "Who did it? Why? It wasn't a student, was it?" Her voice became shrill and she reached for the back of a chair. "Oh, God! Don't tell me he was shot by a *student!*"

"No," I said quietly. "He wasn't shot by a student. He was shot by Angela Lopez's mother."

Chapter Seventeen

The evergreen rosemary is the symbol of faithfulness and fidelity
in marriage, and of the married couple's never-ending desire for
one another.

What happened after that was mostly anticlimactic. I gave
Sheila the address of Margarita Lopez's house in Friendship,
and a description of the car I had seen in her driveway—a mid-eighties
Mercury Marquis, maroon. Sheila phoned an APB on the car to the Texas
state police and a request for assistance to the Friendship police, asking
them to watch the Lopez house.

Lisa Simon said she wanted to see the coach's body for herself, but
when she got out to the truck, she decided she didn't, so she went to her
office to call the school superintendent and Claude Leglar, the lawyer who
decided there wasn't enough on Duffy to open a formal investigation.

Odell came in to say that the TV crew was giving him all kinds of
bullshit about going on the air with breaking news, and the chief went
out to deal with them. I went to my car and fetched Angela's teddy bear,
with its Denver Broncos football stuffed full of incriminating letters, and
gave it to Officer Murdock. The letters were part of the body of evidence
that would go into the prosecutor's case against Mrs. Lopez. Ironically,
they'd be an important part of the defense's case, too, since they were so

clearly an indictment of Tim Duffy and his extracurricular relationships with underage girls. I could see the headlines now: MOTHER KILLS COACH WHO MOLESTED DAUGHTER. This was going to be an explosive case, but it probably wouldn't be tried in Pecan Springs. Duffy was the town's Golden Boy, and feeling was going to run high against the woman who killed him.

Jake's mother and father arrived and were tearfully reunited with their daughter. When Sheila got back from dealing with the television reporter, she was confronted by the Keenes, demanding to know the full story. Smart Cookie had just begun to explain the situation when Odell came back into the office to say that while the first TV crew had packed up and left, a second had just driven up, and did the chief want to do another interview?

And at that point, Judge Maude Porterfield, justice of the peace, arrived to inspect the crime scene. In addition to issuing search and arrest warrants, holding traffic and small claims court, and performing marriages (the judge married McQuaid and me), Texas law requires that a JP rule on every suspicious death. Judge Porterfield has presided over a great many of these cases, although she usually withholds her final ruling until she's seen the medical examiner's report. She has served Adams County for half of her seventy-five-plus years. Her right knee can't always be trusted, and she wears a hearing aid, but the rest of her operates at an optimum level. She is sharp as a tack and (as we say in Texas) she don't take no bull from nobody.

"Evenin', Chief," the judge said to Sheila, adding, "Same to you, Miz Bayles," to me. She pulled off her gloves and fished a handkerchief out of her coat pocket. "Cold as a witch's tit tonight." She took off her gold-rimmed bifocals and began to polish them.

212

I tried not to smile, since the occasion did not allow for smiling. "Pretty cold," I agreed. The judge and I are on first-name terms, but when she's on a case, she's all business.

"You need me out there, Judge?" Sheila asked, her cell phone in her hand.

"Nope," the judge said, putting her glasses back on her nose and the handkerchief back in her pocket. "Figger I can pretty much see what happened if I use my eyes—now that I got my spectacles clean." She shook her head. "Hard to believe, though. Fine, upstanding man like that. Why, he got the Chamber's Lifetime Achievement Award just last week—I know that for a fact, 'cause I handed it to him m'self. Big silver cup, with an inscription. Big check, too."

"Pillar of the community," I murmured dryly, passing up the opportunity to remark that the coach's lifetime had turned out to be fairly short.

The judge gave me a look. "Well, I guess somebody didn't think so, unless it was simple robbery. Shot him through the truck window, huh? Any idea whodunnit?"

"We have a photograph," Sheila said, punching a number into her phone. "It was taken just seconds after the shooting. And there were witnesses. But no, the motive wasn't robbery."

"Golly," the judge replied approvingly, pulling off her knitted wool cap and ruffling her sparse white hair with one thin hand. "Witnesses and a photo. That oughtta make Howie happier 'n a hog in a mud hole." Howie Masterson is the recently elected Adams County district attorney. "Who was he? Can you tell from the photo?"

Sheila was speaking into the phone, so I answered. "He was a she. Margarita Lopez, from Friendship."

213

"Ah-ha," Judge Porterfield said. She wiggled her sparse white eyebrows at me. "Same family as the Lopez girl you phoned me about today, I s'pose. Sorry I wasn't in the office to get your call." She paused. "There's a connection between the Lopez suicide and this killin', you reckon?"

Carrying her phone, Sheila walked out into the main office, motioning to me to go on with the conversation.

"Yes, there's a connection," I said. "Margarita Lopez is Angela Lopez's mother. When you get some time, Judge, I'd like to talk about the girl's death."

"Tomorrow," the judge said, putting her wool hat back on and pulling it over her ears with both hands. "Give me a call and we'll set a time to get together. I gotta go to work now. We need to get that body outta here before it freezes." She grinned to show that she was making a little joke, pulled on her gloves, and left, a glint in her eye and a jaunty spring in her step. Judge Porterfield is some three decades older than I am, but she never seems to run out of steam. And she does enjoy her job, even when it involves dead bodies.

By that time, it was after midnight. With Sheila's permission, I took Brian, collected his bicycle from the front of the building, and maneuvered it into the trunk of the Toyota. And then we drove home—carefully, because although it had stopped snowing, the streets were glassy. Brian didn't say much, and I didn't either.

When we got home, I made some hot chocolate and got out the cookie jar. We sat at the table and I told him, as gently as I could, what I knew about Angela Lopez's relationship to the coach, and that Mrs. Lopez must have followed Coach Duffy and shot him because she blamed him for her daughter's death. We wouldn't know the whole truth until she told her side of it, of course. But that's what it looked like to me.

He listened carefully, sipping his chocolate and munching a cookie.

"It's just so hard to believe," he said at last. "I mean, I was there when she shot him, and I still don't believe it. The kids at school—they're not going to believe it, either. And they're going to be mad at Jake and me. Lots of them will think we knew he was going to be shot."

There was nothing I could say to refute that. Brian was right. Given Duffy's status in the community, there would always be a certain number of people, teens and adults, who blamed Brian and Jake for Duffy's death. Regardless of the facts, people were going to spin all kinds of stories. They were likely to make things very uncomfortable for both kids, in small ways and large. It would be difficult for Brian, but probably much harder for Jake.

I cleared my throat and said the only thing I could think of. "They'll get over it."

It didn't sound at all comforting or convincing, even to me, but Brian only nodded. "Yeah. Well, just the same, I think I'd like to stay home tomorrow if it's okay with you."

"It's okay," I said. "But you and Jake will have to face people sooner or later, you know. You can't put it off forever."

"I know," he said bleakly. "Just tomorrow." He gave me a sideways glance. "I wish I could call Jake, but I know it's not a good idea. Her mom wouldn't let me talk to her, anyway."

I chuckled. "You're probably right there. When your dad gets home, we'll sit down with Jake and her parents and talk this whole thing out. I want them to know that we're behind the two of you, all the way."

He brightened at that, and squared his shoulders. "Yeah, good idea. Thanks, Mom."

I put my hand over his. "Jake will survive," I said. "And so will you.

The people who know you will understand that you had nothing to do with Duffy's death, and those who don't won't matter, in the long haul. You're both strong, and you've got good heads on your shoulders. You'll get past this."

I hugged him very hard, then, and kissed him and sent him off to bed. Then I went into the bedroom I share with McQuaid and closed the door. It had been an utterly awful evening, and the utter awfulness of it was going to hang over us like a cloud until Duffy's killer was apprehended and brought to trial. It wouldn't take long to find and arrest Mrs. Lopez. But the trial was months away, and after that, the appeals—Brian was right. The kids would be exonerated, but there would always be people who thought that the coach had been set up, and that Brian and Jake had been somehow complicit in his murder. The two of them might be in college before this ugly affair was settled and they could get on with their lives.

Howard was asleep on the bed, and I pushed him over to make room for me. I stripped off my clothes and pulled my old pink T-shirt over my head, the one I sleep in. I crawled under the covers, but there was something I had to do before I could go to sleep. I picked up the handset on the phone beside the bed and punched in McQuaid's hotel room in Albuquerque. It was an hour later there, Mountain Time. He was still up, watching television.

"We need to talk," I said soberly, and gave him an account—as concise as I could make it—of the entire Lopez-Duffy matter, ending with a report of what had gone down tonight, and Brian's part in it. He listened carefully, with muted exclamations of disgust and horror, with a heartfelt "Oh, shit," at the end.

"So I guess it's all over but the shouting," I said, wrapping up my story. "Sheila was dealing with the Keenes and the media when Brian and I left. Maude Porterfield was doing her JP thing. And Lisa Simon was calling the superintendent and the district lawyer." Cradling the phone against my shoulder, I reached over to turn up the electric blanket another notch. "I'd like to have heard what Claude Leglar said when she told him."

McQuaid asked the cop's natural question. "Have they caught Lopez yet?"

"No, but they will. There can't be too many of those old maroon Mercurys on the road. And if they don't stop her on the highway, they'll pick her up when she gets home."

"How's Brian?"

"He's pretty shaken. It's just beginning to dawn on him that people are going to think that he and Jake were involved with the shooting. And of course, the plan that the kids cooked up was stupid and dangerous—but I'll let you tell him that when you get home."

"You will, will you?" he remarked. "How come I get that duty?"

"Oh, I'll be right behind you," I said. "It's important for parents to put on a united front when it comes to discipline, don't you think?" Without stopping, I added, "Don't be too hard on him. He kept his head through the whole thing. If it hadn't been for him and his camera, there wouldn't be a photo of the shooter."

"Yeah." McQuaid sounded as relieved as I felt. "Conclusive, is it?"

"Absolutely. With that as evidence, maybe she'll be persuaded to plead, and the kids won't have to testify at the trial. Without it— Well, she might have gotten away with murder. Nobody would have suspected her."

There was a dry chuckle. "Geez, China," McQuaid said. "I don't know how you manage to get into so much trouble when I'm not around."

"Hey, wait," I said indignantly. "I didn't get into trouble. I just—"

"Yeah, I know. It's just your dumb luck that you talk to Mrs. Lopez on Monday and she kills the coach on Wednesday." Another chuckle. "And in between, you interview enough of the principals to put the whole story together, so that when Lopez blows Duffy away, you can tell the police what happened, and who and how and why."

"Well," I said defensively, "I personally think it's a good thing that I met Mrs. Lopez, because I could identify her from Brian's photo. And that I talked to Christie and Tyler, because that was what gave us the link between Jake and Angie. And—"

"Hey, you," McQuaid said tenderly, "it's okay. I was just teasing. It's lucky for Sheila that you could fill in the blanks. And lucky for me that you were there for Brian." He paused. "How about you? Are you all right?"

"Yeah," I said. "Except that I'm really tired. Even before the shooting, it was a busy evening. Ruby did her Ouija board thing." I stopped. I hadn't told him about the word *broncos*. I thought that could wait until he got home and we were face-to-face. It's not the sort of thing that can be explained over the telephone. "And afterward, we talked to Ruby's heartthrob." I paused, remembering that McQuaid had said once that he thought he might have known Colin, back when he was with the Houston PD. "By the way, I've been meaning to ask—did you ever remember where you met Colin Fowler?"

There was a moment's hesitation, then, "Nope, sorry. I guess he's just got one of those ordinary faces. Probably reminds me of somebody else I used to know. Why are you asking?"

Having spent a substantial part of my adult life listening to people who might be lying under oath—or at least not telling the whole truth—I get a prickly feeling when somebody's lying. It was happening now. My husband was lying to me about his acquaintance with Colin Fowler. But I was too tired to pursue it. And anyway, this was another of those face-to-face topics.

"Just wondering," I said vaguely. I rolled over onto my side. Howard Cosell was sleeping on his back, his paws in the air, his ears flopped over McQuaid's pillow. He was snoring gently. "I miss you," I added. "I really miss you."

"I miss you, too," McQuaid said. "How would you feel about a little phone sex?"

"Phone sex?" I asked innocently. "What's that?"

"You're a married woman and you don't know about phone sex?" he asked, pretending to be surprised.

"Never heard of it," I said. I giggled. "I guess that makes me a phone sex virgin, doesn't it?"

He laughed, in that low, throaty way that never fails to turns me on. "Well, we can take care of that."

So we did.

Howard Cosell didn't pay any attention to us, though. He just kept snoring. And after a while, McQuaid and I said good night, exchanged phone kisses, and I went to sleep.

But not for long. When the phone woke me up, I opened one eye and looked groggily at the clock. It was not quite two a.m.

"What?" I growled, into the handset. "Who?" Then, thinking it had to be my husband, said seductively, "Back for more phone sex, babe?"

It wasn't McQuaid. "Sheila here, China," Smart Cookie said crisply. "Have you gone to bed?"

"You bet. Haven't you?"

"Not yet. I'm thinking about tomorrow morning."

"Yeah, well, it's still tonight. Tomorrow morning is a ways away."

"I want you to go to Friendship with me to pick up Lopez."

"Hang on," I said, and rolled Howard over. "The dog was snoring and I couldn't exactly hear. I thought you said you wanted me to go to Friendship with you and pick up Lopez."

"Right. I'll come by your house at five." She yawned. "I'd make it earlier, but I've got to get a couple of hours of sleep. I'm just about dead."

"Wait," I said, alarmed. "Why me? I don't—"

"Because you know Margarita Lopez," Sheila said patiently. "Because it was your son who witnessed the murder and took her photo. Because you talked to her daughter's roommate and you understand the story behind the story. Because she's already met you." She paused. "And because a friendly face might make all the difference. I've got an arrest warrant. I'm hoping for a confession."

"Who said my face is friendly?" I muttered. "Anyway, I can't go. I told Brian he could stay home from school tomorrow. I need to be here. I don't think he should be alone all day. He seems okay with what happened, but something like this might have delayed repercussions."

"You're right," Sheila said. "He shouldn't be alone. I'll send Murdock over to stay with him until we get back. I've just talked to the Friendship chief. Lopez got home about twenty minutes ago and went to bed. I asked him to put somebody on the street in front of her house to make sure she doesn't leave. You and I will be knocking on her door at sunrise."

"You're serious about this, aren't you?" I replied glumly. "You really want me to go."

"Yeah." Her voice softened. "I wouldn't ask if I didn't need you, China. Five o'clock, sharp." She paused. "Oh, by the way. What's phone sex?"

"Something private between me and my husband," I said shortly, and hung up.

I set the clock, knowing that without an alarm, I wouldn't wake up until I heard Sheila pounding on the door. Howard was on his back again, snoring. I lay there for a moment, wondering how Mrs. Lopez was going to react when Sheila confronted her, and then I fell asleep.

Chapter Eighteen

The marigold has a mournful reputation, associated as it is with grief, pain and chagrin. It expresses ennui and despair. Dedicated to the Virgin Mary and known as Mary's gold, it was held in high esteem by herbalists, who recommended it "to comfort heart and spirits."

Pamela Todd
Forget-Me-Not: A Floral Treasury

Marigold (*Tagetes sp.*) figured in Aztec beliefs about the seven-year journey to and from the afterworld, which must be completed before the dead could rest. In search of nourishment, souls returned to the land of the living each year. They carried strong-smelling marigolds to drop behind them, marking the trail they would take on their return the following year. Often, the living create such trails, from the cemetery (where marigold flowers decorate the grave) to the home.

China Bayles's Book of Days
365 Celebrations of the Mystery, Myth, and Magic of Herbs

We got such an early start that Lila's Diner wasn't open, but we made do with coffee out of Sheila's thermos. Black, without sugar, because that's the way she likes it. Strong enough to stop a charging buffalo.

Sheila was in uniform and driving one of the PSPD's newer squad cars, which was equipped with a laptop computer, radio, cell phone, radar—all the impressive modern gizmos that are supposed to make law enforcement easier. There was a partition between the front and back seats. Sheila was obviously hoping that Mrs. Lopez would consent to go back to Pecan Springs.

There had been plenty of snow in Pecan Springs when we started out, but I-35 was mostly just wet. We were early enough so that there wasn't much traffic except for the usual fleet of all-night NAFTA truckers piloting their eighteen-wheelers through the dark, heading for the border crossing at Laredo or McAllen. Sunrise was still a couple of hours away, and the stars were out. When dawn began to streak the sky to the east, it looked as if the day would be pleasant—cold and bright, with none of the ice and snow we'd had in Pecan Springs the night before. Winter in Texas is like that. The cold air spills rapidly down from the Plains and then retreats back north before a flood of Gulf warmth. We were headed south, where it was bound to be warmer.

Sheila took a more direct route than the one Brian and I had taken on Sunday: south on I-35 and west on the outer ring road around San Antonio, where we found an open McDonald's and made a quick pit stop for more coffee, orange juice, a sack of hot biscuits to go, and the ladies' room. Then west again on US 90 to Uvalde, and south on US 83 to Friendship. Taking the main roads and with lead-footed Sheila at the wheel of her cop car, we'd be there by the time the sun rose.

As we drove, Sheila told me that Lopez had left enough tracks in the snow so that the investigating officers could track her to the point where she had parked her car outside the gate. The headlights Brian had seen had been hers. She had entered the parking lot on foot, shot Duffy, and gone back to her car. She then drove back to Friendship and went to bed. The Friendship PD had the Lopez house under surveillance, but were under orders not to pick her up until we got there.

223

Sheila filled in a few other gaps, as well. The Keenes had insisted—reasonably, I thought—that their daughter have a lawyer. Jake would not be interrogated until counsel had been arranged, so there was not yet a firsthand account of what had transpired between her and Duffy.

An officer had gone to the Duffy home to inform Mrs. Duffy of her husband's death; understandably, she had collapsed in hysterics and a doctor had been called. Before she was sedated, however, she had managed to offer a little information about her husband's activities that evening. Duffy had been home for dinner as usual, had then gone next door to talk to Chuck Manning about some Booster Club business—the meeting that Chuck's wife, Audrey, had mentioned at Ruby's Ouija party, I surmised. A little before nine o'clock, Duffy had come home and told his wife he had an errand to run and would be back in an hour. He never returned.

Judge Porterfield had done her JP's duty, and when she finished, had released Duffy's pickup truck to be towed to the police impound lot. The area behind the field house was still a crime scene and off-limits to students, however. Lisa Simon had scheduled an emergency assembly during home-room period; the district superintendent would be there to make the announcement of Duffy's death, and counselors would be available to any students who wanted to talk about their feelings—which would undoubtedly be a great many. The kids had idolized the coach. Some students would have heard the story already, or the dozens of variants that were no doubt making the rounds. As I said, news travels fast in Pecan Springs. Once the Nueces Street Diner opens and Lila Jennings gets the first installment, it's Katie-bar-the-door. But while the grapevine is fast, it's never accurate. Heaven only knows what speculations were being offered as truth around the courthouse square or in the halls of the high school. Sheila and Lisa and I would probably be horrified to hear them. I was glad that Brian had decided not to go to school.

I looked out the window as we drove through the quiet Hill Country landscape, thinking about all that had transpired since Monday, when I had driven to Friendship to check out the anonymous tip Lisa Simon had received. All she had asked me to do was to find out whether there was anything of substance to the caller's claim that Duffy had been in some sort of trouble at his previous school. How complicated was that?

Very complicated, as things had turned out—although Sheila and I agreed that Margarita Lopez's action the night before had in some ways simplified the situation. Whatever Duffy's past transgressions, there would be none in the future. He might at this moment be answering for his sins to the Universal Judge of All, but he wouldn't have to undergo those painful hearings before the State Board for Educator Certification. His teaching certificate would never be revoked, he would not be fired from his coaching position, and he wouldn't have to face the humiliation of looking for work other than coaching or teaching. That part of the process had been entirely short-circuited by a bullet to the heart.

Which opened the further question of Margarita Lopez, and gave Sheila and me a new field for speculation. When I had talked to the woman, she hadn't even seemed to know that her daughter and Tim Duffy were both in Pecan Springs. And while she had appeared, in a general way, to blame Angela's death on her relationship with the coach, she hadn't given any hints that she suspected there might be a specific connection. I couldn't help but wonder what had happened between Monday morning and Wednesday night to make Mrs. Lopez angry enough to pick up a gun and shoot the man. Had my questions prompted her to think, instead of washing her thoughts away with alcohol? Had she looked through Angela's things and uncovered some evidence she had over-looked earlier?

If that's what had happened, she might have gone to the high school and found out where Duffy's new job had taken him—or simply asked at the local liquor store, since most people in Friendship had probably kept track of him and knew where he'd moved. Finding him in Pecan Springs wouldn't have been hard, either; all she needed was a phone book. Once she had his address, then what? Had she simply parked on the street out-side his house, running the heater on that old maroon Marquis to keep her warm while she waited? Maybe she'd been watching as he came home to dinner, then went next door to talk to Chuck Manning. Maybe she'd been waiting when he came out of his house alone, close to nine o'clock, got into his truck, and drove off.

Following him wouldn't have been difficult, either. Traffic was light, and the school was only a few blocks away. They didn't have far to go. Watching him drive, alone, into the empty school parking lot, she must have exulted, thinking that her victim had led her to a perfect place to confront him, whether she meant to kill him or merely to threaten him. And it would have been perfect, except for the ironic fact that Duffy was there to meet Jake, and that Brian was there too, with his camera. If Lopez had seen Jake get into the truck, it might have fueled her anger, and per-haps even spurred her to use the gun as a weapon, and not just a threat. But whether she saw the girl get in or not, she had killed her victim in front of witnesses, and she knew it. She had to have known it the minute Jake began screaming, and when the flash on Brian's camera went off.

But those were simply speculations. The true facts would have to wait until Sheila questioned Lopez, who might or might not be persuaded to answer. And in the meantime, there was still another unanswered question, which now loomed larger in my mind than ever before: the mystery of Angela's death. Personally, I doubted that she had killed herself. There were the letters she had kept as proof of what Duffy had done, the hints she had dropped to Tyler and Christie, her friendship with Jake. It seemed more likely to me that Angela had threatened Duffy with what she knew, and that he had killed her. Had Margarita Lopez somehow come to this conclusion, too?

Yes, indeed. There were several important questions. And Margarita Lopez was the only one who could answer them.

THE sun was rising on the street on the outskirts of Friendship where Margarita Lopez lived, gilding the roofs of the shabby houses and brightening the yards and driveways. The maroon Mercury Marquis was parked in the driveway, where I had seen it on my first visit. The house was still and quiet, the shades in the front rooms pulled all the way down. In a police car some three doors down the street, an officer sat, eating a doughnut and drinking coffee out of a cardboard cup. As we drove past him, Sheila frowned and muttered something, from which I gathered that she would have preferred that the house be watched by a plainclothes officer in an unmarked car.

We parked, got out, and went toward the house. The officer, a beefy, sandy-haired male who must have weighed in around two-twenty-five, left his car and walked toward us. The three of us met at the end of the sidewalk.

The officer nodded curtly. "Sheldon," he said, loosening his gun in its holster.

"Chief Dawson," Sheila replied, equally curt, "and Bayles." She paused, her eyes narrowing slightly. "You've been here long, Officer Sheldon?"

He hitched up his sagging pants. "Since before she drove in. She got out of her car, went straight in the house, and turned on the light in that back room—the bedroom, I guess. After a while it went out. Figure she went to bed."

Down the block, somebody kick-started a motorcycle and revved it up. In a nearby house, a child began to wail. Somewhere else, a door banged and a dog barked. The street was waking up.

Sheila turned to look at the house. The gray tabby was sitting on the porch, gazing at us. "Who's watching the back door?"

"The back?" Sheldon pulled his sandy brows together. "Chief didn't say to put nobody on the back. Just told me to park on the street and keep an eye on the car, so she don't turn tail and head for the border." He gave Sheila a bold, head-to-foot glance, then turned aside to spit disapprovingly. I had the idea that there were no women cops in the Friendship PD. He turned back, frowning. "Ain't true she shot Coach Duffy up there in Pecan Springs, is it? That's what the chief said, but I don't believe it."

"That's what's on the arrest warrant," Sheila said, still studying the house.

Sheldon let out a long breath. "Sweet Jesus. What'd she want to go and do that for? Best coach we could ever hope to have. I was one of his biggest fans." He shook his head somberly. "Hell, still am. Can't hardly believe he's dead. He was a good man. Had a good heart."

I could see the muscle working in Sheila's jaw. But all she said was, "Okay, here we go," and started up the walk, past the bed of yellow pansies, past the handsome blue agave. I noticed that its bloom stalk seemed to have shot up several inches since Monday—several inches closer to blooming, to bearing its fruit, to dying. I thought of Margarita Lopez, and wondered if there was a metaphor there. But if there was, I didn't have time to ponder it, because Sheila was telling me to stay behind on the sidewalk, while she and Officer Sheldon went to the door.

Sheila knocked.

No answer. She knocked several more times and called, "Mrs. Lopez. Open up, Mrs. Lopez, it's the police."

"You looking for Margarita?" A motherly looking Anglo woman in a brown suit and low heels, a handbag over her shoulder, had come out on the porch of the neighboring house and was locking her door.

"Yes," Sheila said. "I'm Chief Dawson from Pecan Springs, and this is Officer Sheldon, from the Friendship PD. We—"

"I can see you're cops, can't I?" the woman said darkly, eyeing them. "If you're looking for Margarita, you're not going to find her here."

"Oh, yeah?" Sheldon said in a blustery tone. "Car's here."

"I can see that." The woman was scornful. "But *she* isn't. I was brushing my teeth fifteen or twenty minutes ago, getting ready to go to work, when I looked out the bathroom window and saw her. She was headed down the alley, same as she always is this time of day."

Sheldon shuffled his feet, not looking at Sheila.

"Down the alley?" Sheila asked. "Where does she go?"

"To the cemetery," the neighbor replied, getting out her car keys. "She says good morning to her daughter every day. Always takes something with her, flowers, a trinket, some little something. The girl died last month, you know. I guess Margarita hasn't got her grieving done yet." She looked from Sheldon to Sheila, frowning. "What do you want her for? She didn't get out and get drunk again, did she? I keep telling her she'd better lay off the booze, but she doesn't listen. It's like she's got a death wish."

"We just want to talk to her," Sheila said pleasantly. "Can you give us directions to the cemetery?"

229

I spoke up, feeling suddenly urgent. "I know where it is. It's only a couple of blocks."

"The two of us will go, then," Sheila said, and thanked the neighbor. To Officer Sheldon, she added, with only a hint of mild sarcasm, "You better stay here and keep an eye on Mrs. Lopez's car. If she comes back, we don't want her turning tail and heading for the border."

Sheldon had the grace to blush. "Yes'm. Do you want me to radio for backup?"

Sheila glanced at me, and I shook my head slightly. I doubted if Lopez would put up a fight. And if she was going to talk, she would talk to us, not to the Friendship PD.

"Thanks," Sheila said. "I think we can handle it."

The wrought iron gates to the Cemeterio Guadalupe were closed and padlocked, so we parked the squad car and went forward on foot, under the small palms that had been planted along the gravel drive. The early-morning air was cool and still and very quiet. The sun was lifting above the line of low willows at the back of the cemetery, and the birds were busy about their morning business. I heard the soft cooing of pigeons and white-winged doves, and saw the vivid yellow flash of the Great Kiskadee, one of South Texas' most striking birds.

"Angela's grave is back there," I said, pointing. "The back corner."

We walked quickly, not speaking. Sheila's face was set and angry, and I knew she was thinking that she should have told the Friendship PD to pick Lopez up as soon as the woman showed up at the house. But I also knew why she hadn't. She'd thought she had a better shot at a confession if the two of us—a female cop and a woman with a friendly face—served the arrest warrant. She hadn't counted on a sloppy stake-out that allowed the subject to slip out of the house and make her usual early-morning trek to her daughter's grave.

But maybe things would still work out, I thought. Our conversation might be even more productive here, in a cemetery. There's something compelling about gravestones. They're a reminder of the hereafter, and of the Christian teaching that we must all stand before the judgment bar and be held accountable for our deeds. Surrounded by grave markers and stone crosses, Mrs. Lopez might be more inclined to tell us the truth about her reasons for killing Tim Duffy.

Sheila stopped and glanced around. "Where?"

"There," I said, pointing to the large cottonwood tree that stood like a green guardian over this section of the cemetery. "But I don't see Margarita."

And then I did. Dressed in jeans and the same plaid shirt and green sweater I had seen earlier, she was lying on her side on her daughter's grave, under the figure of the angel, in front of the picture of Our Lady of Sorrows, with the bleeding heart pierced with knives. The plastic carnations had been replaced in the vase with a large bunch of florist's marigolds.

"Mrs. Lopez?" I asked tentatively. She didn't answer.

I thought at first that the woman was weeping, so deep in her grief that she couldn't respond. But then I saw that her fingers were curled around the butt of a Smith & Wesson police revolver, and that a pool of blood had spread across the bare earth of her daughter's grave.

Sheila bent down and put her fingers to Mrs. Lopez's throat, feeling for a pulse. But it was clear that the woman was dead. Angela's mother had shot herself in the heart.

Chapter Nineteen

"Damn," Sheila said softly.

"Yeah," I said. We stood there for a moment, in silence. My gaze went to the picture of Our Lady of Sorrows. I couldn't help remembering what Margarita had said to me on Monday: *See those drops of blood? She lost her only, just like me. She's got knives in her heart, like I've got in mine. Knives in the heart. Never stops hurting.*

Margarita's heart had stopped hurting now.

*   *   *

WE went back to the squad car and Sheila radioed for assistance. After a brief consultation with her, I walked back to the Lopez house. Officer Sheldon, grim-faced, drove past me on his way to the cemetery, lights flashing and siren blaring. I guess he'd gotten the word that his surveillance subject would not be turning tail and heading for the border. He saw me, but he didn't bother to wave.

At the house, I let myself in through the unlocked back door. I went through the kitchen and into the living room. The altar to Angela's departed spirit was still there, and the votive candle was lit in front of the photo. That's where I found the note, handwritten in red ink on white paper: *I did it for you, my Angel.* The words were enclosed in the drawing of a heart.

But that wasn't all. On the sofa, next to an overflowing ashtray and a glass that had once held a Bloody Mary, I saw a copy of the *Friendship Times-Herald*. It was opened to the sports page, which featured a two-column photo of a grinning and confident Tim Duffy, accepting a lifetime achievement award from Judge Maude Porterfield, on behalf of the Pecan Springs Chamber of Commerce. The caption under the photo read: "Coach Duffy earns well-deserved award for outstanding work with the Pecan Springs Panthers." In the accompanying article, the sports editor praised the coach and expressed regret that he was no longer at Friendship High. "Our loss is their gain," the writer lamented. "Too bad we couldn't keep Coach Duffy on our team!"

I stared at the photo. I could picture Margarita sitting here on the sofa with her feet on the coffee table, smoking a cigarette and sipping her drink, opening the newspaper and paging casually through it. I imagined her attention caught by the photo, then by the article. I imagined her swinging both feet onto the floor and sitting up straight, shocked into speechlessness at the discovery that Angela and the man who had sexually abused her had both been living in Pecan Springs. I imagined her pacing back and forth across the living room, imagined her growing conviction that Duffy had been directly responsible for Angela's death, whether he had driven her to suicide, or into a depression that led to an accidental overdose—or had murdered her. And then thinking of the gun she kept hidden somewhere in the house, of driving to Pecan Springs, of stalking the coach until she found him in an isolated place where she could shoot him. Could shoot him and kill him and get away with it, because nobody would ever connect Tim Duffy's murder to a woman in Friendship, Texas. Or perhaps she didn't intend to get away with it. Perhaps she planned, all along, to return to Angela's grave and shoot herself with the same gun that she had used to kill Duffy—yet another victim of the hideous crime that had taken her daughter.

I left the living room as it was and went down the wood-floored hallway, a bedroom on either side, a bathroom at the end. In the bedroom on the right, the bedclothes were flung back and the pillow still bore the imprint of Margarita's head. She'd slept there, at least for a while, last night. Or maybe she just hadn't made the bed since the last time she'd occupied it, a couple of nights before.

But it was the bedroom on the left that interested me. The bed was neatly made with a white cotton spread, and a cluster of stuffed animals—a green plush frog, a pink bear, an orange-and-black striped tiger—waited forlornly on the pillow. A shelf held a row of books and a pink-painted desk displayed photos of Angela in happier times. A fringed pink chenille rug with a rose in the middle occupied the center of the room, which looked just as it might have looked on the day Angela left for college. It was a sad room, bereft and empty.

I opened the closet door. There was no clothing, but on the floor was a large cardboard packing box, the kind you get from U-Haul. I pulled it out into the room and opened it. This was what I was looking for: the things that Mrs. Lopez had brought back from Angela's dorm room. I put the box on the bed and started taking things out, sorting through the books, the papers, the litter of pens and pencils, the random paraphernalia of college life, all embued with the same forlorn sadness that seemed to fill the whole room. The box was full, the search took a while, and I wasn't even sure what I was looking for—except that I thought I'd know it when I saw it.

But I didn't spot anything that looked even remotely promising until I was putting everything back into the box, trying to be neat about it. A piece of pink paper fluttered out of some other papers and fell to the floor. It was a page from a telephone-message notepad, one of those things with "Caller's Name" and a space for the date and the message. The date scribbled on it was December 15—and the cryptic note: *Angie—Glenda called. Wants you to call her back.* A phone number was jotted down, followed by the initial *C.* Christie, probably.

Glenda? I frowned. Glenda *Duffy*? Or maybe not. Maybe Angela had a friend named Glenda. Maybe—

I took out my cell phone and punched in the number, with the Pecan Springs area code. The answering machine picked up on the fourth ring, and a man's recorded voice, heavily laden with sadness, said: "The Duffy family has experienced a great tragedy and will not be answering the telephone for the next few days. We appreciate your call. If you would like us to return it at a later time, please leave your name and phone number. Thank you for your patience and understanding." *Click.*

Yes. It was Glenda Duffy who had left a call-back for Angela Lopez. Why? What possible connection could there be between them—except for Tim Duffy. And then I remembered. Carol Bruce, who coordinated the hospital volunteer services, had said that Glenda worked with the Candy Stripers. Angela had volunteered in that program. Glenda's call probably had to do with a meeting, or something like that.

I tucked the message slip into my shoulder bag and began to put things back in the box. But as I did, my glance happened to fall on a purple pen with a red plastic heart at the top, one of those fancy pens that girls take such delight in. I frowned at it for a moment, thinking. Then I stuck it into my handbag, as well. A few moments later, everything else was back in the box and the box was back in the closet. I looked around the room for a moment longer, and then, with a feeling of deep sadness for the tragic chapter that had just ended, closed the door.

There was only Margarita's bedroom left. In it, there was nothing of interest except for a small cardboard box on the dresser. When the box was full, it had held fifty thirty-eight caliber rounds. Six were missing.

I could do the math. Two of the bullets were in Tim Duffy's body, and one in Margarita's. The remaining three were no doubt still in the gun.

IT was after eleven before Sheila and the Friendship PD finished their own search of the house, coming to the same conclusion I had when they saw the newspaper on the sofa in the living room and the box of cartridges in Margarita's bedroom. Her brother lived in Nuevo Laredo; he'd been notified of her death and was on his way. The body had been taken to the county hospital in nearby Crystal City, where the ME would do an autopsy. But the outcome already seemed clear, and while Sheila might have to come back down to Friendship to testify at the inquest, it was time we headed back to Pecan Springs.

"Did you find anything interesting, other than what we saw?" Sheila asked, putting the key into the ignition.

"Just this." I took out the pink message slip and showed it to Sheila, with a brief explanation of where I'd found it. "The phone number belongs to the Duffys," I added. "I checked it out."

She looked at it for a moment and then at me, frowning. "Glenda Duffy?"

I stuck the slip back into my pocket. "I'm guessing that the call had to do with the Candy Stripers program at the hospital. Glenda is an active recruiter, and Angela Lopez was a volunteer. That's where Angela met Jake."

"Sounds right," Sheila said. She turned the key in the ignition, put the car into gear, and pulled out into the street. "What a morning it's been. I'm ready for some lunch. How about you?"

"Absolutely," I said.

Before we started out that morning, I had phoned Ruby, waking her up with the news that Tim Duffy had been shot and that Sheila wanted me to go down to South Texas with her. Ruby had been shocked almost speechless, then had offered to do whatever she could to pick up the slack in the shops until things got straightened out. While Sheila and I were eating—fast food again—I phoned the Crystal Cave to tell Ruby that we'd be back in Pecan Springs by early afternoon, and to let her know what had happened in Friendship.

"Another shooting?" she asked breathlessly. "My stars, China. Where is it going to end?"

"I think it's ended now," I replied. The ugliness that had begun with

Duffy had come crashing to its fateful conclusion. Angela, Duffy himself, Angela's mother—victims and victimizer alike, all three were gone. There wasn't anybody else.

"Feel free to do whatever you have to do," Ruby said in a comforting tone. "And tell Smart Cookie I said to hang in there. It must be just awful to be the police chief and see such horrible things going on all the time."

I turned off the phone and stuck it in my bag. "Ruby says to hang in there," I reported. "She says it must be just awful to be the police chief and see such horrible things going on all the time."

Sheila chuckled ironically. "That's our Ruby. If she had things her way, the world would be full of nothing but goodness, wouldn't it? The better angels of our natures would win out every time."

We went out to the car, got back on the freeway, and headed north, in silence. Sheila was intent on her driving, I was occupied with my thoughts. What was there to say? There were no better angels.

After a long while, Sheila broke the silence. "I've been thinking about Ruby," she said. She brushed her hair back. "I don't know. Maybe this business with Lopez has got me thinking, or maybe I'm worried about Ruby's love life." She turned to me, grinning wryly. "Or maybe I'm just tired of being a holdout. Anyway, I guess I should tell you about Colin Fowler."

"Well, good," I said. "It's about time, if you don't mind my saying so."

She was staring straight ahead. "You know Ruby better than I do, China—you'll have to decide whether this is something she can handle, or whether it should be kept between the two of us. But whatever you do, don't tell her unless she swears not to tell Colin what I've said." She hit the wheel with the heel of her hand for emphasis. "She absolutely can*not* tell Colin, or anybody else. Under any circumstance, for any reason. Is that clear?"

I frowned. If Ruby couldn't tell Colin, I couldn't tell Ruby. It was as simple as that. So did I want to know, or not?

I didn't even hesitate. "It's clear," I said. "So what's the story?"

"Well, for starters, Colin Fowler isn't his real name."

"Why am I not surprised?" I asked.

She ignored that. "His name is Daniel Reid. I knew him when we both worked with the Dallas police. We were . . . friends."

"Mmm," I said in a skeptical tone, remembering a glance that Sheila and Colin—or Daniel, or whoever—had exchanged at the cast party for *A Man for All Reasons*, the previous October. Whatever their relationship, I was betting that there had been more to it than friendship. I wasn't surprised to hear that he had been a cop, either. I've known enough cops to recognize the general characteristics of the breed.

Her shrug was carefully nonchalant. "Okay, so we were lovers—but not for very long. It never got serious."

"Because?"

"Because . . . well, I was more serious about my work than I was about him." She hesitated. "And because he was married. He and his wife weren't living together at the time, but I wasn't sure it would stay that way."

"Marriage does tend to toss a monkey wrench into the romantic works," I said dryly, watching her profile. Sheila was a beautiful woman, poised and sure of herself. I knew what had attracted him to her. The question—was he still attracted to her?—was not one I wanted to entertain. Not as long as he was with Ruby.

"I don't think he's married now," she said without inflection. "Not to that wife, anyway. They got divorced after he went to prison. Of course," she went on, "I have no way of knowing whether he's gotten married since then. I wouldn't be surprised. He's a man who enjoys the comforts of home." Her voice took on a bitter edge. "He's fond of hot meals, clean sheets, and somebody to pick up after him."

I was staring at her. "Went to *prison*? I thought you said he was a cop."

"So?" She arched a delicate eyebrow. "I thought you were a criminal defense attorney."

"That was in a past life," I muttered.

"He had a past life, too. You've heard of corrupt cops?"

I had—far too often. The world is full of police officers on the make, on the take, and on the wrong side of the law.

"So let's hear it," I said.

Sheila told me the story without emotion or embellishment—and without interruption, for I was fascinated by the tale as it unfurled. For six years, Daniel Reid had been a narcotics agent, conducting undercover investigations of drug dealers for the Dallas Police Department's Organized Crime Division. It was a bottom-fishing job, slimy and dangerous, a difficult job for even the most dedicated cop. But Dan turned out to be exceedingly good at it. He was resourceful, assertive, unafraid, and manipulative—all the character traits that make somebody a good undercover officer.

But Dan was also independent—too independent, as it turned out—and he didn't always communicate regularly with the other members of his team or with his street supervisor or the guys up the line. This must have worked to his advantage, for he was responsible for more arrests than anybody else in his division. But it was probably this same tendency to freelance that got him into trouble. He had developed a productive relationship with a well-connected but nasty dealer—a man called Mario—who had already given him several good leads into the labyrinthine world of narcotics trafficking. When Dan got word that the dealer was about to be taken down, he didn't like it.

"To give him his due," Sheila said, "Dan had been working on Mario for months. He was convinced that the guy was ready to lead him to one of the major suppliers. He thought he could hook even bigger fish if Mario stayed on the street. He was probably right." She gave me a sideways glance. "He also suspected that there might be something funny behind the sudden decision to go with the bust."

I grunted. "Wouldn't be surprised. It's been known to happen."

I was beginning to feel some sympathy for Reid, who was obviously the man in the middle, feeling the pain of losing a source he had spent months cultivating. Most cops are straight arrows, but the system itself is rotten-ripe with potential for corruption, as I knew from cases in which I had been personally involved. For example (just one of a half-dozen I could come up with off the top of my head), somebody a step or two up Reid's chain of command might have had a cozy, lucrative arrangement with that drug lord Mario was about to rat out. Take Mario down, and it was business as usual for the supplier and his cop buddy. And if you don't think this happens, just read the newspapers a little more carefully. From small towns to big cities, there's more than enough official corruption to go around.

"Yeah," Sheila said dryly. "Anyway, this was only Dan's opinion, and he was pretty sure his opinion wouldn't count. So instead of wasting time and effort going through channels to try to keep Mario on the street, he tipped him that the bust was going down. Mario did the smart thing and left town, but it didn't help. He was picked up and interrogated. Dan was indicted a couple of months later."

"Obstruction of justice, I suppose."

Sheila nodded. "Served one year of his three-year term."

I was surprised. "Only three years? He got off light." Obstruction is a third-degree felony. It usually gets you five years.

Sheila gave a wry chuckle. "I'm sure he doesn't think so. If I know Dan, he probably spent the whole year plotting to get even."

"Well, he obviously couldn't go back to law enforcement," I said. Ex-felons are prohibited by law from employment as police officers. "I guess he's had to start over again. Selling environmental products is as good a line of work as any."

"Well, there's some ambiguity here, if you ask me," Sheila said, not looking at me.

I eyed her. "What sort of ambiguity?"

"You know he's into this hemp thing."

"Yeah." I grinned. "A lot of folks are into 'this hemp thing,' Smart Cookie. There's no law that says you can't import hemp products. You just can't grow the stuff in your backyard, that's all."

"I'm not saying Dan Reid is doing anything illegal," she said with a shrug. "I just think it's kind of interesting that his business puts him into contact with people who advocate liberalizing the drug laws, that's all. Some of them are perfectly legit. Others . . . who knows?"

I stared. "Are you saying the guy has gone undercover again? Freelance?"

Of course, it might not have to be freelance. With the right kind of leverage, a criminal record can be expunged. And there are situations where an expunction wouldn't even be necessary. For instance, if the Feds wanted somebody badly enough—if they had a use for Dan Reid's skills, his experience, his underworld connections—they would simply ignore his record. I thought of Ruby, her comfortable, creative life invaded by a man who lived and worked on the margins of the law, and the potential danger to her. I thought of a story I'd read recently, in which a mob hit team entered a house and shot an FBI undercover agent who was getting too close to the big guys. For good measure, they also killed his wife, even though she had nothing to do with her husband's activities. I shivered. Then I reminded myself that I could be making all this up. Maybe Reid—Colin Fowler, I mean—is exactly who he seems to be, a guy who has turned a page. An ordinary guy with an ordinary small business, living in a small town, leading a small-town life. I could be worried for nothing . . . but I doubted it.

"Freelance?" A muscle worked in Sheila's jaw. "I have no idea what Dan is doing at the moment, China. I do know, though, that all kinds of weird things go down in this business. And I care for Ruby. I want her to be safe and happy. That's all."

"You and me both," I said grimly. Unless I missed my guess, Sheila either knew for certain or had a pretty good idea that Colin—Dan Reid, that is—was doing some sort of investigative work, and that his business here in Pecan Springs was only a cover. But she wouldn't say so. Smart Cookie is a cop, first, last, and always. And while I am a friend, I am still a civilian, and a lawyer to boot. She was willing to tell me a part of the story, but only a part.

I sighed. "So now I know—as opposed to simply suspecting—that the guy Ruby is sleeping with isn't the man she thinks he is."

"Yeah." She turned and gave me that dimpled grin that drives so many guys up the wall. "Monkey off my back and onto yours, Counselor. But remember our deal. You can't tell Ruby unless—"

"Yeah, right," I said. "I can't tell Ruby."

I turned to look out the window again. At least part of the mystery had

243

been cleared up: who Colin Fowler was, what his past had been, and how he and Sheila had known each other. But that didn't clear up everything.

There was still the question of what Colin—Dan Reid—was doing here in Pecan Springs.

Chapter Twenty

CHINA'S LEMON-LAVENDER TEA

¼ cup dried lemon grass, chopped
¼ cup dried lemon verbena
¼ cup dried lemon balm
¼ cup dried lavender flowers
¼ cup dried spearmint

Mix tea herbs well and store in an opaque airtight container. Use 2 teaspoons per cup of boiling water. Steep for five minutes. Serve with honey or sugar. This recipe can be varied, using equal amounts of rosemary, rose geranium, and hibiscus flowers. (Be sure to use only plants that have not been sprayed.)

It had warmed up during the day, and while there were still some icy remnants of last night's snowfall on the north sides of buildings and in the shade of trees and shrubbery, mostly the ground was simply wet instead of being pretty and white. Sheila dropped me at home, where I found Sophie Murdock in the kitchen. Brian was in his bedroom, cleaning his lizard cages. He was incensed at the idea that he had been left in the custody of a police baby-sitter.

"It was because I was concerned about you," I said soothingly. "Chief Dawson asked me to go down to Friendship with her." I had decided I would tell Brian about Margarita Lopez's suicide later—this evening, maybe, when we had some time to sit down and talk quietly. "I didn't want to wake you up to tell you," I went on, "and I didn't think we'd be gone so long. When the chief suggested that Officer Murdock come over and stay for a few hours, I thought it was a good idea."

"Well, it wasn't," Brian said frostily. There was a lizard perched on top of the lampshade—Lewis, I thought. (Lewis can be distinguished from his twin, Leonard, because Lewis has an extra toe. Leopold, the third member of this lizard trio, now deceased, was minus a toe. This is the kind of esoteric knowledge that comes with being a mom, you understand.)

Brian plucked Lewis off the lampshade and plopped him back into the cage. "Anyway, you're home now," he added. "She can go back to being a cop."

"I've got to go out again," I said. "I need to drop in at the shop, and I have a couple of other errands. Will you be okay here by yourself?"

"Of course I'll be okay." Brian rolled his eyes to show his utter disdain for the question. "I'm not a baby, am I? I wish I'd gone to school. It would've been better than being baby-sat by a cop, like I'm some kind of juvenile crook or something."

I grinned at this healthy response, ruffled his hair, and gave him a hug. "Phone calls?" I asked.

"Dad called. I told him all about it. Last night, I mean."

"Oh, yeah? What did he say?"

Brian opened the small glass tank where his tarantula—a Costa Rican zebra, in case you're a tarantula fancier—hangs out, mostly in the burrow she's dug in the deep peat-and-vermiculite substrate on the floor of her cage. Her name used to be Ivan—Ivan the Hairible—until Ruby's daughter, Amy, who was staying with us at the time, pointed out that he was really a she. Now she's Ivanova. She is said to be a very attractive female (you can't prove this by me), but Brian hasn't had any luck breeding

246

her, in spite of the fact that she's been introduced to several potential mates. She seems to make them nervous—afraid of being eaten, no doubt.

Brian peered into the tank. "Dad said you told him to tell me that the plan that Jake and I cooked up was stupid and dangerous. But he was proud of me anyway, for getting the photo of the shooter. If I hadn't done that, the person who killed the coach might not ever be caught. He said it was good evidence."

It was my turn to roll my eyes. So much for a united front on important issues of child discipline. "I hope you got the message."

"That it was stupid and dangerous?" Ivanova came out of the plastic flower pot that serves as her burrow, and Brian stroked her gently. Tarantulas don't usually like to be petted, I'm told, but Ivanova makes an exception where Brian is concerned. "Yeah. I woke up in the middle of the night, thinking that Jake could've been shot, too. And me."

"Not a pleasant thought," I said. "We'd certainly hate to lose you. And there wouldn't be anybody to take care of Ivanova and the rest of the gang. Was that the only phone call?"

"Nah." He took out the water dish and went to the bathroom to get some fresh water. Over the noise of the faucet, he said, "Some guy called for Dad. I wrote it down and put it on his desk." He came back into the room and put the water dish into the tank. "And somebody named Buddy called for you. He wanted to know if you've read the letters yet. He seemed kinda worried that maybe you hadn't."

"Let him worry," I said grimly. My long-dead father's love letters to his deceased mistress were the least of my concerns at the moment. "Anything else?"

"Nope." He opened the top of his plastic cricket cage, shook it a bit, and peered in. "Okay," he said pleasantly, "which of you guys would like to go out to dinner?"

I left before Ivanova could begin snacking on her cricket, which is not a terribly appetizing sight. Downstairs in the kitchen, I thanked Officer Murdock—Sophie, she told me to call her—and suggested a cup of tea before she went back to work.

"Back to work, heck," she said, with a grin that showed both dimples and very white teeth. She waved a hand at the stacks of papers on the kitchen table. "I've been working ever since I got here this morning. The chief wasn't going to let me have a day off, even if we did have a late night last night. Did it go okay with Lopez?" she added eagerly. "Did she give you any trouble?"

I put the kettle on, got out the tea canister, and spooned loose tea into the teapot. "No, it didn't go okay," I said, and told her the story.

"Sure beats all," she said gloomily, shaking her head. "Mother and daughter, both killing themselves. You know, I read the other day that twice as many Hispanic girls try to commit suicide as white or black girls. Makes you think, doesn't it?"

"It certainly does," I said, and put a half-dozen of Cass's lemon-rosemary cookies on a plate. Howard Cosell, who had been napping in his bed beside the Home Comfort stove, heard the rattle of the cookie jar lid and lifted his head with the bright-eyed alertness he usually reserves for invading rabbits and squirrels. "You were the investigating officer in the daughter's suicide. Could we talk about that?"

She shrugged. "Sure. Not much to talk about, though. It was a pretty clear-cut case, especially seein' as how she left that note." She put a stack of papers into her briefcase, frowning. "That business last night does trouble me some, though. Mrs. Lopez shooting the coach, I mean. And hearing about what Duffy was up to with those two girls." Her frown became a scowl. "How a man like him, a coach and all, could do that—well, I don't know. You see a lot of things in this business, but that . . . well, that's about the worst, far as I'm concerned. Girls are tender. Don't do for them to be messed with." She reached for a cookie. Howard got up and padded over to sit beside her, gazing with heartfelt envy at the cookie in her hand.

"I was wondering—was there anything in that motel room that made you think Angela might not have been there alone?"

She ran a hand over her clipped gray hair, so short and wiry it looked like steel wool. "Only thing was that thumbprint on the bottom of that plastic pudding cup. It wasn't hers. In fact, her prints weren't on that pudding cup at all. Plenty on the spoon, though. And on the bathroom cup." She looked down at Howard, who was looking up at her. "Can your dog have a cookie? He looks pretty hungry."

"He always looks hungry," I said. "He's on a diet. He's got his own chicken-liver snack bars, with flaxseed and brewers yeast. Good for his heart." I opened the fridge and took one out. "Here, Howard. This is for you."

Howard accepted his heart-healthy snack bar with a mournful glance in Sophie's direction. He took it back to his bed, where he ate it in two bites, no doubt pretending that it was a high-fat people cookie with plenty of sugar.

The kettle squealed and I poured hot water into the teapot. "Her prints weren't on the pudding cup?" I didn't remember that little detail being in the police report. "But don't you usually have to pick up one of those things in order to eat out of it?" The theory, I remembered, was that Angela had put the Nembutal into the pudding—the traditional way of getting it down. "Her prints should be all over it."

249

"You'd think so," Sophie said. "Her prints were on the phone, though."

"But no record of any calls?"

"Nada. I thought maybe she'd called her mother, to say good-bye or something like that. But there wasn't anything recent on her phone card, and no long-distance calls from the room, so I figured it had to be a local."

"And what about the traces of roofie in her system? Wonder where she got that."

She stared at me. "Roofie? You talkin' about that date-rape stuff?"

"You didn't see the autopsy report?"

She shook her head. "My mom had a stroke. I was out for about ten days, and when I finally got back to work, there were a couple of other pending investigations I had to get started on. One of the other officers interviewed the roommate and the counselor, I guess. That wasn't me."

Ah, I thought. That would account for the superficial questioning. That, and the fact that everybody seems to have taken Angela's death for a suicide right from the get-go.

Sophie was staring at me, perplexed. "I heard you right, did I, China? The autopsy report said she had *roofie* in her?"

"Yeah. It seemed a little odd to me. A date-rape drug and Nembutal, both. You ever hear of that in a suicide case?"

"Nope." She shook her head vigorously. "You see roofies and booze all the time, but not roofies and nembies." Her dark eyes widened as she guessed where I was going with this. "You're thinking maybe Duffy was there? That he fed the child some roofie so she'd do whatever he said without putting up a fuss, then finished it off with some nembies for dessert?"

"I don't know," I poured tea into two mugs. "What do you think?"

"If that's how it was," she growled, "it sounds like murder. Now I got to think back and try to figure out if there was anything I missed." She thought for a moment, frowning. "Nope, I just don't see it. The bed wasn't mussed, so I doubt there was sex—unless he straightened it afterward, which it didn't look like. You can always tell when a man makes a bed." She sipped her tea. "What'd the autopsy report say about sex?"

"No recent intercourse." I paused, considering. "That yellow nightie she was wearing—the report described it as new."

"Brand-new, never washed. In fact, the lace was still kinda stiff. And I found the register receipt for it on the floor under the bed." She took another cookie. Howard, watching, sighed heavily and closed his eyes, as if he couldn't bear to watch.

"There was a register receipt? I don't remember seeing that mentioned in the report."

"Oh." She frowned. "Well, heck. I must've left it out, I guess. You don't think it's important, do you?"

"I don't know. Do you remember what store?"

"Oh, you bet. It was Neiman Marcus. Pretty pricey nightgown, too, if you ask me."

"Really?" Neiman Marcus is located in the upscale mall on I-35. It's not exactly the kind of place a student on a limited budget might shop. "How pricey?"

"I don't remember exactly, but it was around forty-five dollars or so." She wrinkled her nose. "If you want to see the ticket, I'm sure it's with the stuff I signed into the property room at the station." She looked at me. "It's not really relevant, is it? If Angela was planning to meet the coach, she could've bought it to look sexy. Or if she wasn't, maybe she just wanted to look pretty when she was found dead. I've seen that happen."

She shook her head. "That's why women almost never shoot themselves in the mouth, the way men do."

"Relevant? Probably not. It's just another loose end." I thought for a moment. "What about the bag?"

"The bag?"

"The sack the nightie came in. The Neiman Marcus bag." If there'd been one of those distinctive bags in that room—they're shiny black, with silver letters—I thought Sophie would have found it. But I didn't remember that being mentioned in the report, either.

She stirred a spoonful of sugar into her mug. "I looked over that room really good, wastepaper baskets, drawers, and all. I wasn't looking for a bag, but I didn't see one. Her purse was one of those little denim things, about the size of a pancake. There wasn't any luggage, either." She narrowed her eyes. "So what'd she do? Carry that nightie over her arm when she checked in? I don't think so."

"And there's one other thing I was wondering about," I said. "The suicide note was written in purple ink on a piece of pink paper. But there's nothing in the report about a purple pen. Was there one in her purse?"

"A purple pen?" She looked troubled. "I don't remember any purple pen, but since I left out the register receipt—" She shrugged. "Maybe I better check and see."

"That'd be great. As far as you know, the evidence you collected is still available?"

"Might be." She picked up her mug. "Or it might not. The case was ruled a suicide, and they might have released the stuff to her mom." She took a long drink. "Hey, this is good tea. What is it? Some of that exotic herb stuff you sell in the shop?"

I grinned. "Not too exotic. Just some mint, lavender, and lemon balm out of my garden. Want some to take home?" Nothing like bribing your friendly neighborhood cop.

"I'd really appreciate that." She paused. "Listen, I've got to get back to the station. Want me to check out the evidence and see if it's still there? I can give you a call and let you know what I find out—if it's okay with the chief, I mean." She eyed me. "I guess you've got some sort of special interest in this case, huh?"

I nodded. "I thought the whole thing was finished after Mrs. Lopez killed herself, but now I'm not so sure." I got up and filled a zipper-lock plastic bag with tea herbs. I gave it to her, with my cell phone number, and thanked her for staying with Brian.

"He's a neat kid." She drained her cup and pocketed the tea. "Got a good head on him. Taking that picture of the shooter last night was real smart—but dangerous, too. That woman could've ripped off a shot at him, grabbed the camera, and run." She regarded me dubiously. "I'll tell you, though. I don't know about that big old spider he's got up there in that bedroom. He was mine, reckon I'd persuade him to find some other kind of pet." She shuddered. "What's a kid want spiders for?"

I was glad she had failed to notice Brian's snakes, which live in another cage on top of his dresser. Sophie stuck her papers into her briefcase, put on her uniform cap, and left.

After she was gone, I headed for the phone, where I found Miles Danforth's office phone number written down on the pad in Brian's careless scrawl, followed by *PLEASE CALL ASAP!!* The words were underlined twice. I tore off the sheet, crumpled it up, and threw it in the wastebasket. I had better things to do than talk to Buddy.

I dialed the shop. Laurel said loftily that she and Ruby and Cass had the place under complete control, and that I didn't have to drop in unless

I felt the need to check up on them. Since she put it that way, I said I'd see her tomorrow, and dialed Maude Porterfield's office number. Her secretary said that she was available, and to come straight on over. I made a pit stop, combed my hair (which hadn't been touched since Sheila got me out of bed), and called upstairs to let Brian know where I was going. In five minutes, I was on my way.

Chapter Twenty-one

It was the custom for judges sitting at assizes to have sprigs of Rue
(*Ruta graveolens*) placed on the bench of the dock against the
pestilential infection brought into court from gaol by the prisoner,
and the bouquet still presented in some districts to judges at the
assizes was originally a bunch of aromatic herbs, given to him for
the purpose of warding off gaol-fever.

Maud Grieve
A Modern Herbal (1931)

Maude Porterfield's Justice of the Peace office is in a low-rent
strip center on the east side of town, and it took a little while
to get there. I had just parked the car when my cell phone rang. It was
Sophie Murdock.

"I've checked out the evidence," she said. "The stuff is still there."

"What about the purple pen?" I asked.

"No purple pen," she said with satisfaction. "At least I didn't leave
that out."

"Register receipt?"

"Yeah. It's there. Neiman Marcus, like I said. It's dated the same day as
the suicide. Funny thing, too." She cleared her throat. "It's a Neiman
Marcus charge account."

Oh, yeah? Now, what were the chances that a college student on a
budget would have a Neiman Marcus charge account? "If you've got time,

could you check that out, Sophie? If the chief says it's okay," I added, not wanting to step on Smart Cookie's pretty toes.

"It's fine with her," she said. "I'm on my way to the mall right now. Oh, and if you want to check out the evidence, chief says that's okay, too. Case is closed, so the stuff was due to be tossed at the end of the month."

Tossed? Already? I shook my head disgustedly. If criminal lawyers had their way, police departments would hold on to evidence forever.

ANY Texas JP who handles more than six hundred cases a year is entitled by law to free office space, to be provided by the county commissioners. Maude Porterfield works so hard that she not only gets an office, but a secretary, to boot. The judge has a reputation as a difficult woman, and there's been quite a turnover. But I recognized this one—Myrtle Means—as having more longevity than most. Myrtle is the same blue-haired, lipsticked lady of uncertain age who had made the arrangements with the judge when McQuaid and I got married. Judge Porterfield officiated at the ceremony (she remembered to turn up her hearing aid but forgot to omit the word *obey*), which Hurricane Josephine turned into an unforgettable experience—not your average wedding, by any means. The torrential downpours spawned by the hurricane not only soaked the entire wedding party but drenched the cake, washed out River Road, and marooned the entire wedding party at the Pack Saddle Inn, where the ceremony took place. McQuaid and I spent our wedding night in a mirrored honeymoon suite with red-flocked walls that might have been designed as a set for *The Best Little Whorehouse in Texas*. But that didn't bother us. We were legal. We could hang out in the honeymoon suite until the floodwaters went down.

"Hello, Mrs. Means," I said to the secretary. "I'm China Bayles. The judge is expecting me."

Mrs. Means, who had been reading the Pecan Springs *Enterprise* spread out on her desk, rose from her chair and reached for a cane propped against the wall. She's younger than the judge by at least a decade, but she's had a hip transplant and doesn't get around as well as she did. "If you'll give me a minute," she said. "I'll see if Her Majesty is available."

I raised an eyebrow. "Her Majesty?"

"Today, anyway," Mrs. Means said in a meaningful tone. "She was out late last night on a case, and she's been in a foul mood all day." She looked solemnly down at the newspaper. "In case you haven't heard, Coach Duffy was murdered. In cold blood, right there at the high school. The judge was called out to examine the body."

I followed her glance, my attention caught by the black headline screaming across the front page: COACH DUFFY VICTIM OF RANDOM SHOOTER. I scanned the first few paragraphs. There was no mention of the fact that Duffy, who was described as the "most popular coach in Panther history," was in the company of an underage girl when the shooter approached the truck. Nothing was said about the shooter, who was identified only as an "unknown woman"—entirely understandable, since the PSPD had not yet released any details by the time Hark Hibler had to put the paper to bed. Nothing was said about Brian or the photo, either. Hark had made up for the lack of hard facts, however, by running a three-column black-bordered photo of Duffy, two page-length columns extolling the man's winning football record, and another column of comments from the mayor ("Shocked! I'm just totally shocked!"), the city council ("We are all in a state of utter shock"), and

257

members of the school board ("On behalf of the entire school district, we can only say how completely shocked we are").

My eyes went back to the headline, and I frowned. Random shooter, huh? I wondered how Hark would feel when he had to print the *real* story. And then I remembered the Seidensticker family's place in the community and wondered if the real story would ever be fully told. Hark is a responsible journalist and a serious news-hound, and I was sure he'd want to print all the gory details of the crime, the arrest, the arraignment, the bail hearing, and the trial, as they emerged over the next months. But blood is always thicker than water, even in the newspaper business. Hark might not get to tell it all.

Mrs. Means was back. "She'll see you now, Ms. Bayles." She glanced down at the paper and back up at me, her face mournful. "You just have to wonder why God lets such terrible things happen in this world, doncha?"

"You're right about that," I said.

She shook her head uncomprehendingly. "It had to've been a crazy woman who escaped from a mental hospital, wouldn't you think? Or maybe a cult thing. You know, witches, black magic. Ritual murder." She fished a handkerchief out of the neck of her navy dress and blew her nose. "It's a sad day for Pecan Springs, is all I can say."

I couldn't disagree with that, either, I thought, as I went down the hall and tapped at the judge's door. However you looked at it, it was a sad day.

Judge Porterfield's office is decorated in what you might call "early utilitarian." She has a metal desk that almost certainly dates back to the Second World War, a floor-to-ceiling bookshelf filled with law references, and a half-dozen metal filing cabinets. There are no photos on the wall, no artificial plants, and no special effects—unless you count the judge herself, who was wearing a zippy black and white polka-dotted dress with a bright yellow scarf and a string of large yellow beads. She does not believe that women past seventy ought to fade into the woodwork.

"Afternoon, China," she said, motioning me to a chair. "I heard that you and the chief drove south to pick up Lopez this mornin'. Everything go okay down there?"

"Unfortunately, no," I said regretfully, and reported what had happened in Friendship that morning. Just that morning? It already seemed like a week ago.

The judge scowled. "Bad news, that is *bad* news. I was hopin' we'd get a motive out of her." She pushed her lips in and out. "You said last night that you thought the shootin' might be connected to the Lopez girl's suicide."

I nodded.

She regarded me darkly. "Don't suppose it'd have anything to do with the fact that Coach Duffy was sittin' out there in the parking lot with a sixteen-year-old girl, would it?"

"I'm afraid it would," I said, and told her the story I had pieced together. "It's clear that Duffy sexually abused Angela Lopez," I said, wrapping it up. "And there's no doubt, at least as far as I'm concerned, that Lopez shot him because of what he did to her daughter."

The judge was silent for several moments, thinking, then shook her head. "Just can't seem to get my mind around that corner, I'm afraid. I've met the man, served on the hospital board with his wife, been a guest in their house. Hard for me to believe he'd do somethin' like that. Reckon it'd be even harder for some of those Boosters. Chuck Manning, f'r instance." She gave me a sharp look. "What evidence d'you have for this accusation, besides the mother's say-so? O'course," she added, "she's dead, so she can't speak up."

I thought of the stash hidden in the football. "There's evidence. The sheriff has Duffy's letters. A couple of Angela's friends recall what she told them. And, of course, there's Jacquelyn Keene, the girl who was in the truck with Duffy last night."

The judge's expression was dour. "I'm just thinkin' about what the media is going to make of this. It'll be a circus like nothin' this town ever saw before. Helluva lot worse than that Obermann business last fall, 'cause it's got sex in it. Folks're always a lot more interested in a murder that's got sex in it than they are in just plain murder." She sighed gustily. "At least there's not goin' to be a trial. All the principals are dead. There's nobody left to put on trial."

"There's that," I agreed. "But I'm still concerned that we don't know the full story of Angela Lopez's death. When you made your ruling, did you—"

"When I made my ruling," she cut in crisply, "I pretty much took the Bexar County ME's say-so, same as I always do. He put down suicide as the cause of death, which in his medical opinion was the correct thing to do, and I couldn't see a reason in this world to disagree. It was Nembutal, as I remember. No sexual activity, no sign that anybody else'd been in that room with her. She just put on that nightgown, wrote a suicide note in pretty purple ink, and laid herself out all pretty and peaceful. Girls do that, y'know." She grinned suddenly. "Doesn't always work the way they think, though. Remember Lupe Velez? The Mexican Spitfire?"

"No, I don't remember Lupe Velez," I said, and added, in a cautioning tone, "But it wasn't just Nembutal, Judge. It was—"

"Well, I guess you're too young." She leaned back and her chair squeaked. "This was in the late thirties, early forties. Lupe was a real beauty. Married to Tarzan for a while."

"Tarzan?"

"You know. Johnny Weissmuller."

"Oh, him." I hid a smile. "Of course."

"Yeah. Had an affair with Gary Cooper, too. Anyway, she put on a sexy nightgown and took a handful of Seconal. Except she had to throw up, and when they found her dead, she had her head in the toilet. Nothin' pretty about that."

"It wasn't just Nembutal," I persisted. "Angela had *flunitrazepam* in her system, too."

She frowned. "I saw that in the report. But it wasn't anything but a trace."

"It metabolizes quickly. The question is why it was there at all. It's not something you'd take if you were alone and planning to do the job with Nembutal. And then there's the matter of that unidentified thumbprint on the bottom of the pudding cup."

"Sales clerk."

"Maybe. But why weren't Angela's fingerprints there?" I paused. "And what about the nightgown? It was brand-new—the investigating officer even found the Neiman Marcus cash register receipt under the bed."

"Neiman Marcus?" Both white eyebrows went up.

"That's right." I could see that the significance of this was not lost on the judge. "And what's more, the gown was charged on a Neiman Marcus account."

"Whose?"

"That's not clear just yet. There was," I added, "no bag. And Angela had no luggage. So how did she bring the nightgown and the other stuff to the motel? And there was no purple pen in her purse, or anywhere in the room. So how—and when—did she write that suicide note?"

The judge leaned forward. "No pen?"

"No purple pen."

She picked up a pencil and turned it in her fingers. "So you're tellin' me that somebody else was there with her." Her tone was brisk. "And that somebody was Tim Duffy, who is right now layin' over there in Love's Funeral Parlor, where every single person in this town will line up to pay their respects."

"Who else would it be?" I asked, spreading my hands.

She squinted at me. "How the hell should I know?" she asked testily. "You're the one arguin' this case, Counselor."

I cleared my throat. So we were being formal. "The preponderance of the evidence suggests that the victim was not alone in that room," I said firmly. "I am asking you to reopen the case, Judge Porterfield." Of course, if she didn't, Sheila could continue the investigation on her own say-so. But in Adams County, where there is no medical examiner, Justice Porterfield serves for the coroner. Coming from her, the ruling would definitely get more attention.

"Reopen the case." The judge pushed her gold-rimmed glasses onto her forehead and rubbed her eyes, as if this was not a vision she wanted to contemplate. "What the hell good would that do, China? The girl is dead, the girl's mother is dead, the coach is dead. If he did it, he's already paid the penalty, hasn't he?"

I felt myself stiffen. All this was true, of course. But what about justice? What about a girl who didn't kill herself? What about—

"If it turned out that Duffy had anything to do with that girl's death, it'd pretty near kill that wife of his," the judge went on, tenting her fingers under her chin.

"That's true," I said. I eyed her. "And of course, the Seidenstickers wouldn't be happy about it at all. Nor would the school board." The judge, who is one of the more liberal citizens of Pecan Springs, has found herself on the wrong side of the conservative Seidenstickers more often than not. She has been known to take on the school board, too.

The corners of her mouth quirked in what might have been a smile, and she leaned back. "Old Claude Leglar," she said. "He would pitch the biggest fit you ever did see."

"That's for certain," I said.

"Howie Masterson would be in a twit, too, since the Seidenstickers put up about half the money that got him elected." She put her glasses back on and tucked her wispy white hair back. "In fact, it'd be a whole helluva lot better for all these folks if everybody thinks it was just some crazy woman from down near Crystal City, maybe high on dope or booze or both, who drives up to Pecan Springs, picks Duffy out at random, follows him around and shoots him, then drives on home and put a bullets in herself. Now, wouldn't it?"

"Yes, it would," I said. "And from the headline in the *Enterprise*, that's exactly what people are going to think."

She narrowed her eyes, smacked her hand against the top of the desk, and sat forward. "How*ever*. In view of Mrs. Lopez's suicide on her daughter's grave, and what appears to be prior sexual misconduct on the part of Coach Duffy, directed to Mrs. Lopez's daughter, last night's shootin' does not seem to me to be a random event. And we cannot have coaches and teachers and priests, however well-connected, foolin' around with young kids." Her voice became sharper. "That's about the very worst thing there is in this world, and it is *not* goin' to happen in my precinct, by heaven."

"I am very glad you feel that way," I said.

She hit a button on the phone and picked up the handset. "Myrtle, you call the police chief and tell her I'm reopenin' the Lopez case. And when you've done that, call Howie Masterson's office and tell him the same thing." There was a pause, and the judge snapped, "Well, do it anyway, Myrtle. He can't bite your head off over the phone, can he?" She banged down the handset and rolled her eyes.

"These girls wanta be part of the action," she said, "but they don't wanta do any of the heavy liftin'. "

Girls? I wasn't sure whether the judge was making a joke about Myrtle Means, or whether from her advanced perspective, any woman who was ten years younger qualified as a "girl."

MY next port of call was the police station, where I planned to check out the evidence Sophie Murdock had collected from the motel room where Angela had died. I had driven only a couple of blocks when my cell phone rang. The caller ID panel displayed an Austin number that I didn't recognize, but I picked it up anyway. My mistake. The caller was Miles Danforth. My brother. Excuse me. My half brother.

"China," he said, in an urgent tone, "I've been trying to reach you for the last couple of days. Where have you been?"

I wanted to tell him that I'd been trying like crazy to stay out of his reach, but I forced myself to be nice. "It's a busy time," I said. "Lots going on at the shop. What's up?"

"Have you looked at the letters?"

"Nope." I signaled for a left turn, waited for the traffic to clear, and went. "Is there some rush about this, Buddy? I mean, why exactly should I be in a hurry to read letters that have been hanging around for . . . well, since he died." I forced myself. "Since our father died, I mean."

There was a silence on the other end of the line. "I thought," he said stiffly, "that you would be interested—especially when you read the last few letters. You'll see. There's a really serious issue that we—"

I had just about had it with serious issues today. "If you don't mind," I said, "I am in the middle of a suicide investigation that's turned into a murder. Maybe two murders. I—"

"I thought you said things were busy at the *shop*," he broke in, sounding confused. "What's with suicide? And *murder*?"

"I was doing a favor for a friend and it got complicated. Anyway, I've barely had time to eat and sleep, let alone read antique love letters." One of the Pecan Springs garbage trucks—the city council had them painted green to denote the community's green consciousness—pulled out of an alley right in front of me. I braked hard enough to send my handbag flying onto the floor. "Hell," I said, tasting blood. I'd bitten my tongue.

"I didn't quite get that."

"I said *hell*. I had to put on the brakes to keep from being smashed by a garbage truck and I bit my tongue. I shouldn't be talking on the phone while I'm driving." Just because everybody else does it, that's no excuse. I'd really have been ticked off if the garbage truck driver had been on *his* cell phone.

"Oh. Sorry." He paused, penitent. "I know you think I'm bugging you about this."

"There's no argument on that score," I muttered.

"I didn't quite—"

"Skip it," I said loudly. "You're bugging me, and it's okay. But I'm curious. These letters have been hanging around almost as long as the Old Testament. Why the rush?"

"Because . . ."

Another pause. The light at Brazos and Third turned red and a teenaged girl in a tight leather skirt and high-heeled boots sauntered across in front of me. I took advantage of the stop to pick up my handbag. As I did, the top came open and spilled out a handful of change and various other artifacts.

"Shit," I said. Then hastily, into the phone, "That wasn't for you, Buddy. I spilled some stuff in the car."

"Because," he went on, as if I hadn't spoken, "when I read the last five or six letters, it looks to me like Uncle Bob—your father, I mean—"

"Our father," I said, eyeing the scatter of coins and stuff on the floor.

"Okay, our father. It looks to me like he was in some kind of trouble. Serious trouble. He mentions death threats and—"

"Death threats? Oh, come on, Buddy."

"Yeah." His voice was flat, but darkened by withheld emotion. "That's what I used to think, too. My mother always insisted that his death was no accident, but I thought she was . . . well, being dramatic. After I read those letters, I changed my mind."

Death threats. I still wasn't sure I believed it, but I don't suppose it should be any surprise. My father's firm was into a lot of pretty sticky stuff, and the people he was involved with—politicos, powerful families, major players in all the big-ticket Texas games—rolled the dice for very high stakes. But this wasn't something I wanted to get into, not at the moment. And probably not ever. I had all kinds of reasons to dislike my father—his betrayal of my mother and me being at the top of the list— and no reason at all to wonder why he died.

"Buddy," I said firmly, "I really don't want to hear this. I've got way too much stuff on my plate to—"

"Don't get mad, China," he replied heavily, sounding defeated. "I don't blame you. You're a busy woman, and it was all a long time ago. I understand why you don't care."

"I'm not mad, and it's not that I don't care. I just don't have time to—"

"You don't need to be defensive. I'm saying it's okay."

"I am *not* being defensive," I yelped. "It's just that—"

"You're right. I understand. I doubt if there's anything we can do, anyway. It was a long time ago. He's dead and she's dead and nobody gives a shit. Just destroy the letters and we'll forget all about it."

"Okay, *okay*," I said. "I'll destroy the letters and we'll forget all about it." I clicked the button and tossed the phone onto the seat. When it began to ring again, I turned the damned thing off. If I ignored Buddy long enough, maybe he'd go away.

But there was one thing I couldn't ignore. It was the purple pen that had spilled out of my purse and lay on the floor of the car—the one I had found in the cardboard box in Margarita Lopez's house that morning. I had forgotten all about it, but suddenly it seemed important.

Very important.

WHEN I got to the police station, I went first to Sheila's office. She turned away from her computer monitor, where she was reading a report. She looked cross.

"What's this about Judge Porterfield reopening the Lopez suicide?" she asked, before I even opened my mouth. "Did you have anything to do with that?"

"Yep," I said. "I confess. I'm the one. I talked her into it."

"Well, I hope you have something more than a gut feeling and a circumstantial argument, China. We've got barely enough manpower to handle the ongoing investigations, without reopening closed ones. Something like this could take more man-hours than we can spare." She ticked her fingers on the monitor screen. "The budget's so tight that we can't afford any more overtime, and one of my best officers has to go on permanent disability. We're going to miss him."

"Here you go, Smart Cookie," I said, and put the purple pen on her desk. "You might want to have this checked out." Most inks can be identified by thin-layer chromatography, a process so simple that it's taught in high school chemistry classes.

She frowned down at the pen. "Refresh my memory."

"The suicide note that was found with Angela Lopez's body was written in purple ink, but Officer Murdock didn't find a purple pen in the motel room. I discovered *this* purple pen in the cardboard box I found in the closet this morning, along with the other odds and ends that Mrs. Lopez brought back from Pecan Springs after her daughter died."

"In the closet?" Sheila regarded the pen with interest. "It's probably nothing, but it won't hurt to take a look." She opened a desk drawer, took out a plastic zipper-top bag, and put the pen in it. "Give this to Dorrie," she said, "and tell her to give it to Kinsey."

"Kinsey?"

"In forensics." She closed the drawer. "She can do a preliminary ink analysis, enough to tell us whether it's the same brand of pen that wrote the note. If it is, we'll send it to Austin." She turned back to her monitor, adding, over her shoulder, "Oh, and be sure to get a Property Inventory form from Dorrie."

Property inventory forms. The Pecan Springs police have come a long way from the days when Chief Bubba Harris kept his office under his

Stetson and wouldn't know what to do with a computer unless it had a drawer for his cigars. I paused at the door. "Murdock said it was okay for me to have a look at the evidence from the Lopez case."

"Right," Sheila said in a preoccupied tone, and waved her hand.

I stopped at Dorrie's desk, filled out the Property Inventory form, and handed over the bag containing the purple pen. "Chief says this should go to Kinsey."

"Sure thing," Dorrie replied, and went back to applying orange nail polish to her nails. Sheila may have updated the department's property inventory management, but there's not much she can do with Dorrie except fire her. But in spite of the nails, the perfume, and the pile of Dolly-Parton hair, there isn't much Dorrie doesn't know about Pecan Springs. It would be impossible to replace her, and Dorrie knows it.

"Can you point me in the direction of the Property Room?" I asked. "The chief says it's okay if I look at the stuff from the Lopez suicide case."

Dorrie frowned. "Carl—our evidence tech—is off this afternoon. Had to take his wife to Austin to get a sonogram. It's twins, which will make six. Four boys, two girls. The twins are girls."

"Six!" One is just about right, as far as I'm concerned.

"Yeah. Well, there was eight of us, including a pair of twins. My mom managed." She recapped the bottle, blew on her nails, and reached for a ring of keys, using the tips of her fingers so as not to damage her orange nails. "I guess I got to take you. Come on."

We headed down a flight of stairs to the basement, made a left turn at the foot of the stairs and another left at the staff bulletin board, which displayed the results of a recent bowling tournament and a request for donations to the Help-A-Family Fund. Careful with her nails, Dorrie unlocked a door marked Property and Evidence Unit, and pushed it open.

The stuffy, windowless room smelled of fresh paint and floor tile adhesive. It was furnished with a desk, a worktable and pair of metal folding chairs, and two long rows of three-tiered gray metal shelves filled with labeled boxes. A clock ticked on the green-painted wall.

"This is where we keep the stuff we don't have to double-lock," Dorrie said. She nodded toward a door that looked like it might lead to a walk-in safe. "There's enough pot and coke in there to make somebody filthy rich. Not to mention guns."

"I'll bet," I said. At first glance, Pecan Springs may look pretty and clean and cozy, the kind of wholesome place you'd love to bring up your kids. But it's located on an interstate highway that serves as a pipeline for illegal drugs smuggled from Mexico to everywhere else in the country— to your hometown, maybe. Under the attractive surface of Pecan Springs, things happen that you wouldn't want to know about.

"I gotta stand here and watch while you look." Dorrie looked stern. "Make sure you don't take anything." She pointed to a box of plastic gloves. "You gotta wear these, too. Don't want no mysterious prints on this stuff. Carl puts the boxes on the shelf by the date. Lopez would be over there, far right."

I pulled on the gloves. Examining items held in a police evidence locker used to be part of my job description as a criminal lawyer, although I haven't done it lately. There's a kind of edgy excitement to it, like going through somebody's underwear drawer, which is heightened by the knowledge that the police would really rather not have a lawyer making free with something that might exonerate the person they've already charged with the crime. And even though nobody had been charged in this case, the thrill was still there, under the sadness evoked by the sight of the items in the box. It was labeled with the name "Lopez" and the date of her death. Clipped to the front was a typed Property Inventory form, listing all the items I had already seen in the police report, with the handwritten addition of "Neiman Marcus register receipt." Sophie had corrected her omission.

I put the box on the table and took the things out carefully. The yellow nightie, with frills of stiff yellow lace at the neck and hem. The Neiman Marcus receipt, with a time-date stamp that showed that the purchase was made about four hours before Angela checked into the motel. The plastic bathroom cup in which the date-rape drug was presumably administered, the plastic pudding cup and spoon—all still bearing traces of fingerprint powder. The denim purse and its contents (no purple pen), and the suicide note.

The suicide note. It was written on lined pink paper, some five inches wide and three inches high, in a young woman's flowing handwriting, with circles instead of dots over the lowercase *i*s. *I'm really sorry. I didn't mean it to end like this. Angie.* The bottom of the note was straight, the top torn jaggedly. The writing began close to the torn top edge, and as I looked at it, I saw it for what it was: the bottom three inches of a page from what had probably been an eight-by-five notepad.

I was frowning at this piece of paper when the door opened and Sophie Murdock came in, slightly out of breath.

"Hey, Sophie," Dorrie said, and put the keys on the desk. "Now that you're here, I'll go back upstairs. Lock up when y'all are done, and bring me the keys. Okay?" She gave a ta-ta wave of her orange fingertips and disappeared.

"The chief told me you were here," Sophie said, when Dorrie had gone. "She said Judge Porterfield reopened the Angela Lopez case. You get her to do that?"

I grinned. "Who, me? You find out anything at Neiman Marcus?"

"You bet," she said, with a flash of her dimples. "I got this guy in Accounting to pull the charge slip. I took the signed original, and he kept the copy. I just put it on the chief's desk. Thought she ought to see it. The nightgown was charged to the Duffy account, all right."

"No kidding?" I felt a great sense of relief, as though we had come to the end of a long and painful journey. "Hey, Sophie, that was great work!"

"Well, maybe." She folded her arms across her uniformed chest. "So what do you think happened in that room?"

I went swiftly through the scenario I'd been working out in my head. "Angela Lopez posed a serious threat to Tim Duffy—a time bomb that could go off anytime in the next eight years, until the statute of limitations ran out. After Angie found out about Jake and began to worry about how many other girls the guy might molest, she decided that the time was now. She wrote to Duffy, telling him that she was going to blow the whistle." I glanced down at the torn pink note. "It might have been a two- or three-page letter, ending with this sentence—*I'm really sorry. I didn't mean it to end like this*—and her name."

"So you're saying that's not a suicide note after all?" Sophie asked, interested.

"Exactly. Her letter must have convinced him that he had to get rid of her. And when he read the last sentence, he saw the potential. He'd kill her and make it look like a suicide. So he set up the date in the motel room, maybe telling her that they needed a place to talk where they wouldn't be interrupted. Then he obtained the roofie, which he knew would make her compliant enough to eat the Nembutal he'd stirred into the pudding. He bought the yellow nightgown to make it look even more like a suicide."

Sophie was shaking her head, but I ignored her. "He probably took

272

her clothes off and put the gown on her after she was unconscious, not realizing that he'd dropped the register receipt under the bed. He—"

"No." Sophie shook her head harder. "Sorry, but it didn't go down like that, China."

I stared at her. "It didn't?"

"Nope. Tim Duffy didn't buy that nightgown."

"But you said it was charged on the Duffy account."

"It was. Only it wasn't Tim Duffy who charged it. It was his wife."

"His *wife?*" I was dumbfounded.

And then, all of a sudden, I wasn't.

I was remembering the scene in the Duffys' kitchen, the week before, when Cass and I had catered their party. Remembering Glenda Duffy's wide-eyed glance at Missy Bowers, a glance of horrified understanding.

Angela wasn't the only girl Tim Duffy had set his heart on, and his wife knew it.

Chapter Twenty-two

According to old legends, deadly nightshade (*Atropa belladonna*)
belongs to the devil, who goes about trimming and tending it in
his leisure, and can only be diverted from its care on one night in
the year, that is on Walpurgis, when he is preparing for the Witches'
Sabbath. The name Belladonna is said to record an old superstition
that at certain times the herb takes the form of an enchantress of
exceeding loveliness, whom it is dangerous to look upon.

Maud Grieve
A Modern Herbal (1931)

 The door opened again, and Sheila came into the evidence
room. She glanced from me to Sophie, shaking her head.

"Do you *believe* it?" she asked.

"Well, yes, I guess I do," I said gloomily, "although I feel like a dimwit
for not figuring it out before."

I didn't know her well, but even a superficial acquaintance suggested
that Glenda Seidensticker Duffy was a beautiful woman with a great deal
to lose—and a very great deal to protect. She must have felt driven to
protect not only her husband but his reputation and his successful career,
which had purchased for her a lifestyle and a place in the community
that many women envied. She must have been struck with fear and des-
peration when she found the letter Angela had written to her husband
and realized that the girl posed an unimaginable danger to both of them.

274

If Angie did what she threatened to do, Duffy would lose his coaching job and Glenda would lose everything. Getting rid of the girl was the only sure way, she must have thought, to save herself and her husband from the threat of loss and public humiliation.

Only it wasn't, of course. As long as Tim Duffy couldn't keep his hands off young girls, there would always be a threat. Angela, Jake, Missy Bowers, others. There was no way for Glenda to know, or even guess, how many young women he had been involved with—and that, I guessed, accounted for the look of horrified recognition I had seen when she glanced at Missy that night in the kitchen, and realized that it wasn't over.

I pushed those thoughts away. We didn't need more speculation. What we needed was forensic evidence so compelling that not even the very best defense attorney could refute it.

"I wonder if Glenda Duffy left any prints on that charge slip," I said.

"Her signature is on it," Sophie replied with a frown. "Isn't that enough?"

"It proves that she bought it, but I wasn't thinking about that. I was wondering whether we could match Glenda's prints against that unidentified thumbprint on the bottom of the plastic pudding cup. The print on the cup was entered into your database, wasn't it?" In most police departments, all prints retrieved from a crime scene—and this had been initially treated as a crime scene—are entered into the computer, for possible matching against nation-wide databases.

"Sure it was," Sophie said excitedly.

"Kinsey's running a print analysis on the charge slip right now." Sheila picked up the keys. "Let's lock up here and go see if she's found anything."

Kinsey had hit the jackpot. There were two viable prints on the charge slip, and one—a thumbprint—matched the unidentified thumbprint on the bottom of the plastic pudding cup, placing Glenda Duffy in the motel room with Angela Lopez. What's more, the purple pen I found in the closet at the Lopez house held the same ink that had written the so-called suicide note. It would be tested further, but there was no doubt now that we were dealing with a planned, premeditated murder—and that Glenda Duffy had done it.

"I don't know what Howie Masterson is going to say when I take him this case," Sheila muttered darkly. "It is going to scare the hell out of him."

"That's what he gets for campaigning on a get-tough-on-crime plat-form." I grinned, thinking of those Texas Tough billboards Howie had put up along the highway when he was running for district attorney. "Howie's in the big-time now. He's got to take the bad with the good—even though, in his worst nightmares, he never imagined that he'd be prosecuting old Joe Seidensticker's granddaughter."

"When are we going to pick Mrs. Duffy up?" Sophie asked.

"Not until Howie's a hundred percent on board with this case," Sheila said, between clenched teeth. "I am not going out on this limb by myself." She paused, frowning. "Anyway, I don't think she's a flight risk. As far as she knows, Angela's death is still considered a suicide."

"And she'll want to show up for her husband's funeral tomorrow," I said.

Sheila nodded. "Howie will want to wait until that's over." She thought for a moment. "In fact, under the circumstances, he might want to talk to the Seidensticker family lawyer and arrange a surrender and a quick arraignment. That might be the easiest thing all the way around—reduce the possible media exposure."

I could have pointed out that if the killer had been a black woman drug addict she wouldn't have merited such tender consideration—but Howie was going to handle things his way, without regard to my opinion. All I cared about was seeing that Angela got the justice she deserved. It looked like the process was underway.

"Well," I said cheerfully, "I'll leave you public servants to get on with protecting the public welfare. I'm a working girl with a business to run."

Sheila walked me to the door. "I owe you for this, China. For being persistent about Angela Lopez, I mean. If you hadn't kept at it—"

"Save it until you get a conviction," I replied. "You know what they say about counting your chicks before they're hatched."

"Seems like a sure thing to me," Sophie said. "There's plenty of evidence. Hard evidence, too."

I shook my head. "You never know," I said. "You just never know."

And we didn't.

I skipped Tim Duffy's funeral. I didn't have any respects to pay, either to the dead man or his widow. Instead, I sent flowers to the Friendship funeral home for Margarita Lopez, with instructions that they be taken to the Cemeterio Guadalupe and placed on the grave. Red and white carnations. Red for blood, white for purity. I couldn't condone what Margarita did, but I understood, and sympathized.

And I didn't pester Sheila with questions about her progress on the case. Given the social prominence of the Duffys and the Seidenstickers, the chief of police and the district attorney were going to have their hands full. I had done all I could, and I didn't want to get in the way. I guessed, though, that Howie had talked to Glenda's lawyer, and that the lawyer was making arrangements for her surrender, the details of which would be kept for as long as possible from the media (meaning Hark Hibler and the Pecan Springs *Enterprise*).

Anyway, I had plenty to do. There was the shop to manage, Brian to look after (he had stoically returned to school), and the various Valentine's events to cope with—not to mention worrying about Ruby's affair with Colin Fowler, or Dan Reid, to give him his real name. But there wasn't anything I could do about that, either, so I just had to grit my teeth and get on with business. I couldn't decide whether I was glad to know about Fowler's past or wished that Sheila hadn't told me. I just knew that I had to keep it to myself. I couldn't tell Ruby.

It was the day after the funeral. Ruby had left early that afternoon, Cass was in the kitchen making up a batch of dinners for her Thymely Gourmet customers, and I was closing the cash register and locking up the shop. I was turning out the lights when Cass came in.

"Would you have time to make a couple of deliveries with me this afternoon, China? My shoulder is giving me problems, and I'd really appreciate it if you'd drive. Big Red Mama is a wonderful gal, but she doesn't have power steering."

"I'd be glad to," I said.

It took only a few minutes to carry Cass's orders out of the kitchen and load them into Mama's capacious rear. I climbed in behind the wheel. "Where are we going?"

"Bronwyn Avenue."

"Bronwyn? Isn't that where—"

"Right," Cass said, fastening her safety belt. "Where Audrey Manning lives. Her husband wants me to put the dinners into the freezer. It's a surprise."

"What if Audrey's at home?"

278

"She isn't. Her husband called this afternoon and said that they were going to Austin for dinner this evening. He left the back door unlocked, and the freezer is in the garage. All we have to do is sneak in, dump the dinners, and run."

I grinned. "I'll bet Audrey will be surprised."

We had no idea.

When we got to the Mannings' house, we parked in the drive, Cass opened the back door and turned on the light, and I carried the boxes into the garage. I set them down on the floor, lifted the lid of the chest-type freezer, and looked inside.

"There'd be more room," I said, "if we took out this big bag of ironing."

"Ironing?" Cass asked.

"Sure. Haven't you ever dampened clothes and stuck them in the freezer to iron later?"

"To tell the truth," Cass said wryly, "ironing is against my principles." She opened the black plastic bag I had pulled out. "And this isn't ironing, either, China. It's a quilt." She frowned. "Wait a sec. This looks like . . . like Carol's quilt!"

It not only looked like Carol's quilt, it was. Even if I hadn't recognized it from the photo Ruby had shown us, I could see Carol's name embroidered on a label sewn in the corner.

Cass and I stared at each other in speechless astonishment.

"So Audrey was the one who stole it," Cass said at last. Her eyes widened. "And Ruby's Ouija had it right!"

I frowned down at the quilt in my hands. "What does Ruby's Ouija have to do with anything?" And then I realized what Cass was talking about. "Never mind," I said ruefully. "I get it." Carol's quilt was frozen— and Audrey had complained of the cold. In fact, the night of the Ouija party, she had been shivering uncontrollably when the rest of us were comfortable. Ouija had pointed to both the thief and the place where she had hidden her ill-gotten goods. Far-fetched? Yes, but Ouija had also hit the jackpot as far as the Broncos football was concerned. So who was I to question its methods or its integrity?

"Audrey must have wanted Best-in-Show very badly," Cass said in a sad voice.

"I guess she did it on impulse," I said. "What do you want to bet that she was sorry afterward? Especially after Ruby began playing Nancy Drew. She probably invited herself to the Ouija party just to make sure that her name didn't come up as a suspect."

"So what do we do now?" Cass wondered.

That was easy. "We put Audrey's dinners in the freezer," I said decidedly. "And we return Carol's quilt to her. The show is still up. The quilts won't be judged for another week, so there's no harm done."

"Except to Carol's and Audrey's relationship," Cass said with a sigh.

"I don't know about that," I said. "Carol strikes me as a forgiving person. Maybe she'll just hang the quilt again, without saying a word to Audrey." And maybe she won't—but that was up to Carol.

"We've probably lost a customer, too," Cass added. "When Audrey finds the food, she'll know exactly who took the quilt."

"This particular customer is well lost, if you ask me," I said sourly, stuffing the quilt back into the plastic bag. "Who wants to cook for a thief?"

"I suppose you're right," Cass said with resignation. She followed me out of the garage and closed the door, still shaking her head. "I can't wait to tell Ruby. She is going to be totally amazed."

I opened Mama's rear door and shoved in the plastic bag. "Okay. What's the next stop?"

Cass jerked her thumb. "Across the street. The Duffys."

I let out my breath in a whoosh. Why hadn't I recognized the Duffy house? But I knew why. It had been dark when we drove up, the night of the party, and it just hadn't registered—even though Audrey had mentioned that they were neighbors. But it registered now.

"We can't!" I exclaimed. "We can't leave those meals because—"

And then I stopped. I couldn't tell Cass why. She didn't know what Glenda had done. Nobody would know until the DA was good and ready.

"Why not?" Cass asked reasonably. "Sure, her husband's dead, and it's a great tragedy. But she'd surely be comforted to know that he planned a Valentine surprise for her. And it's great food. What's more, she won't have to cook. Come on, China." And with that, she marched across the street to the Duffys' front door.

I had no choice but to pick up the box of dinners and follow Cass. She was knocking for the second time when I stepped up on the front porch behind her. She waited a moment, then knocked again. After another moment, she gave the door a little push, and it swung open.

"It's unlocked," she said. "Let's go back to the kitchen. Coach Duffy told me to put the dinners into the refrigerator freezer. I'll leave a note."

With a resigned sigh, I followed her down the hall. I was just the delivery girl. Cass was calling the shots, so we'd do it her way.

We went into the kitchen, and Cass opened the freezer, one of those big side-by-sides. "Well," she said cheerfully, "at least there's no stolen quilt. You go ahead and put the dinners away. I'll find something to write on."

I relocated bags of frozen potatoes and packages of hot dogs and made

281

the room to stow all fourteen of Cass's Thymely Gourmet dinners. I was putting the last one in when I heard a noise and turned around to see Cass clinging to the doorjamb. Her eyes were round and her face was ashen.

"What's wrong?" I asked. "Cass, what—"

"She's dead," she gasped in a horrified voice. "Glenda Duffy is dead!"

But she wasn't, quite. She was lying on the sofa, dressed in a pretty negligee, her hair spread out around her, a dish that contained traces of butterscotch pudding on the table beside the sofa. She was breathing, but barely. And she was still breathing when EMS arrived to take her to the emergency room. Another half-hour, the paramedic said, and she would have been dead.

"I guess she just couldn't face the thought of life without her husband," Cass said sadly, as we watched the ambulance drive off, lights flashing, siren wailing.

"She couldn't face what was coming," I said grimly. "I wasn't going to tell you, but since you saved her life, I think you ought to know what's ahead for her."

When I finished the story Cass was crying. "I just can't believe it," she said despairingly. "Tim Duffy and those girls? And Glenda Duffy, a killer? How *awful!*"

"Yes," I said. "There's only one comfort, and it's a small one."

"What's that?"

"Her attorney will request that her trial be moved to another venue. It won't be held in Pecan Springs."

She shook her head. "That's a comfort?" she remarked, wiping the tears from her cheeks with the back of her hand. "If you ask me, most people would want the trial to be held here. The courtroom would be jam-packed."

I had to admit that Cass was probably right. Like every other small town, Pecan Springs loves a scandal, even when it features their favorite football coach.

I got the rest of the story from Sheila. On the day of the funeral, Howie Masterson had confronted the Duffys' attorney—a lawyer named James Matheis—with a warrant for Glenda's arrest on the charge of first-degree murder, which carries a possible life sentence. At first, Matheis was incredulous, but when Howie laid out the evidence, he saw the seriousness of it. He picked up the phone and immediately called the patriarch of the Seidensticker family.

The next morning, Matheis and two senior members of the Seidensticker clan went to break the news to Glenda. She took it hard, but Matheis promised her that they would hire the very best criminal attorney in the country, regardless of the cost. They would do their damnedest to get her acquitted of all the charges. Yes, of course it was all ridiculous, he assured her. But it had to be faced. And the very best way to face it was to get the best attorney on their team. In the meantime, though, she would have to steel herself for some unpleasantness.

The surrender was scheduled to take place on the following day. But sometime after Matheis and the Seidenstickers left, Glenda put on a negligee, mixed a handful of Nembutals into some pudding and ate it. And if it hadn't been for Cass's insistence that we deliver the dinners, she would have died.

The *Enterprise* broke the news—the full story of Tim Duffy, of Angela and her mother, and Glenda Duffy—on the day that Glenda was arraigned on one count of first-degree murder. Bail was denied because she had attempted to take her life, and she was remanded to jail under a suicide watch. The trial, when it finally takes place, will likely be held in San Antonio or Austin, and the sensational details will undoubtedly attract the attention of the national press. It will be an embarrassment for Pecan Springs, but a lesson for all of us. The abuse of children is a tragedy we cannot ignore or wish away.

"We don't understand how this could have happened in our town, in any town," Hark Hibler wrote sadly. "It's a terrible story. Our hearts bleed for everyone involved."

Yes. Our hearts bleed.

Chapter Twenty-three

Valentine's Day wouldn't be complete without chocolate, everybody's favorite herb. But our culture is not the first to treasure this divine concoction. The Mayans worshipped the cacao plant (*Theobroma cacao*), used cacao beans as money, and brewed them in a medicinal drink called xocolatl, to ease fatigue and treat the "faint of heart." The Aztecs added chile peppers to their xocolatl to make an aphrodisiac (a different way, perhaps, of treating the heart).

The explorer Cortez knew a good thing when he saw it. He took the cacoa beans back to the Spanish court, where passions soon ran high over chocolate. Doctors prescribed the new drink for everything from tuberculosis to intestinal parasites and sexual dysfunction, and (of course) to strengthen the heart. Recently, scientists have learned that chocolate has twice as many antioxidants as red wine. New research also shows that the flavonoids present in dark chocolate may help reduce heart disease.

In books, the story of a murder usually ends when the killer is apprehended, usually in a car chase or a shootout, with guns blazing and bullets zinging overhead. The loose ends of the plot are neatly tied up, the ambiguities have been tidily resolved, and the reader closes the book with the satisfaction of knowing that justice has been served and everybody got what they deserved.

It doesn't happen that way in real life. Discovering the killer is only one step in a long and tortuous legal journey. The process of obtaining justice for the victim is never easy or conclusive, and even when the jury renders its verdict and the judge pronounces sentence, there's still a feeling that it's not really over. While Angela's story seems to have been wrapped up with the discovery of her killer, it will be years before it's all over.

Another part of this story hasn't ended, either, and that's what I need to tell you about now. It has to do with the letters Buddy Danforth gave me. I had told him I was going to destroy them and we'd forget the whole thing. I had every right, didn't I? My father had carried on an illicit love affair behind my mother's back, over a period of many years. He had secretly fathered a son, to whom he gave preference when it came to offering a place in his firm. And these were only the betrayals we knew about. How much more deception, how much more hurt and pain, was there to discover?

But Buddy's insistence kept nagging at me, and to be totally honest, my curiosity was nudging me, as well. My father was a good-looking, firm-featured man who exuded self-confidence and personal authority, a man who commanded respect, demanded attention. But in the eighteen years I lived with him—or rather, lived in the house that he provided for the three of us, and where he spent some evenings and weekends— I had always considered him even-tempered but distant, personable but chilly. Since he so rarely demonstrated affection for my mother or me, I had come to define him in that way. He was a man who cared only for his work, who didn't have time for love or family.

But now I knew that his affair with Laura Danforth was something other than a short-term office fling. Somewhere deep within him there must have been a capacity for romance, for passion, for tenderness, none of which I could have imagined. So what kind of man was Robert Bayles, really? What was he like, behind that façade of detached objectivity that was all I knew of him? Was his relationship to Laura Danforth primarily sexual? Or did he love her? If he loved her, why didn't he divorce my mother and marry her? How did he feel about his betrayals? Was there any remorse or guilt, any sense of regret? Any wish that things might have turned out differently, if only he had done this, or that, or something else?

In the end, then, it wasn't simple curiosity that drove me to sit down with the letters. It was a feeling that I needed to know more about a man I thought I had known reasonably well.

So one night after Brian had gone to bed, I fortified myself with a glass of wine and the box of Valentine chocolates McQuaid had sent from Albuquerque and spread the letters out on the kitchen table, in the order in which my father had written them. There were fourteen, dating from two years to a week before he died. Most were written in his neat, precise hand, apparently while he was on one of his frequent business trips; a few were typed. The first eight or ten were informal and chatty, inquiring about news of the office, mentioning friends I'd never heard of, asking after Buddy, who by that time had left Stone and Bayles and taken a new position, with an apparent boost from my father, who showed more concern about him than he ever showed about me. (Was that jealousy I felt? Yes, probably. But didn't I have a right to feel jealous?) They were the sort of letters a husband writes to his wife of many years. They weren't love letters, but there was love in every line—not passion, perhaps, but a certain sturdy tenderness, a deep affection, a long-shared and comfortably reciprocated warmth. Each concluded with the same phrase, "You have all my heart, Laura—Bob."

All his heart, I thought sadly. Would my mother have lived a different life, been a different person, if she had had all his heart? And for Laura Danforth, did the belief that she had all his heart make up for the fact that she didn't have *him,* that he was married (apparently irrevocably so) to another woman? These were sad and unanswerable questions. They left me wanting to know more, and I turned to the next letters with anticipation.

But these were written later, much nearer the time of his death, and they were filled with a certain wary edginess, an undercurrent of apprehension and concern. My father was working on a case for a client he called simply Katz, a troubling client, a troubling case, apparently, that took him to Miami and Mexico City and Rio de Janeiro. He instructed Laura to copy several documents—he identified them by their file numbers—and put them into a safety deposit box she was to rent under an assumed name. He asked her to set up an appointment with a man named Gregory, and mentioned a planned trip to Washington. One of the letters ended with the caution: "Remember, not a word. Not a single word, especially to Buddy."

The last two letters had an even sharper tone. He was writing from Washington (that planned trip?) to tell Laura that he had arranged to purchase a $250,000 insurance policy on his life. It was in her name, to keep it separate from his estate, and to keep my mother from learning about it. "I want you to start looking for another job," he wrote. "I know you don't want to leave the firm, but you have to, and you have to do it as soon as possible. Don't wait until this is over." An insurance policy? Because he expected something to happen to him?

This disturbing question was answered, at least partially, in the final letter, dated the week before his death. The script was hasty, less precise, less careful. Laura was told to leave the firm immediately, even though she had not yet found a position, and to get another apartment. And the last few sentences were chilling: "If something happens to me—I should probably rather say 'when'—you are not to make or encourage any sort of investigation. If you do, you could put your life and Buddy's life in very grave danger, and China's and Leatha's, too. I want your promise on this, Laura. It may be the most important thing you ever do for me." It was the only time, in all of the letters, he mentioned my mother and me.

I sat back in my chair. Howard Cosell was snoring contentedly in his basket, the antique Seth Thomas clock was ticking sedately on the wall, and the peace of the old kitchen was wrapped around me like a familiar shawl, warm and comforting. The letters had given me a glimpse into a man I had barely known, in spite of our intimate acquaintance—and he wasn't the person I had thought.

But I also knew now why Buddy had been so urgent. It seemed very clear that my father—our father—considered himself a marked man. And maybe he had been right. Nobody had ever figured out why his car had gone off that bridge and into the bayou. It could have been a murder instead of an accident.

Which led to more questions. What should be done now? What *could* be done now, after all this time? And if something could be done, why do it? Sixteen years is a long time, and even if I learned who had killed my father and why, bringing the killer to justice would likely be impossible.

And what about Leatha? How much did she have to know about Laura Danforth, about Buddy, about what had happened to Dad? How much would she want to know?

And what about me? How deeply did I want to involve myself in Buddy's crusade?

The clock wheezed, cleared its antique throat, and struck eleven, the hollow tones finally dying into silence. I thought a moment more, and then reached for the telephone and punched in some numbers. He didn't answer immediately, and when he did, his voice was thick with sleep.

"Danforth here. Who is it?"

"China. I've just finished reading the letters."

I heard his sharp intake of breath. "Yeah? What do you think?"

I countered with a question. "What are you planning to do?"

There was a silence. Then, "Look into it, I guess. See what I can find out. I owe it to my mother, and maybe even to him." He paused. "What about you?"

I knew what he meant. I took a deep breath. "Speaking from experience, I'd say that an investigation doesn't have a snowball's chance in hell of turning up anything actionable. But keep me informed. And let's have dinner when my husband gets back."

Another silence. "Maybe you'll change your mind." A dry chuckle. "What're you going to tell him about me? That I'm an old friend from your father's firm? A former associate? The guy who taught you how to smoke?"

"No," I said. "I'm going to tell him you're my brother." I paused. "Half-brother."

"Hey," he said. "We're making progress."

"And after that, I'm going to have a talk with my mother."

He let out his breath. "Good luck," he said.

"Good night," I said, and put the phone down.

I'll probably never know what really happened to my father, and I'm not even sure it matters. But I've learned one thing in the past few days. It's never too soon to start telling the truth.

Truth is the only thing that heals.

Herbs for a Healthy Heart

He that is merry of heart hath a continual feast.
Proverbs 15:15

Heart health—in a broader sense, the health of the entire circulatory system—ought to be at the top of everyone's health
concerns. In these health-conscious days, you no doubt already understand the importance of a low-fat diet, weight control, exercise, hyperten-
sion management, and quitting smoking. But herbs can be an important
part of an overall holilstic program of heart heath—especially if you
grow them yourself and enjoy the beneficial exercise of gardening. Here
are just a few of the herbs that have been recommended for circulatory
health, along with a list of resources for you to explore. (As with any med-
ication, consult your physician before using any herb therapeutically.)

Garlic is among the oldest medicinal plants, and has long been praised
for its antibiotic properties. But modern science has learned that garlic
has a role to play in maintaining heart health. In numerous scientific
studies, garlic has been demonstrated to lower cholesterol, reduce blood
pressure, and help prevent blood clots.

Hawthorn helps to dilate coronary blood vessels, thereby improving
the flow of blood to the heart. The leaves, flowers, and berries contain

antioxidants and flavonoids that seem to strengthen the heart muscle, reduce blood levels of cholesterol and triglycerides, and lower high blood pressure.

Ginger, traditionally used as a digestive aid, helps to control several key risk factors for circulatory disease: cholesterol, blood pressure, plaque build-up, and blood clotting.

Ginkgo (*Ginkgo biloba*) is "good for the heart and lungs," according to China's first important herbal, the *Pen Tsao Ching (The Classic of Herbs)* and is widely used in the East to treat many heart and circulatory diseases. Plant chemicals improve arterial blood flow, reduce the risk of clotting, and enhance recovery from stroke.

Alfalfa isn't just for horses. Experiments suggest that alfalfa leaves help prevent arterial plaque and reduce serum cholesterol. Alfalfa sprouts have a reduced effect.

Turmeric, used in India for millennia, stimulates the production of bile, thereby lowering serum cholesterol levels. It also prevents the formation of dangerous blood clots that can lead to heart attack.

Other heart-friendly herbs: astragalus, cat's claw, kelp, kola, motherwort, myrrh, psyllium, passion flower, red pepper, saffron, skullcap, tarragon, and valerian.

Further Reading

Castleman, Michael. "Heart Healing Herbs," *The Herb Quarterly*, Spring, 1993, pp. 14–20.

Foster, Steven. "Heart Health," *The Herb Companion*, August-September, 1998, pp. 61–62.

Hoffman, David. *Healthy Heart: Strengthen Your Cardiovascular System Naturally*. Storey Books, 2000. Pownal, VT.

Hoffman, David. *The New Holistic Herbal*. Element Books, 1990. Shaftesbury, Dorset, UK.

Khalsa, Karta Purkh Singh. "Heart-Healthy Herbs," *The Herb Quarterly*, Spring, 2002, pp. 19–24.

Recipes

Leatha's Lemon Lovers' Coffee Cake
(Chapter Six)

For coffee cake:

2 cups flour

1 teaspoon baking powder

1 teaspoon baking soda

¼ pound (1 stick) unsalted butter

¼ cup finely minced lemon zest

2 teaspoons finely minced lemon herbs (lemon balm, lemon verbena, lemon thyme, lemon mint)

1 cup sugar

3 eggs

1 cup sour cream (low-fat is fine)

Preheat oven to 350 degrees (325 degrees if using a glass cake pan). Grease a $13 \times 9 \times 2$-inch baking pan well and set aside. Prepare Lemon Pecan Topping and set aside.

Sift together flour, baking powder and baking soda, and set aside. Cream butter with lemon zest and lemon herbs until the butter is soft. Add the sugar and mix well. Add the eggs, one at a time, beating after each addition. Add the dry ingredients alternately with the sour cream, beating only until incorporated. Turn batter into greased pan and smooth the top. Sprinkle evenly with Lemon Pecan Topping. Bake for 30 to 45 minutes, until a toothpick inserted into the middle comes out clean. Serve cake while still warm, or cool to room temperature. Makes about 12 servings.

For Lemon Pecan Topping:

5 tablespoons flour

¼ teaspoon nutmeg

¼ cup sugar

½ cup packed light brown sugar

2 tablespoons cold butter or margarine, cut in ½-inch pieces

2 tablespoons grated lemon zest

¾ cup coarsely chopped pecans

Stir together first 4 ingredients. Cut in cold butter or margarine until mixture looks like coarse corn meal. Stir in lemon zest and pecans and set aside.

Chicken Breasts Stuffed with Chives and Fresh Herbs (Chapter Nine)
(reprinted with permission from Lucinda Hutson's
The Herb Garden Cookbook, p. 46)

4 split chicken breasts with skin

4 cloves garlic, minced

8 teaspoons chopped fresh chives

8 generous tablespoons chopped fresh lemony herbs (see below)

¼ cup herb vinegar or dry white wine

1 teaspoon dried mustard

1 teaspoon honey

¼ teaspoon crushed dried red chile pepper

3 tablespoons olive oil

salt, freshly ground pepper, and paprika to taste

Rinse chicken breasts and pat dry. Gently lift up skin of each and rub each with a clove of garlic and 2 teaspoons chopped chives. Stuff about 2 tablespoons of the fresh lemony herbs beneath skin of each breast. Set aside.

Mix herb vinegar or wine with mustard, honey, crushed red pepper, and any herbs that did not fit into chicken, and whisk in the olive oil. Marinate chicken in this mixture for 2 hours or more, turning occasionally. Sprinkle with salt, pepper, and paprika, and grill over hot coals or under broiler (about 6 inches from flame), skin-side down, for approximately 7–8 minutes. Turn skin-side up and cook another 6–8 minutes, basting occasionally with marinade. Do not burn!

Lemony Herbs (per chicken breast)
1 tablespoon lemon thyme
1 tablespoon lemon balm or lemon verbena
⅛ teaspoon lemon zest

Cass's Lemon-Rosemary Cookies
(Chapter Twenty)

2 cups flour
1½ teaspoon baking powder
2 teaspoons lemon zest
1 cup shortening
1 egg
1 cup sugar
1 teaspoon lemon juice
1½ teaspoon vanilla
2 tablespoons dried rosemary, crushed fine
1 tablespoon fresh lemon balm or lemon balm, minced fine

Mix flour, baking powder, and lemon zest. In large bowl, cream shortening, egg, and sugar until well mixed. Add the flour mixture. Add lemon juice, vanilla, rosemary, and lemon herb. Mix together very well. Divide dough and form into two rolls. Wrap in wax paper and chill, then slice into ¼-inch slices. Bake at 350 degrees until lightly browned, about 10 minutes.

Howard Cosell's Favorite Heart-Healthy
Chicken Liver Snack Bars
(Chapter Twenty)

2 cups flour

¾ cup wheat germ (use cornmeal if your dog is allergic to
wheat)

¼ cup ground flaxseed

¼ cup brewers yeast

⅛ cup vegetable oil

1 egg, lightly beaten

½ cup chicken broth

2 teaspoons parsley

2 garlic cloves, minced

1 cup cooked chicken liver, chopped fine

Combine flour, wheat germ, flaxseed, and brewers yeast. In separate
bowl, beat egg with oil, then add broth, parsley, and minced garlic.
Mix well. Add the dry ingredients gradually, stirring well. Fold in
chicken livers and mix well. Dough will be firm. Turn dough out on
lightly floured surface and knead briefly. Roll out ½-inch thick and cut
into bars. Place on greased cookie sheet 1 inch apart. Bake at 400 degrees for 15 minutes or until firm. Store in refrigerator.